THE HELLFIRE HOUSE

A Novel

MICHAEL PENNING

THE HELLFIRE HOUSE

First Edition. Nov. 2025
ISBN: 978-1-997836–00-1 (Paperback)
ISBN: 978-1-997836–01-8 (Hardcover)

www.michaelpenning.com

For my brother.

Chapter 1

Anna Jacobs stood at the prow of the two-masted yawl like a resolute figurehead, her black hair whipping against her pale cheeks as the vessel pitched through the mounting swells. The Atlantic stretched before her in shades of pewter, the churning waves a reminder that she had crossed into waters where maps grew uncertain and compasses told lies. Thunder cracked like a hunter's rifle somewhere behind her. Or maybe ahead. It was impossible to tell. The Connecticut coastline had vanished long ago, swallowed by the gray marriage of sea and sky, leaving only the rhythmic groan of timber and rope to mark their passage.

Anna's gloved hands clung to the slick railing. Her dark green cloak snapped around her like a broken banner. Beneath her hood, her expression remained implacable, her sharp blue eyes unwavering as they searched the shifting line between sea and sky where the island ought to be.

Brimwatch Isle—that cursed slab of rock and pine that jutted from the horizon like a broken tooth. A blot on no official map, its name whispered like a curse in New Haven taverns by old men with hollow eyes and too many ghosts. Haunted, they said. Hexed. No sane soul ventured there. Better to drown than set foot on it.

Anna heard the two sailors she'd hired moving around on deck behind her with the practiced efficiency of men who had spent their lives at sea. The taller one, a grizzled man with arms like a ship's cable and a face weathered to leather, kept casting glances in her direction when he thought she wasn't looking. His companion, younger but no less hardened by salt and sun, had developed a nervous habit of touching the knife that hung from his belt while he steered the tiller. Neither man had spoken directly to her since they'd cleared Boston Harbor, but Anna had caught fragments of their whispered conversations—words like "witch" and "devil's gold" that carried on the wind.

The storm had been building for the better part of an hour, transforming what had begun as a calm crossing into something altogether more treacherous. Lightning flickered in the distance, illuminating towering columns of cloud that reached down toward the water with grasping fingers. The wind carried the smell of rain and something older and more primeval that made Anna's skin prickle. She had paid these men well to ferry her to an island that most sailors refused to acknowledge existed, but as the weather worsened, she wondered exactly what kind of misfortune her coin had purchased.

The yawl's deck gleamed with the spray of waves that crashed over the sides with mounting ferocity. Salt water ran in rivulets between the weathered planks, and the mainmast groaned against its rigging as gusts of wind tried to tear the canvas free. Anna braced as another swell crashed over the deck, soaking the dark skirts clinging to her lithe form. She gripped the bow rail but maintained her position despite the vessel's violent dance across the swells. She had endured worse storms than this—both literal and metaphorical—and she would not show weakness before reaching her destination.

The wind behind Anna whispered something in her ear. "She paid us double," one sailor grumbled. He was the younger one—Reed, if she remembered correctly. "Let her have her ghost rock and drown."

"Not if the storm gets worse," the older one, Harker, growled.

It was then that the voice began, sliding into her consciousness like ice water poured down her spine.

They mean to kill you, child.

Every muscle in Anna's body tensed, but she forced herself to breathe steadily, her jaw tight. Rebecca Hale's rasping voice was as familiar as her own heartbeat, a poisonous whisper that had haunted her since birth. It had grown stronger in the months since Anna had surrendered herself to her ancestor's dark influence. The dead witch's presence pressed against the edges of her mind like fingers testing the bars of a cage, always seeking weakness, always promising power in exchange for submission.

You know I speak truth, Rebecca continued. *You feel it, don't you? These men have no intention of delivering you to the island. They will wait until the storm provides cover, then slit your throat and feed your corpse to the fishes. One push into the sea, and no one will ever know. Your gold will buy them drink and whores in some distant port, while your bones rest fathoms below.*

The truth of the words frightened Anna the most. She *did* feel it—and part of her thrilled at the promise of bloodshed.

"Quiet," Anna whispered through gritted teeth, the word lost in the howl of wind and crash of waves. She tightened her jaw, knuckles white against the railing, resisting the insidious spirit like a sickness. Her head ached with the effort of fighting the familiar battle between her own instincts and the seductive certainty of her ancestor's counsel. Rebecca's voice always spoke to the darkest corners of her mind, the places where suspicion and aggression festered like infected wounds.

The storm chose that moment to unleash its full fury. Lightning split the sky in jagged ribbons of silver fire, illuminating the churning sea in stark relief before plunging everything back into premature twilight. Thunder followed seconds later, a sound like the very heavens tearing apart. The yawl pitched forward into a trough between waves, and Anna felt her stomach drop as they plunged toward the water before the next swell caught them and lifted them skyward again.

Rain fell in fat, cold drops that quickly became a driving torrent. Within moments, the downpour soaked Anna's clothes, and streams of water ran from her hair. The deck became treacherous, and she heard one of the sailors curse as he nearly lost his footing while securing a loose line.

Look at them, Rebecca hissed, her voice somehow clearer now that the storm raged around them. *See how the younger checks his blade? How the big one watches for your moment of weakness? They are predators, Anna, and you are alone on this floating coffin with no one to hear your screams.*

Anna risked a glance over her shoulder, and what she saw made her stomach twist. The sailors had moved closer together, huddled near the mizzenmast in what appeared to be an urgent conference. Harker's hand rested openly on his knife hilt now, no longer bothering with subtlety, while his shorter companion kept glancing toward the small boat secured near the stern—their means of escape once they finished their grim work.

The wind shifted again, stealing away more fragments of their conversation: "...storm will hide it..." and "...no witnesses..." and finally, clearly enough to freeze her heart, "...witch's blood brings bad luck, anyway."

Anna's hand moved instinctively toward the concealed blade beneath her coat, her fingers grazing the familiar grip. She drew comfort from its solid presence. She had faced monsters both human and supernatural, had exorcised demons and vanquished the restless dead, but there was something particularly chilling about the calculated malice of ordinary men.

Kill them first, Rebecca urged, her voice rising with excitement. *Strike before they can act. You have the element of surprise, and I can guide your blade true. Their deaths will be swift. It is what they deserve, these faithless dogs. Men like that do not see women like us as people. Just coin to be pocketed. Secrets to be sunk.*

Another lightning bolt, this time nearer. In its brief illumination, Anna saw Brimwatch Isle rising from the storm-lashed sea like a fortress of rock and misery. The sight of her destination so close at hand filled her with desperate resolve, even as Rebecca's poisonous counsel threatened to overwhelm her better judgment.

The storm raged with renewed fury as Anna watched the sailors make their final preparations for murder. The younger one had moved to check the small boat's securing lines twice in as many minutes, his movements quick and nervous like a rat testing the walls of its cage. His companion stood with the confidence of a man who had killed before, one hand resting on his knife while the other gripped a coil of rope—perfect for weighing down a body before it went over the side.

Salt spray and the threat of violence filled Anna's quick and shallow breaths. The deck beneath her feet pitched wildly as the yawl fought through swells that seemed determined to tear the vessel apart, but she had found her sea legs hours ago. Rebecca was right, she realized with crystalline clarity. These men intended to use the storm as both cover and accomplice. Lightning would mask the flash of steel, thunder would swallow her screams, and the hungry sea would claim all evidence of their crime.

You see it now, Rebecca's voice purred with satisfaction, sliding through Anna's mind like oil over water. *They have already decided your fate. The only question remaining is whether you will die like a lamb led to slaughter, or whether you will paint this deck red with their blood first. I can show you how to make them suffer, child. I can guide your hand to places that will make them beg for the mercy they would have denied you.*

Anna's pulse quickened as Rebecca's influence pressed against her consciousness, seeking the cracks in her resolve like water finding fissures in stone. She was no lamb, and these men would learn the danger of cornering a thing that fights. Part of her—the part that had inherited more than just blood from her ancestor—whispered that the sailors deserved whatever fate she visited upon them.

But Anna's life had been a lesson in separating justice from bloodlust, and necessary violence from the tempting darkness. Her mother's teachings echoed in her memory: *Power without principle is merely another form of evil, no matter how righteous it feels in the moment.* She would defend herself, yes, but she would not become the monster that Rebecca urged her to embrace.

Harker straightened from his conversation with his younger companion and began walking toward her, his gait sure despite the pitching deck. His weathered face wore an expression of grim determination, and Anna noticed he had loosened his knife in its sheath. Behind him, Reed remained near the stern, blocking any retreat toward the small boat.

"Beggin' your pardon, miss," Harker yelled over the wind and rain, his tone lacking any real politeness. "But we need to have ourselves a word."

With a flick of her wrist, Anna threw back her hood, turning to face him. Her hand remained steady on the bow rail as she ignored the ship's violent rocking. Rain plastered her black hair to her skull and ran in rivulets down her pale cheeks, but her blue eyes remained fixed on the approaching threat with unwavering intensity. "I trust we are maintaining our course to Brimwatch Isle," she said, her voice carrying clearly despite the storm's fury.

The sailor laughed, a harsh sound like scraping metal on

stone. "Course? Miss, ain't no course to that devil's rock. Ain't no sailor worth his salt who'd set foot on cursed ground like that." He took another step closer, and Anna could see the knife's handle protruding from his belt like a steel fang. "And ain't no Christian who'd ferry a witch to her unholy business."

His companion had moved closer as well, Anna noted from the corner of her eye. Reed's nervous energy had transformed into something more focused and predatory, his hand now gripping his own blade. They had her trapped between them, or so they believed. She was a dozen steps ahead of them, and still they thought themselves in control.

Kill him now. Feverish excitement laced Rebecca's voice. *While he speaks, while he thinks you helpless. Drive your blade up under his ribs and twist. Watch the light fade from his eyes as his life spills across the deck. Show these dogs what happens when they threaten the blood of Rebecca Hale.*

Anna's jaw clenched as she fought against the witch's influence, her white-knuckled grip on the rail betraying the fight raging within. The familiar weight of her concealed knife seemed to burn against her side, and she could almost feel Rebecca's spectral hands guiding her own toward the weapon's grip.

"You've made an error in judgment," Anna said, her voice piercing the roaring storm. "I am not helpless, and I am not your victim."

Harker's grin widened, revealing teeth stained yellow by tobacco and neglect. "Pretty words from a pretty witch," he said, drawing his knife with practiced ease. The blade gleamed dully in the storm's light, its edge keen and hungry. "But words won't save you when you're feedin' the sharks."

Lightning cracked the sky again, closer now, illuminating the scene in stark black and white. In that moment of electric clarity, Anna saw everything with perfect detail: the sailor's confident stance, his companion moving to flank her, the way both men's eyes reflected the lightning like those of hunting wolves. She also saw something else—the fear beneath their bravado, the knowledge that they sailed in cursed waters toward an island that existed on no honest chart.

"No one goes to that devil's rock," the sailor continued, taking another step forward. The deck pitched beneath his feet, but he compensated automatically, a lifetime of sea legs keeping him steady. "And no one will miss a witch like you."

The words hung in the air for a moment, suspended between the crash of waves and the rumble of thunder.

Then Harker lunged.

His blade caught the next lightning flash like a falling star. Behind Anna, Reed moved as well, seeking to pin her between them and end this business quickly.

But Anna Jacobs hadn't survived nineteen years of monsters and magic by being unprepared for violence.

As Harker's knife swept toward her throat, she threw herself sideways, her hand finally closing around the grip of her own weapon. Thunder crashed overhead like the sound of the world splitting in half, and in that cacophony of storm and steel, the real battle began.

Chapter 2

Anna twisted away from Harker's blade as it sliced through the rain, missing her throat by a hairsbreadth. The deck pitched violently beneath her feet, nearly sending her sprawling into the big sailor's waiting arms. Lightning cracked open the sky, freezing the scene in electric clarity. Harker's face contorted with murderous intent while his companion circled like a shark, the horizon tilting at an impossible angle as the yawl fought against the storm's fury.

Anna yanked at her concealed knife, but her rain-slicked gloves fumbled against the leather sheath. The blade clattered to the deck, skittering across wet planks before disappearing into shadow.

Harker laughed, a sound like gravel rattling in a tin cup. "Seems your luck's run out, witch," he snarled, advancing with the confidence of a wolf who knows he has cornered his rabbit.

Anna's mind raced through her options, each one more desperate than the last. The bow offered no escape, only the churning black water beyond. Reed blocked the stern, his own blade gleaming dully in the storm's light. But there, just beyond the mainmast—the narrow door to the galley. She had noted it earlier, part of her habitual assessment of any space she entered. A potential refuge, or at least a source of weapons.

Kill them both! Rebecca's voice thundered, vibrating through Anna's skull like the ship's timbers in a gale. *Tear out their throats with your bare hands if you must. They are nothing! Insects beneath your boot!*

Anna ignored the witch's commands, though her blood sang with her desire for it. Instead, she feinted left, then dove right as Harker lunged again. His knife slashed through her cloak, tearing fabric but missing flesh. She rolled across the tilted deck, using the ship's violent motion to her advantage, and scrambled toward the galley door.

"She's running!" Harker shouted over the storm's howl. "Cut 'er off!"

Anna reached the galley door just as Reed's fingers grazed her shoulder. She slammed the door behind her and threw her weight against it, searching frantically for something to bar it with. The small space reeked of old fish and stale beer, illuminated only by the erratic strobe of lightning through a tiny porthole. The ship pitched again, sending pots and cups clattering across the floor.

A heavy body crashed against the door. It shuddered under the assault, the wood splintering around the hinges. Anna had seconds, not minutes.

They're going to kill you slowly, Rebecca whispered, her voice almost gentle now. *Let me help you, child. Let me in, and I'll paint this ship with their entrails. I'll make them scream for death long before it comes.*

Anna's hands trembled, not from fear but from the effort of restraining the darkness that Rebecca offered. The witch's power beckoned—seductive, easy, complete. But Anna knew the price of that surrender. She wouldn't relinquish herself and become the monster her ancestor urged her to be, not even to save her own life.

Her gaze fell on the small iron stove bolted to the floor, its meager fire still burning despite the ship's wild motion. Beside it lay a broken belaying pin, likely used to stir the coals. The door shuddered again, a crack appearing down its center.

"I'm gonna cut out yer heart, witch!" Harker's voice carried through the splintering wood. "Feed it to the fishes!"

Anna darted for the belaying pin and gripped it in her right hand. With her left protected by her glove, she reached for the iron plate atop the stove. Heat seared through the leather, but she gritted her teeth and pried the plate loose. It glowed a dull red in the dim light, hot enough to burn flesh to the bone.

The door exploded inward in a shower of splinters just as Anna turned to face her attackers. Harker's massive frame filled the doorway, his knife raised high. Behind him, Reed peered over his shoulder, eyes wide with murderous anticipation.

"Nowhere left to run," Harker growled, stepping into the tiny galley.

Anna didn't hesitate. She swung the belaying pin in a vicious arc, connecting with Harker's forearm with a sickening crack. The bone shattered beneath the impact, and the knife fell from his nerveless fingers. Before he could register the pain, Anna lunged forward, slamming the glowing stove plate against the side of his face.

The smell came first—burning hair and scorching flesh—then the sound: a high, animal scream that seemed to bubble up from somewhere deep inside the sailor's chest. He staggered backward and collided with Reed, his hands clutching at his ruined face as they both stumbled out the door. The storm unleashed another volley of thunder, swallowing his screams in its fury.

Feeling cold and detached, as though watching herself from a great distance, Anna followed through with mechanical precision. The belaying pin connected with Harker's temple—once, twice—each impact sending shock waves up her arm. Teeth flew from his mouth and blood sprayed across the rain-slicked deck in a dark arterial fan, mingling with the puddles already gathering at their feet. The sailor went down like a felled tree, his body twitching once before growing still.

Yes! Rebecca hissed in triumph, her voice thick with satisfaction. *Feel the power in your hands. Feel how easily you snuff out their lives. This is what you were born for, child.*

Anna's stomach clenched, not at the violence she had just committed, but at the pleasure she had taken in it. Her hands were numb from the impact, but she felt a warmth in her chest, an uncomfortable heat she recognized as Rebecca's influence—the witch's dark joy seeping through the cracks in Anna's defenses.

Reed stood frozen in the rain, his face a mask of horror as he stared at his companion's body. Harker's blood ran in rivulets between the deck planks, disappearing into the bilge below. For a moment, the only sounds were the howl of the wind and the creak of straining timber as the yawl fought against the mounting swells.

Then something changed in Reed's expression. Horror gave way to rage, fear transmuting into a desperate courage. His grip tightened on his knife, and his eyes fixed on Anna with the intensity of a man with nothing left to lose.

"*Devil-loving witch!*" he snarled, and launched himself at her, his blade slashing through the air.

Anna raised the belaying pin, ready to meet his attack, but her foot slipped in Harker's blood. She stumbled backward, colliding with the galley door. The belaying pin slipped from her grasp, clattering across the deck and disappearing beneath a storage bench.

Reed was on her in an instant, his greater weight bearing her down. His blade flashed downward. Anna caught his wrist with both hands, straining to keep the knife from her throat as they crashed to the deck together. The smell of the sea filled her nostrils, along with the metallic tang of blood and the sour stench of Reed's breath.

"You'll not have me too," he growled, his face inches from hers, spittle flying from his lips to mix with the rain on her cheeks. "You'll not murder me like you did Harker!"

Reed's weight crushed against Anna's chest, driving precious air from her lungs. His fingers, calloused and strong from years of hauling rope, found her throat and squeezed with the desperate strength of a man who had witnessed death and refused to join it. The knife hovered inches from her face, its blade catching lightning in brief, terrible flashes.

"Witch! You'll not drown me!" he snarled. His eyes had gone wild, pupils dilated with fear and rage until they seemed to swallow the irises entirely. "I seen what you are!"

Anna clawed at his wrists, her vision beginning to darken at the edges as her lungs screamed for air. She bucked beneath him, trying to dislodge his weight, but he was solid as iron and twice as unyielding. The ship pitched violently, and they slid several inches across the blood-slicked deck, the sailor maintaining his deadly grip.

Kill him! Rebecca urged, her voice more distant now as Anna's consciousness faded. *Let me in, child! Let me save us both!*

Anna's fingers scrabbled against Reed's arms, her strength ebbing with each passing second. The knife descended, pressing against her cheek, drawing a thin line of blood that was washed away by the driving rain. The sailor's face twisted into a grimace of triumph as he felt her resistance weakening.

Suddenly, the hold door burst open with a bang that was nearly lost in the storm's fury. A small figure emerged, moving with startling speed across the heaving deck. Reed had only an instant to register the newcomer before a blade—small but wickedly sharp—plunged into the meat of his thigh.

He howled, a sound more animal than human, his grip on Anna's throat loosening just enough for her to drag in a desperate breath. Reed jerked the knife away from her cheek as he twisted to confront this new threat.

Anna's vision cleared enough to see her unexpected savior. A girl, no more than twelve or thirteen, with hair so pale it seemed to glow in the gloom. One of her eyes caught the lightning and burned with a brilliant shade of crimson. The other, a pale blue, remained in shadow. A sodden dress clung to her thin frame, and something that looked like soot or ash streaked her arms.

Mercy Alden.

The strange albino girl from the haunted village of Sévérité, whom Anna had rescued months earlier from the clutches of the dead witch, Angéle de la Barthe. The child should have been safely hidden away in Boston, not on a storm-tossed vessel bound for an island that didn't exist on any official chart.

Reed lunged for Mercy, his knife slashing through the rain toward the girl's face. "Devil's get!" he roared, his leg trailing blood across the deck. "I'll gut ya both!"

Mercy ducked beneath his wild swing with surprising grace, her mismatched eyes wide but determined. She darted past him, putting the mainmast between them as Anna scrambled to her feet, throat burning, legs unsteady beneath her.

"The pin!" Mercy called, her voice barely audible above the storm. She pointed toward the belaying pin that had skittered beneath the storage bench.

Anna dove for it just as Reed changed direction, charging toward her with murder in his eyes. Her fingers closed around the smooth wood, and she rolled to her side, bringing the makeshift weapon up just as the sailor reached her. The pin connected with his knee with a sound like a tree branch snapping in a gale. Reed stumbled, howling in pain, but kept his feet, slashing wildly with his knife.

"Behind you!" Anna shouted as Reed turned toward Mercy

again, determined to eliminate the smaller threat first.

The girl feinted left, then darted right, leading the limping sailor on a desperate chase around the heaving deck. Blood trailed behind him, quickly washed away by the rain and spray that crashed over the rails with each passing swell. Mercy's face was a mask of intense concentration, her pale hair plastered to her skull, her small hands balled into white-knuckled fists.

Anna circled behind Reed, waiting for her moment. When Reed lunged for Mercy and missed—his wounded leg finally betraying him—Anna pounced. She brought the belaying pin down on his wrist with all her strength, and this time his knife went flying, disappearing into the churning water beyond the rail.

Reed turned on her with animal ferocity, his teeth bared in a feral snarl. He tackled Anna backward, his superior weight bearing her down despite his injuries. They crashed against the gunwale, the wood digging into Anna's back as Reed's hands found her throat once more.

"Die, witch," he hissed, fingers tightening. "Die and let the sea take what's left."

Through the curtain of rain, Anna saw Mercy approach from behind, her face set in grim determination. The girl leaped onto Reed's back, her thin arms wrapping around his throat in a mirror of his own stranglehold on Anna. He released one hand from Anna's neck to claw at the girl behind him, buying Anna precious seconds to gulp air into her burning lungs.

"Push!" Anna gasped, seeing their chance. She braced her feet against the deck and shoved with all her remaining strength.

Mercy seemed to understand instantly. She threw her weight backward, pulling Reed off-balance. The sailor teetered at the gunwale, arms windmilling as he fought for purchase on the rain-slick deck. For one suspended moment, he hung there, his eyes wide with the sudden knowledge of his fate.

Then he was gone, tumbling backward into the churning black water below. The crash of a wave cut his scream short, and then there was only the endless howl of the wind and the rhythmic thump of the rigging against the mast.

Anna sagged against the rail, one hand massaging her bruised throat, the other still gripping the belaying pin. Across from her, Mercy stood trembling, her pale skin ghost-white in the storm light, her strange mismatched eyes fixed on the spot where Reed had vanished.

For a moment, neither spoke. What was there to say? The girl who should have been safe in Boston had just helped Anna kill a man, sealing his fate with the same calm efficiency with which one might swat a fly. And yet, without her intervention, it would have been Anna's body feeding the fishes in the Sound.

"You're supposed to be with William," Anna finally managed, her voice a raw croak against the storm's backdrop as she went to retrieve her knife from where it had fallen. "In Boston."

Mercy pushed a strand of wet hair from her face, revealing the lattice of scars that crisscrossed her wrists—remnants of her time under the evil Cotton Barlow's influence. "I followed you," she said simply, as though this explained everything.

Before Anna could respond, a monstrous wave crashed over the starboard rail, nearly washing them both overboard. The yawl lurched sickeningly, timbers groaning in protest at the ocean's assault. Through the curtain of rain, Anna spotted something that turned her blood to ice: jagged black shapes emerging from the storm-tossed sea like the teeth of some primordial beast.

"Rocks!" she shouted, the word torn from her raw throat. "We're being pushed toward the shoals!"

Chapter 3

Mercy's eyes widened with understanding. Without a word, both of them lunged for the stern, fighting their way across the pitching deck toward the tiller. It swung wildly, the rudder at the mercy of currents that seemed determined to dash the vessel against Brimwatch's unforgiving shore.

Anna reached the tiller first, her gloved hands closing around the wooden handle with desperate strength. She threw her weight against it, trying to bring the yawl's bow around, away from the deadly rocks that grew more distinct with each flash of lightning. Mercy joined her, adding her slight weight to the effort, her face set in a grimace of determination.

"Pull harder!" Anna commanded, feeling the rudder beginning to respond beneath their combined strength. The yawl shuddered, fighting against their efforts like a living thing, the sea clutching at its hull with greedy fingers.

For one brief, hopeful moment, Anna thought they might succeed. The bow began to swing away from the rocks, the vessel responding sluggishly to their desperate steering. Then she felt something give beneath her hands, a subtle shift in resistance that sent a spike of dread through her chest.

The tiller snapped with a sound like a pistol shot, the wood splintering in Anna's grip as if struck by an invisible ax. Fragments scattered across the deck, skittering away in the wind and rain, leaving her holding nothing but a useless stump. The force of the break knocked both women off balance, sending them sprawling across the slick planks as the yawl, suddenly masterless, spun like a child's top in the grip of the current.

"No!" Anna's cry was swallowed by the storm's fury. She scrambled to her feet, still clutching the broken piece of tiller, her mind racing through increasingly desperate options. Without steering, they were at the mercy of the wind and waves—and neither seemed to be forgiving.

Mercy pulled herself up using the gunwale, her thin face taut with determination despite the fear that widened her mismatched eyes. "What do we do?" she called, her voice barely audible above the tempest.

Anna didn't answer. There was nothing to say. The yawl had surrendered to the storm, spinning in lazy, nauseating circles as the current dragged it inexorably toward the jagged teeth of the shoals of Brimwatch Isle. Each flash of lightning brought the rocks into sharper relief—black, slick with spray, and utterly merciless.

"Brace yourself!" Anna shouted, throwing aside the useless tiller remnant and grabbing for a rope secured to the mainmast. She tossed the end to Mercy, who caught it with surprising dexterity despite the pitching deck. "Tie it around your waist! Quickly!"

The girl obeyed without question, her nimble fingers working the knot. Anna did the same, looping the rope around her own waist and securing it with a sailor's knot that would tighten, not slip, when wet. They had barely finished when the storm unleashed a fresh assault. A wave crashed over the starboard rail with enough force to send them both skidding across the deck.

The rope went taut between them, a tenuous lifeline in the chaos. Their eyes met briefly across the surging water, a moment of shared understanding that transcended words. They were no longer hunter and child, protector and protected. They were simply two souls facing the same deadly storm, bound by circumstance and a length of salt-stained hemp.

Lightning split the sky, illuminating the scene in stark monochrome: the yawl spinning toward destruction; the shoals waiting like executioners; the two women braced against the inevitable. In that flash of electric clarity, Anna saw Brimwatch Isle looming behind the rocks, a dark mass of pine and stone that watched their approach with malevolent patience.

The impact, when it came, defied description.

One moment they were riding the swells, the next they were hurled forward as the yawl's hull connected with submerged stone. The sound was primal. Wood splintered and timbers groaned as the sea rushed in to claim what it had broken. Anna felt the deck buck beneath her feet like a living thing in its death throes, sending her crashing against the gunwale hard enough to drive the breath from her lungs.

Mercy fared worse. The girl was airborne for a sickening

moment before the rope connecting them went taut, yanking her back like a puppet on a string. She landed on the deck with a cry that was half-pain, half-surprise, one hand clutching at her ribs where the rope had dug into her flesh.

"Hold on!" Anna cried. She reached for the girl as the yawl shuddered and groaned, listing heavily to port where the rocks had torn a gash in its hull. Water rushed in, black and hungry, flooding the lower deck and cargo hold. The ship's death knell played out in a symphony of breaking wood and rushing water, punctuated by the crash of waves and the banshee wail of the wind.

Mercy crawled toward Anna, her face a pale oval in the gloom, her eyes wide with a fear she seemed determined not to voice. They met at the base of the mainmast, clutching at each other as the deck tilted beneath them at an increasingly precarious angle.

"We need to stay with the ship as long as possible," Anna said, her voice steady despite the maelstrom around them. "If it breaks up completely, grab onto something that floats. The current's pushing us toward the island. We might make shore if—"

A tremendous crash cut her words off as another wave slammed into the stricken vessel. The mast creaked ominously above them, its rigging hanging in loose loops like the entrails of a gutted animal. The yawl shuddered again, more violently this time, as another submerged rock tore at its wounded belly.

Water surged across the deck in a freezing torrent, soaking them to the skin and numbing extremities already chilled by fear and exposure. Anna felt it rising around her legs, creeping upward with inexorable purpose. The hatches to the lower deck burst open under the pressure, releasing a geyser of seawater that had already filled the cargo hold.

"It's sinking fast," Mercy said. She wasn't panicking, Anna noted with a mixture of pride and concern. The girl had already seen too much horror in her young life to be undone by the prospect of drowning. "Should we try to swim for it?"

Anna shook her head, droplets flying from her sodden hair. "Not yet. The current around those rocks would tear us apart. We need to ride this out as long as we can."

As if in response to her words, the yawl shuddered one final time, then slipped sideways off the rock that had impaled it. The sudden movement sent both women crashing against the port gunwale, which was now nearly level with the churning sea. The deck listed at almost forty-five degrees, making it impossible to stand without clinging to something.

"The mast is going to go," Anna said, eyeing the main spar as it swayed drunkenly above them. The wood groaned under stress it was never meant to bear, and several of the supporting lines had already snapped, lashing the air like deadly whips. "We need to move aft. Now!"

They began a desperate crawl up the tilted deck, using whatever handholds they could find: cleats, gunwales, the splintered remains of hatches. The rope between them went slack, then taut, as they navigated the treacherous terrain of the dying ship. Rain lashed their faces, and waves crashed over the lower rail, each one threatening to sweep them into the hungry sea.

Halfway to the stern, Anna's hand closed around something solid. Her leather satchel, somehow still secured to a cleat where she had left it hours earlier. She grabbed it without thinking, slinging it over her shoulder by its strap. Whatever came next, she would need its contents.

They reached the stern just as another section of hull gave way with a sound like the world tearing in half. The yawl lurched again, tilting ever further, until the deck was almost vertical. Mercy lost her grip on the gunwale and would have slid into the water if not for the rope connecting her to Anna.

"I've got you!" Anna braced herself against the stern rail and hauled on the rope. Mercy scrambled upward, her fingers bloody from clutching at wooden seams and metal fittings. Their hands met, fingers interlacing in a grip that defied the storm's attempts to separate them.

For a breathless moment, they clung there, suspended between the broken vessel and the heaving sea. Lightning illuminated the scene again, and Anna saw they were closer to Brimwatch than she had realized. The island's western cliffs rose less than a quarter-mile away, black against the storm-darkened sky. Atop the highest bluff, she glimpsed something that made her blood run cold despite the chaos. A structure, massive and jagged, like a cathedral built by hands that had never learned mercy.

Hallowspire.

The mansion she had come to find. It watched their approach from its perch on the cliffs like a patient bird of prey.

"Look!" Mercy gasped, following Anna's gaze. "Is that—"

Her words dissolved into a cry of alarm as the stern where they clung suddenly lifted, propelled by a wave that seemed determined to finish what the rocks had begun. The yawl's bow plunged beneath the surface, and water rushed up the deck toward them with terrible speed, swallowing hatchways and cleats and anything else in its path.

"Hold on to me!" Anna commanded, wrapping her arm around Mercy's thin shoulders. "Don't let go, no matter what happens!"

The girl nodded, her face pressed against Anna's side, her small hands clutching at Anna's coat with desperate strength. They braced themselves as the wave reached them, lifting them from the dying ship as casually as a child might pluck petals from a flower.

Chapter 4

The cold hit like a fist, a shock that drove the air from Anna's lungs and replaced it with salt and pain. The Atlantic didn't embrace; it devoured—and she was plunged into its black mouth with the violence of a birth into hell. A thousand tiny needles stabbed at her skin as she broke the surface and gulped a half-breath before another wave smashed her under again. Timber and rope thrashed past in the undertow, battering her legs, clawing at her clothes. Overhead, the sky was a writhing bruise, split by the strobe of lightning that revealed the remains of the yawl scattering like a carcass before wolves.

She surfaced again, coughing brine, eyes stinging as she fought to orient herself. Somewhere—impossibly distant through the roaring in her ears—she felt the tug of the rope still connecting her to Mercy. The girl surfaced behind her, sputtering and coughing, her white hair plastered to her skull like wet parchment. The rope between them had tangled around Anna's arm, cutting into her flesh with each pull of the current.

"The ship!" Mercy choked out, water streaming from her mouth.

Anna turned in time to witness the yawl's death throes. The vessel had rolled completely onto its side, its mast parallel to the churning surface. As another wave struck, the mainmast gave way with a crack like splintering bone, toppling into the sea in a tangle of canvas and rigging. Timbers shrieked as they tore apart, the hull breaking open like a rotten fruit to spill its contents into the hungry water.

A cask bobbed past them, followed by the broken remnants of a hatch cover. Anna reached for it, her numbed fingers struggling to close around the splintered wood. She pulled the hatch toward them, offering Mercy something to cling to besides the rope that bound them.

"Hold this!" she shouted over the storm's roar. "Don't let go!"

The last of the yawl disappeared beneath the waves with a final, bubbling sigh, leaving nothing but scattered debris. Anna's gaze fixed on the shore of Brimwatch Isle, a jagged silhouette barely visible through sheets of rain. Lightning forked overhead, illuminating towering cliffs and the mansion perched atop them like a crouching predator.

"We need to swim!" Anna called, already pulling herself through the water with powerful strokes. Her boots filled with water, and she kicked them off, but she refused to abandon the leather satchel still slung across her body.

Instinct took over. She struggled free of the tangle that threatened to drag her under and struck out with desperate, disciplined strokes, using the flash of distant cliffs as a point of reference. Her waterlogged cloak tried to pull her down, but she couldn't shed it. The cold would murder her as surely as the sea, and every layer was one more chance at living. She couldn't hear anything over the howl of the wind and the roar of her own heart, but her mind kept a running tally: direction, distance, survival.

Lightning forked overhead, painting the ocean in negatives. She glimpsed the mass of Brimwatch Isle. It was closer than she dared to hope now. Another stroke, and another, her legs kicking rhythmically despite the weight of her waterlogged skirts. Her arms threatened to seize, and the cold chewed at her bones. The current fought her, trying to pull her back out to sea or dash her against the rocks that jutted from the water like rotted teeth. But there was no time for fear. There was only the rhythm: breathe, stroke, breathe, stroke.

She didn't look back.

Not until she heard the scream.

It was thin—a child's pitch—but raw and animal, the sort of sound that even a hurricane couldn't drown. Anna turned her head, vision blurring from salt and rain, and scanned the rolling chaos behind her. For a moment, she saw nothing but wreckage and foam; the churn of the dying vessel. Then lightning fired again, and there was Mercy—twenty yards away, perhaps less. The makeshift float had slipped from her grasp, and she now thrashed in the water, pale hair splayed like a corona, her arms chopping at the waves with none of a swimmer's logic, only panic. The rope that had tethered them in their final moments aboard the yawl now wrapped around Mercy's leg, dragging her under with every convulsion. Anna watched as the sea claimed the girl once, twice, each time slower to let her rise.

It occurred to her she could let it happen. She could keep swimming for the rocks. It was what anyone would do.

Anna felt the thought crystallize, cold and perfect as a splinter of ice in her skull. Rebecca's voice slid in behind it, sly as a knife between her ribs: *Let her go, child. That one is only ballast now. She will drag you down with her. You are so close! What is one child against your greater purpose?*

"Shut up," Anna hissed through chattering teeth, though the wind tore the words away before they could reach anyone but herself and the dead witch who haunted her thoughts.

She is dragging you down, Rebecca insisted, her voice gaining strength as Anna's resolve wavered. *She followed you uninvited. Her fate is not your burden to bear. The knife in your belt would sever the rope in an instant. One quick slash, and you would be free.*

Anna clenched her teeth against the voice, against the part of herself that thrilled to its logic. She had survived so much that she had learned to measure cost and consequence like a butcher weighing cuts. Now, she calculated the odds with merciless precision. The shore was still distant. The storm showed no signs of abating. Her own strength was waning with each passing moment spent fighting the current. Mercy was slowing her down, increasing the likelihood that neither of them would reach land alive.

But the memory of Mercy's face—her mismatched eyes, the dogged hope that had outlasted beatings and exorcisms and a haunted life—shoved itself between Anna and the cliff. If she let Mercy die now, the ghost of her failure would follow her to the grave.

And she had enough of those already.

She sucked in a raw lungful of air and veered off course, kicking hard against the undertow. Every stroke away from the shore was a gamble, each second closer to hypothermia. But Anna had always courted risk the way other girls courted suitors. The storm made distance a joke—one moment she was yards away, the next within reach, as if the ocean itself wanted to see what she would do.

Mercy went under again. Anna dove, eyes wide open in the stinging salt, and snared the girl's arm just as she began to sink. For a moment, the dead weight dragged Anna down, the water trying to wedge itself between their bodies, trying to claim them both. Then Anna wrenched Mercy up, and they broke the surface together in a violent spray of foam and spit.

Mercy coughed and sputtered, eyes rolling, her lips already tinged purple in the lightning's sick glow. "Let go," the girl managed. "You'll drown too."

Anna spat water and forced her voice steady. "Shut up and kick. Help me or die—I don't care which."

She slung an arm around Mercy's chest, treading water as best she could, then began the grim slog back toward the cliffs. The weight of the girl—so slight on land, so damn heavy in water—threatened to pull them both under with every yard. Anna kept her chin above water by force of will, swimming with her legs while Mercy managed weak, dogged kicks of her own.

Rebecca's presence writhed in the back of her mind, a coiled serpent of disapproval and scorn. The witch offered no further counsel, but Anna could feel her ancestor's contempt like a physical weight.

The shore didn't seem to get closer. Each time Anna risked a look, the cliffs loomed unchanged, mocking her. The rain stung her eyes. Her fingers numbed, and she lost feeling in her legs below the knee. Mercy had gone silent, limp but breathing, her head lolling against Anna's shoulder.

A quieter, older memory replaced Rebecca's voice: Anna's mother, Abigail, teaching her to swim in the icy shallows of Boston Harbor. "*The sea doesn't care about you,*" Abigail had said, voice matter-of-fact. "*If you want to live, you have to care for yourself.*"

Anna cared about living. But she cared, against her own design, about this girl too.

Mercy went under again, her pale arms vanishing beneath the froth. Anna barely caught her by the collar as the undertow tried to suck her down for good. There was no grace left, just the ugly, animal instinct to grab and hold. Anna's grip found the sodden linen of Mercy's dress and yanked upward with a force that felt borrowed from some other, stronger body. The girl surfaced with a gurgling gasp, water streaming from her nose and mouth, eyes wide and wild. For a moment, she was dead weight, her limbs limp, until Anna shook her hard enough to startle the life back into her.

The shore of Brimwatch Isle loomed before them, a jagged strip of black rock that offered little welcome. Waves broke against its edge in explosive bursts of white foam, the water receding to reveal barnacle-encrusted stones glistening like wet bones in the storm light. Beyond the narrow beach, cliffs rose in sheer walls of dark granite, their faces scarred by centuries of wind and salt.

"Kick," Anna commanded, voice shredded by cold and sea. "Now."

Mercy obeyed, coughing but alive, her feet scrabbling against nothing until Anna hoisted her half over the next breaker. The surf was a white blur of violence. Anna's arms screamed with fatigue, but she kept her grip, hauling Mercy's head above water even as her own dipped below with every swell. The leather satchel still slung across her body had become a waterlogged anchor, dragging at her shoulder with each movement. She considered abandoning it, but the contents were too valuable—if they survived this.

A massive wave caught them from behind, lifting them high before hurtling them forward with terrifying speed. For one suspended moment, Anna thought it might carry them safely to shore. Then she saw the rock directly in their path— a jagged spire that would impale them as readily as any executioner's spike.

"Hold your breath!" she shouted, releasing Mercy's collar to grab her around the waist instead. With the last of her strength, Anna twisted in the water, positioning her own body between Mercy and the approaching stone. The impact drove the air from her lungs in an explosive gasp. Pain blossomed across her shoulder blade, sharp and immediate, but the thick leather of her satchel had absorbed the worst of the collision.

As the wave retreated, threatening to drag them back out to sea, Anna dug her fingers into a crevice in the rock, anchoring them against the pull. Blood mingled with seawater—hers or Mercy's, she couldn't tell—and her vision swam with black spots that had nothing to do with the storm's darkness.

"Almost there," she said, though she wasn't sure if she spoke to Mercy or herself. "One more push."

A chunk of hull tumbled past, nearly striking Mercy's skull. Anna twisted to shield her, taking the blow on her own shoulder. Pain flared—sharp, hot, then gone, replaced by a deeper numbness. Together, they closed the gap to shore in a series of desperate, ugly lunges. The current seemed to sense their intention, pulling them sideways toward a cluster of rocks that jutted from the sea like broken teeth. Waves crashed against the stones with enough force to shatter bone, sending spray twenty feet into the air.

The next wave lifted them again, this time carrying them past the worst of the rocks and spitting them into the shallows of the stony beach. Anna's knees scraped against rock, and by the time her feet found pebbled ground, her legs trembled so badly she nearly dropped Mercy. She half-dragged, half-carried the girl as they stumbled forward through knee-deep water that seemed bent on pulling them back. She hauled Mercy a few more feet, then collapsed beside her, face pressed to the wet stones.

The sky above was a convulsion of lightning and clouds. Thunder rolled over them in long, overlapping bursts, each one vibrating through the ground beneath their bodies. Rain hammered the shore, drenching Anna's face and pooling in the hollow of her throat. Her green traveling cloak, rent in three places, fanned out behind her like a spill of ink. Blood trickled from a dozen small cuts on her hands and face, and a deeper wound on her shoulder throbbed in time with her pulse. She stared at the sky, too empty for words, while her breath slowed from frantic to merely desperate.

Mercy lay on her side, curled up, coughing until her chest was empty of water and full of raw, ragged air. Her wrists, marked with those ghastly scars, seemed even more prominent against her blue-tinged skin. The water plastered her bone-white hair to her skull in stringy clumps, revealing her delicate ear and vulnerable temple. Her lips had gone a startling shade of blue, but her eyes—one crimson, one blue as a glacier—remained open, fixed on Anna with a look that was part fear, part awe. She didn't speak, not at first, but her gaze was as loud as any scream. It was a look Anna had seen before, on the faces of those who believed she had saved them from monsters, never realizing that she carried a darkness inside her that was more dangerous than any external threat.

For a long minute, neither moved. The world had narrowed to this: the rhythm of lungs, the metallic taste of blood, the ache in every joint. Anna propped herself on one elbow and spat out another mouthful of salt. She felt the cold more now that she was free of the water. It was sharp enough to make her teeth chatter and her fingers clumsy. She fumbled for her satchel, still miraculously strapped to her, and thumbed its contents through the waxed-canvas wrapping: knife, phosphorus matches, vials of ritual components, a couple of tallow candles. All there. Some god had decided she would live, at least for a while longer.

Mercy broke the silence first. Her voice was thin, a thread in the storm. "I thought you'd let me drown."

Anna looked at her, searching for sarcasm or resentment, but found only honest bewilderment. "I thought about it," she said. There was no point in lying.

Mercy blinked, as if she hadn't expected to be addressed so

plainly. She swallowed, coughed once more, then hugged her knees to her chest. "Thank you."

Anna nodded, then rolled onto her back, staring at the bruise-colored sky. She was too tired for triumph, too battered for self-recrimination. The only things that mattered were the breathing girl at her side and the rocky, indifferent land that waited for them both.

Lightning forked behind the cliffs, sketching the distant silhouette of Hallowspire in lines of blinding white. Anna stared at the outline, her heart thudding slow and heavy, and felt something new. Not hope, but the certainty of purpose. She had come this far. She would see it through, for both their sakes.

Chapter 5

The rain relented as the first hints of twilight gathered in the hollow between cliffs, turning the ocean from black glass to the muted pewter of old cutlery. Every muscle screamed in protest as Anna sat up and tried to take stock of their surroundings. The beach was less a true shoreline than a dumping ground for the island's broken bones—splintered logs, heaps of pebbles slick with algae, and spurs of rock that jutted from the sand like the ribs of a whale carcass. The sea had already reclaimed the debris of their shipwreck, and the yawl's corpse was nowhere to be seen, consumed by the patient appetite of the tide.

Mercy shivered beside her, arms locked tight around her knees, the thin dress now a shroud of sodden misery. Anna studied her in profile—hollow-cheeked, lashes sticky with salt, lips blue and bloodless—and marveled at the grimness that kept her upright. Most girls would have curled up and wept. Mercy did not. She simply stared at the sea with the fixed attention of a starving wolf, as if the water had something it owed her.

Anna's own body was a map of injuries. Her scalp wound oozed hot down her temple. Barnacles had cut her palms, and bruises were already purpling on her ribs and shoulder. But she found that if she moved slow and breathed shallow, she could ignore the worst of it. Her cloak had lost most of its warmth, but she cinched it tighter regardless, gathering her satchel and scanning the length of the cove for any sign that the path to Hallowspire would be less lethal than the swim.

They didn't speak for a long while. The silence wasn't comfortable, but it was honest; a mutual contract to let suffering run its course before inviting words back in. Anna was the first to break it.

"We need to get higher," she said, testing her voice. "The tide's coming up. If we don't move, we'll freeze."

Mercy nodded, pushed herself to standing with difficulty, and followed as Anna limped toward the bluff at the back of the cove. The incline was steep, tangled with roots and trailing ferns, the stone slick with moss and the runoff of centuries. There was a faint path worn into the cliff face by feet long since gone to dust. Anna took the lead, her stockinged feet finding purchase where they could, one hand always testing the holds before trusting her weight. She heard Mercy's footsteps behind her, slow but relentless. Somehow, the girl had managed to keep both of her shoes—a small blessing on this rugged landscape.

Wind funneled through the pines above, making the whole island groan like a wounded animal. Twilight draped itself across Brimwatch Isle, the fading light reluctant to touch the twisted pines that clung to the cliffside. The storm had exhausted itself to a sullen drizzle, but the rocks remained treacherously slick. Anna dug her fingers into a crevice, ignoring the pain that shot through her torn nails as she hauled herself upward. She kept her eyes up, searching for a shape on the horizon, the promise of their destination.

Behind her, Mercy's labored breathing punctuated the damp silence. She didn't complain once during their ascent, though Anna could hear her slipping frequently, catching herself with small, bitten-off gasps. The rope still connected them. Anna had considered cutting it once they reached shore, but something had made her reconsider. Perhaps the practical knowledge that the climb would be dangerous, perhaps something less pragmatic that she refused to examine too closely.

Anna's hair was a tangle of black vines whipping against her face when the wind gusted. The soles of her feet were raw from sharp rocks and her skirts, still damp and torn in a dozen places, clung to her legs like needy hands, restricting her movement with each step. The leather satchel had survived their ordeal, its contents protected by the waxed canvas. Her shoulder throbbed where the rock had struck it, the pain a dull companion to the sharper sting of cuts on her palms and the persistent ache in her lungs from the seawater she had swallowed.

With a grunt of effort, Anna pulled Mercy up beside her onto the final ledge. They remained side by side at the top of the cliff wall, catching their breath. Below them, the narrow beach where they had washed ashore had disappeared into shadow, the tide reclaiming it inch by inch. Anna saw a trail fifty yards ahead, likely leading from a better landing to the distant mansion.

"We'll rest here," Anna decided, easing herself into a sitting position, her legs dangling over the precipitous drop. "Five minutes, no more."

Mercy sank down beside her, wincing slightly as she stretched her legs. The girl's homespun dress had become little more than rags, revealing the thin arms and legs of a child on the cusp of adolescence. Despite her fragile appearance, she had kept pace with Anna's climb with stubborn determination, never asking for help unless Anna offered it.

They sat in silence as twilight deepened around them, the light bleeding from the western sky. From somewhere in the pine forest that crowned the lower slopes of the cliff, an owl called three mournful notes that went unanswered.

"I followed you from Boston."

Mercy's voice was so unexpected in the gathering gloom that Anna nearly startled. The girl spoke softly, but with a certainty that suggested she'd been rehearsing these words.

"I saw you take the coach to the wharf," she continued, her gaze fixed on the mansion rather than on Anna. "I paid a boy to tell me which ship you'd hired, and I stowed away until it was too late for you to turn back." A hint of pride crept into her voice at this last revelation, as though her resourcefulness might somehow mitigate the foolishness of her actions.

Anna's mouth worked, but no words came. Her first urge was anger—rage at the stupidity, the audacity, the risk.

"Why?" she demanded, her voice stripped of any warmth.

Mercy turned to her and held her gaze. "Because I want to learn. I want to know what you know—the craft. The power. I know the supernatural is real. I've seen it. Felt it." She raised her wrists, the hideous scars clearly visible even in the fading light. "I need to understand it. Control it. Like you do."

Anna's laugh was sharp and bitter, a sound like breaking glass. "Control? You think I control this?" She gestured vaguely toward her own chest, where Rebecca Hale's insidious presence lurked like a tumor. "You have no idea what you're asking for."

"Then teach me," Mercy insisted, a desperate edge creeping into her voice. "I need to know how to protect myself. How to fight back. William tries, but he doesn't understand. Not like you do."

"And what of William now?" Anna demanded, thinking of Mercy's brother waiting in Boston, likely sick with worry for his missing sister. "Did you spare a thought for him before you decided to chase after ghosts and monsters?"

A flicker of guilt crossed Mercy's face, but her resolve remained unshaken. "I left him a letter. Told him I was safe with you."

"With me!" Anna's voice rose despite the danger of drawing attention on this hostile island. "You were never with me! You were following me, like a shadow I never asked for! Do you have any conception of where we are? What awaits us up there?" She thrust a finger toward the looming silhouette of Hallowspire. "This is not some adventure from a penny dreadful, Mercy. This is death and worse than death."

Mercy flinched at Anna's tone but didn't retreat. Instead, she straightened her thin shoulders, facing Anna's fury with a courage that would have been admirable in any other circumstance.

"I know it's dangerous," she said. "But so is ignorance. So

is being helpless when the darkness comes again." Her hand unconsciously moved to her throat, where Anna knew the spiritual scars of Angéle de la Barthe's possession ran deeper than any physical mark. "And it will come again. For both of us."

The simple truth of the girl's words deflated some of Anna's anger, leaving behind a hollow exhaustion. She knew better than most that darkness rarely passes by those it has touched once. It returns, again and again, drawn by the scent of previous violation. One dead witch had already claimed Mercy. Without protection, without knowledge, she would be easy prey for other spirits.

Anna shook her head, almost laughed again, then refocused on the mansion. Hallowspire rose from the northern cliffs like a cathedral torn from the bones of some ancient continent. Its walls were black in the gathering night. The windows seemed to leak shadow, not illumination. Vines climbed the stonework like desperate hands reaching for heaven, and the roof—steep-pitched and adorned with iron finials shaped like twisted creatures—cut a jagged line against the starlit sky.

"You don't want this life," Anna said, her voice weighted with a fatigue that went beyond physical exhaustion. "You think you do, but you don't. It's not a gift. It's a curse. Every spell has a price. Every power demands payment in blood or sanity or soul. And every day you wake up knowing something is waiting to eat you—and one day, it will."

Anna turned back to Mercy, her face harsh in the deepening shadows. "Is that what you want? To be haunted? To live knowing that the darkness isn't just around you, but inside you as well? To never be certain if you're the one hunting the monsters, or if you've become the very thing you hunt?"

Mercy didn't flinch at the questions. Instead, she nodded once—a simple gesture that contained volumes of understanding beyond her years. "I already live that way," she said. "The only difference is whether I face it armed or defenseless."

Anna didn't answer. There was nothing to say to that.

Chapter 6

The last rays of daylight died with surprising quickness behind the bristling pines, as if even the sun wanted nothing to do with Brimwatch Isle after nightfall. By the time Anna and Mercy reached the upper rise of the plateau, their wet clothes clung to them in damp sheets, drawing the heat from their bodies in long, steady pulses. The climb bruised and bloodied them both. Fresh cuts ribboned Anna's hands, and Mercy moved with the stiff, shuffling gait of someone whose limbs had gone almost numb.

They crossed what might once have been a formal garden, now a tangle of wild rosebushes and thorns that snagged at their already-torn clothing. Stone benches, cracked and covered in lichen, stood along the overgrown path. They paused at the edge of a broken yew ring, catching their breath and taking in the massive structure that now loomed over them.

Hallowspire was larger than it had appeared from a distance—much larger. The black-veined granite of its outer walls rose straight and sheer for two stories before breaking into a riot of spires, minarets, and angular gables, all capped in the same slate as the cliffs beneath. Ivy climbed the walls in thick, ropey tendrils, pulsing slightly in the breeze—or perhaps it was merely a trick of the failing light. The windows —set deep behind gothic arches and wreathed in stonework —caught what little light remained and reflected it back as featureless eyes.

Staring up at it, Anna felt the peculiar weight that comes with proximity to greatness, or perhaps only to old, deliberate evil.

"It's watching us," Mercy whispered, her mismatched eyes fixed on the mansion's facade.

Anna didn't dismiss the observation. Mercy wasn't wrong; there was a presence to Hallowspire that transcended mere architecture. The building seemed aware, patient in the way only things born of stone and darkness can be.

The main entrance awaited them at the head of a short flight of steps, flanked by two weathered gargoyles whose features were so eroded by time and lichen that Anna couldn't determine if they were human, beast, or something in between. The ironbound oak doors were easily twelve feet tall and appeared, at first, not to have a handle at all. Above the arch was a stone shield, carved with a seven-pointed star surrounded by serpents devouring their own tails.

The sigil of The Crucible of Night.

Mercy felt Anna tense beside her at the sight of it. "What is it?" she asked. "Is something wrong?"

Anna hesitated, then shook her head. "It's nothing. Just the cold."

Mercy gave a skeptical squint. "You're lying. You're

scared."

Anna shot her a glance. "Only fools and dead men don't get scared walking into places like this."

"You don't look like someone who gets scared."

Anna smirked without humor. "That's why I'm still alive."

She gave the door an experimental shove. It didn't move. Anna gritted her teeth, planted both boots on the top step, and put her shoulder into it. The hinges didn't so much as squeak. It was like trying to budge a section of the cliff itself.

Mercy's voice was thin, barely audible above the wind that knifed across the steps. "What if we're not meant to get in?"

Anna shot her a look that carried every ounce of her exhaustion. "There's always a way in, especially if you know how to look." She turned, scanning the facade for alternatives.

To the left of the main doors, hidden behind the shadow of one jutting gargoyle, Anna spied a narrow postern gate, its metal studs corroded to green. She led Mercy down a slippery cobblestone path and found a servant door's lock so rusted that the bolt itself seemed fused to the jamb. Anna reached for her belt, her fingers closing around the bone-handled knife she'd managed to keep through the ordeal. The blade wasn't designed for this task, but it provided sufficient leverage. After a dozen grunting attempts and a blow from a loose stepping stone, Anna forced the latch open with a sound like an old bone breaking.

An ancient, stale smell, like a tomb's centuries-old breath, emanated from the opening. Mercy wrinkled her nose but didn't hesitate, her eyes huge and glassy in the dark as she slipped past Anna into the relative shelter of the corridor.

Anna followed, the knife still in her hand, her eyes adjusting to the deeper darkness within.

Beyond the door, frigid air instantly frosted Anna's breath, despite the hallway's protection. The walls sweated with moisture that stank of iron and brine. Just inside the threshold, they found a couple of pairs of leather boots and a set of moth-eaten cloaks hanging from pegs, their outlines thick with salt and ancient mildew. Anna ripped one free and handed it to Mercy. It was too big for her, but the girl accepted it without a word, pulling it tight, though her shaking hands made the cloth twitch like a frightened creature's hide. Anna's raw and tender feet throbbed as she slipped them inside a worn pair of boots, grateful for their protection.

After a few yards, the short passage opened into the grandest chamber Anna had ever seen outside a cathedral. The ceiling soared overhead, lost in darkness and supported by fluted columns the color of old teeth. The floor was a chessboard of black and gray marble, the squares so large that Anna's outstretched arm would barely span two of them. At the far end, occupying the width of the hall, was a fireplace so immense Anna could have stood upright inside it with room to spare. The firebox was empty, but on the hearth sat a tarnished brass grate, half-filled with the desiccated remnants of old logs.

Most striking, however, was the cold. The hall was freezing —a deep, penetrating chill that seemed to radiate from the stones themselves.

Mercy's breath clouded before her face, and she noticed with alarm that a thin layer of frost had formed on the flagstone hearth despite the mild October evening outside. "Something's wrong," she murmured. "This cold isn't natural."

"It's the stone," Anna said, though she knew the real reason was the way Hallowspire hunched against the Veil—the spiritual border between the living world and the other. She kept this thought to herself. Instead, she set about examining the chamber with a hunter's eye for shelter, weapons, and weaknesses.

The Grand Hall was mostly devoid of furniture except for a couple of moth-eaten couches, a few broken chairs stacked in one corner, and what looked like the remains of a banquet table pushed up against the far wall. Stone columns, each carved to resemble a different creature—some human, some decidedly not—supported a gallery that ran the perimeter of the hall. Tattered tapestries hung between the columns, their once-vibrant scenes now reduced to ghostly outlines of hunts and rituals.

Mercy had stopped in the middle of the hall and hugged her arms close in her borrowed cloak, shivering so violently Anna worried she'd break a rib. Her lips had lost their color entirely, and each breath came out in thin, whistling gasps.

Anna frowned. The hall's air wasn't just cold, but actively drawing the warmth from their bodies—as if the house, deprived of living company for decades, was desperate to fill its own emptiness. She approached the fireplace and poked at the remains of the old logs. Dry rot had turned them into a kind of pitted sponge, but the core was solid. Anna set about building a fire, arranging the biggest pieces on the grate and scavenging strips of wood from the broken chairs for kindling.

"Come closer," Anna said, not looking back. "You'll freeze if you stay over there."

Mercy obeyed and inched a couch closer to the hearth, the frosted floor seeming to hinder her progress. She curled up into a tight ball, her eyes following Anna's movements with the intensity of someone for whom fire meant the difference between life and death.

Anna dug her flint and steel from the bottom of her satchel. Her fingers, still numb from the cold ocean, fumbled with the tools. The first strike produced only a sad shower of sparks that fizzled against the damp kindling. Anna muttered a curse, then closed her eyes briefly, steadying her breathing.

"Come on," she whispered, striking again. This time, a spark ignited a splintered piece of kindling, a tiny point of orange that threatened to die with the slightest breath. Anna hunched over it, sheltering the ember with her body.

The fire spread, reluctantly at first, then with growing appetite, as the core of the old wood smoldered to life. Soon, the chimney drew a thin but steady column of smoke upward, and the feeble light pushed back a few feet of shadow from the hearth.

Mercy left the couch and crouched by the growing fire, holding her hands so close Anna worried she'd burn herself in desperation. The child's fingers were nearly translucent, the knuckles swollen and red. She rocked back and forth, eyes locked on the dancing flames with a hunger that went deeper than cold.

"You did it," she said, her voice small but admiring.

Anna nodded, feeding another piece of broken chair leg

into the growing flames. She shed the remains of her own cloak, wrung it out, and laid it near the edge of the hearth to dry. "It won't last long without more fuel. I'll have to search for—"

She broke off as a low, resonant groan echoed through the hall. Not the familiar sound of settling timber or cooling stone, but something deeper and more deliberate. The noise seemed to emanate from the very walls, traveling through the floor beneath their feet, vibrating in their bones.

The flames flickered wildly for a moment, then steadied. Mercy's eyes darted to the shadows beyond their small circle of light.

"What was that?" she whispered.

Anna's hand moved to the knife she had laid on the floor. "The house," she whispered. "It knows we're here."

The crackling of the fire filled the silence that followed Anna's words, a sound too small and ordinary for the vastness it fought to warm. Mercy drew her knees closer to her chest, her mismatched eyes reflecting twin flames—one blue, one red—as she stared into the darkness beyond their small circle of light. Neither of them spoke for several long minutes, listening for more of the mansion's unsettling groans.

"How does a house know anything?" Mercy finally asked, her voice barely above a whisper. She had arranged her tattered dress to dry near the fire, the fabric steaming slightly as the heat drew out the seawater. "Is it… haunted?"

Anna considered her next words. Mercy had earned some answers, if only enough to keep her from acting foolishly. Anna knew from experience that children filled the gaps in adult stories with the most disastrous possibilities.

"Haunted implies ghosts—the lingering spirits of the dead. This is something else." Anna gestured to the vast hall around them, its corners still shrouded in darkness. "Hallowspire was built to be a warded temple, not just a dwelling. Its stones were quarried at night from a haunted quarry, its timbers harvested from trees that grew on old gallows grounds. Every inch of this place was designed to amplify spiritual energy."

"Who built it?" Mercy leaned forward, her face a study in fascination and dread. Her skin was no longer blue, but she sat so close to the fire that Anna worried she might tip forward and sear herself on the brass fender. The darkness beyond the circle of light felt absolute, every noise amplified by the stone chamber: the tick of the fire, the slow drip of water somewhere in the walls, the wind shoving fitfully at the windows high overhead.

Anna sat back against the stone column, positioning herself so she could see both Mercy and the main entrance to the hall. "His name was Alistair Gilead Thorne," she said, letting the name roll off her tongue. It sounded right in this room, the way a curse fits its victim. "He was obsessed with the Veil —the boundary between the living and the dead. He believed it could be breached, not just temporarily, as in a haunting or visitation, but permanently torn open."

Mercy shivered, though whether from cold or fear was impossible to tell.

"Thorne was born to wealth in Boston, a brilliant mind warped by ambition and arcane knowledge. By seventeen, he'd been expelled from Harvard for what they called *unnatural inquiries into the human soul.* Later, he joined a secret society called the Crucible of Night—wealthy elites who make pacts with demons in exchange for knowledge and power."

Mercy's face darkened in the firelight. "Like Cotton Barlow."

Anna nodded, her attention unintentionally drifting to the ghastly scars on Mercy's wrists.

A log shifted in the fire, sending up a shower of sparks. One of them landed on Mercy's sleeve, and she brushed it away with a quick, nervous gesture.

"Thorne became fixated on immortality—not just extending life, but transcending death itself." Anna leaned forward, her face half-illuminated by the firelight, the other half lost to shadow. "His methods grew so extreme even his fellow cultists feared him. They called him *The Severed Hand* behind his back. Eventually, he vanished from Boston society, purchasing this island—which appears on no official map—and beginning construction of Hallowspire in 1799."

Mercy glanced around the hall with fresh eyes, seeing beyond its decayed grandeur to the sinister purpose in its design. "What did he do here?"

Anna hesitated, measuring how much to reveal to the girl. "He conducted experiments, what he called *transcendental vivisection*—an unholy blend of ritual magic, anatomical dissection, and spiritual coercion."

"Did he succeed?" Mercy's voice had grown so quiet that only the hall's unnatural acoustics allowed her words to reach Anna.

Anna shrugged. "One night, he simply vanished. No one ever saw him die. But the house..." Anna trailed off, watching Mercy.

Mercy fixed her eyes on the fire, yet Anna knew the girl was listening intently. "Is that why you're here?" Mercy asked. "To solve the mystery of Thorne's disappearance?"

Anna's expression shuttered, becoming deliberately opaque. "We're here because we needed shelter from the storm." The lie hung between them, as palpable as the chill that permeated the hall beyond their small circle of warmth.

Mercy studied Anna's face for a long moment, then nodded slowly, accepting that there were things Anna wouldn't—or couldn't—share. "What happened after Thorne disappeared?"

"The island was abandoned. Sailors avoid it, claiming it's cursed. Over the years, various expeditions have attempted to explore Hallowspire, seeking Thorne's legendary wealth or the arcane knowledge he supposedly uncovered." Anna's mouth tightened. "None returned."

The implications of this statement settled over them like a shroud. Mercy drew her damp cloak tighter around her shoulders, though the fabric offered little protection against the pervasive cold.

"Yet here we are," she murmured.

"Yes," Anna replied, something flashing in her eyes that might have been doubt or determination. "Here we are."

She didn't elaborate on what had brought her to Brimwatch, what she hoped to find in Hallowspire's moldering halls, or why she was willing to risk not only her own life but that of the girl sitting across from her. There were truths too dangerous to speak aloud.

Another groan emanated from deep within the mansion's walls, this one accompanied by a faint but discernible tremor in the floor. The fire flickered wildly for a moment, then steadied, though it seemed to burn with less vigor than before.

Mercy shrank closer to the fire, the tension in her body drawing her knees to her chest, her hands tight around her shins. "I think it's listening," she whispered.

"Good," Anna said, her voice dry. "That's half the battle. If it's paying attention, it can be distracted." She pulled her coat tighter, feeling the dampness returning despite the fire's efforts. "The other half is making sure it never learns what you're really afraid of."

Chapter 7

Night enveloped Hallowspire, erasing the line between the house and the heavens, leaving only their weak firelight to mark their presence against the void. With the last of the kindling consumed hours ago, Anna fed the flames with whatever scraps of wood she could pry from the rotting wainscoting near the hearth. Mercy had finally surrendered to exhaustion, curled on the moth-eaten couch like a pale question mark, her white hair splayed across the faded upholstery. The girl's face had softened in sleep, her habitual wariness giving way to something closer to her actual age.

Anna sat with her back to a stone column, her knife across her lap, its blade glinting in the firelight. Though her body screamed for rest, she kept her eyes open, scanning the darkness with the practiced vigilance of someone who had learned early that sleep was a luxury afforded only to the protected, never to the protector.

The fire had settled into a steady glow, more embers than flame now, casting just enough light to transform the hall into a cavern of dancing shadows. The stone creatures perched on the columns seemed to shift and breathe in the unsteady light, their granite faces twisting into expressions of malice and hunger that vanished when viewed directly.

As the mansion settled deeper into the night, the quality of the silence changed. The ordinary creaks and groans of an old structure gave way to something more deliberate—pauses that stretched too long, followed by sounds that came too precisely, like footfalls measuring the exact distance between heartbeats.

It was in this altered silence that the voice came, as inevitable as the cold.

Child. So cautious, so clever. You would not have survived the crossing without my counsel. Or my hunger.

Anna's right hand flexed, nails digging crescents into her palm. The familiar shudder ran through her body. Rebecca's possession was never total, but it was always there, as if a cold thumb pressed against the back of her skull, ready to push through. Anna fought it, as she always had, with sheer force of will.

"You're not helping," she murmured, too low for even Mercy to hear.

On the contrary. Without me, you would be feeding the eels at the bottom of the Sound. Or floating, bloated, until the crows opened your eyes for you.

Anna's jaw clenched until she thought she might break her own teeth. She kept her eyes fixed on the fire.

You waste precious time, child. The answers lie deeper, not in this empty hall. Thorne's secrets beckon. Yet here you sit, playing nursemaid to a girl who should never have followed you.

Anna squeezed the knife handle so tightly her knuckles

turned white. A faint tremor ran through her right hand—the first sign of Rebecca's growing control, a physical manifestation of the dead witch's will imposing itself on Anna's flesh.

"Not now," Anna breathed, her voice nearly lost in the quiet crackling of the dying fire. She glanced at Mercy, ensuring the girl still slept before continuing her one-sided conversation.

Time grows short, great-granddaughter, Rebecca persisted, her voice carrying the weight of centuries, thick with malice and something like hunger. *I have kept my part of our covenant. I have guided you to this place, shared my knowledge of the Veil and its thinning. Without me, you would never have discovered Thorne's writings, never learned of his power to restore souls lost beyond the Veil.*

The tremor in Anna's hand worsened, spreading up her arm until her elbow twitched against her will. She clutched the affected limb with her other hand, pressing it against her side as if the physical restraint could contain the spiritual intrusion.

Our bargain was clear, was it not? Rebecca's voice had taken on the cadence of formal recitation, each word precise and weighted. *My guidance and power in exchange for flesh to house my spirit. Your body as my vessel, that I might walk again among the living.*

"Not until we restore my mother's soul," Anna hissed through clenched teeth. "That was our bargain, witch. I am your tether to this world, only so long as you help me bring my mother back from beyond the Veil."

She closed her eyes briefly, fighting for control over her

own limbs as Rebecca's influence surged against her will. When she opened them again, the shadows in the corners of the hall seemed to have deepened, gathered, become more attentive.

"That's why we're here," Anna continued, her voice steadying as she reasserted her dominance. "That's the only reason I let you in. You promised Thorne found a way to open the Veil without sacrificing the summoner. A way to reach through and retrieve a specific soul."

And so he did, child. But such power is not given freely. It demands payment, as all magic does. Are you prepared for that cost?

The question hung in the air, unanswered, as the fire in the hearth suddenly hissed and flared, the flames leaping three feet high before collapsing back to embers. The unexpected illumination cast the hall in harsh relief for a moment, revealing details previously hidden by shadow: strange symbols carved into the ceiling beams, a dark stain on the floor near the main entrance that might have been old blood, faces carved into the stone wall behind the tapestries—hundreds of them, mouths open in silent screams.

Darkness fell again, even more profound than before. Mercy stirred on the couch, murmuring something unintelligible before settling back into her troubled sleep.

She senses it too, Rebecca observed, a note of approval in her spectral voice. *The girl has potential. The mark of another's possession still lingers on her soul—a door once opened is never truly closed again.*

"Leave her out of this," Anna warned, though she knew the futility of threatening a spirit that existed partly within her own mind. "She's under my protection."

Protection? Rebecca's laugh was dry and brittle, like autumn leaves crushed underfoot. *You can barely protect yourself from me, let alone shield another from what dwells within these walls.*

As if summoned by Rebecca's words, a series of distinct footsteps sounded from the floor above—slow, measured, deliberate. Not the random settling of an abandoned structure, but the purposeful tread of something with weight and intention. The footsteps crossed the ceiling directly above them, paused, then continued toward what would be the eastern wing of the mansion.

Anna rose silently to her feet, knife ready, her eyes tracking the sound as it moved overhead. When the footsteps faded, she remained standing, every sense alert to the sudden, oppressive stillness that followed.

We are not alone, Rebecca whispered, her voice now almost gentle, seductive in its certainty. *Thorne's work continues, even in his absence. This house will try to kill you. It will enjoy it. Let me guide you, or die shrieking in the dark like all the others who thought they could walk here uninvited.*

Anna moved closer to the couch where Mercy slept, positioning herself between the girl and whatever might emerge from the darkness. The fire had dwindled to almost nothing now, the circle of light shrinking by the minute. Soon they would be left in complete darkness, with only touch and sound to guide them through Hallowspire's treacherous halls.

You were born for this moment, Rebecca continued, her voice rising with excitement. *Our blood mingled with Thorne's power. We need only find its source—and pay its price.*

"My mother's soul first," Anna insisted, though there was a slight tremor in her voice. "Then we discuss your freedom. Not before."

The flames guttered suddenly, as if an icy breath had passed over them. Anna tensed and raised her knife as she scanned the darkness beyond their tiny island of fading light. For a moment, nothing moved.

Then she heard it. A slow, deliberate exhalation from the shadows just beyond the firelight's reach. Not the random draft of an old building, but the measured breath of something alive and aware.

Something that had been watching them all along.

Anna froze, every sense straining. The sound didn't repeat, but she knew it was not the house settling.

Something was moving, testing the limits of their intrusion.

A cold wind slipped down the corridor and across the floor, swirling the ashes in the fireplace and making the embers flicker almost out. Anna remained perfectly still, letting her eyes adjust to the new patterns of dark and light. She focused on her own heartbeat, slow and steady, and waited for the next noise.

It came, eventually. Another footstep, closer this time. And then a long, slow exhale from somewhere just beyond the edge of the firelight. The house had awakened, and Anna was certain she wasn't the only predator within its walls.

She bared her teeth, not in fear, but in challenge, and stared into the dark until the sun began to rise.

Chapter 8

The morning brought no relief from the gloom. Hallowspire's windows, thick with years of salt and dust, admitted only a thin gray light. Anna rolled the stiffness from her shoulders, the remnants of her sleepless vigilance turning her movements sharp and abrupt. Beside the ash-flecked embers of the hearth, Mercy stirred beneath her ragged cloak, her white hair tangled across her face like spun cobwebs. She blinked her mismatched eyes and pushed herself upright on the couch, wincing at muscles gone rigid with cold and fear.

"You didn't sleep," she observed, her voice scratchy from salt and exhaustion.

Anna shook her head and sheathed her knife in her belt with practiced efficiency. "This house doesn't want us to rest." She kept her voice neutral despite the certainty that eyes had watched them through the night—eyes that belonged to neither the living nor precisely the dead. "We need to move," she said, scanning the cavernous hall one more time. "We're not safe here."

They gathered their meager possessions in silence. Anna's

clothes had dried unevenly, stiff with salt in some places and still damp in others. Her leather satchel hung at her side. Mercy wrapped herself in the tattered remains of her borrowed cloak, her thin shoulders squared with a defiance that belied her years.

The Grand Hall was bitterly cold and held the silence of a mortuary. When the two of them set off, their steps echoed in the vastness as if they'd woken the bones of the house itself.

Anna led them across the expanse of the chessboard floor. At its heart, a seven-pointed star was worked into the stone, just as it was in the carvings, in the very architecture of the house. Anna skirted the mosaic with care, not out of superstition, but out of memory. Circles and stars meant boundaries, and boundaries meant traps. It never paid to tread carelessly in a place built by a mind like Alistair Thorne's.

The night's supernatural pressure had subsided, but the emptiness of the house now felt predatory—watching, coiled, waiting for some cue. Anna kept Mercy close as they found the wide marble staircase that spiraled up from the side of the hall and followed it to the next level.

The second-story gallery opened to the hall below, but off its length branched a corridor of arched doors and balustraded balconies. Anna chose the leftmost hall, scanning for signs of disturbance—old scuff marks, new dust patterns, the subtle chemical scent of spent candles. The mansion's stone walls seemed to press in, lined with warped portraits whose eyes had not clouded entirely with age.

Anna continued without stopping. She wagered that the library would be somewhere in the western wing, isolated from the bedrooms but accessible to the master's offices.

After three turns and a narrow stairwell that smelled of mice and mold, they found it: a double set of black walnut doors, inset with panels of scarlet glass. Across the lintel, words had been carved in a language that shifted and changed even as Anna tried to read them.

"What does it say?" Mercy asked, squinting at the inscription.

"It's in Enochian," Anna replied, her finger tracing the symbols without touching them. "The language of angels, corrupted by men who thought themselves worthy to speak it." Her lips moved silently for a moment before she translated: "*Knowledge bleeds. Wisdom hungers. Enter and feed both.*"

Mercy shivered. "That doesn't sound like an invitation."

"It's not." Anna frowned. "It's a warning."

She pressed her palm to the cold wood. For a moment, she thought she heard the faintest hiss, like breath held for a century. She pushed, and the doors opened on silent hinges, as if someone had oiled them within the last week.

Thorne's library was nothing Anna had prepared herself for.

It was a cathedral in miniature, three stories high, the air so cold it burned her sinuses. Walkways and spiral staircases of iron lacework circled the perimeter, each level crammed with shelves that reached up into shadow. At the room's heart, beneath a glass dome painted with star charts and phases of the moon, stood Thorne's magical Veiled Flame.

It floated three feet off the floor, encased in a thick cylinder of glass. It didn't flicker, and though its shape was that of a fire, the color was a blue so deep it threatened black. The light it shed had no warmth and cast no shadow, but it etched every object in the room with the sharpness of moonlight on a winter night. Beneath the flame, the floor dropped away to form a shallow pit lined with polished obsidian, its bottom lost in reflection.

Mercy's breath misted in the air. She moved toward the flame, stopping at the edge of the pit. "Why does it burn blue?" she asked, her voice barely more than a breath.

"Not all fire is for burning," Anna replied, studying the runes etched into the pit's rim. "This is a sigil-fire. Thorne used it to bind knowledge and test truth. Books read too close to it sometimes whisper or weep."

The library's shelves were the real macabre attraction. Most were lined with tomes bound in animal skin, some chained to the shelves, others locked inside iron cages or encased in glass boxes surrounded by sigils of containment.

Anna surveyed the ground floor. The arrangement of the books wasn't by author or subject, but by some arcane taxonomy: alchemical, daemonological, necromantic, cosmic. Near the spiral stairs, she found a cluster of shelves whose contents seemed to hum, the vibration setting her teeth on edge. The further she walked, the more oppressive the sense of being watched became, until even the pressure of her own footsteps felt rebuffed by the air.

Mercy wandered to a reading table, examining the thick, chained tomes with a mixture of awe and disgust. She pulled a random volume toward her, dust ghosting upward in a lazy arc. "Can I—" she began, but Anna shot her a look sharp enough to cut.

"Don't open anything you don't want living inside your head," she warned. "These books can read you back."

Mercy withdrew her hand, eyes wide.

Anna's attention fixed on a row of black leather tomes, each secured with a different metal chain—iron, silver, copper, gold. The chains disappeared into the shelf itself, as if the books had been physically incorporated into the library's structure. Behind them, barely visible in the dim light, she detected a seam in the woodwork, a line too straight to be natural.

"A door," she murmured, her fingers tracing the nearly invisible outline. Symbols had been etched into the frame—warding signs meant to keep out the uninitiated, to blind the eye and confuse the mind. Anna recognized them from her Book of Shadows—containment sigils, binding runes, markers of forbidden territory.

She glanced back at Mercy, who was still examining the contents of the shelves. The girl wouldn't understand what Anna was about to do, and it was better that way. This door concealed something unfit for innocent eyes, however much darkness those eyes had already witnessed.

Anna removed a small vial from her satchel and unstoppered it carefully. The contents—grave dust mixed with her own blood, collected during the full moon—had a sharp, metallic scent that made her nostrils flare. She dabbed a small amount on her fingertips and began to trace counter-sigils over the wards, her lips moving in a silent incantation taught to her by Rebecca Hale in the dark hours between midnight and dawn.

The wood warmed beneath her touch, the sigils glowing

briefly with a sickly green light before fading back to black. A low grinding of stone against stone emanated from within the wall as hidden mechanisms shifted and released. The shelf slid backward, then to one side, revealing a narrow staircase beyond.

Anna hesitated at the threshold, aware that crossing it would commit her to a course that might have consequences far beyond her understanding. But she hadn't come this far to turn back now. Her mother's soul hung in the balance, trapped beyond the Veil, destined for Hell if Anna couldn't restore her to the living world.

"What is it?" Mercy called from across the library, finally noticing Anna's discovery.

"Stay there," Anna commanded, her voice firm but not unkind. "If I'm not back in five minutes, light this and run for your life." She tossed the girl a packet of phosphorus matches from her satchel and waited for acknowledgment before descending the stairs.

Chapter 9

The air inside the stairwell tasted of rust and old water. The walls were damp, the passage barely wide enough for Anna's shoulders. At the bottom, she found herself in a cramped, barrel-vaulted room lined with shelves of journals and ledgers, some chained, others locked in glass-fronted cabinets. At the center, a heavy table supported an array of documents—letters, folded packets, brittle yellowed sheaves arranged with obsessive neatness.

This was Thorne's archive, his private repository for his most personal secrets.

Anna approached with caution. The Veiled Flame's cold light filtered through a narrow slot above, giving the room an underwater quality. The only sound was her own breathing, amplified by the arched stone. She scanned the shelves, her gaze fixing on one bundle of letters that stood out from the rest. It was tied with a black ribbon and sealed with wax the color of dried blood. The impression in the wax was unmistakable: a seven-pointed star surrounded by serpents devouring their own tails.

The sigil of the Crucible of Night.

Anna's pulse raced. Her hands weren't entirely steady as she reached for the first letter. Whatever she read here could never be unlearned.

She broke the seal.

The immaculate script was written in a hand so precise it could have been typeset. Anna read, her lips barely moving:

To A.G. Thorne, Guardian of the Womb Below, Keeper of the Nocturne Gate:

The Order has received your latest communication regarding the Tenebric Sequence and finds your progress both commendable and concerning. While we acknowledge the potential of your work on soul-stripping and restoration, we must caution against proceeding to walk the final spiral.

The specimens you have prepared—those you call the "Quiet Ones"—represent a significant advancement in our understanding of spiritual anatomy. However, by your own account, the stripping process has rendered them less than ideal as vessels. A soul-stripped body without proper containment sigils becomes vulnerable to possession by entities from beyond the Veil —entities whose allegiance cannot be guaranteed.

We implore you to delay the opening of the Nocturne Gate until you can verify the integrity of your wards. If, by fate or by failure, the wards should break, the consequences of an uncontrolled breach in the Veil could prove catastrophic, not only for our Order but for the fabric of reality itself.

In blood and shadow,

—Exaltus D.

Anna's blood ran cold as she absorbed the implications of the letter. Soul-stripping. Vessels. Entities from beyond the Veil. These were the very powers she sought to understand, to harness. But to what terrible purpose had Thorne directed them?

Her eyes fixed on the phrase "Nocturne Gate." Was this why Rebecca had led her here? Was this the key to reaching beyond the Veil and retrieving her mother's soul?

The possibilities were as horrifying as they were tantalizing. A way to strip souls from living bodies. A way to restore them. A gateway to the realm beyond death itself.

Anna folded the letter with unsteady hands, her mind racing with questions that chilled her more deeply than the mansion's supernatural cold. What exactly had Thorne been attempting in the final days before his disappearance? And if his experiments had succeeded, what manner of entity now walked the halls of Hallowspire?

The air in the archive clung to Anna's skin. Every inhale felt like it left a permanent residue on her lungs. She pressed both palms flat to the table, grounding herself in the chill, then forced her fingers to open the second of the sealed letters.

Someone else wrote this one—a slashed, almost desperate script that tilted hard left, as if the writer were racing the end of the world to finish his thought. The wax seal was newer than the rest, brittle, and snapped in her fingers with a satisfying crack. She unfolded the parchment. The edges were crisp but yellowed. Small eruptions of mildew clustered in the margins where fingers had lingered too long.

She read:

Midsummer's Eve, June 21, 1813—Brimwatch Isle, Hallowspire

The moon has begun her descent. She glowers tonight, bloated and red, as though wrenched from some deeper sky. The wind does not move, and yet the trees strain as if listening. It is nearly time.

I do not expect to survive this night—not as I am. And should these pages endure, let them serve as testimony, not a warning.

I was born to open the Wound.

For fifty-three years I have studied the pulse behind the Red Silence of the Veil. In the screams of the dying, in the silence of graves, in the language of flame and shadow, I have heard them —the Watchers Beyond. They wait behind the mirror of death, not asleep, not awake… merely hungry.

They gave us souls only to see how long we would last in the cage. Now I will break the bars.

The Thirteen are prepared. I have plucked their spirits like weeds, stripped them bare of name and memory. They weep without cause. They breathe without meaning. Perfect vessels. I envy their peace.

Below the mansion, the Spiral sings again. The black stone hums when I walk near it. The Antiverb scratches itself into the walls at night. Sometimes, I find it under my nails.

The Crucible counsels caution, but they are blind to the magnitude of what approaches. The prophecy is clear: 'When the

Red Silence is torn, not merely pierced, the Old Ones shall return through gates of bone and flesh to reclaim what was stolen.' The Crucible's elders interpret this as mere metaphor, but I have glimpsed beyond. I have seen the truth.

My ancestors did not create this Order merely to commune with petty demons or harness trivial magics. They foresaw the Fourth Turning—the apocalyptic conflict that will cleanse this world of the unworthy and elevate the enlightened. The Crucible of Night was never meant to prevent this war; we were meant to trigger it, to serve as catalysts for the rebirth that follows destruction.

There is one last thing: I saw her again. In the glass. My sister. Dead these forty years, and yet she stood behind my reflection, her mouth sewn shut, her eyes full of wings. She placed her hand on my shoulder—from the other side. Whispered into my ear: "It isn't a gate. It's a mouth."

To any who dare open this, know that you are now a custodian of the Womb. If you lack the courage, burn this note, pray, and resign yourself to the gnawing that will follow. If not, meet me where all things begin and end.

I have no more blood to give. Only soul. One last Spiral remains to be walked. Let the Nocturne Gate open. Let the Inmost Dark dream me whole.

If I am undone, let it be in full.
If I return, do not trust the skin I wear.

A. G. Thorne
Midnight minus one bell

Anna's face had drained of all color by the time she finished reading. Her fingers were numb, but she felt a warmth in her chest, an uncomfortable heat that she recognized as fear mingled with something worse—a terrible fascination with the power Thorne had sought to harness.

The letter vibrated in her hand—not because of her trembling—but from a faint, almost heartbeat-like pulse emanating from the parchment. She set it down, wiping her fingers against her skirt as if to remove some invisible contamination.

These weren't the ramblings of a madman, but the calculated designs of someone who had glimpsed something terrible and embraced it. And if Thorne had indeed opened this "Nocturne Gate," what had come through in his wake? What still lurked in the depths of Hallowspire, waiting to be released again?

We have only to finish what he began.

Rebecca's voice slid into Anna's mind, smooth and elusive, like oil on water. There was a new quality to it now—excitement, eagerness, a hunger that had not been present before they'd entered Hallowspire.

This is what I have been guiding you toward all along, child. The means of bringing back your precious mother—and so much more. Thorne found a way to part the Veil permanently. With such power, we could retrieve Abigail's soul... and reshape the world in our image.

"No," Anna whispered aloud, though the word was barely audible even to her own ears. "That's not what I came for. You promised me a way to save my mother, not to unleash hell on earth."

Hell, heaven—such childish concepts. The dead witch's voice carried a note of amusement now. *What lies beyond the Veil is neither punishment nor reward. It is power in its rawest form, waiting for those with the courage to claim it. Thorne understood this. Why do you resist what is inevitable?*

Anna's jaw clenched as she fought against Rebecca's influence. The witch's presence seemed to swell within her, pressing against the boundaries of her consciousness like water testing a dam for weakness. For a terrible moment, Anna felt her right hand move without her permission, reaching for Thorne's letter again.

"Stop," she hissed, grabbing her wrist with her left hand, forcing the rebellious limb back to her side. "This is still my body."

For now. Rebecca's voice receded slightly, though her amusement lingered like the aftertaste of bitter medicine. *But time grows short, Anna. The Gate awaits... and your mother's soul hangs in the balance. How much longer will you deny what you know to be true? That power demands sacrifice. That resurrection requires death.*

Anna was still shuddering when she heard the faintest noise behind her—the soft click of a foot on stone, the careful weight of someone trying not to be heard. Anna's instincts kicked in. She swept the letters into her satchel and turned, knife already in hand.

Mercy stood at the top of the stairwell, pale as the smoke from a guttered candle. The girl's eyes went straight to Anna's face, registering the wildness there, then to the knife, and finally to the satchel.

"I heard your voice," she said. "I thought—" She stopped,

clearly at a loss.

Anna realized her own posture—coiled, violent, a hair away from an attack. She forced herself to lower the knife and softened a fraction, uncurling her body so as not to terrify the girl further. "It's nothing," she said. "Just old letters. Useless now. Let's get out of here."

She led the way up the stairs and into the relative brightness of the library. There, the Veiled Flame still burned in the ghostly cold, a blue-black promise in its prison of glass.

They were halfway down the main aisle, Mercy trailing two steps behind, when the girl stopped dead.

"Look at that," she whispered, pointing at a niche in the wall.

Anna turned and saw an oval mirror, framed in ornate silver, set between two crumbling busts. The glass was fogged and slightly convex, warping the reflection of the room behind them.

Mercy stepped closer, as if drawn by gravity. "Why does it look like that? It's like the air inside is… thick."

Anna watched, unease crawling down her spine. She had seen many tools for scrying and divination, but none that gave her quite this sense of foreboding. The mirror's surface caught the cold light from the Veiled Flame and seemed to pulse, very faintly, in time with the beating of her own heart.

Mercy moved until she stood directly before the mirror. She gazed into it, and for a moment, all was normal: her pale face, her thin frame wrapped in the borrowed cloak, her eyes mismatched but alive. She raised a hand to touch her cheek, and her reflection did the same.

Then the image began to change.

It started subtly—a darkening around the eyes, a pallor that spread across her skin like frost across a window. Mercy's reflection opened its mouth slightly, as if to speak, but no sound emerged. Instead, its jaw continued to stretch, wider and wider, until it gaped open impossibly far, revealing a throat that seemed to extend into infinite blackness.

The reflection's tongue was gone, replaced by a raw, red stump that glistened wetly in the half-light. Its eyes, once mismatched and human, rolled upward in their sockets until only the whites remained—lidless, staring, inhuman. The skin of its face grew translucent, revealing the skull beneath in ghastly detail.

Mercy didn't move, transfixed by the horrible transformation of her own image. Her real face remained unchanged, but her reflection had become something else: one of Thorne's soul-stripped victims, a vessel emptied of its essential humanity and waiting to be filled with something else.

"Anna?" Mercy whispered, her voice thin with terror. "What's happening to me?"

Just as Anna tried to pull her away from the awful sight, the mirror's surface started to fracture. It started as a single line across the glass, a hairline crack that spread outward like a spider's web, accompanied by a sound like ice breaking on a frozen pond. More cracks appeared, racing across the reflective surface until the entire mirror was a maze of splintered silver.

Mercy finally broke free of her paralysis and stumbled backward, colliding with Anna, who wrapped protective arms around the girl's shoulders. Together they watched as the cracks in the mirror continued to spread, each new fissure appearing with a sharp, musical sound, like tiny crystal bells being shattered one by one.

The reflection itself remained visible through the broken glass, still showing the grotesque, soul-stripped version of Mercy. But now it moved independently, its head tilting at an impossible angle, as if studying the two women through the fractured barrier. Its lidless eyes fixed on Anna, and she felt a chill of recognition—not of Mercy, but of something else that wore the girl's shape like an ill-fitting mask.

The thing in the mirror opened its lipless mouth again, and this time a sound emerged—not speech, but a high, thin keening that seemed to come from everywhere and nowhere at once. The noise built in intensity, rising to a pitch that made Anna's teeth ache and Mercy clamp her hands over her ears in pain.

Just as it became unbearable, the mirror shattered into a million pieces. Silver shards exploded outward, glittering in the blue-black light like deadly stars, then froze in midair, suspended impossibly for one breathless moment before falling to the floor with a sound like rain on a leaden roof.

Mercy screamed, the sound torn from her throat as if by force, and buried her face against Anna's shoulder. Anna held her, one hand moving to the knife at her belt, her eyes fixed on the now-empty frame where the mirror had been.

Only darkness remained where the glass had shattered—a void deeper than the absence of light, a hole torn in the world's fabric itself. And from within that darkness, something watched them with patient, ancient hunger.

As she gathered Mercy to leave, Anna risked a glance back

at the Veiled Flame. In its depths, she could have sworn she saw, for a fraction of a second, the reflection of her own ancestor, Rebecca Hale, in the torn black of her wedding shroud. Her eyes were bright as cinders, watching her with a hungry, patient smile.

And behind Anna's own eyes, Rebecca's voice cackled with unholy delight.

Chapter 10

The iron-strapped door groaned as Anna heaved it open, particles of rust drifting like copper snow as the ancient hinges protested their movement after decades of stillness. Beyond lay what had once been Hallowspire's walled garden. The grand terrace was now claimed by wilderness, where twisted rosebushes reached with thorny fingers toward a sky heavy with salt and mist. It clung to the very edge of the northern cliffs, suspended between the mansion's dark embrace and the endless gray canvas of the Atlantic. Anna stepped through first, her boots crunching on gravel long ago buried beneath moss and creeping vines. Her eyes narrowed as she scanned this unfamiliar territory for threats both seen and unseen.

The garden stretched outward in the vague shape of a formal labyrinth. Stone paths meandered and doubled back, their once-precise lines now devoured by the opportunism of wild roses and the relentless march of vines.

Mercy lingered at the threshold of the mansion, her eyes tracking Anna's every move. Her thin hands, already chewed by the cold, clung to her cloak. She hadn't spoken since leaving the library. Her last words—*What's happening to me?*—still knotted somewhere in her throat. Anna didn't blame her.

"Come on," she murmured. "We need to understand the full layout of this place."

Mercy stepped into the garden, hugging herself as if she feared the open air would swallow her whole. The mirror's shattering had left her shaken, her mismatched eyes darting to every shadow cast by the overgrown foliage.

"You're looking for a way off this island, in case we need to leave quickly," she said. It wasn't a question.

Anna stayed quiet. Her attention was already fixed on the garden's perimeter, measuring distances, cataloging obstacles, calculating risks with the cool efficiency of someone whose survival had long depended on such assessments. The garden stretched perhaps a hundred feet in each direction, enclosed by a stone wall that stood chest-high where it bordered the mansion, but grew progressively lower as it approached the cliff's edge, as if surrendering to the inevitable pull of the sea below.

The wind here was different. It was sharp with salt, but also laced with something older, the mineral scent of stone flayed by centuries of weather and neglect. The cries of gulls cut through the gusts, never visible but always overhead, their complaints echoing from the house's high windows and giving the impression of perpetual aerial surveillance. Below, at the cliff's edge, the sound of waves colliding with rock was a ceaseless reminder of their isolation. No boats would approach these shores willingly. No help would come from the mainland. Whatever dangers Hallowspire harbored, they would face them alone.

"This would have been beautiful once," Mercy ventured, her fingertips brushing the velvet petals of a rose that somehow thrived amid the chaos. The bloom hung heavy, too large and full for a plant that should have withered without tending.

They hadn't gone a hundred paces when Anna saw the first of the cairns. It stood beside the path, where the roses thinned to reveal a patch of bare earth. At first glance, it was just a pile of wet, sea-rounded stones, no taller than Mercy's knee. But the closer Anna drew, the clearer it became that this was a deliberate construction. The stones were stacked with uncanny precision, each one balanced on the point of another so that the whole looked less like a monument and more like an assertion of dominance over the land it occupied.

Mercy edged up beside her. "What is it?" she whispered, as if the stones might overhear.

Anna crouched, one palm pressed flat to the ground to steady herself, and studied the cairn at eye level. Between the stones she saw a scatter of snail shells and fragments of white bone. Animal, probably, but the shapes were so clean, so carefully chosen, that it was hard to imagine this as the random detritus of island wildlife.

"It's a marker," Anna said. "Boundary or warning. Or both."

She reached out and gently nudged the topmost stone. It didn't move. Instead, Anna's fingertip traced a groove running the length of the rock, a deliberate scoring that repeated on the others below it. Some marks were faded by rain and wind, but on several she could make out the shape of an arrow, always pointing north, toward the furthest extent of the garden.

"They're marking a path," Anna observed, her eyes following the line of cairns as they wound through the garden's wild heart.

Mercy drew in a shuddering breath. "Should we follow it?"

Anna glanced over her shoulder at the solid bulk of Hallowspire, its black silhouette now looming with a different kind of menace. She straightened, dusting her hands on her skirt, and resumed her march along the path. Mercy followed, silent but close. The path narrowed, the cairns now packed tighter together, their arrangements growing in complexity. The salt wind intensified as they neared the cliff, whipping Mercy's pale hair across her face and forcing Anna to squint against the spray.

They emerged onto a second, smaller terrace that jutted out over the cliff face like a stone tongue. The view was breathtaking and terrible. The whole of the Atlantic spread before them, gray and endless, with Brimwatch Isle's jagged shoreline visible far below. Waves crashed against the rocks with hypnotic violence, throwing spray fifty feet into the air before retreating to gather strength for another assault.

Dominating the terrace's center was the largest cairn yet: a man-sized formation that resembled nothing so much as an altar. The stones were arranged in a rough cylinder, topped with a flat slab of granite that bore more symbols carved deeper, with greater precision, than those they had seen before.

Anna approached cautiously. The symbols were familiar variations on the sigils she had seen in Thorne's private archive. Runes that spoke of binding, of opening, of crossing boundaries not meant to be crossed.

Her fingers traced one symbol, a seven-pointed star surrounded by what appeared to be flames or perhaps reaching hands. Despite the cool sea air, the stone was unnaturally warm beneath her touch, as if heated from within.

"Thorne wasn't just studying the Veil," she murmured. "He was preparing locations all over the property—focusing points for whatever ritual he performed on the night he vanished."

Mercy had gone very still, her mismatched eyes fixed on the stone altar. "Is that... blood?" she asked, pointing to a dark stain that had seeped into the granite's porous surface.

Anna nodded grimly. "Old, but yes. Blood and something else." She leaned closer, detecting faint traces of other substances. Wax perhaps, and the residue of burned herbs or incense.

"These stones aren't just markers," she concluded, straightening. "They're anchors—physical touchpoints meant to secure something that exists primarily in the spiritual realm. Like nails pinning a sheet to a wall."

The implications chilled her more deeply than the sea wind that cut through her damp clothes. Thorne had created a network of ritual sites across Hallowspire's grounds, all connected, all focused on whatever lay beneath the mansion —the Nocturne Gate he had spoken of in his final letter.

"We need to keep moving," Anna said, her steady tone

betraying none of the unease that crawled along her spine. "The garden might hold more answers—or at least give us a better understanding of what we're facing."

The garden's far corner curled away from the ocean like a wounded thing, shielded by a crumbling section of ivy-covered wall. Here, the rose bushes gave way to stunted, leafless trees whose branches reached skyward like supplicating hands, their bark blackened as if by intense heat.

Anna halted abruptly at the clearing's edge, instinctively pulling Mercy back with an outstretched arm. Suspended from the lowest branches, twisting slowly in the salt breeze, hung the first of the effigies—a construct of delicate bones lashed together with fraying black ribbon. Its avian skull tilted at an angle that suggested a macabre curiosity about those who had disturbed its vigil.

"It's ghastly," Mercy whispered, her voice barely audible above the persistent crash of waves against the cliffs below.

Anna's eyes traced the lines of the effigy, noting the precise placement of each brittle bone. Its wings were outstretched in a pose between flight and rest, its ribs interwoven with strange symbols made from smaller bones. The whole construction was no larger than a child's doll, but its presence dominated the clearing with an authority that transcended its size.

"Crow bones," Anna finally said, moving closer with the caution of someone approaching a sleeping predator. "Used in binding spells."

More effigies hung from other branches, forming a grotesque constellation, outlining the clearing's perimeter. Each was unique in its construction. Some were more bird than humanoid; others struck poses suggesting interrupted movement, as if frozen mid-flight or mid-scream. Black ribbons, faded by exposure but still recognizable, bound the bones together in intricate knots that Anna recognized from her Book of Shadows.

Mercy joined Anna, her face stony with horrified fascination. Her hand trembled slightly as she reached toward the nearest effigy with the hesitant curiosity of a child encountering something both beautiful and terrible.

"Don't touch it!" Anna's command cut through the air as her hand shot out, closing around Mercy's wrist with enough force to make the girl wince. She pulled Mercy back, her eyes never leaving the gently swaying effigy. "These are still active."

"Active?" Mercy rubbed her wrist where Anna's fingers had pressed, but she made no move to approach the effigy again. "You mean they're… magic? Still working after all this time?"

"Some rituals never end," Anna replied. "The purpose determines the duration. These were meant to bind something permanently."

She circled the clearing, noting the arrangement of the hanging effigies. They formed a perfect hexagram, with additional constructions marking each intersection of the invisible lines that connected them. This wasn't the work of a lunatic; this was calculated, precise magic performed by someone with intimate knowledge of binding rituals.

The earth beneath the effigies had its own tale to tell. Where normal grass should have grown, only blackened soil remained, forming perfect circles that seemed to have been scorched by intense heat. Anna knelt beside one such circle, her fingers hovering just above the ground, feeling the residual energy that still pulsed faintly, decades after whatever ritual had been performed there.

"He burned something here," she murmured, more to herself than to Mercy. "Something that resisted."

Mercy watched Anna's examination with growing unease, her thin arms wrapped around herself as if for protection against more than just the ocean chill. "What was he trying to bind?"

Anna bit her lip and moved to the center of the clearing, where the largest of the effigies hung from a branch that had been bent and secured to create a natural arch. This construction was more elaborate than the others—a skeletal puppet whose limbs were articulated with tiny wire joints, allowing it to move with the breeze in a grotesque parody of life.

She reached up and carefully detached the effigy from its perch, cradling it in her hands with the reluctant respect of someone handling a venomous snake. Up close, the craftsmanship was even more disturbing. Each bone had been selected for its specific shape and function, the connections reinforced with some dark substance that might have been tar or resin.

Anna's fingers probed between the bones, her expression hardening as she discovered what she had feared. "These aren't all crow bones." She held up a small, yellowed segment that was unmistakably a human finger bone, its surface etched with the same symbols that marked the stone cairns.

Mercy's face drained of what little color it had. "Is that—"

"Human," Anna confirmed, her mouth a thin line.

"Specifically, the distal phalanx—the bone at the fingertip." She turned the effigy, revealing more such bones incorporated into its structure. "There are at least five different human finger bones here, all from different hands. And I'd wager each of these effigies contains similar… components."

The implications hung in the air between them, as heavy as the fog that had crept into the garden from the sea. Mercy swallowed hard, her mismatched eyes fixed on the bone construction in Anna's hands.

"Why would he mix human bones with crow bones?" she asked, though her tone suggested she didn't really want to know the answer.

"Crows are messengers between worlds," Anna explained, carefully replacing the effigy on its branch. "In many traditions, they carry souls to the afterlife. By binding human remains to crow remains, Thorne was creating anchors to keep specific souls from passing beyond the Veil."

She wiped her hands on her skirt, as if trying to remove some invisible contamination. "This isn't just binding magic. It's necromancy of the most fundamental kind—using death to control what comes after."

Mercy's gaze swept the clearing, taking in the dozen or more effigies that swayed in the salt breeze. "Were these… his victims?"

Anna nodded grimly. "Some of them. The people he used in his experiments—the *vessels*." She picked up a fragment of black ribbon that had fallen to the ground, rubbing it between her fingers. "The ribbon is significant. Black for mourning, but also for binding. He was keeping them here, tethered to this place, unable to move on."

She let the ribbon fall, watching as the wind caught it and carried toward the cliff edge. "Thorne didn't just kill them. He harvested their souls, stripped them of identity, and then bound whatever remained to serve his purposes."

The wind shifted suddenly, carrying the scent of decay from somewhere deeper in the garden. Anna tensed, her hand moving to the knife at her belt as she scanned the perimeter for movement.

"Is that what happened to Thorne himself?" Mercy asked, picking up on Anna's sudden alertness but misinterpreting its cause. "Did he become one of his own vessels?"

Anna shook her head slowly, her gaze fixed on a point beyond the garden wall where the fog seemed to gather with unnatural density. "No. I think Thorne got exactly what he wanted. And I think part of him is still here, watching us even now."

The words were barely out of her mouth when a crow landed on the branch above the central effigy, its black eyes fixed on the two women with an intelligence that seemed more than animal. It opened its beak but produced no sound —a silent scream that sent chills racing down Anna's spine.

"We need to move," she whispered, taking Mercy's arm and guiding her firmly away from the clearing. "Don't run, don't look back. Just walk."

As they retreated, the crow remained motionless, its head rotating to follow their progress with the mechanical precision of a weathervane tracking the wind.

Anna traced her palm along the weathered stone wall as they walked, leaning slightly to survey the endless gray canvas of sea and sky. This vantage point revealed the hopelessness of their situation: no ships on the horizon, no lights from distant shores, only water, rock, and indifferent birds circling above the foam.

Mercy walked beside her, close enough that their shoulders nearly touched. The girl's white hair whipped around her face, tangling in the salt wind. For several minutes, neither spoke, allowing the constant thunder of the waves to fill the silence between them. It was a respite, however brief, from the horrors they had witnessed in the garden.

"Is this why you came here?" Mercy finally asked, her voice almost lost in the wind. "To find evidence of Thorne's victims?"

Anna kept her gaze fixed on the horizon. "No," she said simply. "The victims are incidental. Collateral damage in something much larger." She didn't elaborate further, and Mercy seemed to sense that pressing for details would yield nothing.

The girl traced her finger along a crack in the balustrade, following its jagged path across the weathered stone. Her face was drawn, her shoulders hunched against more than just the cold. When she spoke again, her voice had changed—softer, more vulnerable, as if she'd decided to reveal something long kept private.

"I didn't tell you everything," she said. "About why I followed you from Boston."

Anna gave a sideways glance, studying Mercy's profile against the gray backdrop of sea and sky. The girl's eyes—one red, one blue—reflected nothing but troubled depths.

"After what happened in Sévérité… After Angéle…" Mercy swallowed hard; the name of the witch who had possessed her was still difficult to speak aloud. "I tried to go back. To be normal. I know you thought it would help—working in the taverns, being around people who didn't know what happened to me. William thought so too."

She held up her wrists, where the hideous scars from Cotton Barlow's ritual remained visible—permanent reminders of how close she had come to being consumed entirely by another's spirit. "But these aren't the only scars I carry."

Anna remained silent, allowing the girl's confession to unfold at its own pace. The wind had calmed momentarily, as if even the elements recognized the importance of what was being shared.

"I serve ale to sailors who laugh about ghost stories," Mercy continued, her voice gaining strength as she spoke. "I deliver trays to merchants who argue about politics and prices. I clean the kitchen and sweep floors for women who gossip about who's marrying whom." Her hands tightened on the stone balustrade. "And all the while, I see things they don't. Shadows that move when no one is casting them. Reflections that linger after people have walked away. Whispers in empty rooms."

She turned to face Anna directly, her mismatched eyes fierce with a need to be understood. "They smile and talk about the weather while I see shadows moving behind their eyes," she said, her voice cracking. "I can't pretend anymore. Not after what I've seen."

The raw honesty in Mercy's words stirred something in Anna, a recognition that cut deeper than she'd expected. She thought of her own isolation, the weight of carrying knowledge that would drive most people to madness. The burden of seeing the world as it truly was, not as most believed it to be.

"The Veil never closes completely once it's been torn," Anna said, surprising herself with the admission. "Not for people like us."

Mercy's eyes widened slightly at the inclusion—*us*—a tacit acknowledgment of their shared condition.

"That's why you followed me," Anna said. "Because you can't unsee what you've seen?"

Mercy nodded, her relief clear in the slight softening of her shoulders. "William tries to understand, but he can't. Not really. He still believes there's a way back to normal." She looked down at her scarred wrists again. "But I know better. There's only forward now. Through the darkness, not around it."

Anna felt a sudden, unexpected kinship with the girl. How many times had she herself stood at the edge of normalcy, looking in at a world she could never fully rejoin?

"The path you're asking for isn't easy," she said, her voice gentler than it had been since they'd washed ashore on Brimwatch Isle. "It's not heroic or romantic. It's blood and fear and doubt, and moments where you're not sure if you're the one hunting monsters or if you've become one yourself."

"I know," Mercy replied. "But at least it's honest. And I wouldn't be alone."

The implication hung between them—a request, an offering, a possibility. Anna's mother—Abigail—had walked this same path, had tried to protect Anna from it even as she taught her its rules and dangers.

"Mercy, I—"

The words died in Anna's throat as a prickling sensation swept across the back of her neck—the unmistakable feeling of being watched.

Her hand moved instinctively to her knife, fingers tightening around the hilt as her body tensed. Her eyes narrowed, scanning the garden's perimeter where tangled hedges and overgrown rose bushes created countless hiding places.

"What is it?" Mercy whispered, instantly alert to the change in Anna's demeanor.

"We're not alone," Anna murmured.

Mercy nodded once, her strange eyes never leaving the hedgerow.

They stood that way for a long time, Anna shielding Mercy with her body, both of them staring into the mouth of the garden as the surf below hammered its rhythm into their bones.

The watcher didn't reveal itself. But a shape—a sliver of shadow denser than the rest—peeled away from the yew and glided noiselessly along the wall, gone almost before Anna could blink.

It was enough.

Anna put her hand on Mercy's shoulder. "Stay behind me," she said. "And if I tell you to run, you don't stop. No matter what."

Chapter 11

Anna drew a line in the gravel with the toe of her boot—a silent command for Mercy to keep behind her. The mist was rolling in thick from the sea now, coiling through the garden like spectral fingers, caressing the edges of crumbling statues and twining through the branches of dead trees.

Anna let her gaze slide away from the hedge where the watcher had vanished, feigning indifference as she scanned the garden's far boundary. Her real focus was a narrow gap in the overgrown brambles three paces to the left, where footprints in the mud revealed an earlier passage. That's where she'd circle.

She moved low and silent along the edge of the terrace, her path shielded by the wild rosebushes and the standing stones that jutted from the ground at uneven intervals. The fog muffled sound, blurring the edge of every shadow and making distances uncertain. She circled wide, using the garden as cover. A lifetime of hunting had taught her that direct pursuit only alerted prey. Better to anticipate, to cut off escape, to become the unexpected threat from an angle never considered. The shadow had moved with purpose. Not the random drift of a lost spirit or the meandering of a curious animal, but the deliberate progress of something that knew this place, that had purpose here.

Anna kept her breathing shallow, her senses attuned to the slightest disturbance in the fog's languid flow. Behind her, Mercy had become a pale ghost, a reference point slowly consumed by the encroaching mist.

There. A flicker of darkness against the lighter gray of the fog, heading toward the westernmost corner of the garden where a clutch of stone cairns formed an uneven line.

Anna matched pace with the fog, letting it eat her as she drifted along the old stone path. She counted the crunch of gravel beneath her boots, matched it to the rhythm of her own breathing, and then, by increments, slowed both until even the crows in the bone-trees seemed to pause and listen.

The watcher moved with unnerving patience. Its walk— determined, quiet—showed no fear or curiosity, only the grim assurance of a seasoned hunter.

Anna could have shouted. Could have called Mercy forward, made a show of strength in numbers. But she knew from the set of the shoulders—broad, arms held loose and ready—that the watcher wouldn't be spooked by words, nor intimidated by threats. This was the measured approach of a living, thinking adversary. Anna found herself relishing the moment, the seconds stretching into a deliberate anticipation, like the pause before a knife's plunge.

The watcher turned at the last bend, pausing before the crow-bone effigy. Anna closed the distance. She stepped behind a tangle of bramble, slowed her breathing to the barest whisper, and waited until the watcher drew level with the cairn. She gathered herself, muscles coiling with potential energy, and measured the distance, calculating the force required.

Only then did Anna move, exploding out of the cover and driving her shoulder into the figure's lower back with enough force to upend an ox. They tumbled together into the rose beds, the watcher twisting in mid-air to land hard, catlike, in a defensive crouch. Anna didn't hesitate. She brought the heel of her palm down toward the watcher's clavicle, aiming to stun, but the figure caught her wrist, reversed the leverage, and Anna felt herself slammed sideways into the earth.

Wet grass and thorns bit through Anna's skirt. The watcher's grip was firm—callused fingers encircling Anna's wrist—but Anna had wrestled with worse in graveyards and haunted charnel houses. She knew how to slip a hold. She brought her knee up, caught the watcher in the stomach, and for one clean second their faces hovered inches apart.

Not a man. Not a ghost. A Black woman—a head taller than Anna. She was built like a boundary stone, her hair in thick braids wound with copper wire and bone charms. Her eyes were black, bottomless, and alive with something more dangerous than hate… calculation.

The woman reacted with startling speed. Her strong hands found Anna's wrists, her fingers like iron bands trying to pry the knife away. One powerful leg hooked around Anna's waist, and suddenly the world tilted, positions reversed. The woman straddled her, one hand pinning Anna's knife arm, the other drawn back in a balled fist.

Anna sucked in a deep breath and spat a gob of blood and

saliva directly into the woman's left eye. As the stranger recoiled, Anna twisted her hips and uncoiled a leg, catching the woman behind the left knee with the blade of her boot.

The kneecap buckled, just enough. Anna threw her full body weight into the motion, using the torque to roll them both. The move worked. Anna came up on top, her own knees pinning the woman's arms, her left hand catching the woman's throat in a claw. With her right, Anna pressed the point of her knife to the hollow at the base of the woman's neck. It was not a bluff.

"Stop," Anna growled. "One word and I'll open you from ear to breastbone."

The woman's lips curled back, but she held still, eyes glittering through the blood and spit now dripping into them. Her voice, when it came, was low and resonant, edged with a Virginia accent that time and travel had sanded down to its core.

"Wouldn't be the first to try," she said, and Anna realized with an electric shock that the woman wasn't afraid. Not at all.

For several heartbeats, neither moved. They both breathed hard, fog swirling around them in agitated eddies. The woman beneath her might have been twice Anna's age—forty, maybe more, though her body was all sinew and muscle. Anna considered how best to keep her alive and get her talking. "Who are you?"

The woman's gaze flicked to the left, just a hair, but Anna caught it. The signal wasn't for Anna—it was for someone else.

A shape burst from the undergrowth on Anna's right, low

and fast, and she only had time to recognize it as a child before the blur hit her square in the ribs. She kept her grip on the woman's wrist, twisting so she rolled with the impact, but the newcomer was bigger and heavier than she expected. Anna lost her position, felt the edge of her blade slide away from the woman's neck, and suddenly she was grappling not one, but two bodies on the slick ground.

The child—no, a Black boy, maybe twelve or thirteen, tall for his age and wiry as a steel cable—grabbed Anna's knife hand and tried to wrench it upward. Anna slammed her head backward, catching the boy in the nose with the crown of her skull. His grip faltered just long enough for her to draw the blade back down and reverse the hilt, striking him in the temple with the butt end of the bone handle.

The woman lunged, but Anna anticipated the move and let herself go slack, rolling into the blow so that she landed on top of the woman again, pinning her more effectively this time. The boy scrambled to his feet, wiping blood from his nostrils. Anna spared a glance upward, just enough to see the shimmer of rage and confusion in his eyes before he darted for a chunk of granite at the base of the nearest cairn.

"Stop," Anna commanded, her knife pressing a crescent of blood into the woman's dark skin. "One more step and she's dead."

From the direction of the terrace came a cry—Mercy. Anna risked a glance back and saw the girl running toward them, her pale hair a beacon in the gathering dark. "Anna, wait! Don't!"

The boy froze, the stone raised in both hands. Anna saw the whites of his eyes now, but his face had set in an expression that was more calculated than afraid.

There was a long, tense silence until the woman breathed in hard, then exhaled with the controlled slowness of someone who had practiced turning pain into discipline. "He won't listen," she said. "Not unless I tell him myself."

Anna didn't relax her pressure on the blade, but she nodded once. "Speak. But no tricks."

The woman grunted. "Micah. Drop the stone. I'll live."

The boy—Micah—obeyed instantly, the rock thudding to the dirt with a dull, reluctant clack.

The garden held its breath. Fog drifted between the four figures, obscuring and revealing their frozen tableau. The only sounds were their collective breathing and the distant crash of waves against the cliff far below.

Anna took her next gamble, betting that she could keep control. "On your knees. Hands on your head. Both of you."

She let the woman up, her blade never more than a finger's width from the vital arteries. The woman rose with a defiant dignity. She kneeled with her back straight, her hands laced atop her head. The boy joined her, slow and resentful, but his eyes never left Anna's face.

Anna stepped back, just out of reach, and let her gaze dart to the garden's entrance, checking for more threats. Mercy hadn't moved. Her lips were bloodless, her fists clenched so tight her knuckles shone through the thin skin. Anna's respect for the girl notched higher. She'd followed instructions even in the face of violence, and now she watched the scene with unblinking attention.

Anna shifted her weight, keeping both prisoners in her peripheral vision. "Who are you?" she asked again, this time with enough menace to chase away any pretense.

The woman didn't answer at once. Her eyes flicked briefly toward the cliff, then the house, then back to Anna. "Juba," she said finally. "My name is Juba."

Anna filed the name away. "And the boy?"

"He's mine," Juba said. "My son."

Micah glared, but didn't contradict her.

Juba's eyes, black as a well, flicked again to the edge of the terrace. "I have another child. A girl. Her name's Euphemia. Small, quiet." She jerked her chin at the tangled bramble where Anna had first spotted her. "She's hiding. Don't hurt her."

Anna weighed the risks. "Call her out."

Juba did. "Effie!" she called, then said something else in a language Anna didn't recognize. The words had the rhythm of a prayer or a curse, but the meaning was clear.

A figure moved from behind a low stone cairn—a girl, no more than eight, dressed in rags and wrapped in a length of faded red kerchief that matched Juba's own. The child's eyes were enormous, black as pitch, and fixed on Anna with a gaze that was neither pleading nor afraid.

Mercy bent at the knees and lowered herself to Effie's height. She smiled, slow and deliberate. In that instant, something passed between them—something Anna couldn't see, but felt all the same.

"You're safe," Mercy said.

"You're like me," Effie said to Mercy, her voice soft and melodic, carrying easily across the garden despite its gentleness. "You hear them too."

The simple statement landed between them all like a stone

dropped in still water, ripples of implication spreading outward. Mercy's face registered shock, then a hesitant recognition. Anna felt Juba tense beneath her, a mother's protective instinct surging against the cold reality of the blade at her throat.

Anna lowered her knife, just a hair. Enough to signal that the violence was suspended—for now.

"You can all stand," she said, and Juba did, rising with the careful economy of someone who had been made to kneel before men with less reason and more hate.

The boy, Micah, stood next, never taking his eyes off Anna.

Anna studied Juba, noticing for the first time the old scars: burns, welts, a half-healed gash along the jawline. Not all were the marks of punishment, but of work, of battle, of survival against enemies that didn't care if you lived so long as you suffered.

Anna felt an unbidden flicker of sympathy. She killed it.

"If you're not my enemy," she said, "then tell me what you know of this place. Why are you here?"

Chapter 12

Juba waited for Anna to come closer before moving. She kept her arms loose at her sides, as if still half-expecting another attack, but it was a calculated posture. Nothing about her suggested panic or submission, only a tightly coiled readiness. She rose with a grunt and signaled for her children to join her.

They regrouped near a lichen-stained bench whose back had long ago surrendered to rot, so that it listed backward like a rowboat after a storm. Juba sat and Effie climbed up to nestle against her side. The boy, Micah, remained standing, his body interposed between Anna and his family like a sentry.

Juba's eyes swept Anna and Mercy with the measured detachment of someone who'd grown used to being studied. The knife at her throat had left a crimson crescent, but she touched the wound with the indifference of one who had endured far worse.

"I reckon you might know what it's like to have the devil's shadow hanging over your neck," Juba said at last, her gaze straying to Mercy. "And maybe you know what it's like to have the devil's mark on your skin from the day you draw your first breath." Her voice was deep and slow, carrying a tidewater drawl that made every word feel deliberate.

Effie burrowed tighter into Juba's ribs, drawing comfort from the cadence as much as the contact. Juba's arm encircled the girl with automatic protectiveness, but there was nothing soft in the gesture. It was the reflex of someone who expected the world to snatch away anything she dared to love. Micah said nothing, but Anna saw how his shoulders eased, just barely, when Juba's storytelling voice took hold.

Juba began in fragments—geography first, as if the land itself mattered more than her own history. "Southampton County, Virginia. Hot as blazes in August, wet as a baptism in April, and so full of misery you could drown in it standing upright." Her hand moved unconsciously to a raised scar along her collarbone. "I was born property."

The stark and ugly word lingered in the air. Anna had encountered the children of slaves in Boston, but the raw nearness of Juba's experience made the horror immediate.

"Worked the fields since I was eight," Juba continued, her voice matter-of-fact. "Sixteen hours, sunup to sundown. Picked leaf, hung leaf, stripped leaf. Hands bleed first month, then they harden." She held up her palms, callused ridges crossing them like ancient roads on a weathered map. "Tobacco gets in your skin, your hair, your dreams. Never washes out."

Micah shifted his weight, his eyes darting between Anna and Mercy with the wary calculation of someone who had learned to measure threats by instinct rather than reason.

"There was always someone with an eye on us," Juba said. "Overseer, driver, White men drunk or bored. If it wasn't the whip, it was the hunger. If not hunger, it was the sickness. But I watched my mama work her rootcraft, and I learned to watch, too. Watch for the holes in the fence, for the hush in the wind when bad news was 'bout to blow through."

Anna noticed Juba's hands never stopped moving as she spoke. Even seated, her fingers wove invisible cords in the air —making knots, unmaking them, as if tying her story to the world to keep it from slipping away. Effie watched the hands, eyes wide and reverent, while Micah scanned the garden for threats, his own fists clenched around nothing at his sides.

"Master Devereaux wasn't the worst," Juba said, her tone suggesting this was faint praise. "Didn't beat us without cause. Fed us enough to work. But his overseer—" She broke off, a muscle tightening in her jaw. "Whitaker. Man had the devil in him. Liked to hear screams. Made examples of folk. Once saw him whip a boy till his back was nothing but red strings, just for dropping a basket."

Effie pressed against her mother with her eyes shut tight, as if trying to block out memories that weren't even her own. Juba's hand moved to stroke her daughter's hair, the gesture absent and automatic, like breathing.

"When I had Micah," she continued, glancing at her son, "they left me alone three days, then put me back in the fields with him tied to my back. When I had Effie, they gave me two. We lived that way until the old Master died. Then we lived worse." Juba's face went flat at this; it was not a subject for embellishment. "His son took over—Benjamin. Young man with books full of numbers and not much else." Juba's lips thinned. "Started selling people off. Breaking up families. Said it was just business." She looked down at Effie, then up at Micah, something fierce and terrible passing across her face. "He beat my husband so bad the man couldn't stand straight. Sent him south, never saw him again."

Anna's skin prickled with the image—the sort that had nothing to do with bloodlines or ghostly whispers, but the common, base cruelty that stitched the world together more tightly than any magic ever could. She glanced at Mercy, who stood rigid and pale, unable to look away.

"When the Nat Turner rising came last August, we heard it in the fields before the White folks did," Juba continued, voice lower now. "Word spread in the hush—slaves rising up, cutting down their masters with axe and knife. Happening not twenty miles from where we was." She described the days that followed, a fever of hope and terror so thick it choked the air. "We knew what would come next. Retaliation. Killing ten for every one. So I waited for the blood to start, then I took my children and ran."

Here, she curled her arm tighter around Effie, who had begun to hum under her breath. Anna felt her own nerves spark in response. The girl made her uneasy. There was a static charge to Effie, a sense that her awareness extended in directions not visible to the human eye.

Juba went on: the escape undertaken "by moon and starlight only"; hiding in the swamps when patrols came; wading rivers in the dead of night with children half-drowned and shivering but too afraid to cry out. "Micah got so sick I thought I'd bury him right there by the riverbank, but he lived." She nodded at the boy, who met Anna's gaze with a level, unsmiling defiance.

"Somehow we made it north. Delaware at first, then all the way to Connecticut. There were White folk who helped us, but never for free. The cost was different, that's all." Juba's mouth twisted. "Some wanted prayers. Some wanted a little of your blood, or your sweat, or your time. I paid what I had to."

Anna knew the familiar pain of making deals out of desperation, debt mounting instead of decreasing, each step toward freedom creating new burdens. "I understand," she murmured.

Juba shot her a look that was more challenge than thanks. "Do you? Because the woman who first helped us in New Haven, she was a conjure woman, like my mama. She put us in the hands of a preacher and a ship captain who promised passage to Canada. I believed them. Paid with the silver buttons I'd cut from the Master's coat the night we fled."

Anna could guess what had happened next. "They betrayed you."

The laugh that followed was bitter and hollow as a burned-out log. "They took us all right. Locked us below decks. Three days at sea. Then the Revenue Cutter Service appeared on the horizon, looking for smuggled goods, not people. The captain panicked. Said they'd hang him for transporting fugitive slaves. They put us in a rowboat with a skin of water and a sack of hardtack. Pointed us toward an island they said was uninhabited. Then they cut us loose in the mist."

Juba's arm tightened around her daughter. "We rowed 'til our hands bled. Storm came up sudden—worst I'd ever seen. Waves tall as trees. Thought we'd drown for certain." Her gaze shifted to the towering bulk of Hallowspire behind them. "Then we saw it. Standing there like judgment. Like it was waiting for us."

"How long ago?" Anna asked.

"Hard to say." Juba bit her lip as she thought it over. "Time don't work so well on this island, but I'd say over a month. We made camp in a cave in the cliffs." Her eyes narrowed. "And we'd have stayed there, if the island would've let us be."

Anna considered this. A month was a long time to survive on Brimwatch, especially with children.

"How have you managed to stay alive?" Mercy asked. "This place…"

"We live careful," Juba said simply. "Trap crabs. Collect eggs from gull nests. There's fresh water in the caves." Her expression hardened. "And we stay away from this house. Far away. Until today."

"What changed?" Anna pressed.

Juba's eyes met hers, unflinching. "The storm that brought you. It woke something that was sleeping." She looked toward Hallowspire, its towers now black against the sky. "And now it's hungry again."

"You've been watching the house?" Anna asked.

"Watching you, more like," Micah said, his eyes boring into Anna's. "Waiting to see if you made it through the first night."

Anna felt the island's pressure mounting, a physical sensation not unlike the press of a skull in a vise. Across from her, Juba's family formed a compact, silent triangle: the mother on the bench, Effie curled in her lap, Micah bracing the ground just behind them, a stone pillar against the shifting mist.

"The first night you spent here," she said, directing her words to Juba, "what did you hear?"

Juba's eyes flicked to the ground, then to Effie, as if the answer had to pass through her daughter before it could find air. "I knew something wasn't right. Air too still. Trees leaned like they was listening. Even the birds went quiet when we passed." She drew Effie closer, the child's small form nearly disappearing within the circle of her arm. "We made camp in a cave facing east. Thought we'd be safe there—sheltered from the wind, back to stone, sea in front. Nothing could come at us unseen."

Mercy had drawn her legs up beneath her on the edge of the bench, making herself small. The wind lifted her white hair in spectral tendrils that caught the pale light. Anna remained standing, one hand still resting near her knife, her posture relaxed but ready.

"Three days passed quiet," Juba continued. "Then the whispering started. Just at night, first. Like someone standing just outside our fire, mumbling words I couldn't catch. I'd go look—nothing there but shadows." Her eyes narrowed at the memory. "Thought it was the wind. Wanted to believe that. Then things started moving. Small things—a cup I'd set down, Micah's trap line, Effie's doll. They'd be in different places come morning. Places they shouldn't be." Juba's voice remained steady, but her eyes had taken on a distant quality, as if looking through the present into memories she'd rather forget. "One morning I woke to find all our belongings arranged in a perfect circle around us as we slept."

Anna's expression didn't change, but something in her posture shifted—a slight tensing of the shoulders, a narrowing of focus that betrayed her growing interest.

"That's when Effie started talking to them." Juba looked down at her daughter, her face softening with a terrible mixture of love and fear. "My girl's always been… different. Sees things others don't. But here, whatever she sees saw her back."

Effie stirred against her mother's side, her small voice startlingly clear in the twilight hush. "The Quiet Ones," she said, not looking at any of them but at a point beyond the garden wall where shadows were congealing into deeper gloom. "They sing to me at night. Tell me stories about the island. About the house." Her round and dark eyes fixed on Anna. "About the Gate underneath."

A chill that had nothing to do with the evening air crawled up Anna's spine. Thorne's letters mentioned both the Quiet Ones and a Gate. Rebecca's presence stirred at the back of her consciousness, a sudden alertness that felt like fingers pressing against her skull.

Juba continued, her arm tightening protectively around Effie. "Started small. She'd wake up speaking words I never taught her. Drawing symbols in the dirt with sticks. Talking to empty corners." The woman's voice dropped lower. "Then she started knowing things. Where to find fresh water when our spring dried up. Which berries wouldn't poison us. Which parts of the island to avoid."

"What does she mean by Quiet Ones?" Anna asked, her voice carefully neutral.

Juba's eyes met hers, unflinching. "They ain't like normal

ghosts," she said. "Normal dead still look like people—still got faces, voices you recognize. These…" She shook her head slowly. "These got no faces, just holes where eyes should be. They don't speak so much as push thoughts into your head. And they hungry for something."

"They want names," Effie interjected. "They forgot their own."

Micah let out a sharp, disapproving noise. "Effie, don't—"

"It's all right," Juba cut him off, though her expression suggested it was anything but. "They need to know what walks here." She turned back to Anna. "Few days after we arrived, Micah found footprints in the mud outside our cave. Not animal. Not ours. Perfect circles, like someone walking on the balls of their feet. Followed them halfway around the island before they just… stopped. Middle of a clearing, like whatever made them just floated away."

The wind picked up, sending dead leaves skittering across the terrace like tiny, frantic messengers. In the deepening shadows, the effigies of crow bones rattled against each other, producing a sound like distant, mocking laughter.

"We started seeing them after the first week," Juba continued. "Just glimpses. Movement in the corner of your eye. A patch of fog that moved against the wind. A shadow without a body to cast it." Her hand moved to a crude folk charm at her throat. "But there are places where they gather. Certain stones. The big oak in the east clearing. And this house." She looked up at Hallowspire's looming silhouette, its windows now black against the twilight sky. "Especially this house."

Anna's mind was working, categorizing Juba's observations

against her extensive knowledge of supernatural phenomena. These weren't ordinary hauntings—the patterns were wrong, the manifestations too deliberate. This was something else going on here, something related to Thorne's metaphysical experiments.

"What happened when you tried to approach the mansion?" she asked, her voice carrying the professional curiosity of someone who hunted such things for a living.

A look passed between Juba and Micah, a shared memory neither seemed eager to revisit.

"First week was hard," Juba said after a long pause. "Cave stayed wet. Effie got sick with a fever that wouldn't break. We needed better shelter." Her eyes hardened. "I decided to try the house, just for a night or two. Got as far as those steps." She nodded toward the main entrance of Hallowspire.

"The door wouldn't open," Micah said, breaking his silence. His voice was deeper than Anna expected, though still caught in the awkward transition between boy and man. "Mama pushed and pushed. Then the knocker moved by itself. Three times, like someone on the other side was answering."

Juba nodded. "Then we heard it. Laughing. Coming from inside. Not one voice—many. And footsteps, moving toward the door." Her face had gone still, a mask of controlled horror at the memory. "We ran. All the way back to our cave. When we looked back, every window in that house was lit up bright as day. By the time we reached the cliffs, they were dark again."

Mercy's face had drained of what little color it possessed. Her hands were pressed flat against her thighs now, as if she needed the pressure to ground herself. "You've seen them, haven't you?" she asked Effie, her voice barely above a whisper. "The ones without voices."

Effie nodded, solemn as a priest. "They follow us sometimes. They're curious. They don't remember being people." She tilted her head, as if listening to something only she could hear. "Some of them were children once. Before the house ate them."

Micah moved closer to his sister. "Effie has dreams," he said flatly, as if this explained everything and nothing.

"Not dreams," Effie corrected, her voice taking on a sing-song quality. "They show me things. The hall with all the mirrors. The chapel where the floor bleeds. The spiral that goes down and down and never stops." Her eyes fixed on Anna with unsettling intensity. "They say there's a gate under the house. A door that wants opening."

Anna felt a cold weight settle in her stomach. Rebecca's voice slithered through her consciousness like the mist coiling around the trees: *The child knows. She sees the Gate. Use her.*

"Gate to what?" Anna asked, forcing her voice to remain steady.

Effie opened her mouth to answer, but Juba's hand on her shoulder stopped her. "Doesn't matter," Juba said. "Whatever's on the other side, it's nothing good."

Anna looked at Effie. "Do the Quiet Ones know what happened to the man who built the house?"

Effie's eyes went huge, the pupils nearly swallowing the irises. "He's under the house. Not dead. Just waiting for someone to finish the work." The little girl fixed Anna with a gaze that made her shudder. "But you already know it, don't you?" she whispered.

Anna said nothing, but in her mind a name rang like a cracked bell: Thorne. "If the Quiet Ones want the door opened, why haven't they just done it themselves?"

Juba answered for Effie. "They're trapped. Bound here by something unspeakable. Effie says the only way out is through the bottom."

Anna's memory supplied the word: the Womb Below. She glanced at the cairns, the rose thorns, the crows. There had to be an entrance somewhere—maybe under the house, or maybe in the cliffside. She looked at Effie again, her head pillowed on Juba's lap, one hand curled around her mother's finger like a root seeking water. The fog pressed closer, softening edges, blurring the shapes of the trees and stones. In that moment, at least, Anna knew which side she was on.

The side that kept children alive.

"We're going back into the house," she said, pitching her voice low enough that only the living could hear. "It's dry, there are locks, and a warm place to sleep."

Juba's jaw set hard, the muscles in her cheek flickering as she weighed the offer. "That house ain't dead," she declared, the words carrying absolute conviction. "It's listening. Has been since we washed up here. I feel it breathin' when we pass. Whatever walks there, it's older than anything living… and it's waking up. It ain't just stone and wood anymore. It's grown roots in the world below." Her eyes found Anna's and held them. "We'll take our chances in the caves. Hidden. Safe as anything can be on this rock." She gestured toward the forest that covered the eastern slopes.

Micah had gathered their few belongings: a worn leather

satchel and what appeared to be fishing implements crafted from scavenged materials. His movements were efficient, practiced, the routine of someone who had learned to flee at a moment's notice.

"You should come with us," Effie blurted, her small voice startling in the growing gloom. She was looking at Mercy, not Anna. "The house doesn't like new people. It plays with them first, then takes them down to the Womb."

Mercy's face paled further, the blood draining from her lips until they matched the ghostly white of her hair. Anna stepped closer to the girl, a subtle gesture of protection that wasn't lost on Juba.

Juba held her gaze for a long moment, then nodded once, accepting the situation for what it was. She turned to her children, her posture straightening as she prepared to lead them back into the wilderness that had become their reluctant sanctuary.

"If you change your mind," she said over her shoulder, "follow the eastern path till you reach a lightning-split oak. Turn south there and keep the moon on your right shoulder. We'll hear you coming."

"We'll be fine," Anna said, though the words tasted false even as she spoke them. "I've dealt with haunted places before."

Chapter 13

Anna sat on a tattered velvet settee in the Great Hall, her back to the dying fireplace, and watched the shadows crawl across the soot-dark ceiling. The embers cast no warmth. Their sullen glow illuminated only the bones of the room—the chessboard marble, the ranks of columns, the blackened teeth of candelabras gone decades without flame. The hall's silence was absolute, broken only by the settling sighs of the mansion as it remembered itself.

Mercy slept a few feet away, draped across the couch with her arms locked around a patchwork quilt Anna had scavenged from a trunk. Her white hair lay splayed across the faded upholstery like spilled milk. Each time she exhaled, her lips formed a shape close to a question, then unmade it. Her sleep was a shallow, feverish imitation of peace. Anna envied her ability to rest, even if only for a little while.

Anna herself had not slept since their arrival. She'd tried twice—once huddled against the back of the settee, once curled up beside the fire—but both attempts ended in violent memories, her own or another's. The second time, she'd awakened with her right hand pressed so tightly to her neck that the skin was white and cold. She'd smelled blood, and had checked Mercy for wounds before she realized the scent was inside her own mind, thick and coppery, a memory retched up by the soul intertwined with her own.

Child, said the voice, sudden and close, as if spoken in Anna's own ear. *The slave girl was right. There is a gate below. I can feel it pulsing even now, calling to those with the power to hear.*

Anna shut her eyes. "Leave me," she whispered. "Let me think."

She didn't say the name—Rebecca—because that only encouraged her. The dead witch didn't need an invitation.

The child knows nothing of true power, Rebecca continued, undeterred. *But that woman—Juba—she understands more than she admits. Did you see how she protected the little one? The one who hears the Quiet Ones?*

Effie's words echoed in Anna's memory: *He's under the house. Not dead. Just waiting for someone to finish the work.* The implication was clear enough: Thorne had initiated something he couldn't complete, something that involved the Gate Effie had described. Something that might hold the key to retrieving her mother's soul.

The fire crackled, a sudden flare of light that threw Anna's shadow huge against the wall behind her. In that moment, she could have sworn the silhouette wasn't entirely her own —the shoulders broader, the head shrouded in something that might have been a veil.

The key to your mother's soul is here somewhere, Anna. I can feel it. The power to part the Veil at will. To command the passage of souls between worlds. Thorne discovered it, and now it awaits us.

Anna closed her eyes, willing the voice to recede, but Rebecca's presence only pressed closer, coiling through her thoughts like smoke seeking escape through any available crack.

Abigail's soul hangs in the balance, child. Every moment you delay, her spirit drifts further from your reach, deeper into realms from which there is no return.

"I know," Anna whispered, too softly to wake Mercy. "But I won't be your puppet."

She stared at Mercy, guilt gnawing at her ribs. An unfamiliar protective instinct urged her to wake the child, to flee this place while they still could. Is this what it felt like to have a sister? A daughter?

But even as she opened herself to the unfamiliar sense of connection, her pragmatic mind slammed the door. Where would they go? Back to the caves with Juba? Into the gnashing teeth of the churning sea?

No. There was only forward now.

Anna rose from her settee, the movement so controlled, not even the scrape of its wooden legs betrayed her. She stepped around the couch where Mercy slept, pausing just long enough to tuck the quilt more securely around the girl's thin shoulders. She needed every minute of oblivion she could steal. Then, with the practiced stealth of someone accustomed to moving among the dead and dying, Anna crossed the Great Hall.

Her boots made no sound on the black and bone-white marble. She paused at the edge of the mosaic and looked back. Mercy hadn't moved. Anna watched her for another minute before continuing.

The eastern corridor beckoned—a vault lined with tattered banners and the heads of grotesques, each with a mouth fixed in a rictus of hunger or agony. Anna moved with her usual predatory caution, heels rolling silently from marble to ancient rug. The air here was colder, flavored with mold. She passed three doors. One led to the ruined music room, one to the abandoned conservatory, and a third to what looked, at first, like a broom closet.

That third door should not have been there.

Anna had walked this corridor three times since their arrival. Each time she had noted the run of the paneling, the flaws in the stone, the way the air felt heavier near the base of the wall. But this door—narrow, vertical, oaken—was new. The hinges were tarnished iron, old but recently disturbed, with a halo of dust around the edges as if the house itself had only now exhaled it into being.

Rebecca's presence stirred, eager and insistent. *Yes, child. The house knows. It is choosing to reveal itself to you. To us.*

Anna reached for the handle. It was cold, but not dead. A faint heat lingered, the way iron does after being held in a trembling hand. She pressed her palm against the wood, listening for the telltale click of a trap or the electric shiver of a ward.

Nothing.

The hallway held its breath.

She opened the door. It swung inward without a sound.

A spiral staircase climbed up into darkness, the curve so tight that Anna could see only the first seven steps before the void swallowed them. No banister, no light, only stone steps. A cold draft swept down from above, carrying the scent of dust and something else—something older and sharper, like the air from a newly opened mausoleum.

Anna weighed her options, then reached into her satchel and pulled out the stub of a candle. She struck the flint and lit the wick, cradling it in her hand to hide the flame from anything that might watch from above.

Rebecca's voice came again, soft and hungry: *Hurry, child. Time grows short.*

The spiral staircase wound upward like a corkscrew, piercing the mansion's heart. Anna climbed steadily, one hand trailing along the cold wall for balance, the other holding the small tallow candle. The flame guttered in invisible drafts, casting her shadow in grotesque, elongated shapes that danced across the curved walls.

The staircase defied the mansion's external architecture. Anna had counted over a hundred steps already; far more than she expected given Hallowspire's apparent height. Yet the stairs continued upward, coiling tighter with each revolution, until she felt caught in the grip of some enormous stone serpent. The air grew colder as she climbed, carrying an iron tang that settled on her tongue like old coins.

The staircase ended so abruptly that Anna nearly stumbled. One moment she was climbing, the next her foot met a level floor. She raised her candle higher, its feeble light pushing back the darkness just enough to reveal a long, vaulted chamber stretching before her.

Anna stood frozen at the threshold, overwhelmed by the sudden expansion of space after the stairwell's claustrophobic confines. The ceiling arched high overhead, its beams visible only as darker shapes against the general gloom. But it wasn't the architecture that commanded her attention—it was what lined the walls.

Mirrors. Dozens of them. Perhaps hundreds, their frames and surfaces visible as dull gleams in the candlelight. They covered the walls from floor to ceiling in a bewildering array of sizes and shapes—some tall and narrow, others squat and wide, still others perfectly round or oddly angled. No two frames matched. Anna glimpsed ornate gilt carvings alongside severe iron borders and simple wooden edges.

She crept forward, her candle flame reflected infinitely in the sea of tarnished glass. She kept her light close and her gaze high, refusing to look too long at the mirrors on either side. Some were shattered, the fractures feathering out from a central impact point, their silvering peeling away in ragged strips that reminded Anna of scabbed-over wounds. Other mirrors were veiled in funereal cloth, the black crepe hanging limp as dead skin.

A whisper of unease crawled up her spine. Anna had encountered mirrors with occult properties before—scrying glasses, soul-catchers, windows into other worlds—but never had she felt such concentrated power. Each mirror seemed to vibrate with its own frequency, its own hunger. She had the distinct impression they were watching her, these silver eyes lining the walls, drinking in her presence like parched soil absorbing rain.

The house remembers, Rebecca whispered. *Each mirror, a trap. Each image, a snare. Do not linger. Do not look back.*

Anna nodded, though she couldn't say whether the gesture

was real or only a nervous flicker in the glass. She advanced, favoring the left side of the corridor, where the mirrors were more likely to be broken or shrouded. The right-hand glass was perfect and alive, its surface as still as a frozen pond. The air on that side was colder, and Anna imagined she could hear a faint hiss, like a whisper from lips pressed too close to her ear.

At the midpoint of the gallery, the mirrors grew monstrous. Full walls of glass, over ten feet high, faced one another like the teeth of a beast preparing to close. Between them, yet more mirrors: round, oval, elliptical; some no larger than a serving dish, others the size of a sarcophagus lid. All reflected Anna back to herself, multiplied and scattered into grotesque parades.

Anna advanced to the nearest mirror, unable to resist the lure of its glass. This one was oval, framed in gold and marked with delicate sigils along the rim. The glass was smoked, veiling its reflections as if through a curtain. Anna leaned in.

At first, she saw nothing but her own silhouette. Then the image clarified. Anna saw herself as she might have been, with her mother's soft blonde hair instead of coal black, and a blue dress that belonged to a childhood she never had. The not-Anna smiled, but her lips didn't move. Instead, the eyes widened, and the skin beneath them paled. The next time the mouth opened, it was a perfect black O, swallowing the light. The image flickered, jumped, and then showed Anna as she was now, but with a second face—Rebecca's face—just behind her left shoulder, grinning wide beneath her black veil with a mouthful of too many teeth.

Anna recoiled, heart hammering. The mirror wavered, then stilled, returning her to herself. She tore her gaze away, focusing instead on the wall of glass to her right.

Each massive mirror there showed something different. In one, Anna walked with Mercy, hand in hand, down a spiral staircase that narrowed until it squeezed them into a single strand, then into a dot, then nothing at all. In another, she saw herself standing over a prone figure—Juba, dead, with her own bone-handled knife protruding from the woman's throat. In a third, Anna saw herself in the garden, every bone of her body exposed and weeping blood, while the sky rained petals of white-hot ash.

She forced herself onward, the candle held high, resisting the magnetic pull of the mirrors. Rebecca's voice pressed in again, louder now, echoing off the glass in a thousand overlapping frequencies.

All you see here is possible, child. All you see is true. The mirrors do not lie, but they show you only what you most fear. Find the right one, and you will find the way through.

Anna tried not to look, yet the mirrors insisted on being noticed, each filled with the promise of horror. The gallery itself seemed to flex as she advanced, the walls breathing in time with her own shallow, uneven breaths.

The next uncovered mirror trembled as Anna neared it. Its surface didn't reflect the room behind her, or even her own face, but rippled like a pond stirred by wind. For a second, she saw only blackness. Then the darkness clarified, resolving into a pool of viscous liquid. In it, her mother—Abigail— struggled, her face already half-submerged, arms clawing toward the surface. Anna reached out involuntarily, fingertips grazing the glass, and the image jerked as Abigail's head broke the surface, her mouth open in a scream that produced only bubbles.

"You let it in, Anna," Abigail said, voice bubbling up through the black water, eyes huge and wild. "You invited it."

Anna staggered back, knocking her hip against a second mirror. This one displayed her mother from another angle, walking backward into an inferno, the flames climbing her blue dress, licking at her hair. Abigail never took her eyes off Anna, not even as the fire consumed her and blackened her flesh. Her lips barely moved, but the words repeated, flat and merciless:

"You let it in, Anna. You invited it."

The third mirror waited for her. Abigail again, this time falling down a rift in the earth, her body twisting, limbs flailing as the walls of the fissure scraped skin from bone. Anna watched, helpless, as the image receded into blackness. Just before Abigail's face disappeared, her eyes met Anna's with a gaze that accused and pitied in equal measure.

"You let it in, Anna. You invited it."

Anna spun away, bile rising in her throat. Her breath came in quick, sharp bursts, and her knife-hand shook. For a moment, she thought she might pass out. Rebecca's voice was absent now—not a word, not a snicker, just a pulsing in Anna's head like a drumbeat.

The far end of the gallery held a mirror nearly twice Anna's height. It was framed in tarnished silver carved into a writhing border of snakes, hands, and hollow-eyed skulls. The glass was utterly clear, a perfect window into a darkness deeper than any Anna had seen. The mirror didn't distort her.

Instead, it rendered her with surgical precision. Every scar, every strand of hair, the pulse at her throat; all were visible and real. Anna met her own gaze and saw something behind her: a movement in the dark, just at the edge of sight. She whirled, but the chamber was empty except for the mirrors and her own infinite reflections.

Anna turned back to the glass. Now the movement was closer, a shadow rising from the base of the mirror like a reversed candle flame. It climbed her silhouette, wrapping her in coils of blackness, binding her arms to her sides, then choking off the light at her throat. Anna fought the image, willing her own reflection to move, to resist, to do something other than be so passively consumed. Then, with the subtlety of a bad dream, her features began to run, melting from the bone. Her cheeks grew hollow, her lips thinned, her hair lengthened and grew red. Her blue eyes faded and then reignited, orange-bright and rimmed in sooty shadow.

Rebecca's face looked back at her, shrouded behind the dreadful black veil Anna knew from every nightmare.

Anna gritted her teeth, raised her knife, and stabbed the glass with all the force she could muster. The blade glanced off, the recoil jarring her wrist to numbness.

The mirror didn't crack. Instead, the reflection—Rebecca's face—threw its head back and howled with laughter, the sound so loud and sharp it made the flame of Anna's candle gutter. The hall filled with the noise, every mirror picking it up, amplifying it, until she was surrounded by a wall of cackling that left no space for her own thoughts.

She stepped back, then back again, but the gallery kept expanding, mirrors on all sides now, each one occupied by a different version of herself or her mother or Mercy or some impossible hybrid of them all. The laughter changed pitch, layering into itself until it became less a sound than a physical force, pressing in on Anna's skull until she wanted to scream herself just to make it stop.

"Anna," said a voice, not Rebecca's this time, but Abigail's, weak and plaintive. "Anna, don't let it take you. You're stronger than she is. You always were."

Anna searched for the source, found it in a mirror half-broken and rimmed with old blood. Abigail's face peered out from the fracture, alive with pain but still recognizably her own. The image reached out, palm pressed flat against the glass from the inside. Anna raised her own hand to meet it, but the surface remained cold and unyielding.

"You let it in, Anna," the reflection whispered, softer now. "But you can send it back. You just have to try. Please, Anna. Please."

Anna closed her eyes, tried to shut out the laughter, the agony, the accusations. She focused on the feeling of the knife in her palm, the weight of it, the memory of every lesson her mother had ever taught her about facing fear: Head high. Shoulders square. Show them the monster in you before they can show you theirs.

She opened her eyes. In the main mirror, Rebecca still grinned back at her, veil rippling, teeth yellow as grave worms. Anna locked gazes with the dead witch and bared her own teeth in defiance. She raised the knife again, this time drawing it across her own palm, letting her blood spatter the mirror's flawless surface.

The glass hissed, and the laughter faltered for half a second.

Anna pressed her hand to the wound, then smeared the blood in a line across the bottom of the mirror. Every reflection in the gallery flickered, spasmed, and then stilled.

For a heartbeat, Anna was alone—truly alone—in the gallery. The hush that fell was almost as terrifying as the laughter had been.

She turned to leave, only to find the way out was gone.

Mirrors covered every surface. There was no door, no landing, only endless glass, each pane an eye waiting to see her fail.

She tried to step forward, but her reflection didn't move. It watched her, smirking, then lifted a hand and beckoned her closer.

Anna froze, heart hammering. Behind her, she heard the soft, wet sound of something peeling away from glass. She looked over her shoulder in time to see one of the mirror images—herself, but not herself—crawling out of a cracked oval, nails digging furrows in the marble as it dragged itself into the world.

Another figure emerged from a broken mirror to her left. It was Abigail again, her eyes wild, mouth dripping tar. From every shattered or veiled surface, something crawled or slithered or oozed, filling the gallery with a menagerie of horrors, each one more grotesque than the last.

Anna backed toward the great mirror, unable to stop herself. The Rebecca in the glass widened her grin and opened her arms in welcome. Anna thought about running, about fighting, but she had nowhere left to go.

The horrors from the other mirrors closed in, their hands reaching, mouths open in silent screams. Anna braced herself, knife at the ready. But before any could touch her, Rebecca's arms reached out from the main mirror, impossibly long, and wrapped her in a shroud of black lace.

The sensation was suffocating, absolute, like being drowned in oil. Anna fought, slashed with her knife, but the veil only tightened, squeezing the air from her lungs, the sight from her eyes, the will from her mind.

"You let it in, Anna," Rebecca whispered, voice softer than silk, "but you can let it out again. All you have to do is surrender."

Anna screamed, the sound eaten by the veil, by the laughter, by the thousand mirrored mouths all calling for her in unison. The world narrowed to a single, searing point of pain, and then—impossibly abruptly—everything stopped.

She stood alone in the gallery. Every mirror was empty, every reflection gone.

Anna's hand still bled, the blood dripping from her fingertips. The only sound was her own ragged breathing and the echo of it bouncing back at her from every surface.

She looked for her mother in the glass, for Mercy, for anything human, but found only herself: hollow-eyed, hair wild, lips pressed thin and pale. She straightened, wiped the blood from her hand onto her skirt, and began to walk. The mirrors watched her go, silent and sated—for now.

Behind her, in the main mirror, Rebecca waited, smiling, her hands folded in her lap. Patient as the grave.

Chapter 14

Mercy woke with a start to the sensation of being watched. She didn't remember falling asleep. One moment she was staring up into the ribbed blackness of Hallowspire's ceiling, tracking the slow drift of shadows as the fire crackled, and the next she was vertical, sitting bolt upright on the moth-eaten couch. Her heart thudded as if she'd been running for miles. The only light came from a thread of moon sneaking through the grimy windows, falling in a single, unforgiving stripe across the marble floor.

Anna was gone.

Mercy listened for the familiar sounds of her presence—the measured breathing, the scrape of a boot on stone, the cough or mutter that proved she wasn't alone. But the Great Hall was empty. Even the hush of the ocean, so constant last night, had receded. The quiet was absolute except for the popping of cooling stone and, somewhere deep behind the walls, the tick of ancient wood settling into new shapes. The fire had dwindled to a faint red eye in the hearth, offering neither warmth nor light.

"Anna?" Mercy's voice emerged smaller than she intended, swallowed by the vastness of the hall.

No answer came.

Mercy's quilt pooled around her waist, and the couch creaked beneath her as she shifted her weight nervously, the sound amplified by the hall's strange acoustics until it seemed to echo from every shadowed corner.

Anna's absence changed everything. Alone, Mercy felt the shape of the room differently, as if the house itself had noticed the gap and exhaled to fill it. The cold was more invasive, the air thicker, and the shadows moved with a purpose she couldn't name.

"Anna?" she tried again, louder this time. "Are you there?"

A soft scraping sound answered, so faint that at first Mercy thought she'd imagined it. She held her breath, listening.

There it came again: a delicate pattering, like fingernails tapping against the inside of the wall to her right. Too light for rats. Too rhythmic for settling timber. It moved with purpose, tracing a path behind the wainscoting—*tap-tap-tap-tap*—then halted.

Mercy exhaled, and the moment her breath left her lips, the tapping resumed.

She swung her feet to the ground, her heartbeat pulsing quicker now. Should she search for Anna? Stay put?

The pattering continued, no longer confined to a single wall. It came from everywhere now: behind the fireplace, above the ceiling, beneath the floor. Multiple patterns overlapped, some fast and frantic, others measured and deliberate.

Mercy thought of Effie's words: *The Quiet Ones...*

But these sounds weren't quiet at all. They were insistent, demanding, a hundred tiny fists hammering for attention.

When the tapping stopped again, Mercy held her breath instinctively. As she'd feared, the sounds ceased with her breathing, then resumed the moment she gasped for air.

They were listening. They were responding.

They knew she was alone.

The shadows lengthened as clouds passed over the moon, stretching across the furniture like grasping hands. The grandfather clock in the corner—which hadn't worked since they'd arrived—suddenly ticked once. The sound was so unexpected that Mercy cried out. Its hands remained fixed at midnight, but something inside the case shifted, the pendulum swinging once without human intervention.

Mercy rose to her feet, the quilt clutched around her like armor. The pattering intensified, growing louder and more frenzied. It sounded like dozens of small feet running circuits through the walls. Up to the ceiling, across, down, around— forming patterns that almost made sense.

The wind outside—or was it the wind?—moaned through the chimney, the sound twisting into something that might have been words. Mercy strained to listen, and immediately wished she hadn't.

The pattering paused. In the sudden quiet, another sound emerged. A high, thin voice, not so much speaking as vibrating, like the whine of wind through a keyhole. The syllables were impossible to parse at first, just a sibilant susurration, but as Mercy strained to hear, she realized there was a rhythm, a melody.

Lullabies.

Not sung, but recited, the cadence oddly familiar.

"*Circle round and round again; Count the teeth from one to ten,*" came the first phrase, a rising and falling tone that made Mercy's scalp prickle. Another followed, more insistent: "*Bind the tongue and blind the eye; Swallow the earth and say goodbye.*"

Mercy's skin crawled. The voices were layered, dozens or more, and all of them children's. They threaded through the architecture, sometimes close enough that she imagined a mouth pressed to the other side of the wall.

"*Twist your name into the floor; Knock three times upon the door. If it opens, don't look in—that's where all the screams begin.*"

Mercy took a single step backward. The footfalls raced to keep pace with her, first overhead, then along the floorboards at her feet, then, horrifically, beside the couch itself.

She jumped away and collided with a low table. The impact sent a candle rolling onto the marble, its stubbed end spinning in a slow, lazy circle. Mercy followed it with her eyes, too afraid to look up, knowing that whatever was moving in the walls could see her hesitation as clearly as a wound.

The lullabies continued, overlapping, a choir of desperate children singing the only songs they remembered from lives stolen away. Mercy clamped her hands over her ears, but the sound found new entry through her teeth, her bones. Some voices sang in English, others in tongues she couldn't recognize but whose melodies were as old as grief itself. All of them sounded wrong, every note a little sharp, a little flat, as if the house delighted in ruining the music.

She gathered her courage and called again for Anna, louder this time: "Anna! Please… where are you?"

Silence.

Then the voices erupted all at once, the footfalls now a frantic dance, up and down the stairs, in and out of the closed doors, through the walls and under the floor. It was as if the children in the walls were circling her, drawing ever tighter, waiting for something to break.

Mercy stumbled backward, tripping over the uneven flagstones of the hearth and sprawling on the cold marble. The impact sent a jolt of pain through her hip, but she barely felt it. She pressed her palm to the wall, feeling the cold vibrate through the stone, and then pressed her ear against it.

The voices had changed. They were lower now, pitched in the murmur of secret-sharing, of confessions made in the hope of rescue. At first, only scraps of meaning broke through. Mercy concentrated, willing her mind to untangle the words.

"…*he comes at night, slicing, slicing…*"

"…*cuts away your name first. Says you don't need it anymore…*"

"…*the room where the floor drinks blood…*"

"…*seven cuts. Always seven…*"

Mercy's flesh prickled with gooseflesh, her white hair standing on end as if electrified. The voices overlapped and doubled back, some trailing off into whimpers, others rising in pleading calls for "Ma," "Maman," "Nana." The languages shifted, but the sense of longing, of abandonment, was always the same.

Mercy gathered her nerve, drew a shaking breath. "Who

are you?" she whispered against the wood. "Tell me your names. Please."

The tapping stopped instantly.

The silence that fell was as complete and final as a coffin being sealed. Even the house seemed to recoil at the audacity of her question.

Mercy pulled away from the wall, suddenly terrified she had made things worse. For a moment, she could almost believe she had dreamed the entire episode—except the cold sweat on her skin and the raw ache in her throat said otherwise. She forced herself upright, knees buckling as she half-crawled, half-staggered to where the candle had come to rest.

Her fingers shook so badly she fumbled the stub twice before closing it in her fist. She patted her cloak and found the packet of phosphorus matches Anna had given her in the library. She lit the first match with a trembling strike. It flared hot, nearly burning her fingers, but she set it to the candle's stub and coaxed a guttering flame into being.

Instantly, the shadows retreated from the immediate space, but the comfort was short-lived. The darkness beyond was now a living wall, bristling with anticipation. She tried to steady her hands. The candle flame danced, wavering with each uneven pull of air from her lungs.

The hall was empty. But the voices were back.

They were quieter now, a subtle weeping that seemed to trickle from the baseboards and the cracks in the stone. Mercy moved slowly, her candle in front of her like a holy talisman, and the sound moved with her—first to her left, then behind her, then spiraling up into the high black reaches of the Great Hall's vaulted ceiling. Sometimes the voices overlapped, a girl's lilt layered over a boy's growl, sometimes they braided together into a chorus of lost longing.

"Amma…mama…mãe…mother…"

Always the same plea, repeated in every tongue.

Mercy's throat tightened with recognition. She thought of Juba's children, Effie's haunted eyes, her words: *They want names. They forgot their own.* The idea that these lost souls—these Quiet Ones—were simply children looking for someone to call them home was almost more than she could bear.

She pressed the candle closer to the wall, hoping for some physical evidence—a crack, a crawlspace, anything to explain the voices. The warmth of the flame gave her courage, so she knelt and pressed her ear to the wood paneling.

For a moment, nothing.

Then a whisper so close and clear she recoiled: "Behind you."

Mercy turned sharply, nearly dropping the candle. The darkness behind her was impenetrable, but as the flame shook, she glimpsed, for a split second, the ghost of a face no more than a foot away.

The features were wrong, as if drawn from memory by a blind hand. The eyes were too large, lips too pale, teeth like pearls. The face vanished when the candle stilled, but Mercy could still feel the cold where it had been.

She remembered what Anna had said about the crow effigies anchoring the souls of Thorne's victims to this place, and a realization struck her with the force of certainty. The walls of Hallowspire weren't just walls; they were cages, prisons, tombs. And the spirits of those who had died here remained trapped in the spaces between spaces, unable to escape the house that had devoured them.

The candle flame convulsed, stretching tall and thin, then shrinking to a blue nub before flaring again with unnatural brightness.

In that moment of disturbed light, the air around Mercy filled with faces.

They materialized like ink bleeding through paper—first outlines, then features, then eyes that fixed on her with desperate intensity. Children's faces, dozens of them, floating in the darkness beyond her candle's reach. Some were as young as five or six, others were on the cusp of adolescence. Their appearances varied, but all were Black children with skin tones ranging from deep ebony to warm chestnut, some with African features, others bearing the unmistakable stamp of mixed heritage. All of them shared the hollow-eyed look of the long-dead.

And all bore the marks of Thorne's cruelty.

A boy no older than ten hovered near the ceiling, his mouth sewn shut with thick black thread that had been embedded in his flesh for so long it had begun to fuse with it. The stitches pulled his lips into a grotesque rictus that might have been a smile or a scream. His eyes, though—wide and aware—conveyed everything his silenced mouth could not.

Near the hearth floated a pair of twin girls, perhaps seven years old, their spectral forms partially translucent so that Mercy could see the fireplace grate through their tattered dresses. Their wrists and ankles bore the marks of iron manacles, the flesh beneath rubbed raw and never healed. But it was the strange symbols carved into their foreheads that drew Mercy's horrified gaze: seven-pointed stars surrounded by serpentine shapes that seemed to writhe even as she looked at them.

A smaller child—barely more than a toddler—drifted near the floor, his round face innocent except for the perfect circle punched through his forehead, revealing the darkness behind. The wound was surgical, precise, the skin around it bearing the marks of careful, methodical experimentation. His transparent hands reached toward Mercy with an infant's instinctive trust, unaware that his touch would bring only terror.

Everywhere Mercy looked, the air was thick with ghostly children. Some bore signs of physical torture: broken limbs never set, burns that had melted flesh to bone, weals from whips that had cut to the spine. Others showed evidence of Thorne's more esoteric cruelties: eyes replaced with smooth river stones, throats opened to reveal crystalline structures growing where vocal cords should be, chests carved open and ribs spread wide like wings to expose hearts wrapped in copper wire.

One girl, perhaps Mercy's own age, hovered directly before her. Her transparent form was more defined than the others, her presence stronger, as if her will to communicate transcended the barrier between their worlds. Her hair had been shaved, her scalp mapped with tiny silver pins driven into her skull in a pattern that matched the heptagram on the Great Hall floor. When she opened her mouth, no sound emerged, but her lips formed a word Mercy understood:

"Mercy."

The shock of hearing her name spoken by the dead girl sent her stumbling backward, the candle nearly snuffed.

The faces receded at once.

Mercy sagged against the wall, the stub of the candle burning close to her skin. She clutched it tighter, willing its flame to burn brighter, to push back the darkness that pressed against her tiny circle of light.

The flame responded by guttering violently, stretching tall and thin, then curling in on itself like a dying thing. Mercy cupped her hand around it protectively, but the gesture was futile. Without a draft, without a breath, without any natural cause, the candle went out.

Darkness fell like an axe. One moment, Mercy stood in a fragile bubble of light; the next, she was drowning in blackness so complete it felt like physical pressure against her eyes. She gasped, instinctively backing away from where the wall had been. But in the absolute dark, direction lost all meaning. She might have been moving toward the wall, not away from it.

"No," she whispered, her voice small and frail in the vastness. "Please, no."

Her eyes strained to adjust, to find any scrap of light, but the Great Hall offered none. The moonlight that had filtered through the high windows earlier had vanished, as if the night itself had drawn closer to witness her fear. The darkness pressed against her, thick as tar, heavy as lead. She felt it on her skin, in her lungs, behind her eyes—a living presence that knew her name and her weakness.

Mercy stood paralyzed, the useless candle still clutched in her rigid fingers, her breath coming in sharp gasps. The air around her felt charged, as if a storm were gathering in the confined space of the hall. She sensed movement in the darkness—not the pattering of small feet behind walls now, but the deliberate shifting of presences in the open air around her.

They were no longer hiding.

They were here, with her, in the Great Hall.

Something brushed against her skirt—the lightest touch, like fingers plucking at the fabric. Mercy bit her lip to keep from screaming. Another touch followed, against her arm this time, cold and tentative. She stood rigid, afraid that any movement might provoke whatever surrounded her in the darkness.

A small, cold hand slipped into hers.

The sensation was so unexpected, so intimate, that Mercy nearly dropped the extinguished candle. The hand that held hers was solid yet not—present enough to feel, but with a quality like water about to turn to ice. Small fingers curled around her palm with the perfect trust of a child who had once known safety, once known love.

Mercy couldn't move. Couldn't breathe. Couldn't do anything but stand there in the absolute dark, her hand clasped by something that should not exist.

The child's lips pressed directly against her ear, close enough that the words seemed to form inside Mercy's head rather than in the air around her:

"He's coming back. The Gate is opening."

The hand slipped from hers, leaving a bone-deep chill that spread up her arm like poison. Mercy felt the presence withdraw, sensed the shifting of the air as the spirits retreated

—not far, just beyond immediate reach. They remained in the hall, watching, waiting.

Mercy stood alone in the perfect darkness, her body rigid with terror, her breath shallow and quick. The silence settled around her again, but now she recognized it for what it was: not an absence, but an expectation. The entire mansion—every brick, every board, every soul trapped within its walls—was waiting.

Chapter 15

Anna left the mirror gallery without looking back. The sensation of a thousand eyes scraping her skin followed her up the corridor, but she refused to acknowledge them. Attention was fuel for things like that, and she had no intention of feeding anything more in this place. Her hand dribbled blood, smearing the wall as she groped in the dim candlelight for the hidden stair she'd glimpsed earlier—a narrow, vertical throat of stone that spiraled up into darkness.

The air grew thinner and colder as she ascended, but not in any natural way. It was the chill left behind when all the living air had been consumed by other, hungrier things. Anna pressed her free hand to the wall, feeling for vibrations and any sign of human or inhuman presence above. The stone was warm at first, then abruptly cold, then—impossibly—warm again, as if she passed through alternating bands of dead and living tissue.

She counted exactly a hundred and forty-nine steps before the spiral spat her out into the tallest of Hallowspire's three towers: the Astral Spire.

A domed ceiling rose high above. Its enchanted glass panels, warped and veined with lead, filtered the night sky through a prism of arcane design. The glass allowed an uninterrupted view of the stars, but not as they truly were. Instead, certain stars drifted across the dome's interior as if orbiting some invisible gravity. The air here was different. Thinner, charged with potential, as if the boundary between earth and cosmos had worn tissue-thin in this forgotten observatory.

Anna paused at the threshold, one hand still braced against the cold stone wall, letting her eyes adjust to the strange illumination. After the horrors of the mirror gallery, she half-expected another assault of reflections and distortions. But this chamber offered a different kind of disorientation, one of scale and perspective.

The circular room stretched perhaps thirty feet across, its perimeter ringed with brass instruments of astronomical study: telescopes with lenses like lidless eyes, quadrants inscribed with symbols no university would recognize, and charts marked in ink that seemed to shift and flow when she wasn't looking directly at them.

The centerpiece of the observatory was a massive orrery—a complex machine of planetary spheres, moons, and other questionable satellites, crafted from blackened brass and moving with impossibly precise, gravity-defying motion. No clockwork mechanism was visible, no weights or pendulums to drive its movement, yet the celestial bodies traced their orbits with meticulous care.

Anna stepped forward, her boots silent on the inlaid stone floor. As she drew closer to the orrery, she detected a sound.

It was faint at first, then clearer: a discordant melody like music boxes wound too tight, notes that shouldn't exist played in sequences that hurt the ear.

The orrery's central sphere—presumably the sun—pulsed with a dull, reddish glow that cast Anna's shadow in multiple directions simultaneously, as if she existed in several moments at once. The planets weren't quite right. There were too many, and several bore symbols Anna recognized from her Book of Shadows—sigils for entities that had never been meant to orbit any natural star.

The floor beneath the orrery was inlaid with a glyph Anna recognized instantly: the Spiral of Navigation. It was a twin of the binding glyphs that kept spirits in their graves. But here it was tuned to a different purpose. It was a map, not of space, but of time—or of something even less forgiving. The lines glowed faintly blue, as if lit from beneath by the pulse of some strange energy. Each time one of the orrery's satellites passed a certain point in its orbit, the glyph on the floor would flare, then dim, then flare again in perfect synchronization.

"He mapped more than stars here," Anna said, her voice unnaturally loud in the charged silence.

Rebecca stirred at the edge of Anna's consciousness, a coiled presence waiting for an opportunity. When she spoke, her voice was a dry whisper, like pages turning in a forgotten book.

This chamber is a crucible, child. Look how the brass mimics the movement of worlds. Feel how the air bends to touch you. He built this place to peer beyond the Veil.

Anna focused on the details of the room. She crossed to a

telescope, noting how the shadows seemed to resist her passage and clung to her skirts like reluctant children. The instrument was unlike any she had seen before. Its main barrel was crafted of obsidian rather than brass, with an eyepiece shaped like a serpent's head, mouth open to receive the observer's gaze. Anna bent to look through it, then hesitated, remembering the mirrors below and the horrors they had shown her.

Look, Anna. See what he saw.

Rebecca's urging only strengthened Anna's resolve not to peer through the telescope. Instead, she examined the base. A series of dials and calibrations allowed for precise adjustments, but the markings weren't degrees or minutes. Instead, they were set in units called "Whispers", "Griefs", and "Veilwidths". As her fingers brushed the cool metal, the orrery's mechanical music shifted key, the discordant notes aligning briefly into a harmony so perfect it made her teeth ache.

The air pulsed once, like a heartbeat, and Anna felt something pass through her. Not a spirit or a presence, but a kind of attention, as if the chamber itself had noticed her at last.

She stepped back from the telescope, turning in a slow circle to take in the chamber's entirety. The domed ceiling's enchanted glass had changed while she explored. The stars beyond now seemed closer, brighter, arranged in constellations that matched nothing Anna had ever seen. Not the night sky as it was, but as it might be—or as it had been, eons ago.

He sought to chart the passage between worlds, Rebecca

murmured, her voice almost wistful. *To map the doorways that exist in the spaces between stars.*

"He was mad," Anna replied aloud, her words echoing in the chamber.

Madness is merely perception that others cannot share, Rebecca countered. *Look around you, child. Does this strike you as the work of a disordered mind?*

It didn't, and that was the problem. The Astral Spire showed evidence of meticulous planning, of a vision executed with surgical precision. Every instrument, every calculation, every angle of the dome's glass panels—all served a singular purpose that Anna was beginning to understand all too clearly.

This room was more than an observatory. It was a calculation, a working model designed to predict celestial alignments and their effect on the Veil between worlds. Thorne hadn't simply studied the stars; he had mapped the precise moments when their positions would thin the boundary between life and death, between the physical world and whatever lay beyond.

A long, curved table of polished stone stood beyond the orrery, partially hidden in the room's unusual shadows. Its surface caught the fractured starlight from above, holding it like black water. Anna approached cautiously, her fingers brushing the cold edge before registering what lay upon it: maps, but unlike any she had seen before. They charted a geography that existed in no atlas, inked in silver that crawled across the page like mercury searching for a home.

She found an oil lamp on the table and lit it, grateful for the steady yellow flame after the treachery of the mirrors below. She held it higher, its warm glow at odds with the spectral illumination filtering through the dome. The maps were extensive, overlapping like scales on some great serpent, each one revealing different layers of the same territory. Anna recognized the shoreline of Brimwatch Isle—its distinctive hook-shaped cove, the western cliffs where she and Mercy had washed ashore, the rocky southern peninsula jutting into the Atlantic like an accusing finger.

But superimposed over these familiar contours were lines of force that no cartographer had ever charted. Three distinct currents of energy converged directly beneath Hallowspire—ley lines marked in inks of different hues and consistencies.

The first—labeled in Thorne's cramped script as "The Silver Thread"—appeared as a thin, brilliant line originating somewhere in the dense forests of Connecticut, snaking through the earth in a meandering path before terminating at the island. The second—"The Bloodline Vein"—was drawn in a rust-colored ink that still gleamed despite the decades since its application. It flowed from the Appalachian Mountains in a more direct route, its course marked by small annotations in what looked like Hebrew mixed with alchemical symbols.

The third line was labeled "The Void Spiral". Drawn in black ink, it twisted its way from deep beneath Long Island Sound, coiling tighter as it approached Brimwatch, until it converged with the others precisely where Hallowspire now stood. Beside it, Thorne had sketched a spiral glyph identical to those Anna had seen in the garden cairns.

"*The Trivium Tenebris,*" she murmured, reading the inscription where the three ley lines converged.

She traced her finger along the Silver Thread, and the ink responded. It shimmered like liquid under her touch, the line brightening momentarily before settling back into the parchment. Anna snatched her hand back, but curiosity overcame her caution. She touched the Bloodline Vein next, and a faint warmth spread up her finger, through her hand, and into her wrist, where her pulse quickened in response.

When her fingertip hovered over the Void Spiral, Rebecca's presence surged forward with sudden intensity, as if drawn by magnetic force.

Yes, the witch's voice hissed in her mind. *This one. This is the channel through which true power flows.*

Anna hesitated, then deliberately placed her finger on the black line. Cold shot through her arm, a numbing sensation that traveled straight to her heart, stealing her breath.

"What was that?" she whispered, flexing her numb fingers.

The Trivium acknowledges you, Rebecca replied, her tone almost reverent. *These are not mere drawings, child. They are windows into the world beneath the world.*

Anna studied the maps more carefully, noting how Thorne annotated each ley line with his observations:

"Silver Thread amplifies spectral resonance—ghosts drawn to its path like moths to flame."

"Bloodline Vein responds to lineage rituals—bloodletting near convergence points produces visions of ancestral memory."

"Void Spiral exhibits temporal anomalies—clocks run backward, pendulums swing counter to gravity. Possible gateway to the Inmost Dark?"

The notations continued across multiple maps, documenting decades of meticulous research. Thorne had charted how the ley lines shifted with lunar cycles, how their intensity varied with the seasons, how certain rituals performed at intersection points yielded different results depending on the phase of Venus or the position of Saturn.

"This is why he chose this place," Anna said, comprehension dawning with cold clarity. "Hallowspire wasn't built here by chance."

Of course not. Rebecca's voice was smug, satisfied. *He positioned it precisely to harness the Trivium's power. The entire mansion is an instrument, a focusing lens for energies that existed long before the stone was quarried or mortar mixed.*

Anna moved her lantern across different sections of the map, noticing how the flame responded—flaring bright over certain intersections, guttering almost to extinction over others. When she held it above the point where all three ley lines converged—directly beneath what would be the foundations of Hallowspire—the flame turned an unnatural blue-green, casting sickly shadows across the maps and her own face.

The convergence creates a wound in the world, Rebecca whispered, her words tinged with something close to ecstasy. *A tear in the fabric that separates realms. Most such wounds heal over time, closing like flesh knitting together. But this one... this one Thorne kept open.*

Anna set the lantern down, disturbed by both its unnatural behavior and Rebecca's growing excitement. Her scholarly fascination was rapidly giving way to a deeper dread as the implications became clear. Thorne had not merely studied the power of the Trivium Tenebris; he had constructed his life's work atop its open nerve. Hallowspire wasn't just a mansion built atop the powerful ley lines; it was a machine designed to split open the world and let something in.

Anna's gaze swept over the length of the curved table and came to rest on a massive tome obscured in shadows. The cover wasn't leather—at least, not animal hide. The skin was too smooth, too pale, stretched taut over boards of some dark wood. Human skin, prepared with meticulous care, bearing the unmistakable pattern of pores and the faint shadow of what might have been a tattoo or birthmark. Anna ran her fingers over the surface, feeling the ridged letters burn into her nerves:

CELESTIAL CODEX OF THE CRUCIBLE OF NIGHT
A.G. THORNE
MIDSUMMER 1812

Anna lifted the book carefully, surprised by its weight. It was easily two feet tall and half as wide, bound with iron clasps that had turned black with age. Along the spine, arcane symbols had been burned into the flesh-leather, forming a vertical sentence in a language that seemed to blur before her eyes, refusing to resolve into recognizable letters.

Anna unlatched the iron clasps, which released with reluctant sighs. The cover fell open, revealing pages of vellum so thin they were nearly transparent. The first page was a palimpsest of celestial diagrams, over-written with looping marginalia in Thorne's cramped, angular hand. Most of the text was ciphered, but Anna's training—and Rebecca's voice —made quick work of the substitutions:

"Beneath the foundations of Hallowspire lies a natural chasm

formed by this convergence—a bottomless void I have named the Womb Below. It is not merely a physical space, but a wound in the world, a birth canal through which the Red Silence might be breached."

Anna turned the page, sweat breaking on her brow despite the frigid air. The next folio was a diagram of the mansion's foundation, a spiral staircase below what appeared to be a chapel, and at the center, a deep black hole rendered in thick, almost oily pigment. Beneath it, Thorne had written: "Nocturne Gate / Womb Below." Around it, thirteen points marked in red ink indicated positions for "the anchors".

"Where the Trivium converges, the world's membrane thins. To breach the Red Silence, a living soul must unmake itself— stripped, rung, and reassembled by the Tenebric Sequence. Thirteen echoes suffice for the first opening, but permanence requires a soul that will not die."

Anna turned the page, finding diagrams of human figures with their spirits seemingly pulled from their bodies—souls depicted as luminous clouds tethered by slender threads to open mouths or empty eye sockets.

A shiver ran through Anna, but she forced herself to read further.

Each page delved deeper into Thorne's obsession with what he called "the Inmost Dark"—a realm beyond death that he believed contained entities of immense power. The text described experiments, failed attempts to create stable passages between worlds, rituals abandoned when they proved too costly or dangerous. Among the pages was a ledger of names, dates, and annotations in a code that, once cracked, told the story of every soul harvested for Thorne's experiments. There were dozens—all slaves from the South. Some were adults, but most—Anna's stomach turned—were children, their ages noted with a precise, almost scientific detachment. Next to each was a note of method and result: *"Satisfactory yield. Vessel did not rot. Memory intact."* Or, more chilling: *"Soul returned in other shape. Host unstable. Do not attempt again."*

Anna's hand shook as she turned the pages. Her pulse was a drum in her ears. One page, written in what looked like Thorne's own blood, read:

"If the Nocturne Gate is to remain, the Keystone must be a living child, shorn of name and memory. Only such innocence may hold the breach until the Inmost Dark is born through."

Anna's pulse quickened, her shoulders tensing as she absorbed the full scope of Thorne's ambition. He hadn't merely sought to commune with the dead or command spirits. He had attempted to tear open a permanent passage between worlds, to breach the Veil—what he called the Red Silence—and allow entities from the Inmost Dark to enter the physical realm.

The next pages detailed the ritual components: astronomical alignments, blood sacrifices, the precise placement of thirteen soul-stripped victims around the spiral's edge. Thorne's handwriting grew more frantic as the instructions continued, the neat script deteriorating into a desperate scrawl that betrayed his growing obsession:

"Final phase requires living conduit—thirteen anchors insufficient for stable breach. Nocturne Gate requires consciousness to bridge final gap. Volunteer must step willingly across threshold—"

Anna's grip on the book tightened, her knuckles whitening as the implication became clear. Thorne himself had been the final component—the living mind that would bridge worlds and allow whatever waited on the other side to cross over.

And he succeeded, Rebecca hissed. *Not fully, not completely, but enough. He crossed the threshold and returned… changed.*

Anna's mind reeled with the knowledge she'd absorbed, pieces falling into place with terrible clarity. The Quiet Ones that Effie spoke of were Thorne's anchors, their souls stripped by the ritual he called the Tenebric Sequence, their empty bodies positioned around the Womb Below to stabilize the Nocturne Gate. And Thorne himself had become something else entirely—not quite dead, not fully alive, but a hybrid entity existing in both worlds simultaneously.

"For what purpose?" Anna asked aloud, though she feared she already knew the answer.

Power, of course, Rebecca replied. *The power to transcend death. To become the gatekeeper between worlds.*

The power to retrieve a soul lost beyond the Veil, Anna thought, but did not say.

But her thoughts were never safe from Rebecca. *Now you begin to understand,* she purred. *Why I guided you here. What waits for us beneath.*

Anna tasted bile. She thought of Abigail's soul, adrift beyond the Veil, waiting for rescue. Of Mercy, trembling and alone in the Great Hall. Of Juba's children, hiding in their cave, praying the darkness would never find them.

Her whole life had been shaped by wounds—by inheritance, by sacrifice, by the endless appetite of the dead for the living. Here, in this room, on this spot, Anna understood she was not the hunter. She was the prey. She was the raw material for a ritual centuries in the making.

She closed the codex with trembling hands, unable to read more. The moment the cover closed, the orrery stopped moving. The sudden silence was profound, almost deafening after the constant mechanical music. The lantern flame stood perfectly still, as if time itself had marked the significance of what Anna had discovered.

Then, from far below—beneath the foundations of Hallowspire, beneath the floor of the Great Hall where Mercy slept, beneath the very bedrock of the island—came a low, resonant rumble. It wasn't the familiar groan of an old house settling, but something deeper, more purposeful. The vibration traveled up through the stone, rattling the instruments around the chamber's perimeter and sending ripples across the surface of the maps.

The Astral Spire held its breath, waiting, as the rumble faded to silence. But Anna knew with cold certainty that it wasn't over. Something deep below had awakened—had perhaps been stirring since she and Mercy arrived on Brimwatch. And now, with every piece of knowledge she uncovered, with every secret she brought to light, it drew closer to the surface.

Rebecca's laughter echoed in her mind, soft and triumphant.

The Gate waits, child. And it knows we're here.

Chapter 16

Water dripped from the limestone fangs above, each drop a metronome counting seconds in the darkness of the sea cave. The sound mixed with the murmur of waves, creating a lullaby that had rocked Effie to sleep hours ago. Now, something else woke her. Whispers thin as spider silk threaded through the cracks in the stone, seeking her out with desperate purpose.

Effie lay nestled between the warm, solid weight of her mother and the bony angles of her brother's back. Juba slept hard, breath shallow but determined. Her arm stretched protectively across her daughter's small chest even in sleep, a reflex born of years spent shielding her children from harm. Micah faced the cave entrance, curled on his side, his body a barrier between his family and whatever might enter from the night. Their breathing formed a steady counterpoint to the dripping water; deep exhalations of exhaustion that the whispers didn't disturb.

It was well past midnight when the temperature changed. Not the natural ebb and flow of oceanic damp, but a sudden, precise stillness like the inhalation before a scream. The sound of the sea dropped away, replaced by a brittle clarity that made the ticking of the water from the stalactites seem monstrously amplified. The blackness outside the cave mouth thickened, as if even the moon had drawn back in revulsion. Something else pressed in with the cold. A presence—or maybe a collection of presences—crowded the air and made the already-limited oxygen taste of iron and salt.

Effie's eyes snapped open. For a moment, she saw nothing at all. Her gaze met only the undifferentiated blackness overhead.

The first whisper slid into her ear like cold water, making her small body stiffen beneath the threadbare blanket Juba had tucked around her. The words came clearly to Effie in a way she couldn't explain:

Come to us, little one.

Her eyes opened wider, adjusting to a darkness she'd never really been afraid of. The cave's interior took shape around her—the rough stone walls slick with salt and moisture; the narrow ledge where Juba had placed their meager belongings; the low ceiling from which water beaded and fell. All familiar, all unchanged, but the air itself had shifted. It felt heavier, charged with expectation.

We have been waiting.

Effie's small body tensed all at once, every muscle tightening in anticipation. Gooseflesh rose on her thin arms, not from cold but from recognition.

The Quiet Ones had found her again.

They always did eventually.

She was careful not to move too suddenly. Juba had a hair-trigger sense for trouble, and a single twitch might wake her. Instead, Effie regulated her breath, slowed it, then eased herself up onto one elbow, moving with the liquid caution of a child raised on secrets. The blanket slid away, leaving her exposed to the cave's frigid air. She didn't mind. If anything, she welcomed the cold—it meant the Quiet Ones were near.

The voices coalesced, overlapping less, the cadence sharpening into something close to music. A faint and lilting lullaby.

"Rock-a-bye baby, the cradle was bone. Hung from a tree where the Quiet Ones moan. When the wind whispers, the cradle will creak. Down will come baby, tongue gone to speak."

Effie's heart beat faster, not with fear but with a strange, solemn recognition. The Quiet Ones never harmed her. They only wanted to be heard, to be named, to be remembered by someone who still breathed.

She looked over at her mother and saw the heavy line of Juba's jaw set in sleep, the deep furrow between her brows. Even when dreaming, her mother looked afraid—afraid for Effie, for Micah, for what waited outside the cave and what might still follow them inside. Effie spared a glance at Micah, too. Her brother was dreaming as well, mouth open a little, one leg spasming now and then with the phantom sensation of running. He was always running, even here, even safe, never quite letting the world catch him.

Effie sat up fully, her bare feet flat against the stone. The cold bit at her soles, but she barely registered it. The whispering had grown louder, enough that she was sure her mother would wake. But Juba slept on, either deaf to the spectral lullabies or too exhausted to care. Effie pressed both palms to her ears, not to block the sound but to amplify it, as if her own skull might be a better receiver.

"Cradle is cracked, and mother is flame; Baby's forgotten her soul and her name. Sing with the silence, soft as a knife; Sleep with the Gate, and trade in your life."

The whispers intensified as Effie moved, as if encouraged by her attention. They seeped from every crack in the stone, from the dark pools where seawater gathered, from the very air itself. One voice broke away from the rest and slithered to the front, whispering directly into Effie's ear:

"The Gate opens...

He is coming back...

Give us your name..."

Effie's heart thudded, but it wasn't fear, only anticipation. She nodded, then stood, careful not to step on her mother's outstretched arm.

The cave's temperature dropped again as she rose, this time so sharply that Effie's exhaled breath hung before her face. The air tasted of brine and decay, undercut by a sweetness Effie couldn't name. Maybe it was just the faint scent of salt marsh flowers caught in the mist, but she doubted it.

A lone wisp of vapor, faintly lit by moonlight filtering into the cave, snaked around Effie's ankles like a hungry cat. It was colder than the air around it, colder than anything natural. Effie felt a jolt of connection where it touched her skin, the same spark that passed between her and Mercy back in the garden—a recognition of shared sight.

Never before had the whispers felt so pressing. Usually, they came in her dreams or in quiet moments when she wandered the shoreline, collecting shells under Juba's watchful eye. Now they pressed against her, insistent as hunger, desperate as thirst.

Something had changed on the island. Something had awoken.

Effie felt her skin prickling, tiny hairs rising along the dark skin of her arms and the back of her neck. Her loose cotton shift, one of Juba's old kerchiefs re-sewn to fit her small frame, suddenly seemed too thin against the unnatural chill. Yet she wasn't afraid. The Quiet Ones had never shown her anything but a terrible, broken kind of kindness—like creatures who remembered how to be gentle but had forgotten why.

More vapor tendrils slid across the cave floor, twisting into shapes that almost resembled hands before dissolving back into formlessness. They moved with purpose, encircling Effie's thin ankles, tugging gently as if to lift her from her feet. The whispers grew more frantic, a chorus of disjointed pleas.

"He will steal your memory…
You can help us…"

Effie stood perfectly still, her amber-flecked eyes reflecting nothing but the dim glow of the vapor as it swirled around her. Her wild hair, untamable even by Juba's careful braiding, framed her small face like a dark halo. She looked both younger and older than her years; a child touched by something ancient and marked by knowledge no child should possess.

The whispers changed, becoming a single voice—higher, clearer, closer to her ear.

"Effie."

Her name sent a shiver down her spine. None of the Quiet Ones had ever used her name before. They had forgotten their own names; how could they know hers?

"Effie, come. The house calls. The Gate waits."

She understood then what they wanted, why they had come to her in this new, urgent way. The Quiet Ones weren't just calling to her anymore; they were coming for her. Something was happening at Hallowspire. Something involving the Gate beneath the house, the one they had told her about in fragmented whispers and half-formed dreams.

And deep in her bones, in the place where dreams and knowing lived, Effie understood she needed to go with them.

The mist grew thicker around her feet, no longer just tendrils but a swirling pool of silvery vapor that glowed with its own pale light. It cast strange shadows on the cave walls— childlike silhouettes that moved independently of their source, hands reaching, mouths open in silent cries.

Effie moved with the careful grace of a child accustomed to silence, to making herself unnoticed when necessary. Each step was deliberate, placed to avoid the loose stones and shallow puddles that might create noise. She paused only once to glance back at her family, the two bodies so still they might have been laid out for burial. Micah had rolled onto his back, one arm flung across his eyes as if to shield them from sights that pursued him even in slumber. Effie thought about kissing her mother's cheek, but something in the air warned against it. Any sudden motion, any break in the ritual, and the spell would be lost, or worse: the attention of the Quiet Ones would shift from her to Juba, and that could not be allowed. Instead, Effie pulled her thin shift tighter around her shoulders and tiptoed forward, out of the makeshift nest and into the stinging cold.

At the threshold, the world was all fog and darkness. The mist rolled in slow, intelligent curls, sometimes splitting to reveal glimmers of starlight or the bone-white slash of the moon overhead. Effie stood on the slick, uneven rock at the mouth of the cave and listened as the lullabies redoubled, now joined by a second, fainter melody that echoed her own heartbeat.

She didn't shiver, though the temperature had dropped far below what any normal child could tolerate. Instead, she held her arms out, palms up, as if expecting to receive a gift. The air pressed in, thick as syrup, until she felt the first touch: a brush of cold across her knuckles, then a sharper jolt as something unseen wrapped around her left hand.

Effie squeezed her eyes shut, as if she might see better in the dark that way. The voices no longer whispered but hummed, surrounding her with a cocoon of sound. They called her by name—Euphemia, Effie, Little Echo—always in the same eerie cadence. The message was unmistakable: she was one of theirs. It felt like a thousand invisible hands wrapped around her chest, each tugging in a different direction, but all converging on the same point just outside the cave's shelter. The sensation was not pain, not exactly, but an ache. It was a loneliness so profound it had become physical, a gnawing need to step forward and fill the hollow space the Quiet Ones had made for her.

She took another step forward, toes sinking into the thin film of silt at the cave's lip. The mist parted like a curtain drawn back by invisible hands, and through it she caught the first true glimpse of the visitors.

They stood at the edge of the fog, their forms flickering between visibility and absence with each pulse of the mist's inner light.

The Quiet Ones.

Black children like her, yet not like her at all. Their bodies were translucent, the rocky cliff face visible through their emaciated frames. Their skin—if it could be called that—was ashen gray, stretched too tight over their bones and pulsing faintly with the same sickly light that filled the mist.

A boy no older than Micah stood closest, his hollow frame draped in what had once been a sailor's shirt, now tattered and stained with decades-old blood that would never dry. His face was hideous to look upon. Where eyes should have been, only empty sockets gaped, weeping black tears that evaporated before they could fall. His mouth hung open in a silent scream, tongue missing, leaving only a raw, dark cavity that seemed to drink in the night around him.

Beside him, a girl perhaps Effie's age wore a faded dress that might once have been white but now hung in ragged strips from her spectral form. Her hair floated around her head as if underwater, moving independently of the night breeze. Like the boy, her eyes were gone, replaced by shadow, but the socket edges were burned, cauterized by some unimaginable heat. Her hands reached toward Effie, fingers too long, joints bending in ways no living child's could.

More forms materialized in the mist. Thirteen of them, all children, all bearing the same terrible hallmarks of violation. Some were missing limbs; others had gaping wounds where their hearts should beat. One small figure, barely more than a toddler, floated several inches above the ground, head tilted at an impossible angle, neck clearly broken. Another dragged itself forward on arms that ended in raw stumps, legs long since severed at the knee.

The Thirteen moved with jerky, unnatural motions, as if their spirits had forgotten how bodies were meant to behave. They shuddered and twitched, limbs lagging behind as if struggling to recall the purpose of joints and tendons. Despite their horror, Effie felt no fear—only a profound sadness and a strange sense of kinship. These were the voices that had whispered to her for weeks, the presences that had guided her to fresh water and safe paths.

"You can be one of us...
You are the one who believes...
You are ours..."

Effie stood at the threshold between the safety of the cave and the unknown that waited in the glowing mist. Behind her lay her mother and brother, the only constants in a life defined by flight and fear. Before her, these strange, broken children offered something else—understanding, purpose, belonging. They saw her as no one else did, recognized the part of her that had always felt out of step with the world.

Her small hand hovered at the edge of the mist, fingertips tingling with cold where they nearly brushed the luminous vapor. Frost formed on her skin, tracing delicate patterns across her palm—the same symbols that marked the Quiet Ones, that adorned the walls of Hallowspire, that appeared in her dreams.

She looked forward again. The mist beckoned, swirling around her ankles, climbing her calves with cool, insistent hands.

"I hear you singing," she said, softer now, her words barely more than vapor.

The Thirteen sang back. This time, the syllables came forward, then backward, then forward again, like water running in and out with the tide. Effie felt the song wrap around her spine and settle into her lungs, a weight that was somehow less than air. She clutched her arms around herself, teeth chattering now, though whether from cold or anticipation she couldn't tell. The longing was a living thing inside her. She wanted to run, to call for her mother, to sink back into the shelter of the cave and never move again.

But she also wanted to know what awaited her in the fog. She wanted to belong. She could almost hear Juba's voice behind her, calling her name, but the sound was as distant as a dream at dawn. Effie looked at the door, then at the ghosts, then at her own trembling hands. She closed her eyes and said, to no one and everyone: "I'm coming to help you."

Then she stepped forward, leaving everything behind.

And in the shivering black, the Thirteen sang their thanks.

Chapter 17

The Great Hall of Hallowspire held its silence like a catacomb. It was the blue hour before dawn, and the vast chamber lay wrapped in that peculiar stillness that comes before morning, when even ghosts retreat to whatever passes for rest among the dead. The only movement was the almost imperceptible twitch of Anna's right thumb as it traced the raw edge of a page.

She sat alert on the moth-eaten settee across from Mercy, Thorne's codex clutched in her white-knuckled fingers. Adrenaline and dread kept her awake, her senses stretched to their limits, though the climb to the Astral Spire and the horrors of the mirror gallery should have exhausted her. The mansion's breathing—expanding and contracting with subtle creaks and settling groans—had taken on a different rhythm since her discovery. As if it knew that she knew. As if it were watching her watch it.

The fire had burned down to nothing, leaving only ghost-white ash. Anna hadn't bothered to relight it after returning from the Astral Spire to find Mercy awake and distraught by her encounter with the dead children in the mansion's walls.

Now, Anna watched the girl's chest rise and fall in dreamless sleep. She lay wrapped in the quilt that was more holes than substance. Mercy's hands clung to the rag as if, even in sleep, she suspected its shelter was a lie.

Pale light filtered through the glass of the windows high overhead, throwing fragmented patterns across the cold marble floor. Outside, the wind had died, leaving behind a silence that felt expectant rather than peaceful.

The knowledge Anna carried from the tower pressed against her skull like hands trying to reshape her thoughts. Thirteen souls, stripped and bound. A keystone child to hold the breach. A living sacrifice to open the way. Thorne had built Hallowspire not as a mansion but as a machine, a device to tear open the Veil between worlds and let something terrible in. Or perhaps, Anna thought with a cold shiver, to let something out.

Rebecca's presence had grown subdued since they left the tower, as if satiated by Anna's discovery. But Anna felt her there still, coiled and waiting at the base of her mind like a serpent pretending sleep. The witch-ghost was playing a longer game, and Anna's growing suspicion of her ancestor's true intentions gnawed at her confidence.

Mercy stirred in her sleep, mumbling something unintelligible. Anna's fingers traced the edges of Thorne's codex, weighing what to tell the girl when she woke. The truth would terrify her, but ignorance might kill her faster. Anna's own mother had made that calculation many times—how much knowledge was too much, how much too little—and Anna had resented her for it. Now, she understood the impossible balance.

Anna's fingers brushed the knife at her side, taking comfort in the cold metal. She could feel dawn approaching in her bones, that subtle shift in the air that came before the first light. If they survived until morning, perhaps—

The pounding broke the silence like an ax through glass.

Not the delicate patter of spectral children in the walls. Not the hollow echoes of wind. This was the sound of a full-grown fist, balled tight and striking wood, each blow reverberating through the frame and into the marrow of the house itself. The rhythm was frantic, desperate, each impact layered with a second, lighter percussion—maybe a boot, or a shoulder, or another body pressed into the task.

Mercy jolted upright, her eyes wide and unfocused, the quilt sliding to pool around her waist. Anna was already on her feet, knife ready, her body between Mercy and whatever waited outside.

"Stay here," Anna commanded. "Behind the couch if you can."

Mercy nodded, still disoriented from sleep but alert enough to recognize danger. She slid from the couch to the floor, making herself small against its bulk.

The pounding came again, more insistent this time—five blows in rapid succession, each one harder than the last. Not the measured knock of a casual visitor, but the frantic tattoo of desperation. Someone was trying to get in, or perhaps to warn those inside.

Anna moved toward the entrance, boots silent on the marble, knife reversed in her grip. The Great Hall narrowed to a short corridor before opening onto the massive oak doors that formed the mansion's main entrance. These doors—twelve feet tall and carved with scenes from myths no church would recognize—had remained sealed since Anna and Mercy's arrival. The iron latches had rusted shut from disuse.

Yet someone was outside, hammering with enough force to make the ancient wood shudder.

Anna flattened herself against the wall beside the doors, knife raised. "Who's there?"

A woman's voice answered, ragged with emotion but unmistakable: "Please! We need help!"

Juba. And where Juba was, her children would be close.

Anna hesitated only a moment before reaching for the first of the door's three locks. The metal was ice-cold against her palm, and it resisted her first attempt to turn it. She set her knife between her teeth, freeing both hands to grasp the iron bar. It yielded with a protesting groan, decades of rust crumbling to dust beneath her fingers.

She pulled the right-hand door open just wide enough to see through, keeping her body braced against it should someone try to force their way in. The gap revealed Juba and Micah on the threshold, both disheveled and frantic. The woman was soaked in brine, her clothing torn at the knees and crusted with salt. Her braids had partly unraveled, giving her the wild look of someone who had been searching through brush and bramble. Her hands trembled as she gripped the doorframe, her fingers leaving smudges of blood where thorns or sharp rocks had cut them. Her dark eyes were red-rimmed, the whites shot through with pink threads.

Micah stood hunched against the wind, his arms limp at his sides, lips pressed flat in a line that betrayed both exhaustion and something more complicated—a private shame or a wound he wouldn't let bleed.

Anna had a half-second to process this before Juba blurted out: "She's gone. Effie's gone."

The words hit the air like a cannon blast. Anna felt her stomach drop, the implications unfolding with terrible clarity in light of what she'd just learned in the Astral Spire.

"Gone?" she repeated, though she already knew what Juba meant. "Since when?"

"Before dawn," Juba said, and her jaw worked against the words. "Slept with her right by my side. Micah woke me, said Effie was gone from the blankets. Searched all the caves along the eastern shore. The cove where we first landed. The old garden with the crow bones. Every godforsaken inch of this island."

Anna let her gaze flick to Micah, whose eyes never left the ground. "And you? You saw nothing?"

The boy shook his head once, but the movement was neither shameful nor evasive. It was stubborn, a refusal to let his own fear show through. "She was there," he said, his voice thicker and more adult than Anna remembered from the garden. "She was right there, and then she wasn't."

Juba's next words came out in a rasped staccato: "There's something wrong with this place. The fog don't move right. You walk the same path, it curves under your feet. The air's got a taste to it, like meat gone sweet. We kept close together, but—" Her breath hitched, eyes hard as granite. "I failed her."

Anna's jaw tightened as she processed this information. Her fingers flexed around her knife as she considered the implications of Effie's disappearance, considering what she now knew about Thorne's ritual.

A keystone child. A living tether to hold the breach between worlds…

Rebecca's voice slithered up from the depths of Anna's consciousness, soft and satisfied: *The house has chosen, child. And soon the Gate will open.*

"Come inside," Anna said, pulling the door wide. "Quickly."

Juba stood at the threshold like a woman facing execution, her body rigid with reluctance. The entrance hall yawned before her, its marble floors gleaming with the dull patina of age and neglect. She exhaled once, hard, as if expelling whatever courage she'd mustered to knock, then stepped inside with the careful tread of someone crossing thin ice. Her eyes darted from shadow to shadow, mapping escape routes even as she surrendered to necessity.

Anna closed the door behind them and threw the locks, the sound making Juba flinch. "You came here for help," she said, not unkindly. It was not a question.

Juba looked at her, and for the first time, Anna saw the full desperation in the woman's eyes. "You're the only thing here that ain't afraid of this house. If Effie went anywhere, she went to you."

Anna almost laughed. "Nobody comes to me for comfort," she said, a bitter edge to her tone. "Not even the dead."

Mercy approached from the Great Hall, still keeping the ruined quilt wrapped like a barrier between herself and the world. "Effie's like me," she whispered, voice tremulous but sincere. "She can hear them—the Quiet Ones. If they wanted her—"

Juba cut her off, a sharp gesture that might have been a curse in another language. "Don't say that," she hissed. "My child's not dead. Not yet."

Micah's gaze never settled in one place for long. He'd positioned himself slightly ahead of his mother, his body angled to shield her from whatever might emerge from the mansion's depths. For all his youth, there was nothing childlike in his posture—only the wary readiness of someone who had learned early on that safety was an illusion.

"She's been like that since we got to the island," he said, his voice low. "Worse this past week. Drawing symbols in the sand, singing songs we never learned before." His shoulders hunched inward. "I should've watched her better. Should've woken up when she—" He broke off, fists clenched at his sides.

Mercy moved closer to Anna, her thin fingers gripping the older woman's sleeve. "The Quiet Ones," she whispered. "Like the voices in the walls last night."

Anna nodded, pieces fitting together with terrible precision. Effie, with her strange sensitivity to the island's spirits. The Quiet Ones—Thorne's soul-stripped victims, bound to the Nocturne Gate. The keystone child needed to complete the ritual.

"I'll search the mansion," she announced. "Every room, every hidden passage. Mercy will help me."

Juba's head snapped up, her eyes fixing on Anna with a pleading that was almost animal. "You'll help us?" she asked, as if the cost didn't matter.

Anna nodded once. "We'll find her… or we'll find what

took her."

The promise was a small thing, brittle as the dawn light that now bled through the high windows. But it was enough.

"I'm coming too," Micah declared, stepping forward with his chin raised. The boy was tall for his age, but painfully thin, his wrists protruding from sleeves that had once been the right length. His eyes held the determination of someone far older, tempered by a fear he refused to acknowledge.

"No," Juba cut in sharply, grabbing his arm with fingers that dug deep enough to bruise. "You ain't setting foot further in this house."

As if in confirmation, a soft sigh seemed to pass through the room—not wind, for the air remained still, but a sound like distant satisfaction. The shadows in the corners deepened slightly, and the clock on the mantelpiece that hadn't worked since Anna's arrival ticked once, the sound unnaturally loud in the tense silence.

"Mama, please," Micah pled, his composure cracking to reveal the frightened child beneath. "She's my sister. I'm supposed to protect her."

"And who protects you?" Juba demanded. "You think I can lose both my children to this place?"

Anna watched the exchange with growing unease. The mansion seemed to be drinking in their fear, feeding on the conflict. She caught Mercy's eye and nodded toward a side table where an oil lamp sat. The girl understood immediately, moving to light it while Anna intervened.

"Micah," Anna said. "Your mother's right about this house. It's dangerous in ways you don't understand." She chose her next words carefully, aware of balancing truth against terror. "But there's something else you could do. Something equally important."

Micah's eyes narrowed with suspicion, recognizing an adult's attempt to placate. "What?"

"Someone needs to wait at the cave," Anna said. "In case Effie returns on her own. In case she's just lost, or hiding."

The lie tasted bitter, but Anna couldn't bring herself to tell him what she truly suspected: that if the Quiet Ones had taken Effie—if she had become part of Thorne's unfinished ritual—they might never find her intact again.

"She's right," Juba said, her grip on Micah's arm loosening slightly. "Someone's got to be there if she comes back, scared and alone."

Micah's jaw worked, anger and fear warring for dominance. "And you?" he asked his mother. "You'll stay outside? Where it's safe?"

A long silence followed, heavy with the weight of impossible choices. Juba looked around the room, her gaze lingering on the shadows that seemed too dense, too attentive. When she spoke again, her voice had changed—resolved, fatalistic.

"I'll go with them."

The surprise on Micah's face mirrored Anna's own. Juba, who had warned them all away from Hallowspire. Juba, who had felt its breath and heard its heartbeat. Juba, who knew better than any of them what waited in its depths.

"Mama, no," Micah protested, but the fight had left his voice. He recognized the look on his mother's face. It was the same expression she'd worn when she'd decided to flee Virginia, when she'd stolen them away from certain death into uncertain freedom. Once Juba made up her mind, nature itself would break before she would.

"My baby is in there," Juba said simply, as if those five words explained everything. And they did.

Micah hesitated, then reached inside his tattered shirt and removed something small that gleamed dully in the half-light. A knife, its blade no longer than a finger but honed to wicked sharpness. He pressed it into his mother's palm and closed her fingers around it.

"Took it from a dead overseer," he said, a world of history conveyed in six simple words. "It finds blood easy."

Juba tucked the knife into the folds of her shawl, her expression unchanged except for a slight softening around her eyes.

Mercy returned with the lamp, its golden light pushing back the darkness but revealing the exhaustion etched into Juba's face. The woman who had survived slavery, flight, and abandonment on a haunted island now faced something that terrified her more than all of those combined: entering Hallowspire to search for her missing child.

"You said Effie hears them," Anna said quietly, meeting Juba's eyes. "The Quiet Ones. Did she ever say what they wanted from her?"

Juba's face hardened. "They want what all ghosts want. Someone who can hear them. Someone who believes them." She looked toward the depths of the mansion, where corridors branched like arteries from a black heart. "But these ones want something more. Something worse."

"What?" Mercy asked, her voice barely above a whisper.

Juba's eyes glistened with unshed tears. "Freedom."

Chapter 18

Anna led them through Hallowspire's intestinal corridors, each turn revealing passages darker than the last. The mansion's layout seemed to rearrange under their feet. Halls stretched longer than architecture should allow. Doorways appeared where none had been before. She kept her knowledge close, a bitter weight in her chest. If the Quiet Ones had taken Effie, Anna knew exactly where they would have led her: the Nocturne Gate that waited beneath the foundation stones.

But she couldn't tell Juba. Not while there was still hope.

"We'll start with the rooms below," Anna said, her voice deliberately steady. "If Effie came to the mansion in the night, she didn't come through the front doors. The only way in would be through a window or a servant's door."

She left unspoken what else might wait in the lower levels: the spiral staircase descending to the foundations; the Sanctum of Sundering where Thorne had arranged thirteen soul-stripped victims in a perfect circle; the bottomless chasm he had called the Womb Below.

"I know what's down there," Juba said quietly, her gaze fixed on Anna. "Effie told me. The spiral that goes down and never stops."

Anna glanced at her, a current of understanding passing between them. Juba might not have Anna's education in the occult, but she possessed an intuitive grasp of darkness that books could never teach. She knew what awaited beneath Hallowspire. She had sensed it from the moment she had washed ashore on Brimwatch.

Juba narrowed her eyes. "You know more than you're saying," she said. But her accusation lacked conviction, just the hollow desperation of a mother who would accept any knowledge, no matter how terrible, if it led to her child.

"My Effie..." she pressed, her stride lengthening to match Anna's. "What do they want with my girl?"

Anna's jaw tightened. She wouldn't lie, but neither would she speak the full truth—that Thorne's ritual required a living child, innocent and open, to serve as the keystone for his Gate. "She can hear them," she said instead. "That makes her valuable."

They moved deeper into the mansion's northern reaches, where the air hung heavier and the walls seemed to lean inward. Dust lay thick on the floor with no sign of the passage of Effie's bare feet. The wallpaper, once rich burgundy, had faded to the exact shade of dried blood, and peeled away in long strips that resembled flayed skin. Mercy stayed close to Anna's elbow while Juba walked with her back never fully turned to either wall, her eyes constantly scanning for movement.

The corridor narrowed, then opened suddenly into a small

antechamber. Beyond it stood a bent-iron arch, coiled with carvings of tongueless figures that seemed to undulate in the flickering lamplight. Through this archway lay Thorne's Chapel of the Crucible, its door ajar, as if beckoning them inside.

Juba skidded to a halt at the threshold, her hand flying to her throat where her charm hung. "This place breathes wrong," she whispered, her words carrying the weight of folk wisdom passed down through generations. "Air moves the wrong way. In when it should go out."

Anna felt it too—a subtle reversal in the natural order. The chapel seemed to inhale as they approached, drawing them in with each breath instead of expelling them with natural drafts.

"My grandmother would say a place like this got a hunger," Juba continued, her deep voice dropping lower still. "Not just for bodies, but for souls. She'd say it's best to walk backward inside, so it can't see your face."

Mercy shivered, her thin shoulders hunching as if against a physical blow. "I hear them," she whispered. "Not like before. Clearer now. They're… singing."

Anna stepped through the archway first, holding the lamp high. The chapel opened before them, its architecture a perversion of a sacred space. Where churches reached upward toward divinity, this room pressed downward, its vaulted ceiling forming a reverse dome that created the sensation of being pulled into the earth. Stained glass etched with inverted iconography filled the narrow, arched windows—crucified goats, crowned serpents, and trees with black fire blooming from their roots.

The floor was black slate veined with crimson marble, laid out in a spiral labyrinth that drew the eye inward toward the central altar. The pattern was deliberate, forcing visitors to follow a winding path that echoed the journey of descent—not into Hell, but into something older and more primordial. Patterns of light filtering through the windows shifted and crawled across the floor as if alive, illuminating the crimson threads in the slate until they pulsed like exposed arteries.

Juba was the last to enter, her steps hesitant, her back rigid with the effort of confronting something that violated every spiritual principle she recognized. "There's wrongness built into the bones of this place," she murmured. "Like it was made to mock what's holy."

The altar stood at the room's center, a slab of obsidian so dark it seemed to swallow light rather than reflect it. Four chained statues of weeping monks supported its weight, their faces contorted in agonies that bordered on ecstasy. An ancient spiral etched the stone surface, and at its center rested a basin of congealed black wax and what could only be old blood.

Anna approached it cautiously, her fingertips hovering just above the surface, careful not to make contact. The spiral pattern matched those she had seen in Thorne's journals, in the garden cairns, in the orrery above—all pointing to the same cosmic arrangement, the same tear in the fabric between worlds.

"Don't touch it," Anna warned. "It's… hungry."

Juba kept her distance from the altar. Her fingers traced protective symbols in the air as she moved, muttering prayers or curses under her breath.

"There are children here," Mercy said suddenly, her head tilted as if listening. "Not just spirits. Their bones. Their… parts." She looked ill, her skin taking on a greenish cast in the unnatural light.

Anna nodded grimly. She turned slowly, taking in the chapel's full scope. This was where Thorne gave offerings and erased names before opening the Gate; where he made his final preparations before descending to the Womb Below.

Mercy's breathing quickened, her chest rising and falling with shallow gasps. She turned in a slow circle, eyes half-closed, as if following sounds only she could hear. Then she stopped, her gaze fixing on a section of the wall behind the altar, where the slate appeared slightly different—newer, perhaps, or more deliberately set.

"There's something behind here," she said, moving forward with the fluid grace of someone following music. She pressed her palm against the cold stone, her white hair standing on end with static electricity. "I can hear them. Behind this wall."

Anna joined her, examining the section Mercy had identified. The slate here did appear different. The veining pattern was interrupted; the stones fitted with fractionally more care. She ran her fingers along the seam, feeling for any irregularity, any mechanism that might reveal a hidden passage.

"The spiral," she murmured, her gaze dropping to the floor where the crimson veins formed a pattern identical to the one on the altar. "It's not just decoration. It's a key."

Kneeling, Anna traced the spiral with her fingertips, following its winding path inward. As she neared the center, she felt subtle indentations—pressure points carved into the stone with surgical precision. She pressed them in sequence, following the pattern's flow: one, three, seven, thirteen.

The wall responded with a low grinding sound, like bones shifting in a mass grave. Stone grated against stone as a section of the wall behind the altar slid aside, revealing a narrow spiral staircase carved from the living bedrock. The opening exhaled a breath of ancient air, carrying the metallic scent of old blood and the mineral tang of stone that had never seen sunlight.

"A way down," Anna said, straightening. "Into whatever waits below."

The staircase coiled downward into perfect darkness. No light penetrated beyond the first few turns, but a subtle vibration seemed to rise from the depths—not sound exactly, but a presence, a waiting.

Juba stared into the opening, her face set in hard lines of determination that couldn't quite mask her terror. "If my baby's down there, I'm going after her," she said, though her voice trembled. "Even if the devil himself is waiting at the bottom."

Anna liked her then. Really liked her, for the first time.

Mercy took Juba's hand, a gesture so unexpected that the woman startled. "We'll find her," the girl promised, her strange confidence cutting through the chapel's oppressive atmosphere. "The voices are louder now."

Anna didn't contradict her, but as she peered into the stairwell's throat, Rebecca's voice stirred in her mind, a silken whisper she could no longer silence: *The Gate awaits, Anna. And so does the keystone. The child has heard the call. She has answered.*

The spiral staircase descended into the island's hungry throat. Anna led the way, lantern in hand, its flame guttering in currents of air despite its glass globe. The light spilled over rough-hewn walls glistening with condensation, revealing chisel marks from hands long dead. Behind her, Mercy and Juba followed in silence, their shadows dancing against the curved walls like prisoners circling a cell.

The staircase coiled ever downward, its rotations so tight that Anna's shoulder scraped the inner wall while her opposite elbow brushed the outer one. The space was a vise, tightening with each revolution, as if designed to compress not just bodies but courage.

Anna counted thirty-seven steps, and the bottom still remained invisible beyond the lantern's reach.

The air changed as they descended, growing dense and metallic, coating their tongues with the taste of iron and salt. It grew colder too, not with the natural chill of the underground, but with a deliberate, penetrating cold that sought out joints and settled in marrow. Anna's breath clouded before her face, the vapor hanging unnaturally still before dissolving into nothing.

Juba kept one hand trailing along the stone for balance, the other gripping the knife Micah had given her. Her braids had come further undone during their journey, framing her face in a chaos of dark vines that caught the light like coiled wire. Her lips remained set in a perpetually crooked line of determination that masked her terror.

"We're being followed," she blurted, her voice unnaturally loud in the confined space. She stopped, glancing back up the staircase where darkness consumed their path. "Something's coming down behind us."

Anna paused, holding the lantern higher. The flame illuminated only empty steps, but the air did seem thicker somehow, disturbed by more than just their passage. "What do you feel?" she asked, eyes fixed on the darkness above.

"Not feel. Hear." Juba's jaw tightened. "Little footsteps. Too many to count. And breathing that ain't breathing—more like the sound air makes when it's being pulled through cloth."

Mercy placed a steadying hand on Juba's arm. "I hear them too. But they're not following us to hurt us. They're… curious. They want to see what we'll do."

The revelation did nothing to ease Juba's tension. If anything, her posture grew more rigid, her eyes wider. "You say that like it's better," she muttered. "Nothing in this place is curious for good reasons."

They continued downward, the spiral tightening further until each revolution brought them only a body's width lower than the last. The walls changed texture, transitioning from quarried stone to raw bedrock, as if they had passed beyond Hallowspire's constructed foundations into something older and unplanned.

Mercy trailed her fingers along the inner wall, then pulled back with a gasp. "It's freezing," she said, showing Anna her fingertips, which were rimed with delicate frost despite the absence of any window or outside air. "Like touching winter itself."

Anna inspected the wall. In the light, she could see crystalline patterns forming on the stone—not natural ice, but frost that crept along the surface in deliberate whorls and spirals, mimicking the same patterns they had seen throughout the mansion. The ice formed and melted in cycles, as if the wall itself were breathing cold.

"It's responding to us," Anna said, her voice steady despite the chill that ran down her spine. "To our presence."

They had descended at least a hundred steps when the staircase finally ended, opening onto a wide, vaulted chamber that stretched beyond the reach of their lantern. Anna stepped out first, holding the light, allowing the others to join her on level ground.

The Vault of Echoes unfolded before them, vast and ancient. The chamber's basalt walls curved upward to form a ceiling that disappeared into shadow, creating the impression of standing inside a massive bell. Salt streaked the black stone in pale tributaries, crystallizing where moisture seeped through hidden fissures. The mirror-finish floor reflected their lantern as a distant star in a bottomless night.

"Can you hear that?" Mercy asked, her head tilted as if listening.

At first, Anna heard nothing beyond their own breathing. Then it came—a subtle reverberating sound, as if distant voices were bouncing off the curved ceiling, too faint to make out words but unmistakably human in tone. The acoustics of the chamber caught these whispers and amplified them, sending them circling the room in overlapping waves of sound.

"The room remembers," Anna murmured, her eyes tracking the invisible paths of sound. "Holds onto every word ever spoken inside it."

She moved forward cautiously, her boots silent on the polished floor. Recessed shelves lined the chamber's perimeter. Carved directly into the basalt, each alcove housed objects of a strange and terrible nature.

A glass jar containing what appeared to be a mummified tongue, blackened with age but perfectly preserved, sat in one niche. The muscle was unnaturally long and narrow, with a forked tip that pressed against the glass as if still seeking to speak. Beside it, a rectangular case of saltglass held what could only be described as a shadow—a three-dimensional darkness that moved independently of any light source, coiling and stretching within its prison like sentient smoke.

The most disturbing artifact occupied a place of prominence: a child's skull, small enough to have belonged to a five-year-old. Its bone surface was blackened as if by fire, yet intricately carved with symbols that matched those Anna had seen in Thorne's codex. The eye sockets had been inlaid with scarlet obsidian that caught the torchlight and reflected it as tiny pinpricks of red.

"Don't touch anything," Anna warned, though neither Juba nor Mercy showed any inclination to approach the grotesque collection.

At the far end of the vault, directly opposite from where they had entered, stood a massive iron door. Unlike the rough-hewn nature of the surrounding chamber, the door was a work of precise craftsmanship. Eight feet tall and over half as wide, it was studded with iron rivets arranged in spiral patterns. Runes had been etched into the metal, their shapes unfamiliar yet somehow threatening, each line pulsing with a subtle energy that made the air around the door waver like heat over summer stones.

Anna approached it slowly, drawn forward despite the mounting pressure in the air. She felt resistance as she neared —not physical, but a force pushing against her intent, against her very will to advance. Static electricity crackled in her hair, and the skin of her face tightened as if exposed to intense cold.

Juba remained several paces back, her body rigid with the effort of not fleeing. She clutched Micah's knife in her hand, though what good steel would do against whatever waited beyond the door, she couldn't say.

"There's power here," Anna said, holding her hand near but not touching the door's surface. Heat radiated from the metal, not the honest warmth of a forge, but something fevered and wrong. "Whatever's behind this door wants out... And it's been waiting a long time."

Chapter 19

The cave was dark—the kind that drowned shapes and left only sound and memory. Micah preferred it this way. Sight was unreliable here. It played tricks, conjured threats where there were none, transformed every harmless shift of shadow into a hungry, lurching figure.

But sound… Sound was honest, if you knew how to listen.

He sat with his back pressed into the stone, legs drawn up, hands cupped around a bit of carved wood. It was a cog of his own making, carefully whittled from driftwood and studded with tiny iron nails he'd scavenged from the wreckage along the shore. He rolled it in his palm, feeling each notch, each imperfection, each gouge where the grain had fought his blade. He'd made dozens like it since coming to Brimwatch, each one a fraction better than the last, each one built to a specific, private logic that only he understood. Sometimes he buried them outside the cave entrance; sometimes he broke them into pieces and scattered them in the tide pools, as if the ocean could grind his failures into something less shameful. But this cog, the one in his hand, was the best he'd ever made. He'd saved it, maybe as a gift for Effie, or maybe just to prove he could.

His hands trembled anyway.

He tried to focus on the cold—the way it crept up his bare ankles, climbed his calves, nested in the bend of his knee. The way it turned his breath to visible fog, a miniature storm that he could exhale, shape, and destroy at will. He preferred that pain—clean, honest, the kind you could name—to the other kind, the kind that came crawling out of the dark with memories attached.

Effie had said the Quiet Ones sang to her in her sleep. Said they were cold, and always so hungry.

Now Micah heard them, too.

The first indication was the drop in temperature, a sharp, surgical chill that cut through even his layered coat and the sailor's shirt beneath. It was the kind of cold that came with no warning, no wind or draft; just the sudden, absolute certainty that you were not alone.

Micah braced himself, counting the seconds. When the voices came, they were almost a relief.

At first, just a whisper.

"Micah…"

Not his name exactly, but the echo of it—drawn out, fractured, spoken as if the speaker's tongue had never learned the sound. It slid past his ear, then vanished. He ignored it. He'd heard worse from overseers, from the White children who used to throw stones at him just to see if he would cry. He was good at ignoring voices.

But the cave wasn't satisfied. The voices doubled back, louder now, layered.

"Miiiiicahhhhh... come and see, come and see, come and see..."

Each repetition grew less human, as if the voice was decomposing in real time, sloughing off vowels, replacing consonants with a sound like grinding bone. Still, Micah kept his eyes shut, focusing on the cog, the pressure in his palms, the memory of Big Joseph's warm hands guiding his own as he worked. He could survive this.

Then the Quiet Ones arrived.

He didn't see them at first; he felt them. First, there was a cold brush at his ankle, then a static tingle crawling up the back of his neck. His hair prickled. The cog slipped in his hand and tumbled to the stone with a click that should have been deafening, but was somehow instantly absorbed by the cave. Micah reached for it blindly, but his hands met only the slick, pitted rock.

He looked up.

There were three of them—translucent shapes, bodies shaped like starving Black children but with faces all wrong. Their eyes were just black holes—no shine, no soul, just the memory of something gouged out and never healed. Their mouths hung open, but the jaws didn't move. They advanced in a stuttering, jerky motion, sometimes floating, sometimes flickering closer in a way that made Micah's stomach twist.

One of them wore a dress that had once been white, but now looked like it had grown out of mold and nightmares. Another had no shirt at all. His ribs were like harp strings, his fingers longer than seemed possible. The third—shortest of the three—dragged one foot, leaving a smear of nothingness in its wake, as if it were erasing the world behind it with every step.

They clustered around the dropped cog, drawn to it like dogs to a bone. The girl in the dress bent low and reached for it, her hand passing through the wood and sending up a ripple of cold that danced over the surface, then vanished. The cog rolled away and bumped against Micah's toe. He snatched it up, clutching it to his chest. The ghosts retreated, but only a little, their heads twitching in unison, as if watching him from three directions at once.

Their silence was worse than the voices.

Micah thought about running. He thought about screaming. He thought about Effie, somewhere in the mansion, maybe alone, maybe surrounded by these things. The thought made his skin crawl and his throat tighten. He forced himself to sit perfectly still, to breathe in through his nose, out through his mouth, in the pattern his mother had taught him when he was young.

"You want to stop a fit," she'd whispered once, the night he'd watched Big Joseph bleed out on the dirt, "you have to slow your body down. Make the fear wait for you."

But the ghosts waited, too.

The cave began to change. The walls pulsed—not with light, but with a kind of afterimage, as if Micah's eyes were failing to keep up with reality. Each pulse brought the ghosts closer, their bodies flickering between child and skeleton, between present and absent. Their faces blurred, smoothed, sometimes replaced by the faces of people Micah had known, or maybe just remembered. There was Joseph, teeth broken and blood in his beard. There was Effie, but her hair was gone, and her eyes were glass. There was his mother, face twisted in the rictus of fear she never let him see when she was alive.

He closed his eyes again, but the images remained.

The voices returned, thicker now, overlapping, the words smeared and sticky.

"Micah, Micah, little clock boy, little wire boy, little bones for the making…"

They laughed, but the sound was all wrong, like the cackle of a crow or the scraping of nails on slate. The laughter grew, feeding on itself, until it filled the cave, filled his head, left no room for thought.

Then silence. Just like that.

He opened his eyes. The ghosts had drawn back, rearranging themselves in a semicircle just out of reach. They watched him, waiting.

Micah wiped his nose with the back of his hand and realized it was bleeding. The cold had split the skin. He stared at the blood for a moment, then wiped it onto his pants, smearing the stain into the cloth. He drew his knees up tighter and pressed the cog into the hollow beneath his chin. He started to hum a tune from Virginia, something Joseph used to sing on the walk to the tobacco fields. It wasn't a happy song, but it was his, and the words were safe in his head.

He remembered the lash. The way it sounded when it split the air, the way it sounded when it split flesh. He remembered the hot, slick feel of blood running down his back, the taste of iron on his tongue. He remembered his mother binding his wounds with dirty rags, singing to him in a voice that shook but never broke.

He remembered the promise she'd made the night they fled Virginia: "I won't let him take you, Micah. I won't let him sell you like a thing. You are mine, and you are Effie's, and you belong to yourself."

He thought about that promise now, with the ghosts crowding around him, with the walls of the cave pulsing and the air freezing in his lungs. He wondered if the promise still held now that Effie was missing, now that he was alone in the dark with no one to hear him but these things that used to be children.

"Not real," he muttered, rocking slightly. "Not real, not real, not real—"

But they were real. The cold was real. The fear was real.

The girl in the dress leaned in closer, her mouth almost touching his ear. Her voice came again, but this time it was different—softer, almost sad.

"*Micah,*" she said. "*We remember.*"

He flinched, but the voice persisted.

"*We remember,*" the ghost repeated, and the other two joined in. "*We remember. We remember. We remember…*"

Micah pressed the cog so hard it left grooves in his palms. He shook his head, but the words wouldn't leave.

"*We remember you. We remember Effie. We remember the stick. We remember the dog.*"

Micah's breath hitched. He had told no one about the dog. He'd killed it to keep them from being caught. The overseer's hound—big and stupid and always hungry—cornered him in a gully outside Petersburg. Micah had sharpened a stick, just like Joseph had taught him, and when the dog jumped, he drove the stick into its throat. It died with its teeth around

Micah's arm, and he had to pry the jaws open with his free hand. He didn't talk about it, not even to Effie. But the ghosts knew.

They always knew.

The girl in the dress moved away, but the other two closed in. The boy with the long fingers touched Micah's shoulder, and the cold went straight to the bone. The shorter ghost, the one with the broken foot, brushed his cheek with a hand that felt like a spider crawling across his skin.

Micah squeezed his eyes shut and focused on the cog. He waited a full minute before looking up again.

There were more this time.

Six? Nine? The number shifted each time he tried to count. They pressed in from every angle, crowding the narrow cave ledge, filling the air with the high, trembling hum of their collective need.

He kept his eyes low, watching their feet—some with shoes, some without; all wrong, all too small or too twisted or floating a few inches above the stone. They ringed him, forming a spiral that curled tighter with each heartbeat. Their faces vibrated, mouths stuck open, sockets blacker than the inside of a mine.

The first ghost to reach him was the boy with the harpstring ribs. He stopped just beyond the reach of Micah's boot, bent double, and let his arms dangle almost to the floor. His mouth stretched wide. The words came out as wet, rotted music:

"Not alone, not alone, not alone…"

The echo multiplied, each child picking up the refrain, their voices overlapping until it sounded like a hundred birds shrieking into a well.

"Not alone, not alone, not alone—"

"Shut up," Micah muttered, but his own voice was a whisper, crushed beneath the avalanche of theirs.

The ghosts surged closer. One reached for his shoulder, passing its hand through the coat, the flesh, the bone, all the way to the ache living inside his chest. He gasped, the sound pulled from the bottom of his lungs. Instantly, the others closed in, hands overlapping, reaching through him, each touch colder than the last.

Micah's thoughts fractured.

He was back in Southampton County, the slave quarters lit by the glare of burning tobacco, the air thick with the smell of hot ash and iron and fear. He was running, Effie in his arms, Juba's hand pressed hard against his mouth to keep him from sobbing. He was hiding beneath the floorboards, the creak of White boots overhead, the whip's shadow on the wall. He was by the river, holding the broken compass Joseph had left him, fingers sticky with the blood of the dog he'd killed. He was in the woods, Effie's voice in his ear, saying, "Don't let them see you. Don't let them hear you. Don't let them name you."

He was in the cave, the Quiet Ones pouring into him, tasting his memories, sucking the marrow from his bones.

He fought to remember the present. He fought to remember who he was now, not what the world had done to him. He forced his eyes open, forced his hands to move, forced himself to speak.

"You can't have her," he said. It came out thin, almost comical, but it made the ghosts pause.

"You can't have her," he repeated, louder. "You can't have any of us. Not unless I say so."

The ghosts didn't back away, but their hands wavered, their heads cocking in a grotesque imitation of curiosity.

The girl in the moldy dress leaned close, her hair swimming around her face like black seaweed. Her voice was full of needles and salt:

"Then let us in."

Micah shook his head. "No."

"Let us in. Let us in. Let us in."

"No!" His shout startled even him, and for a moment the cave was full of nothing but the echo of his own fear, thrown back at him by the dead. The ghosts flickered, their edges growing jagged, the spiral of bodies tightening into a noose. The cold doubled, then doubled again, until Micah's teeth chattered and his fingers went numb.

He fumbled for the fisherman's needle and clutched it in his palm. The wire he'd sharpened still sat by his knee. With sudden clarity, he snatched it up and began to dig at the cave wall, scraping a slow, deliberate spiral into the limestone.

He didn't know why he did it. Maybe it was the memory of the symbols Juba had drawn on Effie's arms to protect her. Maybe it was the only way left to fight back.

The needle bit into the soft rock, leaving a pale groove. He worked in silence, tongue pressed to the roof of his mouth, eyes fixed on the spiral. The ghosts watched, their heads swinging back and forth in unison, the chorus of *Not alone, not alone, not alone* fading as they struggled to understand.

Micah finished the spiral, then pressed the point of the needle into the center and twisted, gouging a tiny well in the shape's heart. He withdrew the needle, looked down at his hand, and saw blood welling from his palm where he'd gripped the wire too tight. He smeared the blood across the spiral, rubbing it in with his thumb, leaving a red trail in the blue-black dark.

The Quiet Ones recoiled as one, their bodies blurring, their mouths opening wider. The boy with the ribs let out a sound that wasn't human, a shriek that peeled the cold from the walls and left only emptiness. They staggered back, forming a loose ring, their faces turned toward the spiral. The blood sizzled on the stone, then cooled, then vanished.

Micah sagged, his strength spent. His breath came in ragged pulls. He wiped his hand on his coat, then curled into himself, arms wrapped around his knees.

The ghosts stayed, but at a distance now, uncertain. They circled the spiral on the wall, eyes fixed on its shape, mouths working soundlessly. Some pressed their faces against the stone, as if trying to breathe it in; others slashed at the air with their too-long fingers, desperate to touch but unable.

Micah watched them for a while, then closed his eyes. The spiral was burned into his vision, a beacon in the dark.

He thought of Effie, wherever she was. He thought of Anna, of Juba, of Mercy. He thought of all the people who had ever wanted something from him, and all the things he had failed to protect.

He thought of his mother, her voice hoarse from years of smoke and sorrow, singing him to sleep after a beating.

"You are mine," she'd said. "You are Effie's. You belong to yourself."

He believed it. For the first time, he believed it.

He sat up, spine pressed to the cave wall, and waited. The Quiet Ones circled, silent but ever present, their eyes never leaving him. He waited for Anna and the others, or for the ghosts to try again, or for the world to end, whichever came first.

He would not be taken. Not by anyone. He belonged to himself.

And he would do anything to survive.

Chapter 20

Anna stared at the iron door, its surface so black it seemed to drink in the lamplight. The door was engraved from top to bottom with spirals, interlocked and knotted until the eye couldn't find a single beginning or end. Every line was filled with a silvery alloy that shimmered when the lantern's flame shifted.

Anna tried the obvious first. She pressed her palm against the metal, expecting heat, cold, or at the very least some shudder of recognition from the occult mechanism. The metal was colder than the grave. Her fingers traced the spiral patterns of rivets, searching for hidden triggers, for seams, for any weakness in its construction, anything that might grant them passage to whatever chamber lay beyond.

"It's sealed," she muttered, withdrawing her hand when the cold intensified to just below burning. "Not with lock and key, but with something... else."

Juba stood several paces back, her spine pressed against a basalt column as if anchoring herself. The knife in her hand caught the lantern light, its edge winking like a promise. "Is my Effie behind there?" she asked, her voice cracking slightly on her daughter's name. "Tell me true."

Anna didn't turn. She kept her eyes fixed on the strange symbols etched around the door's perimeter. They seemed to crawl when viewed from the corner of her eye, then solidify when directly observed. "I don't know," she replied.

Mercy stood a pace behind Anna with the lantern lifted, her face thrown into sharp relief by the flame. Every time her hand trembled, the shadows on the wall swelled and writhed as though preparing to slip loose from their anchors. Her white hair looked almost blue in the vault's airless dark. She shifted her weight from foot to foot, her thin frame swaying as if moved by unseen tides.

The vault's air hung thick around them, heavy with dust and the lingering scent of old incense. Anna took the lantern from Mercy and lifted it higher, illuminating the door's full height. The runes seemed to create pockets of deeper darkness within their curves and angles.

"Stand back," Anna instructed, setting the lantern on the floor and retrieving a small leather pouch from her satchel. She withdrew a pinch of gray powder—graveyard dust mixed with dried sage and bone shavings—and whispered a phrase in a language neither Juba nor Mercy recognized. The powder ignited as it left her fingers, flaring blue-white, before settling onto the door in a perfect arc along its upper edge.

Nothing happened.

Anna frowned, then removed her knife from her belt. She pressed the blade to her already wounded palm, hesitated, then made a shallow cut across the meat of her thumb. Blood welled dark and thick. She smeared it across the central rune

—a spiral within a spiral—and repeated the incantation, louder this time.

The door remained motionless, though the blood sizzled briefly before vanishing into the metal like water into sand.

Juba's voice was low, almost reluctant. "The one who made this, he didn't mean for it to be opened again. 'Least not by you. You're not the right one."

Anna's hands dropped to her sides, numb from more than just the cold. Her shoulders slumped as she stepped back from the door, defeat clear in every line of her body.

"We can't open it," she admitted, the words bitter on her tongue. "Not from here. Not like this."

She slumped back against the wall, breath misting in the gloom. She felt the world close in around her. Every failure, every dead-end hunt, every missed chance to save her mother or anyone else—now it all compressed into this moment, her entire future on the other side of an immovable door.

The silence stretched. Anna realized with a throb of humiliation that she had no plan beyond this. She closed her eyes, forcing herself to breathe. Rebecca's voice was mercifully absent. Even the witch seemed to understand that this was defeat.

When she opened her eyes again, the Vault of Echoes seemed to breathe with relief at her failure. She turned to face the others, her expression hardening into renewed determination despite the admission of failure.

"We're wasting time," she said, the words flat and bitter. "Effie's not here. Or if she is, we need to find another way in. Another passage."

Anna retrieved her lantern from the floor, its light

throwing wild shadows across the basalt walls. She cast one final, bitter glance at the door before turning away. It was then that something caught her eye. A glint of silver nestled in the deepest alcove, half-hidden behind a curtain of shadows.

"Wait," she said, the word halting Juba and Mercy in their retreat toward the spiral staircase. The two women turned, their faces round disks in the lantern light, eyes like bruises from exhaustion and fear.

Anna approached the alcove cautiously, holding the lantern at arm's length. The recess was deeper than the others, carved into the living rock with such precision that no chisel marks remained. At its center sat an object unlike any of the grim specimens that populated the surrounding niches.

It was a box—no, a bone reliquary—blackened by fire or time, polished to an unnatural sheen and fitted together with a silver filigree that crawled across its surface like frozen mercury. The silver formed intricate spirals that matched those on the iron door, each whorl ending in tiny, perfect emblems: a child's silhouette, a severed tongue, an eye with no pupil.

"Don't," Juba whispered, but there was resignation in her voice.

Anna stepped toward it, ignoring Juba's warning. She ran her thumb over the lid, feeling the prick of tiny, sharp ridges. The surface was warm—warmer than the vault, warmer than her own blood. She worked the simple catch, expecting it to be locked, but the lid slid open on silent, greased hinges.

Inside lay a book, thicker than her own palm and wrapped in what could only have been human skin. Soot edged the pages, blackened at the corners as if the reliquary itself had tried to burn the contents to death. Where the light hit the parchment, it shimmered with a sickly, almost organic sheen, like the lining of a gut or the skin inside a fresh wound.

Anna's hands trembled as she reached for the book. The closer she got, the more the world seemed to narrow. Sound faded, and the chill of the vault retreated to a distant memory. She could feel the pulse of the book before she touched it—a low, steady throb, a heartbeat with its own intelligence.

She opened the cover. The title, written in a hand she recognized from the codex in the Astral Spire, read:

THE TENEBRIC SEQUENCE: THE FIVEFOLD
UNBINDING
A.G. THORNE

A rush of exhilaration hit Anna. "Thorne's grimoire," she breathed, recognition and dread mingling in her voice. "The *Tenebric Sequence.*"

Her hands trembled slightly as she lifted the book from its resting place. It was unexpectedly heavy, as if the words inside had physical weight beyond the paper that contained them. The binding creaked as she cradled it, a sound like arthritic joints forced into motion after decades of stillness.

Mercy moved to Anna's side, her mismatched eyes wide with a mixture of fascination and fear. "Is this what he used? To make the Quiet Ones?"

Anna nodded, her thumb caressing the cover with a strange intimacy. "This is his life's work. The rituals he used to strip souls from bodies, to bind spirits to his will." She swallowed hard, her throat suddenly dry, and opened the grimoire carefully. Its pages were yellowed and brittle, covered in dense, spidery script interspersed with diagrams that seemed to shift slightly when viewed directly. The language was a blend of Latin, Enochian, and something older that tasted of copper and ash when Anna silently shaped the words with her lips.

She read aloud, not even realizing she'd done so, the words dry and metallic in her throat:

"*Per venam, per nomen, per carnem excoriatam*—let the spiral drink, let the echoes hunger. In the wound, the Key is shaped—"

Anna's voice froze. For a moment, she couldn't breathe, couldn't even blink. When she did speak again, the voice that emerged from her throat belonged to someone else. It was lighter, softer, infused with an intimate familiarity that made her blood run cold.

It was her mother's.

"You always were too curious, Anna," said Abigail Jacobs's voice, and the sound of it coming from Anna's mouth—so familiar it was almost a comfort—made the hair on Anna's arms stand straight.

Juba and Mercy whipped around at the sound. Juba's eyes went round as coins. Mercy backed away a step, her free hand moving to her throat as if to hold her head on her shoulders.

Anna tried to shut her mouth, tried to will her jaw to clamp shut, but the words kept coming. The tone was warm at first, maternal, exactly as Anna remembered from childhood. Then it shifted, hardening into something cruel.

"Should I tell your new friends what you did to that boy in Lowell? Or how you enjoyed watching that woman burn?"

Anna's face drained of color, her fingers clutching the grimoire so tightly that her knuckles blanched white. She tried to close the book, to stop reading, but her hands remained frozen in place as if bound by invisible restraints.

"Mother," she gasped, the word barely audible. "That's not true."

The voice continued, pouring from Anna's lips but unmistakably Abigail's—the same inflection, the same slight accent that Anna had spent years trying to erase from her own speech.

"Tell me, daughter, do your friends know about the ritual in Providence? How you held that child under until the bubbles stopped, just to see if Rebecca's power would manifest? Or what about Boston, when you stood by and watched while that woman was dragged into Hell itself?" A soft, terrible laugh followed. "You enjoyed that, didn't you? The smell of her skin as it blistered. The sound of her screams as the shadows took her apart. Sure, they were monsters. But what might you have done if I wasn't there to stop you and save you from yourself?"

Anna's hands shook harder now. The grimoire was burning hot against her palm, and she realized that if she didn't close it, if she didn't fight, the voice would keep going, would unravel her in front of the others.

"Stop," she hissed, fighting for control of her own voice. Her shoulders hunched as if bearing a physical weight, her neck straining with the effort of resistance. "You're twisting the truth."

The voice dropped to a whisper, but in the vault's perfect acoustics, every syllable remained audible. "You pretend to save them, but you're just like her. Like Rebecca. The blood you've spilled would fill this chamber. The lives you've taken would populate a small town." A pause, then softer still: "And the worst part? You enjoyed every moment."

Tears gathered in the corners of Anna's eyes; whether from effort or emotion, she couldn't say. Her breathing came in shallow gasps, her entire body rigid with the struggle to silence the voice that wasn't hers.

"Shut the book," Juba commanded from across the chamber, her own voice steadier than seemed possible given the circumstances. "Shut it now!"

"Tell the little one," Abigail hissed. "Tell her what you did to the girl in Boston, the one who begged you for help. Tell her how you almost turned her away, let the nosferatu drain her, all because you wanted to see how long she would scream."

Mercy's head snapped up. She stared at Anna as if she'd never seen her before.

Anna said nothing. She just stood there, her jaw locked, her eyes open and unblinking. Her fingers twitched, fighting whatever force held them in place. With agonizing slowness, she began to force the grimoire closed, its pages seeming to resist, to cling to her hands as if alive.

"Maybe you should tell them why you really came to Brimwatch," the voice continued, rising in volume until it bounced off the vault's ceiling, returning as a chorus of identical accusations. "Tell them what you'd trade for my return. Tell them whose soul you'd sacrifice to buy back mine."

Anna snapped the book shut with a sound like a gunshot. She stumbled backward, nearly dropping the book. Her face was ashen, a sheen of cold sweat glistening on her brow. Her chest heaved with each breath, as if she'd been running for miles.

"That wasn't her," she said hoarsely, though whether to convince herself or the others remained unclear. "My mother wouldn't… she never…"

Mercy stepped forward, her eyes wide with terror but also —horribly—a kind of understanding. "You heard her," she said. "The thing behind the door. It knows us now. All of us."

Anna found her voice at last, but it was a thin imitation of her usual self. "It's not my mother. Just what's left of her. Or what this house wants me to believe."

But she knew, with the certainty of bone, that part of Abigail's soul was tangled up in this ritual, this house, this island. And that the only way to save Effie—or herself—was to finish what Thorne had started, or die trying.

A profound silence settled over the vault, weighty and tangible, pressing against their ears like the deep ocean. Anna clutched the closed grimoire to her chest, its edges digging into her skin through her clothing. The lantern flame steadied, casting their three shadows in sharp relief against the basalt wall. Except where they should have stood as dark silhouettes, the shadows appeared to move independently, rippling like figures underwater.

Mercy was the first to sense the change. The lamplight flickered despite the stillness of the air. The flame bent sideways, then righted itself, then bent again, as if unseen breaths were teasing it from all directions. In that stuttering light, something moved at the edge of her vision—not a shift of shadow, but a face, pressed against the darkness as if trying to push through from the other side.

"Anna," she whispered, her voice thin with fear. Her mismatched eyes fixed on a point just beyond her protector's shoulder.

The face appeared again as the candle flame dipped. A child's visage, skin gray and taut over bone, eyes hollowed into black pits, mouth a gaping wound where lips should have been. It lingered just long enough for Mercy to register its features before vanishing with the candle's recovery.

But it wasn't alone.

With each subsequent flicker, more faces emerged from the vault's shadows. There were dozens of them, crowding the darkness like specimens pressed between glass. Children with their mouths sewn shut, the thread crusted with decades-old blood. Women with their throats opened in precise, surgical lines, the wounds revealing not gore but empty space, as if their very substance had been scooped out. Men with partial skulls, their brains exposed and etched with symbols that matched those on the iron door.

Slaves from the South. All of them.

Mercy's free hand flew to her own throat, fingers splayed across her pale skin as if to protect it. "They're everywhere," she breathed, backing away until she collided with a stone column.

Anna remained frozen, Thorne's grimoire clutched to her chest like a shield. The book pulsed against her ribs, each throb synchronized with her heartbeat but a half-second ahead, as if anticipating the next surge of blood through her veins. The faces appeared and vanished too quickly for her to focus on any single one, but their collective presence filled the vault with a desperation that was almost tactile.

"The Quiet Ones," she murmured, recognition dawning in her eyes. "Not just the children. All of them. Every soul Thorne stripped."

The temperature in the vault plummeted without warning, dropping so rapidly that their breath bloomed in front of them in pale clouds. Frost formed along the edges of the floor and climbed the basalt columns in crystalline patterns that mirrored the spiral glyphs etched throughout Hallowspire. The cold wasn't natural. It carried intent, seeking out exposed skin with predatory precision, numbing fingers and ears first, then settling deeper into joints and lungs.

Juba finally broke. Her eyes, wide with undisguised terror, darted from face to face as they closed in. Her breathing became quick, shallow pants that spoke of barely contained panic. The knife in her hand juddered, its edge catching the lantern light and throwing fractured reflections across the vault's ceiling.

"We need to go!" she gasped, her voice raw with fear. "Now!"

With those words, some final barrier within her shattered. She turned and bolted toward the spiral staircase, taking the steps two at a time, her footfalls echoing in sharp, panicked percussion as she fled upward. The faces nearest the staircase parted to let her pass, their hollow eyes tracking her retreat with what might have been amusement or envy.

Mercy pushed forward, but her foot caught on something

soft. She bent blindly, and her fingers met hair—long and fine, attached to a head smaller than her fist. The scalp was cold, wet, and as she snatched her hand back, she realized it left a trail of salt water on her palm. The taste of iron and brine filled her mouth, and she shuddered, barely resisting the urge to vomit.

"Go!" Anna said. "Just go now!"

They hurried up the stairs, the lantern's light stuttering as Anna jostled it. But with every step, the crowding presence intensified. The walls bulged, the stone felt softer, and more and more of the faces became visible. There were infants now, too—dozens of them—arrayed along the lowest level like a choir of silent witnesses, their lips locked in expressions of infinite betrayal.

Mercy's breathing came in squeaks. She reached the chapel first, and as the light widened, she backed herself into a corner and slid down until she was sitting, knees drawn up. Her hands were shaking so violently she couldn't wipe the tears from her eyes.

Juba was already gone, her footsteps echoing from somewhere deeper in the mansion.

Anna made it into the room last, lamp swinging, the *Tenebric Sequence* pressed so tightly to her chest she thought it might crack a rib. She closed the door to the spiral stairs behind her, knowing it would do nothing to hold back what followed.

Mercy looked up at Anna, her white lashes wet with tears. "Is it really true?" she whispered. "Those awful things your mother said?"

Anna almost answered. Instead, she bent her head, refusing

to meet Mercy's gaze. She forced herself to move and kneeled beside the girl, placing a shaking hand on Mercy's shoulder.

"We have to go," she said, the words barely more than a hiss.

Mercy nodded, but didn't look up.

Chapter 21

Their panicked footsteps thundered through Hallowspire's twisting corridors, echoing their racing hearts. Anna clutched Thorne's grimoire to her chest, its weight an anchor against her ribs, while Mercy scrambled to keep pace behind her. Ahead, Juba's fleeing silhouette appeared and disappeared around corners, her desperate flight guided by nothing but blind terror.

The house seemed to contract around them as they ran. Marble busts tracked their progress with eyes that gleamed too brightly in the dim light. Doorways yawned and then narrowed, as if the mansion itself were breathing. Anna felt as if the spirits of the vault were still trailing them, not in hot pursuit but with the patient certainty of predators who knew their prey had nowhere to run.

They burst into the Great Hall like swimmers breaking the surface after too long underwater. It was afternoon now, but the cavernous space was darker than when they'd left it. The fire in the enormous hearth was a ribcage of red coals, casting faint, crawling shadows up the soot-stained stone.

Juba staggered across the hall, her legs finally surrendering to the weight of her panic. She collapsed against the ornate fireplace mantel, her body folding in on itself like paper in a flame. Her shoulders shook with sobs wrenched from the deepest part of her soul, each breath a raw, wounded sound that filled the hall with grief.

"My baby," she moaned, the words dissolving into incoherence as she pressed her forehead against the cold stone. "My Effie. I left her. I let her…" She couldn't finish, her voice breaking on the jagged edges of her guilt.

Anna watched from the center of the hall with Thorne's *Tenebric Sequence* still clutched in her white-knuckled fingers. Her face was a mask of exhaustion and determination, the skin beneath her eyes bruised with fatigue. The book pulsed against her chest like a second heart, each beat a whispered promise of knowledge and power that might yet save them all —if she was willing to pay its price.

"We don't have time for this," Anna said, her voice sharp enough to cut through Juba's sobs. She crossed the hall in quick strides, setting the grimoire on the settee where she'd left Thorne's codex earlier. "We need to think. To plan. Falling apart won't help Effie."

Mercy moved past Anna, her feet silent on the marble. She approached Juba with the cautious grace of someone who understood grief too intimately to fear its contagion. She knelt beside the older woman, her pale hand coming to rest on Juba's shaking shoulder.

"My mother used to say that tears are the water that keeps hope alive," Mercy whispered, her mismatched eyes solemn in her thin face. "Cry if you must, but don't let go of hope.

Not yet."

Juba's weeping quieted to hiccupping breaths. She straightened slightly, turning to look at Mercy with eyes swollen and fierce. "Hope?" she repeated, the word bitter on her tongue. "Hope died the moment I set foot on this island." She shook her head, braids swinging like clappers in a funeral bell. "You saw what lives in the walls. You saw what that man did to those children. And now my Effie—"

"We don't know what's happened to Effie," Anna interjected, pacing a tight circle in the center of the hall. Her boots struck the marble in deliberate rhythm, as if she were counting out the seconds they had left. "Those spirits in the vault, the Quiet Ones—they're Thorne's victims, yes. But they're also still bound to serve him—or whatever he's become. And he *needs* Effie. Needs her alive. That's why they called to her."

"Like they called to Mercy," Juba said, understanding dawning in her eyes.

Anna nodded, her gaze fixed on the grimoire. Its binding seemed to absorb the dim light that filtered through the windows, the human skin stretched across its cover growing taut as if with anticipation. "The *Tenebric Sequence* contains the ritual Thorne used to strip their souls," she explained. "To bind them to the Nocturne Gate. It might also contain the key to releasing them."

Juba pushed herself upright, her grief momentarily eclipsed by a flare of anger. "And what happens if we release them? Where do they go? What do they become?" She took a step toward Anna, her jaw set in defiance. "You talk about these things like they're puzzles to solve. Like they're not people's souls—*children's* souls—trapped and tortured."

"I'm trying to save your daughter," Anna snapped, her composure cracking to reveal something darker beneath. "And anyone else this house has claimed. If you have a better understanding of what Thorne did, I'm eager to hear it."

The three women formed a tense triangle in the center of the hall: Anna with her icy determination, Juba with her raw maternal rage, and Mercy caught between them, her own fears momentarily forgotten in the face of their conflict. The air between them seemed to thicken, charged with emotion and the lingering miasma of the vault below.

"Thorne opened a gate," Anna continued, her tone steadier now. "A passage between worlds. He used thirteen souls as anchors, stripped them of identity and memory, and bound them to hold the breach open. But something went wrong. The Gate didn't stay open, not completely. And now the thing below—Thorne, or whatever's left of him—needs Effie as the last piece."

"Using my daughter as bait," Juba said, the words flat with dread.

"Not just bait," Anna said. "A keystone. A living child to hold the breach open."

The implications hung in the air between them, too terrible to voice aloud. If Effie had been taken to serve as the keystone for Thorne's unfinished ritual, they had precious little time to find her before Thorne's undead servants completed the rite.

"We need to search the island again," Anna decided, her gaze sweeping the hall as if cataloguing resources. "Starting with the places Thorne marked in his—"

The boom of the front doors being thrown open cut

through her words like cannon fire. The sound reverberated through the Great Hall, setting the iron chandelier to trembling, disturbing the dust that had settled in the corners. All three women turned as one, their postures instantly defensive.

The rectangle of cold daylight from the open doors threw a long shadow across the threshold. Micah staggered forward, his thin frame silhouetted against the gray morning light spilling through the open doors.

His eyes were wide and wild, the whites shining, and his hands clutched something to his chest: a lump wrapped in cloth, stained dark and dripping. His gaze darted frantically around the hall until they found his mother, then locked onto her with the desperate intensity of a drowning man spotting shore.

"Micah!" Juba cried, her own turmoil momentarily forgotten as she lurched forward. Her hands reached for him, checking for injuries with the automatic efficiency of a mother who has bandaged too many wounds. "You were supposed to stay at the cave. You were supposed to—"

"She left this behind," Micah interrupted, his voice cracked and dry. He extended his right hand to Anna, and in the wavering light of the lantern she saw it was a piece of birchbark, cracked and splintered, with something scrawled on it in charcoal.

A map.

Anna moved closer, her steps measured and cautious, as if approaching a wild animal. The boy's eyes shifted to her, wary but determined. There was something changed about him, a hardness that wasn't there before. A fragile shell formed over fresh wounds.

"Let me see," Anna said, her voice deliberately soft.

Micah hesitated, then offered the birchbark, but kept a hold of it. Anna bent to examine the drawing without taking it from him. The bark was torn from a living tree, the inner face scraped almost clean. The charcoal lines were deliberate, too precise for a child's casual sketch. They depicted a sea cave with a distinctive mouth—narrow at the waterline but widening into a cathedral-like chamber within. Spiral markings identical to those in Thorne's codex were rendered in careful, obsessive detail along the walls of the cave.

"Effie drew that," Micah said, his voice dropping to just above a whisper. "Before she left. I found it outside the cave."

Anna stood up straighter, recognition dawning in her eyes. She hurried to the settee where she had left the codex earlier, its binding still warm to the touch despite the chill of the hall. She flipped through the pages with practiced efficiency, stopping at a section near the center where Thorne's meticulous hand had drawn a metaphysical map of Brimwatch Isle.

"Here," she said, her finger landing on a small notation at the island's northern shore. "The Tidal Confluence. Where the Silver Thread meets the island."

The others gathered around her, drawn by the urgency in her voice. Mercy peered over Anna's shoulder, her white hair falling like frost across the yellowed page. Juba stood slightly apart, her body rigid with tension, her eyes never leaving the drawing in Anna's hand.

"Thorne marked three points on the island where the ley lines make contact," Anna continued, her finger tracing a path across the map. "The convergence of the Trivium is beneath Hallowspire itself, but this one—" she tapped the western shore notation, "—this one he describes as '*a wound that opens and closes with the tide, a door that breathes salt and drinks light.*'"

Micah nodded, a quick, jerky movement. "We seen that cave for ourselves, didn't we, Mama? That's where the markings are. Inside the cave, high up where the water doesn't reach. They glow when the tide is coming in, like they're being… fed."

Anna's eyes narrowed as she studied Thorne's map more closely. The notation was accompanied by a small sketch that mirrored Effie's drawing with uncanny precision—the same cave mouth, the same spiral glyphs etched along the walls. Beside it, Thorne had written: "*Secondary threshold. Viable only at spring tide when the moon is thrice-waned. The sea provides what blood alone cannot.*"

The implications cascaded through Anna's mind. If the Silver Thread's energy was enough to tear open the face of the island, how deep did that cave go? All the way to the convergence beneath the mansion? To whatever waited behind that iron door beneath the chapel?

"Effie drew this?" she asked, looking up at Micah.

He nodded again. "She's been drawing them for weeks. The spirals. The faces. The door that goes down and down." His voice faltered. "I didn't think they were real."

Juba stepped forward at last, her movements deliberate and heavy, as if she waded through invisible currents. She studied the codex with reluctance, her eyes skimming the page as if the words might burn her. When she spoke, her voice was low, stripped of everything but the raw truth of experience.

"There's something in that tide cave that don't belong in water," she warned, the words dropping from her lips like stones into a well. "When you talk, it don't echo. It eats the sound, and it don't let go." She met Anna's gaze directly, unblinking. "First time we sheltered there, Effie said she heard singing from deep in its throat. I thought it was just the wind, the way it gets funneled through those passages. But then..." She paused, her fingers absentmindedly tracing a protective sign against her collarbone. "Then I heard it too. Not words. Not music exactly. But a pattern. Like breathing, but not a living thing's breath."

The lantern flickered without cause, its flame stretching tall and thin before settling back into a steady glow. The walls of the Great Hall seemed to contract slightly, the shadows in the corners deepening as if the mansion itself listened with keen interest.

"We have to go there," Anna said, closing the codex with a decisive thud. Her jaw was set with determination, her eyes bright with purpose. "If there's any chance Effie is in that cave, we need to find her before the tide rises."

"The tide's already rising," Micah said. "That's why I came. The entrance will be underwater in just hours."

Anna returned the codex to the settee alongside the *Tenebric Sequence*, her mind already racing ahead to what they might find in the tide cave. She looked at Micah. "Do you remember the way?"

Micah nodded. "Down the cliff path there's a mark. A circle with a line through it, carved on the stone. Then a ladder, but it's rotten. We climbed anyway." He coughed, a wet, hacking sound, and Juba pressed his head back against her chest.

Anna considered the map, the timing, the risk. The tide would soon be at its highest, flooding the cave for hours. But if Effie had entered ahead of the water, there was a chance—if only a slim one—she might still be inside, alive and untouched.

She turned to Juba. "You stay here. Guard the door. If Effie comes back, you keep her here. Safe. You understand?"

Juba nodded, though her eyes betrayed the shame of her fear. Anna almost softened, almost said something to make it easier, but the urgency was already tugging at her to leave. "Juba," she said, keeping her voice as level as possible. "You're safe now."

It was an absurd thing to say, but Anna had learned from her mother that even lies could be lifelines. Sometimes the only way to drag a drowning person ashore was to promise them dry land, whether you believed it or not.

Anna's gaze drifted to the blade still clutched in Juba's fist. "Does Micah know how to handle that?"

Juba's laugh was hollow, devoid of humor. "Boy's been handling a blade since he was six. Survival don't wait on childhood." She turned to her son and returned his knife to him. "You sure about this place? You sure that's where she went?"

Micah's shoulders straightened as he took the weapon, the momentary vulnerability replaced by a fierce, protective determination that made him look older than his years. "She's there," he said with quiet certainty.

"Then we go now," Anna says as she moved toward the

door. "Before the sea claims what's left of our time."

Chapter 22

The path to the sea cave cut across Brimwatch like a scar. Anna followed Micah's slim frame as he navigated the rocky terrain with the dexterity of one who had traversed it many times before, his movements betraying both impatience and reluctance. Behind her, Mercy's breathing punctuated the constant roar of waves breaking against the island's jagged shore. The sky hung low and heavy above them, a bruised canopy threatening to split open at any moment, while the wind carried the sharp scent of coming rain.

"How much farther?" Anna called over the wind's howl, her eyes fixed on Micah's back as he clambered over a ridge of black rock. The boy didn't answer immediately, his attention focused on the crude map clutched in his thin fingers. The birchbark had curled at the edges, its charcoal lines blurring under the assault of salt air.

"Not far," he finally replied, his voice carrying a strange, flat quality that might have been fear. "Just past the headland." He pointed toward a jutting spur of land where the island's western face plunged directly into the churning sea.

Anna glanced back at Mercy, who struggled to maintain her footing on the uneven ground. The girl's white hair whipped around her face like frayed rope, her mismatched eyes narrowed against the stinging air. Her breathing came in labored gasps, but she pressed forward with silent determination, one pale hand clutching the collar of her dress as if to anchor herself against the wind's persistent shove.

"We should hurry," Micah said, his tone suddenly sharp with urgency. "The tide's coming faster than I thought."

He wasn't wrong. The gray-green water surged against the island's base with increasing force, each wave climbing higher than the last. What had been exposed rock when they left Hallowspire was now submerged beneath the churning foam. The sea was reclaiming the island inch by inch, and somewhere in that narrowing margin between water and cliff, Effie might still be trapped.

They rounded the headland, and the full force of the wind struck them, nearly knocking Mercy off her feet. Anna grabbed the girl's arm, steadying her against the gale. The path, if it could still be called that, narrowed to a treacherous ledge barely wider than Anna's boot. Below them, the ocean boiled against the jagged rocks, the white froth spewing high onto the side of the cliff.

"There," Micah pointed to a dark gash in the cliff face about thirty yards ahead. "That's the entrance to the tide cave." His eyes darted nervously toward the horizon, where dark clouds gathered like bruises against the sky's pale skin. "We need to hurry. When the tide peaks, there won't be a way out until it drops again."

The urgency in his voice propelled them forward, despite the danger of the narrowing path. Anna led the way now, her steps careful but quick. She sensed Micah behind her, his body practically vibrating with tension. Something about his behavior struck her as odd—not just the understandable fear of the rising tide, but a deeper anxiety, as if he dreaded what they might find in the cave as much as he desired to reach it.

They reached a crude mark carved into the stone: a circle bisected by a vertical line—exactly as Micah had described. Anna traced it with her fingertips, feeling a warm pulse beneath the etching, as if something inside the rock itself responded to her touch.

"Down there," Micah said, pointing to a wooden ladder that disappeared over the edge of the cliff. The ladder was ancient, its rungs gray with salt and age, the wood splintered and worn to the texture of old bone. It swayed slightly in the wind, creaking with each gust.

Anna tested the first rung with her weight. The wood groaned but held. "I'll go first," she said, tucking her knife into her belt. "Mercy, you follow. Micah, you come last."

The boy nodded, his gaze fixed on the darkening horizon rather than on Anna's face. His hands clutched Effie's drawing with white-knuckled intensity, the birchbark crackling beneath his grip.

The descent was harrowing. Each rung threatened to crumble beneath Anna's boots, the entire structure shuddering with every movement. Halfway down, she paused to look below. The cave mouth gaped like a wound in the cliff's face, black and unwelcoming. Water already lapped at its lower edge, surging in and retreating with each wave.

"The tide's coming in fast," she called up to the others. "We need to move quickly."

The final rungs of the ladder ended several feet above a narrow ledge of slick stone. Anna dropped the remaining distance, landing with practiced grace despite the treacherous footing. She turned to help Mercy, whose slender arms trembled with the effort of the climb. The girl landed awkwardly, one knee striking the rock hard enough to scrape her skin and draw a hiss of pain from her lips.

Micah descended last, moving with the fluid confidence of youth and familiarity. Yet when his feet touched the ledge, he hesitated, as if some invisible barrier separated him from the cave's dark maw. His eyes darted from the entrance to the horizon and back again.

"What is it?" Anna asked, sensing his reluctance.

"Nothing," he replied too quickly. "Just... the tide. It's higher than I expected." He gestured toward the entrance, where water already flooded the lower portion of the opening, forcing them to wade ankle-deep to enter.

The cave's throat swallowed them in cold darkness. Anna fished a match from her satchel and struck it to light their lantern, its flare momentarily blinding in the gloom. The light revealed a narrow passage that cleaved right through the bedrock, following some natural fault in the island's foundation. Water surged around their feet, already deep enough to soak through their clothing, its chill seeping into their bones.

The passage widened as they ventured deeper, opening into a vast chamber that the lantern's meager light could barely illuminate. The ceiling soared beyond visibility, lost in shadows that seemed to swallow sound and light. Moisture and salt crusted the walls, and intricate patterns carved into them caught the lantern's glow.

"More spirals," Anna murmured, stepping closer to examine the nearest sigil. It was identical to the ones in Thorne's codex: concentric circles broken by sharp angles, curving inward toward a center point that drew the eye with irresistible force. As the seawater lapped against the wall, the engravings emitted a faint, bluish glow, pulsing in rhythm with the tide's advance.

"Effie watched them for hours," Micah said, his voice oddly flat.

Shells and the bleached remains of marine life littered the cave floor where it wasn't submerged. Among these, something moved—small, darting shapes that scuttled across the stone with unnatural precision. Anna lowered her lantern, illuminating a cluster of crabs unlike any she had ever seen. Their shells weren't the expected oval but perfect spirals, like miniature nautili carved from bone-white chitin. Dozens of them moved in synchronized patterns, forming and reforming spiral patterns that mirrored the sigils on the walls.

"That isn't natural," Mercy whispered, pressing closer to Anna. She had been a six-year-old when her family fled Penance Cove; old enough to remember the ways of the sea. "Nothing moves like that."

Anna nodded, her attention divided between the unsettling crabs and the glowing sigils. She recognized the patterns now, not just from Thorne's books, but from older texts she had studied under her mother's guidance. These weren't decorative markings, but keys—psychic locks designed to hold something in. Or keep something out.

"These markings," she said, moving closer to the wall. "They're part of a binding ritual. Ancient. Powerful." She traced one spiral with her fingertip, feeling a subtle vibration beneath the stone, like a pulse. "Thorne didn't create these. He found them here and used them in his rituals."

The water around their legs had risen to mid-calf now, its surface alive with swirling patterns as the unnatural crabs navigated its depths. The air in the chamber tasted of salt and rot, undercut by something metallic that coated the tongue like old blood.

"We need to go deeper," Micah said, pointing toward a narrow opening at the chamber's far end. "There's another passage. It leads to where the... where I think Effie might be."

Anna studied his face in the lantern light. His eyes refused to meet hers, fixated instead on the glowing spirals that lined the walls. His breathing had quickened, a fine sheen of sweat visible on his brow despite the cave's chill. Something about his demeanor set off warning bells in Anna's mind, but the rising tide and the knowledge that Effie might be trapped deeper in the cave's winding passages overrode her caution.

"Stay close," she said, gesturing for them to follow.

Micah nodded, relief flashing briefly across his features as he fell in behind Mercy, Effie's map still clutched in his trembling hand.

Anna led the way into the narrow passage, her lantern held high before her. The water had risen to their knees, each step producing a hollow splash that echoed against the constricting walls. The tunnel narrowed like a throat as it cleaved deeper into the island's foundation. Here, the spiral sigils grew more elaborate, no longer mere carvings but complex patterns that seemed to pulse with their own inner light, independent of the lantern's glow or the lapping water's touch. The air thinned, replaced by a heavy miasma that tasted of copper and decay, forcing them to breathe in shallow gasps that never quite satisfied the lungs.

"It gets narrower ahead," Micah called from behind them, his voice bouncing oddly against the slick stone. "There's a gate, but it's not locked. We can pass through."

Anna glanced back at him, noting how he hung several paces behind Mercy, his shoulders hunched as if bearing an invisible weight. The boy's eyes kept darting to the spirals on the walls, following their inward coil with an intensity that bordered on reverence. His fingers still clutched Effie's drawing, though it had gone limp with moisture, the charcoal lines bleeding into the sodden bark.

"How much farther?" Anna asked.

"Not far," Micah replied, the same answer he'd given on the cliff-side. But this time, something in his tone—a certain finality—raised the fine hairs at the nape of Anna's neck.

The passage widened into a modest grotto where the ceiling dropped so low they had to stoop. Water dripped from above, each droplet striking the rising pool at their feet with hypnotic regularity. At the chamber's far end stood a rusted iron gate, its bars twisted into the now-familiar spiral pattern, the metal eaten through in places by decades of salt and damp.

"That's it," Micah said, pointing toward the gate. "Beyond there, the cave opens wide again. There's a high ledge where the water doesn't reach, even at full tide." He paused, swallowing visibly. "That's where I think Effie might be."

Anna approached the gate cautiously, holding the lantern close to examine its construction. The rust had formed in strange patterns—not the random spread of natural oxidation, but deliberate whorls that mimicked the sigils on the surrounding walls.

Micah's gaze fixed on the water swirling around their legs. It had deepened while they examined the gate, now past their knees and rising with visible speed.

"We should hurry," he said, his voice thin with what might have been fear or anticipation. "The tide won't wait."

Anna pushed against the gate. It swung inward through the water with surprising ease, its hinges silent despite their apparent age. Beyond lay a cavern that plunged deeper into darkness, its walls lined with more spirals that glowed with increasing intensity, as if responding to their proximity.

Rebecca stirred at the edge of Anna's consciousness, a warning hiss like steam escaping a kettle. *Something's wrong here, child. This boy is not what he seems.*

Anna hesitated, one hand still on the gate, her instincts warring with the urgency of their mission. The water continued to rise, its chill seeping through her boots and into her bones. Mercy stood just behind her, shivering visibly, her thin arms wrapped around herself for warmth.

"Anna," Mercy whispered, her mismatched eyes wide with unspoken fear. "I don't think we should—"

"We have to find Effie," Anna cut her off. But what she really meant was they had to find a way into the sanctum beneath Hallowspire—and this fissure created by the power of the ley line could be it. She stepped through the gate, boots splashing in the rising water. "There's no time to wait for the tide to turn."

Mercy followed reluctantly, casting one uncertain glance back at Micah, who remained on the other side of the threshold, his face half-hidden in shadow. The boy made no move to follow, his body rigid with some internal struggle that played across his features like lightning behind storm clouds.

"Micah?" Mercy called, her voice small against the growing roar of water surging through the narrow passages behind them. "Aren't you coming?"

The change came over him in an instant.

The hesitation vanished, replaced by a cold certainty that straightened his spine and hardened his gaze. His lips pressed into a thin line, jaw setting with grim resolve. In one fluid motion, he seized the gate with both hands and slammed it shut, the iron bars clanging together with terrible finality.

Anna lunged forward, but too late. Her fingers closed around the bars as a metallic click echoed through the chamber—the sound of an ancient mechanism engaging, locking the gate from the outside. She rattled the bars, but they held fast, the rust flaking off beneath her grip to reveal the iron beneath.

"Micah!" she shouted, fury and disbelief mingling in her voice. "What are you doing?"

The boy stepped back, the water splashing around his legs as he retreated. The dim light cast his face in sharp relief, transforming his features. Gone was the frightened child who had guided them from Hallowspire. In his place stood someone older, harder—a face carved from the same unforgiving stone as the island itself.

"You never should've come here," he said, his voice no longer a child's, but layered with something else, something that echoed in the chamber like distant thunder. "This place belongs to something worse than ghosts."

Mercy pressed herself against the bars, her white fingers clutching the metal as if she could bend it through sheer desperation. "Micah, please," she begged, her voice cracking. "Don't leave us here. The water's rising. We'll drown."

The boy's expression flickered, a brief shadow of remorse crossing his features before being swallowed by determination. "I'm sorry," he said, though the words carried no warmth. He turned away, his shoulders straight, his steps measured as he moved back toward the tunnel entrance. "I'm protecting what's mine. Just like you would."

Mercy called after him, her voice rising to a desperate shout that broke against the stone walls and returned as fragmented echoes. "Micah! Don't do this! Please!"

But the boy didn't look back. Water sloshed around him as he reached the chamber's entrance, his slight frame a silhouette against the faint glow of the outer cave. For a moment he paused, as if considering some last word of explanation or apology. Then he was gone, swallowed by the darkness, leaving only the sound of splashing footsteps that gradually faded to nothing.

Chapter 23

The tide surged into the sea cave with a thunderous roar, the icy seawater rushing up to their knees in seconds. Anna's rage burned through the chill that clawed at her flesh as she lunged against the iron gate, fingers wrapping around bars that wouldn't yield. The passage where Micah had disappeared now churned with foaming water, each new wave pushing higher. The lantern swung wildly in her grip, casting frantic shadows across the glistening basalt walls where ancient spirals pulsed with a blue-green phosphorescence that had nothing to do with her light.

"Damn it!" Anna snarled, slamming her shoulder against the rusted metal again and again. The gate shuddered but remained firmly locked, its ancient mechanism holding fast despite her desperate strength. She ran her fingers along the seam where the metal met stone, searching for weakness, for any gap that might offer leverage.

Mercy pressed her face against the bars, her white hair plastered to her skull, her mismatched eyes wide with betrayal. "Why would he do this?" she whispered, the words barely audible above the hungry growl of the incoming tide. "He was searching for his sister. He—"

"He was protecting her," Anna said, her voice tight as she rattled the gate again. "Or thinks he is. From us. From me."

The water climbed higher, lapping at their mid-thighs now, its grip cold as death. Each wave pushed against them with increasing force, as if the sea itself was trying to drive them deeper into the cave's throat. The light caught the water's surface, turning it into a shifting mirror that fractured their reflections into a hundred broken pieces.

"Search the walls," Anna ordered, passing the lantern to Mercy. "Look for another way out, a weakness, anything. We don't have much time."

Mercy nodded, her thin frame already shivering with cold as she waded toward the chamber's far wall, lantern held high. The light wavered across the glistening stone, revealing more of the spiral patterns they'd seen throughout the cave. Here, however, the carvings were deeper, more deliberate, their edges honed to razor sharpness despite centuries of exposure to salt and sea.

Anna turned her attention back to the gate, examining its construction with methodical desperation. The lock mechanism wasn't visible from their side, but she could feel the solid mass of metal wedged into the stone wall, immovable without a key.

"There must be something," she muttered, fingers probing every inch of the gate's frame. The water had risen to her waist now, each new tide surge sending a fresh shock of cold through her core. Her legs were already going numb, her movements growing sluggish despite the urgency pumping through her veins.

Behind her, Mercy gasped. The sound made Anna whirl, hand flying to her knife by instinct. What she saw froze her blood colder than any tide.

White shapes emerged from crevices in the basalt walls, gaps between the stones barely wider than a finger. There were hundreds of them, each no larger than a child's palm. More crabs, their shells perfect spirals. Their legs moved with unnatural synchronicity, each one keeping perfect time with its brethren as they scuttled through the rising water.

"Anna!" Mercy's voice trembled as she backed away from the nearest cluster.

The crabs moved in formation, dozens at a time, creating living spirals that mirrored the patterns carved into the walls. Their claws clicked in rhythm, a sound like tiny bones knocking together, building to a percussion that somehow cut through the roar of the rising tide. The water swirled around them as they moved, not with the natural push and pull of the waves, but in deliberate currents that twisted into even more spirals, extending from the center of the chamber outward in ever-widening arcs.

"Don't touch them," Anna warned, though Mercy needed no such caution. The girl had pressed herself against the wall farthest from the largest concentration of crabs, the lantern clutched to her chest as if it might offer protection beyond its light.

The water rose with increasing speed now, already reaching their ribs, the current growing strong enough to tug at their limbs. Each new wave lifted them momentarily off their feet before dropping them back. The chamber had become a deadly pool, with no visible means of escape and death measuring its approach in inches of icy seawater.

Mercy's breathing quickened with the sharp pants of encroaching panic. "We're going to drown," she said, the words flat with horrific certainty. "The water's coming too fast—"

"Focus," Anna snapped, more harshly than she intended. "Keep looking. There must be another way out."

But even as she said it, Anna felt doubt corrode her confidence. The gate remained their only visible exit, and it held fast against every attempt to force it. The walls rose smooth and unbroken to a ceiling lost in darkness, offering no handholds, no ledges to climb toward. The water continued its relentless rise, nearly to her chest, each breath becoming more precious than the last.

Mercy had stopped searching. She focused her attention on a section of wall where the carved spirals converged into a single, massive glyph. The lantern light caught the edge of her profile as she stared, transfixed, at the ancient carvings. Her lips parted slightly, moving in shapes that formed no words Anna recognized.

"Mercy?" Anna called, pushing against the current to reach the girl's side. "What do you see?"

Mercy didn't answer. Her free hand rose slowly, as if pulled by invisible threads, and pressed against the central spiral. Her fingertips traced the carved lines with a precision that seemed impossible given the dim light and the turbulence of the surrounding water. When she spoke, her voice had changed—deeper, older, inflected with cadences that belonged to no living tongue.

"Iter ad intra... spirare in abyssum..."

Anna recognized the language, though not the specific words. It was a corrupted form of Latin, blended with something older. The kind of speech that slipped between worlds, that existed in the margins between meaning and madness. The same language she'd seen in Thorne's codex.

But how could Mercy know it?

"Mercy, stop." Anna grabbed the girl's shoulder, but Mercy's hand remained pressed to the wall as if fused there. Her eyes had rolled back, showing only white behind fluttering lashes. The words continued to pour from her lips, a torrent of sound that seemed to rise from somewhere deeper than her throat.

A powerful wave crashed into the chamber, slamming both women against the stone wall. The impact knocked the breath from Anna's lungs and nearly tore the lantern from Mercy's grip. Water splashed into her face, filling her nose and mouth with bitter salt. She coughed, struggling to find purchase on the slick stone as the water receded, only to surge back with greater force.

The tide had reached their chests now. Each new wave lifted them from their feet entirely, forcing them to swim rather than stand. The crabs continued their eerie dance below the surface, their white shells visible as ghostly spirals whenever the water cleared momentarily. Their synchronized movements had accelerated, spinning faster as the chamber filled, as if counting down to some terrible culmination.

Anna pulled Mercy away from the wall with desperate strength. The girl came loose all at once, nearly sending both of them underwater again with the sudden release. Mercy gasped, her eyes clearing as she returned to herself, confusion and terror washing across her features.

"I saw it," she said, clutching Anna's arm with fingers that dug into flesh with bruising force. "I saw what's beneath. What's waiting. It's… It's hungry, Anna. It's so hungry."

Another wave crashed into them, this one powerful enough to send them tumbling through the water like rag dolls. Anna's head struck stone and stars exploded behind her eyes. She surfaced, gasping, to find Mercy struggling to keep the lantern above water. Its flame guttered dangerously as droplets hissed against the hot glass. If it went out, they'd be plunged into endless darkness.

"The spirals," Mercy choked out between desperate breaths. "They're the same as in Hallowspire. The same as what was carved on that altar!"

The connection clicked into place in Anna's mind, pieces fitting together with sudden, terrible clarity. The spiral patterns carved throughout the mansion, the glyphs in Thorne's codex, the ritual chamber beneath the chapel—they all shared the same underlying structure, the same fundamental purpose. They were keys designed to open passages between worlds.

And this chamber, this flood-filled tomb where they now fought for breath, was another kind of door.

The water reached their armpits now, lifting them with each surge until their heads nearly touched the ceiling. The lantern's light caught the surface of the water, transforming the chamber into a cathedral of liquid shadows, the dancing reflections making the spiral carvings seem to writhe and twist with hungry purpose.

Rebecca's voice, silent since they'd entered the cave, suddenly bloomed in Anna's mind: *Blood opens what water only reveals, child. You've seen this pattern before. You know what feeds it.*

Anna's hand moved to her knife, fingers closing around the hilt with grim determination. She understood now, with a clarity born of desperation and the proximity of death. The rituals at Hallowspire had all required blood—Thorne's blood, his victims' blood, blood to open the way between worlds.

And here, in this chamber where the Silver Thread met the island, where the energy of that ley line bubbled up through stone and sea, the same principle would apply.

"Hold the light steady," she told Mercy, drawing her knife from its sheath. The blade gleamed dully in the lantern light, its edge sharp enough to split hair. "And whatever happens, keep the flame above water."

Before Mercy could protest, Anna drew the blade across her palm, wincing as the steel sliced through her existing wound. Blood welled dark and thick, immediately diluted by the seawater that splashed against her skin. She clenched her fist, forcing more blood to flow, then pressed her bleeding palm against the central spiral glyph—the same one Mercy had been tracing in her trance.

The effect was immediate. The carved spiral drank her blood like parched earth absorbing rain, the liquid vanishing into stone that should have been impermeable. Anna felt a pull, not just on her hand but on something deeper—her will, her intention, the very essence that made her who she was. The glyph wanted more than blood; it wanted purpose.

Instinctively, Anna traced her fingers along the spiral, but not in the direction it led. She moved against its flow, drawing a counter-spiral that opposed the pattern's inward coil. As her blood-slick fingertips moved across the stone, the glyph began to glow—not with the faint phosphorescence they'd seen earlier, but with a brilliant electric blue that cut through water and shadow alike.

The crabs reacted instantly. Their synchronized dance faltered, bodies twisting as if in pain, claws snapping at empty water. Then, as one, they reversed direction, their spiral pattern unwinding from the center outward, mimicking the counter-spiral Anna had traced on the wall.

A low, grinding sound filled the chamber, felt more through bone and tissue than heard through water-logged ears. The stone beneath Anna's bleeding palm shifted, the entire section of the wall sliding inward with the ponderous weight of centuries in motion. Behind it, a narrow tunnel appeared. It was rough-hewn but unmistakably man-made, leading upward at a sharp angle that promised escape from the flooding chamber.

Water immediately surged through the gap, sucking Anna and Mercy into the newly revealed passage.

"Hold on!" Anna shouted over the roar of water and grinding stone. She grabbed Mercy's arm, pulling the girl toward her as they tumbled in the flood. Her feet found purchase on the stone beneath her, and she hauled Mercy upright next to her.

Mercy's eyes were wide with shock. She seemed frozen, caught between terror and fascination, until Anna's grip tightened to the point of pain.

"Mercy! Move!"

The command broke whatever spell held the girl. She surged forward with the lantern clutched tight in her white-knuckled grip, its flame miraculously still burning despite the chaos around them. Anna followed, pushing against water that now reached their chins, fighting for every inch of progress toward the tunnel mouth where the passage rose up from the rising water.

A massive wave—larger than any before it—crashed into the chamber behind them. The wall of water struck with the force of a battering ram, lifting them from their feet and hurling them forward into the tunnel's throat. Anna felt stone scrape against her shoulders, tasted blood where her lip split against rock, heard Mercy's choked cry as the current tumbled them deeper into the passage.

Then they were beyond the wave's reach, sprawled on rough stone that sloped upward into darkness. Behind them, water gushed through the opening, but the tunnel's upward angle kept them just above its hungry grasp. The lantern had survived, though its flame now burned low and yellow, its oil nearly spent.

Mercy lay on her side, coughing up seawater, her thin frame wracked with shivers. Anna pushed herself to her knees, wincing at the collection of new bruises and cuts that adorned her flesh. Her hand throbbed where she'd sliced it open, blood still seeping from the wound to mix with the water pooling beneath them.

"We need to keep moving," Anna said, her voice raw from salt and exertion. "The tide will keep rising. We don't know how far up this tunnel goes."

Mercy nodded weakly, struggling to her feet with Anna's help. She held the lantern high, revealing a passage that twisted upward into the island's heart, its walls carved with more of the spiral glyphs, though these were smaller, less elaborate than those in the flooded chamber behind them.

"Where does it lead?" Mercy asked, her teeth chattering with cold and shock.

Anna stared into the darkness beyond the lantern's reach, a grim certainty settling in her bones. "To Hallowspire."

The tunnel seemed to breathe around them, drawing air inward with a soft, sighing sound that might have been the tide or something else entirely. Ahead lay only darkness and uncertain footing, stone steps worn smooth by centuries of use. Behind them, the flooded chamber continued to fill, water lapping at the tunnel's mouth like a hungry tongue testing its next meal.

They had no choice but to climb.

Chapter 24

The chapel floor split open with a scrape of ancient stone against stone. A rectangular section of slate slid aside, revealing a dark aperture from which billowed cold, damp air that smelled of brine and deeper things. Fingers appeared first —pale and bloodied—clutching at the edge of the opening. Then came Anna's face, streaked with salt and grime, her dark hair plastered to her skull like seaweed to rock. She hauled herself up with a grunt of effort, her sodden clothes dripping seawater onto the crimson-veined floor of the unholy sanctuary.

"Mercy," she gasped, turning back to the hole. "Give me your hand."

The girl's white fingers emerged from the darkness, trembling violently with cold and exhaustion. Anna seized them, pulling with what little strength she had left. Mercy surfaced like a drowned thing. Her hair was a shock of white against the gloom, her mismatched eyes wide and glazed. The lantern they'd carried was gone, lost somewhere in the flooded passage, but the kaleidoscopic light through the chapel's stained glass provided just enough to see by.

"We made it," Mercy whispered through chattering teeth. "I thought—" She couldn't finish the sentence, her body convulsing with cold.

Anna glanced back at the passage that had carried them from the sea cave through the island's heart. The journey had been nightmarish: a steep climb through darkness, the water always rising behind them, the walls alive with blind, pale things that slithered away from their touch. By the time they'd reached the chapel's foundation, the lantern had guttered out, leaving them to feel their way through the final stretch by touch alone.

Now, safe in the chapel's confines, they took stock of their condition. Anna's clothes were soaked through, her coat heavy as lead on her shoulders. Her hand throbbed where she'd cut it to activate the hidden passage, the salt water having both cleansed and tortured the wound. Mercy looked worse. Her thin frame was wracked with shivers, lips tinged blue, the hem of her dress trailing water like a ship's banner.

"We need to get warm," Anna said, her voice ragged with salt and fatigue. "Come on."

They staggered from the chapel like shipwreck survivors, trailing water across the floor. The air in the mansion's corridors felt tropical compared to the frigid sea, but it wasn't enough. Without dry clothes and fire, hypothermia would claim them as surely as drowning would have.

The journey to the Great Hall seemed endless. Mercy stumbled twice, her legs buckling beneath her. The second time, Anna had to half-carry her, an arm around the girl's narrow waist, whispering harsh encouragements that were more command than comfort.

"Keep moving. One foot, then the other. Just a little further."

The corridor twisted, then opened onto the Great Hall's vast expanse. Safety—or as close to it as Hallowspire allowed—waited just across the marble floor.

Then Anna saw them.

Micah stood by the fireplace, his slight frame outlined by the glow of freshly added timber. Beside him, Juba. Her posture was rigid with tension, her eyes fixed on something in her hands. They looked whole, dry, warm. Untroubled by the horrors that had nearly claimed Anna and Mercy in the flooded cave.

The cave where Micah had locked them to drown.

Something snapped inside Anna.

The cold vanished, replaced by a heat that started in her gut and spread outward like wildfire, consuming exhaustion, fear, and reason in its path. Her vision narrowed to a tunnel with Micah at its end.

"You," she hissed, the word escaping through teeth clenched so tightly her jaw ached.

Micah's head jerked up, his eyes widening as he registered their sudden appearance—and the murder in Anna's gaze. He took a half-step backward, bumping against the hearth stones.

Anna's hand flew to her belt where her knife waited, drawing it with a motion so practiced it was nearly unconscious. The blade gleamed in the firelight. Her fingers, stiff with cold, wrapped around the hilt with white-knuckled intensity.

"Anna—" Mercy began, but her protest died as Anna

charged forward.

Anna moved with the fluid grace of an assassin, her boots squeaking against the marble floor, leaving twin trails of seawater in her wake. Her coat flared behind her, heavy and dripping. Her face was a death mask of cold fury, eyes narrowed to slits, lips pulled back in a snarl that revealed teeth like a wolf's.

Juba reacted with the speed of a mother defending her young. She stepped between Anna and Micah, her own blade appearing from beneath her shawl as if conjured by the air itself. The knife Micah had given her earlier—the one he said found blood easily—now caught the firelight along its wicked edge.

"You stop right there," Juba commanded, her voice deep and unwavering. She held the knife low, blade angled upward toward Anna's approaching form, her stance wide and balanced. This was not the frightened woman who had fled the vault beneath the chapel. This was a different creature entirely, one who had survived slavery and flight, who had killed before and would kill again to protect what was hers.

Anna's momentum carried her forward until the point of Juba's knife was inches from her sternum. There she halted, her own blade still raised, seawater dripping from her sleeve onto the polished floor. The two women faced each other across the space of a breath, neither flinching, neither yielding.

"Move," Anna said, the word falling between them like a stone.

"No," Juba replied simply.

Micah stood frozen behind his mother, his face a landscape

of conflicting emotions: fear, defiance, shame, and something deeper that might have been resignation. His hands were fists at his sides, but he made no move to flee.

"He tried to kill us," Anna said, each word precise and cutting. "Locked us in that cave to drown."

"I know." Juba's eyes never left Anna's face, her knife never wavered. "And I'll deal with that. But you don't touch my son."

The air between them crackled with tension, a physical force that seemed to push outward against the hall's vast dimensions. Neither woman appeared to breathe. Even the fire seemed to hold its breath, the flames pausing in their dance as if watching the scene with keen interest.

"Please," Mercy's voice broke the silence, cracking with emotion and cold. She had remained where Anna left her, too weak to follow, too afraid to turn away. Water pooled around her bare feet, her white hair hanging in wet ropes around her face. "Please stop. I'm so cold."

For a moment, it seemed as if no one had heard her. Then Anna's blade lowered a fraction of an inch—not a surrender, but the first crack in her murderous resolve.

Juba's eyes flickered toward Mercy, taking in the girl's pitiful state, then returned to Anna with unchanged intensity. "You want blood? Fine. There'll be time for that later. But there's still a child missing. My Effie."

The words hung between them, each syllable weighted with grief and desperation.

Anna's knife trembled in her grip, not from weakness but from the effort of restraint. Her fury had crystallized into something harder, colder, more dangerous than the blind rage that had propelled her across the Great Hall. She took a deliberate step back, creating space between herself and Juba's blade, but her eyes never left Micah's face. The boy, half-hidden behind his mother, whose actions had nearly sealed their doom in the tide-filled cave.

"Tell me why," Anna demanded, her voice so low it seemed to crawl along the floor. "Tell me why you locked us in that cave to drown."

Micah's eyes darted between his mother's back and Anna's murderous gaze. His shoulders hunched inward, making him appear even smaller than he was. The firelight caught the angles of his face, illuminating features that had aged years in mere hours.

"I didn't want—" he began, then stopped, swallowing hard. "They said it had to be this way."

"Who said?" Anna pressed, her grip on the knife tightening. "The Quiet Ones? Those spirits in the walls?"

Micah nodded, a barely perceptible movement. His eyes were haunted, reflecting horrors no child should have witnessed. "They came to me in the cave. Showed me... things."

"What things?" Juba asked, her voice gentler than Anna's but no less insistent. Though her knife remained steady, pointed at Anna's heart, her head had turned slightly toward her son. "What did you see, Micah?"

Micah's confession began like a winter thaw—slow at first, then rushing forth in a torrent he couldn't control. "White faces," he whispered. "Hundreds of 'em. Overseers. Slave catchers. Men who smiled while they hurt us. They showed me every beating I ever got. Every time Effie cried from hunger. Every time you—" he looked at his mother, "—had to bow your head and say 'yes, sir' with blood in your mouth."

His voice cracked, the words spilling faster now. "They showed me how it ends, too. Us caught. Us sold south. Us dead in a ditch with dogs tearing at our bodies." His hands trembled, fingers working at the air as if trying to grasp something that kept slipping away. "They said it wasn't just memories. They said it would happen again—to all of us— unless I helped them."

"Helped them how?" Anna asked, though the cold certainty growing in her stomach suggested she already knew.

"They said the Gate needed Effie," Micah replied, his eyes finally meeting Anna's with a desperate intensity. "Said she was special—could hear them better than anyone. That she was meant to come to the island." His gaze dropped to the floor, shame evident in every line of his body. "But they promised they'd give her back if... if I gave them *her* instead."

His trembling finger pointed directly at Mercy, who stood forgotten near the entrance to the hall, still dripping seawater onto the marble floor.

The room seemed to contract around them. Mercy's face drained of what little color it had, her mismatched eyes widening with horrified understanding. "Me?" she whispered, the word barely audible above the crack and pop of the hearth. "They wanted me?"

"Your white skin," Micah said, unable to meet her gaze. "Your different eyes. They said you were marked from birth."

The chill that ran through Mercy had nothing to do with

her sodden clothes. She took a stumbling step backward, as if trying to distance herself from the truth of Micah's words. "I'm not special," she protested weakly. "I'm just—"

"Twice-cursed," Juba finished for her. "Red eye and moon skin. My grandmother would have said the spirits can see right through you to the other side."

Anna's body went rigid, her breath catching in her throat. The knife in her hand suddenly felt like an extension of her arm, her fingers fused to the hilt by some terrible alchemy of rage and fear. Micah's betrayal was not just a boy's desperate attempt to save his sister. It was part of something larger, something that had been unfolding since before they arrived on Brimwatch.

The Quiet Ones had manipulated Micah, shown him horrors both past and possible, all to deliver Mercy to a watery grave. But to what purpose? Why had they wanted Mercy dead? Anna and Mercy had escaped the tide cave by sheer luck, foiling whatever plan the mansion's ghostly occupants had set in motion.

"I had to choose," Micah said, his voice breaking on the last word. "Between Effie and her." He gestured at Mercy again, tears welling in his eyes. "Between my blood and a stranger."

The raw honesty of his confession hung in the air, neither excuse nor apology but something more fundamental—the terrible calculus of survival that had governed his short life. In his place, Anna wondered, what would she have done? What betrayal wouldn't she commit to save someone she loved?

As if sensing her wavering resolve, Rebecca's voice slithered into Anna's consciousness, soft and intimate as a lover's whisper: *He's not wrong, child. The albino girl has a part in this. Her soul is already half in shadow. And there are always sacrifices in war.*

Anna's jaw tightened at the intrusion, a muscle jumping beneath the skin. Her eyelids fluttered closed for the briefest moment as Rebecca's presence expanded within her mind, cold fingers sifting through her thoughts, weighing and discarding her objections before they could fully form.

The boy merely hastened what was already in motion, Rebecca continued, her tone almost caressing. *The Gate must open. A child must serve. This is why you were drawn here—to rescue your mother.*

Anna's body shuddered, a subtle tremor that began at her spine and radiated outward. Her free hand rose to her temple, pressing against it as if to physically contain Rebecca's invasive presence. Her lips parted slightly, expelling a breath that clouded in the air despite the fire's warmth.

Only Mercy noticed this transformation, this silent battle fought within Anna's flesh. She took a tentative step forward, one pale hand extended.

"Anna?" Mercy asked. "Are you alright?"

Anna didn't answer. When she opened her eyes, they were darker than before, flecked with amber that hadn't been there moments ago. The knife in her hand lowered slightly, its tip now aimed at the floor rather than Micah's heart.

"This changes nothing," Anna said finally, though her voice carried an undertone that hadn't been present before—a harmonizing whisper beneath her natural timbre. "He still betrayed us. Left us to die."

"To save his sister," Juba countered, her own knife still

steady. "What would you have done in his place?"

The question struck Anna like a physical blow. What indeed had she done—was still doing—to save her own mother's soul? What bargains had she struck with Rebecca? What lines had she crossed, what innocents had she endangered in her quest to rescue Abigail from beyond the Veil?

The parallels were too close, too uncomfortable to examine in the harsh light of Micah's confession. She took another step back, her wet boots squeaking against the marble, creating distance not just from Juba's blade but from the truth reflected in the woman's knowing eyes.

"It doesn't matter," Anna said, though the conviction in her voice had hollowed out, leaving only the shell of her earlier rage. "What's done is done."

She sheathed her knife with deliberate slowness, her movement precise despite her trembling fingers. The steel slid into its leather housing with a soft hiss, like a final exhaled threat. Her face settled into something harder than her murderous intent: a mask of cold calculation that transformed her features into marble. When she spoke again, her voice carried no trace of the earlier fury, replaced instead by a deadly quiet that seemed to absorb all other sounds in the Great Hall.

"You'll leave this place," she pronounced, the words falling like stones into still water. "Both of you. Now."

Juba's knife remained steady, her eyes narrowing as she processed Anna's unexpected clemency. "Leave?"

"I won't kill a child," Anna continued, her gaze fixed on a point just above Micah's head, as if she couldn't bear to look directly at him. "Not even one who tried to kill me. But I won't shelter a traitor, either. You have until I count to fifty to gather whatever belongings you need, and then you go."

Juba lowered her knife by inches, incredulity replacing the fierce protectiveness in her expression. "You expect me to leave? With my daughter still missing?" Her voice rose, filling the vast chamber with maternal outrage. "Effie is somewhere on this island—maybe in this very house. Ain't no way I'm leaving without her."

"Your son made that choice for you," Anna replied, her tone flat and emotionless. "When he chose to sacrifice strangers to save his sister, he gambled with all your lives." She gestured toward the massive front doors of Hallowspire. "The island is still there. The caves. The woods. Search them if you must. But not from within these walls."

A chill settled over Anna's features as she spoke. Something alien crept into her eyes; a hardness that hadn't been there before, a calculation that viewed human suffering with academic detachment. Rebecca's influence grew more visible with each passing moment, like ink spreading through water, darkening whatever compassion Anna had managed to kindle.

Wise, child. The witch's voice curled through Anna's mind like smoke. *The boy cannot be trusted. The mother is blinded by love. They will only interfere with what must be done.*

Mercy stepped forward, her thin frame still shivering from the cold and wet, but her mismatched eyes burning with unexpected intensity. "Anna," she pleaded, "they're just trying to survive. Like us." She moved closer to Micah, her pale fingers twisting in the fabric of her sodden dress. "He didn't want to hurt us. The Quiet Ones showed him terrible things."

Anna's gaze snapped to Mercy. "And you believe that excuses what he did?" she asked, each word sharp as broken glass. "He left us to drown, Mercy. For all he knew, we died in that cave."

"I'm sorry," Micah whispered, the words barely audible. His eyes remained fixed on the marble floor, shoulders hunched as if expecting a physical blow. "I didn't know what else to do. They said they'd hurt Effie if I didn't... if I didn't..."

"Enough," Anna cut him off. "I've made my decision. You both leave. Now."

The temperature in the Great Hall seemed to drop several degrees, though the fire still burned in the massive hearth. Shadows lengthened across the marble floor, stretching toward the confrontation like curious spectators. The mansion itself appeared to be listening, its ancient timber creaking in approval as Anna enforced her will within its stones.

Juba finally lowered her knife completely, slipping it back beneath her shawl with practiced ease. Her face had hardened into a mask that mirrored Anna's own—all calculation and cold fury.

"Fine," she said, the single syllable carrying the weight of a curse. "We'll go. But mark me—if my Effie is in this house, if she suffers because you've turned us away, there won't be a place on this earth where you can hide from me."

Anna nodded once, accepting the threat as her due. "Fifty counts," she repeated. "Starting now."

Juba grabbed Micah's arm, pulling him toward the corridor that led to the front of the mansion. The boy stumbled, then found his footing, half-running to keep pace with his mother's determined stride. They disappeared into the shadows of the entrance hall, the sound of their footsteps fading to hollow echoes.

Anna turned to Mercy, who stood trembling with more than just physical cold. "We'll bar the doors once they're gone," she said, her voice softening slightly. "We need to ensure no one else enters—or leaves—until we find what we're looking for."

Mercy didn't answer immediately. "And what are we looking for, Anna?" she asked finally, her voice small but steady. "What's worth all this… this cruelty?"

Anna's hard expression didn't waver. "Effie," she lied. "If she's still alive." She reached out, her fingers barely brushing Mercy's shoulder. "The Gate below is the key."

The touch seemed to both comfort and disturb the girl, who shivered beneath Anna's hand but didn't pull away. "And me?" she asked. "What am I to you? Another key? Another means to end?"

Before Anna could answer, the sound of approaching footsteps forced her attention back to the entrance hall. Juba emerged first, a bundle clutched in her arms—likely food and whatever meager possessions they'd brought to the mansion. Micah followed, his face a blank mask, all emotion carefully tucked away behind eyes that had seen too much for their years.

Anna walked toward the front doors, her wet boots leaving damp footprints across the marble. The massive oak portals loomed before them, twelve feet of ancient wood carved with scenes from myths no church would recognize. She grasped the iron ring that served as a handle, pulling the right-hand door open with effort. Cold air rushed in, carrying the scent of sea salt and impending rain.

"Go," she said simply, standing aside to let them pass.

Juba paused at the threshold, her dark eyes meeting Anna's in silent challenge. "You'll regret this," she said, her voice low and certain. "When the spirits come for the girl—for Mercy —you'll wish you had allies."

"I have what I need," Anna replied, though something in her tone suggested she was trying to convince herself as much as Juba.

Micah stopped beside his mother, his gaze finally rising to meet Anna's. In his eyes burned not hatred, but something worse—understanding. "They're using you," he said quietly. "Just like they used me. Showing you what you want to see. Promising what you need most."

Anna's jaw tightened, the only visible sign that his words had struck home. "Goodbye, Micah," she said, her voice cold once more.

They stepped outside into the gathering dusk, Juba's arm around her son's shoulders as they descended the worn stone steps. Anna watched them until they reached the overgrown path that led away from Hallowspire, then slowly closed the massive door. The sound of the bolt sliding home echoed through the empty entrance hall like a coffin lid being sealed.

Mercy stood a few paces behind her, arms wrapped around herself for warmth, her white hair beginning to dry in wisps around her face. "What now?" she asked, her voice barely above a whisper.

Anna didn't answer immediately. She leaned against the closed door, pressing her forehead to the ancient wood, imagining the fading footsteps of Juba and Micah as they retreated down the path. Her eyes closed, her breathing shallow and controlled.

"Now," she said finally, turning to face Mercy, "we find the Gate. We find Effie. And we finish what Thorne started."

As she spoke, a shudder passed through her body—not from the cold, but from something inside. Rebecca's presence swelled within her mind, a dark tide rising to claim more territory. Anna's fingers pressed against her temple, massaging a pain only she could feel.

You've chosen wisely, Rebecca whispered. *The Gate waits for us both—and for the girl with the strange eyes.*

Anna's lips parted in a silent gasp as Rebecca's influence tightened its grip. Behind her, unseen, a faint smile curved her reflection in the window glass—a smile that didn't belong to her at all.

Chapter 25

Candles guttered in the Great Hall as Anna bent over the *Tenebric Sequence*, her fingers tracing the grotesque symbols that decorated its margins. The grimoire's human-skin cover felt unnaturally warm beneath her palm, almost alive, as if it remembered the body it once belonged to.

Outside, night had fallen completely, transforming Hallowspire's windows into black mirrors that revealed nothing but the occasional flicker of lightning from the approaching storm. The massive hearth still blazed, but its heat failed to penetrate the perpetual chill that hung in the Great Hall's cavernous space.

Mercy lay curled nearby on her couch, her white hair spilled across the faded velvet like scattered frost. Exhaustion had finally claimed her, her small chest rising and falling in the shallow rhythm of troubled sleep. Anna had draped her own coat over the girl, now dry after hanging before the fire for hours. Part of her remained troubled by the strange trance Mercy had succumbed to in the tide cave. What was behind those words she had spoken while being held in thrall? What visions had been revealed to her and—more importantly—by whom? Anna had every intention of demanding answers in the morning, once Mercy had rested and recovered from her trauma.

The pages of Thorne's grimoire rustled beneath Anna's fingers as if eager to reveal their secrets. Written in Thorne's cramped hand, the text was a mixture of Latin, corrupted Enochian, and something older that made Anna's eyes water when she focused on it too long. Diagrams of human anatomy decorated the margins, each labeled with alchemical symbols and notations for precise incisions. The drawings showed bodies in various states of ritual preparation: bound with specific knots, positioned in geometric patterns, marked with spirals that started at the throat and wound down to the soles of the feet.

Anna's head throbbed. She had been reading for what felt like hours, forcing herself to absorb Thorne's methodical madness. Her clothes, though dry, still carried the briny scent of seawater. Her body ached from the ordeal in the tide cave, and the cut on her palm had reopened twice as she turned the grimoire's brittle pages.

Turn to the chapter on severing, Rebecca whispered, her voice sliding through Anna's mind like ice across glass. *The ritual proper begins there.*

Anna's fingers hesitated, then flipped forward several pages, landing precisely where Rebecca had indicated. The text here was darker, the ink mixed with something that had oxidized to a rusty brown over the decades.

"Blood ink," Anna murmured, her own voice startling her in the hall's oppressive silence. The sound didn't travel far before it was swallowed by the shadows that pooled in the corners like living things.

Yes, Rebecca confirmed, a note of appreciation in her spectral voice. *Thorne understood the power of binding medium to message. Each page is inscribed with the blood of its subject. Each ritual preserved in the very essence of its victim.*

The thought turned Anna's stomach, but she forced herself to continue reading. The chapter Thorne called "The Fivefold Unbinding" detailed a process of systematic soul-stripping conducted over five consecutive nights.

The first rite, child, is Severance of Name, Rebecca explained, her tone taking on the cadence of a lecturer. *They are stripped of identity, every record burned, every memory extracted. The name is carved from the tongue and sealed in glass.*

Anna's eyes found the corresponding passage in the text. Thorne described binding a victim's tongue with silver wire, then using a bone needle to extract "the essence of nomenclature" through a precise series of punctures. The diagram showed a tongue mapped with points like a star chart, each prick releasing not blood but *nomina*—the spiritual substance of identity.

The second is Severance of Memory, Rebecca continued, her excitement building. *Memories are stored in the marrow, you see. Thorne discovered this. They must be drained from the longest bones through spiral extractions.*

On the page, Thorne detailed drilling into femurs with specially crafted augers, the bone dust collected and mixed with salt and quicksilver. He packed the resulting paste into the victim's ears and eyes, "sealing the windows through which past experience might re-enter."

Anna's breathing quickened, disgust and fascination warring within her. "This is butchery," she whispered. "Not ritual."

Science and sorcery are twins separated only by understanding, Rebecca countered. *The third rite is Severance of Will—the breaking of the spine's secret architecture. Each vertebra houses a fragment of intention. When realigned according to the pattern...*

The grimoire showed bodies contorted into impossible positions, spines twisted into spirals that mimicked the patterns carved throughout Hallowspire. Thorne wrote of "releasing volitional essence through controlled fracture," describing the sound as "similar to a glass harmonica played with wet fingers—the music of a soul surrendering agency."

The fourth is Severance of Voice, Rebecca purred. *Not just the ability to speak, but to be heard by God or devil. The throat is sealed with nine stitches of iron thread, each knot capturing a different register of spiritual cry.*

Anna stared at detailed instructions for threading a curved bone needle, for the precise tension required to "seal the spiritual aperture without extinguishing the physical vessel." Victims survived this process, Thorne noted clinically, but never spoke again—not even in dreams.

The fifth rite was written in what looked to be a different hand altogether. Shakier and more urgent, it described the Severance of Soul—the final separation that left the body alive but emptied of self.

This is what makes the Quiet Ones, Rebecca whispered, her voice now uncomfortably close, as if she spoke directly into Anna's ear rather than from within her mind. *Empty vessels, perfectly obedient, waiting to be filled with new purpose. Beautiful, isn't it?*

Horror rose in Anna's throat like bile. The academic detachment with which she'd been reading crumbled, replaced by a visceral understanding of what these pages actually described. Real people, systematically unmade through torture disguised as ritual. Children, women, men—slaves chosen because their disappearances would never be investigated, their suffering unmarked by the world.

"Beautiful?" Anna repeated, her voice hoarse with revulsion. "This is monstrous. Thorne was a monster."

Thorne was a visionary, Rebecca corrected, her tone sharpening. *He understood what most never grasp: that souls are malleable. That identity is merely architecture that can be dismantled and rebuilt. The body survives. Isn't that mercy of a kind?*

A new dread wormed its way up from Anna's gut, leaving an icy trail in its wake as Rebecca's words echoed in her mind:

Identity is merely architecture that can be dismantled and rebuilt...

Was this her own destiny? Was this what Rebecca had in mind for her?

Anna's rebuttal died in her throat as the temperature in the Great Hall plummeted without warning. Her breath clouded before her face in a white plume. The fire, which had been blazing merrily in the hearth, suddenly flattened as if pressed by an invisible hand, then shot upward in a column of blue-white flame that nearly reached the mantel.

The candles surrounding her followed suit, their flames

stretching into thin, attenuated pillars that cast no warmth but filled the hall with harsh, unnatural light. Wax wept down their sides in thick rivulets, pooling on the marble floor in patterns that resembled the spiral sigils from Thorne's diagrams.

Anna went very still, one hand resting protectively on the grimoire, the other reaching instinctively for the knife on her belt.

She wasn't alone.

At the edge of her vision, something moved—a figure that seemed to materialize from the shadows themselves. Anna turned slowly, keeping her movements deliberate, controlled.

A young Black woman stood between two marble columns, her form translucent but growing more solid with each passing second. She wore a simple cotton shift, torn and stained with what could only be blood. Her dark hair hung in limp tangles around a face that might once have been beautiful, before horror had claimed it. But it was her mouth that fixed Anna's gaze—lips pulled back in a grimace, sewn shut with crude black stitches that puckered the flesh. A viscous black substance leaked from her eyes, too thick to be tears. It trailed down her hollow cheeks and dripped from her jaw onto the marble floor.

The Quiet One's hollow eyes found Anna's, and in them burned recognition, purpose—and something that might have been a warning.

She wasn't alone. More figures materialized around the hall. Men and women of varying ages, all bearing the marks of Thorne's five rites. A man whose spine twisted in an impossible curve. A child with drill marks visible through translucent skin. An older woman whose throat bulged around iron stitches that glinted in the candlelight.

They moved with jerky, mechanical precision as they formed a circle around Anna. Their steps matched the rhythm of the flames, which now pulsed in perfect synchronicity. The temperature dropped further, cold enough that Anna's fingers grew numb where they rested on the grimoire.

Mercy stirred on the couch but didn't wake, her sleep unnaturally deep, as if enforced by the same will that commanded the ghosts.

The spirits began to move in unison, arms rising and falling, bodies bending and straightening. With dawning horror, Anna recognized their movements—they were reenacting the rituals described in the grimoire. One phantom kneeled, head thrown back as another pantomimed drilling into his temples. A third contorted her body into the spine-breaking position illustrated in Thorne's diagrams.

They remember, Rebecca whispered, her voice thick with anticipation. *The spirit forgets nothing. The ritual lives in them still.*

The first ghost—the woman with the sewn mouth—stepped forward, her bare feet making no sound on the marble. She extended one translucent hand toward Anna, fingers curled as if holding something invisible. Her sewn lips worked against their bindings, forming words she could not speak.

Anna found herself rising from her chair, the *Tenebric Sequence* clutched to her chest, as the circle of ghosts closed around her.

The woman with the sewn mouth turned away first, her movements fluid yet somehow wrong, as if her joints operated on different principles than those of the living. One by one, the other spirits followed suit, forming a silent procession that drifted toward the shadowed archway leading from the Great Hall. They moved with strange synchronicity, their translucent forms flickering like candles caught in a draft, leaving trails of spectral residue that hung in the air for seconds before dissolving into nothing.

Anna hesitated. The spirits paused at the archway, their hollow eyes fixed on her with expectant hunger. They wanted her to follow; that much was clear. The sewn-mouth woman extended one arm, fingers curling in beckoning.

They're showing us the way, Rebecca whispered, her voice coiling through Anna's mind. *The way to salvation for your mother.*

Anna glanced at Mercy, still curled on the couch. The girl hadn't stirred despite the supernatural chill that filled the hall. Her breathing remained deep and regular, almost unnaturally so, as if something ensured she would not wake to witness what was happening.

"I shouldn't leave her alone," Anna murmured. "Not again." But even as she spoke the words, she felt her resolve weakening. The prospect of discovering what the spirits wanted to show her—what secrets might help her rescue her mother—pulled at her with almost physical force.

The child is safer asleep, Rebecca assured her. *Some eyes should remain closed until the proper moment.*

Anna placed the grimoire on the settee and checked that her knife was secured in her belt before moving toward the waiting procession. The spirits parted slightly to admit her, then closed ranks behind her, sealing her within their silent company.

They moved through the archway into the corridor beyond, their passage marked by subtle disturbances in the air: dust motes swirling in spectral eddies, shadows deepening, then lightening without apparent cause. Some spirits glided smoothly for several steps, then suddenly juddered forward as if pulled by invisible strings. Others moved with a strange, sideways gait, their torsos remaining eerily still while their legs worked beneath them.

Most disturbing were the moments when they passed through solid objects. A spirit would approach a side table or decorative urn, then simply phase through it, its form momentarily fragmenting into wisps of translucent matter before reforming on the other side. The sewn-mouth woman led the procession, occasionally turning her head at impossible angles to ensure Anna still followed.

Anna matched their pace, maintaining a precise distance—close enough to follow, far enough to avoid brushing against their spectral forms. The thought of touching one of them, of feeling whatever cold substance made up their being, sent involuntary shivers down her spine.

The corridors through which they passed seemed to stretch and contract, distances warping in ways that defied physical logic. A hallway Anna recalled as being no more than twenty paces suddenly extended before her, its end receding like a tunnel viewed through the wrong end of a spyglass. Doorways appeared where she was certain none had existed before—narrow, arched portals with keyholes shaped like spirals, their wood ancient and black with age.

"This isn't right," Anna whispered, her voice sounding flat and deadened in the strange acoustics of the shifting corridor. "These rooms weren't here before."

Hallowspire has many faces, Rebecca responded, a note of smug satisfaction in her voice. *What you see depends on who leads you. The living view one mansion; the dead know another.*

The procession turned left where Anna would have sworn the corridor continued straight, passing through an ornate door that opened of its own accord at their approach. She felt her sense of direction failing. They had turned and doubled back so many times that she could no longer tell which wing of the mansion they occupied, or whether they were even still within Hallowspire's original architecture.

The procession paused at a junction where three corridors met. The spirits seemed uncertain, their forms wavering like reflections in disturbed water. The sewn-mouth woman turned to Anna, her stitched lips working against their bindings.

Anna's feet refused to move forward. Some instinct, deeper than thought, warned her against proceeding. "I should go back," she said, her voice barely audible. "Mercy shouldn't be alone."

Cowardice does not become you, Rebecca hissed, her voice suddenly sharp as a blade. *Your mother suffers while you hesitate. Every moment you delay, her soul slips further from your grasp.*

The accusation stung like a physical blow. Anna's hand flew to her temple, pressing against a sudden flare of pain. Behind her closed eyelids, she saw her mother's face—

Abigail's features contorted in silent agony, reaching toward her from behind some invisible barrier.

"Show me," Anna whispered, surrender and determination mingling in her voice. "Show me how to save her."

The spirits resumed their procession with renewed purpose, choosing the leftmost corridor, which descended at a steep angle. The passage narrowed as they advanced, the grand architectural features of Hallowspire's upper floors giving way to more utilitarian construction. The air grew increasingly thick and cold, carrying the unmistakable scent of salt and decay. Not the smell of the ocean, but something fouler, like tide pools where dead things had been left to rot. Anna's boots struck stone rather than wood now, the floor transitioning to rough-hewn blocks slick with condensation.

They were descending into the island's foundation again, below the mansion's constructed levels and into chambers carved directly from Brimwatch's rocky heart. The walls wept moisture, glistening in the pale light that emanated from the spirits themselves. In places, the now-familiar spiral sigils marked the stone, carved deep and filled with some substance that caught the light with an oily sheen.

The procession led her down a twisting staircase barely wide enough for a single person. The ceiling dropped lower, forcing Anna to stoop, and the air grew so dense with moisture that each breath felt like drowning, her lungs working harder to extract oxygen from the saturated atmosphere.

At the bottom of the stairs, the passage opened into a cramped antechamber. The walls here were raw stone, roughly shaped and glistening with mineral deposits that formed their own organic spirals. Brackish water pooled in depressions in the floor, reflecting the spirits' ghostly light in fractured patterns.

The procession halted before an ancient wooden door reinforced with rusted iron bands. The door was massive, its timbers blackened with age and constant exposure to damp. The iron bands formed a pattern similar to the spirals carved throughout Hallowspire, though cruder, as if this predated the more refined expressions above.

The sewn-mouth woman placed her translucent hand against the wood. Where her fingers made contact, frost formed in delicate patterns, outlining the shape of her hand before spreading outward in crystalline tendrils.

The other spirits arranged themselves in a semicircle, their hollow eyes fixed on Anna with expectant intensity. They had brought her here for a purpose, shown her a path through Hallowspire that existed in some liminal space between the physical mansion and whatever spectral architecture the dead perceived.

Open it, Rebecca commanded, her voice now a fever in Anna's blood. *What you seek lies beyond.*

Anna stepped forward, her hand rising to touch the ancient door.

Chapter 26

Mercy stirred on the velvet couch, her consciousness returning in reluctant fragments. The weight of Anna's coat still covered her slight frame, but the warmth it had provided was gone, replaced by a bone-deep chill that seemed to seep from the very air. Her mismatched eyes opened to a Great Hall transformed by darkness. The familiar shapes were now rendered strange by shadows, the massive chandelier above her a skeletal thing of iron and unlit candles.

Something was wrong. The fire that had blazed in the hearth when she'd fallen asleep was now a sullen red glow, barely enough to cast light beyond the stone hearth.

And Anna was nowhere to be seen.

"Anna?" Mercy called, her voice thin and small in the cavernous space. The name fell flat, swallowed by the darkness as if the air itself were too thick to carry sound. Memories of the previous night's horrors needled her mind as she pushed herself upright, wincing as her muscles protested. How long had she slept? Hours, certainly, but whether it was still night or early morning, she couldn't tell. The windows revealed nothing but impenetrable blackness, not even the faintest suggestion of stars or moon.

The *Tenebric Sequence* lay on the settee where Anna had been studying it. Next to it was a depression in the cushion where she had sat while reading. The sight of the dreadful grimoire sent a shiver through Mercy that had nothing to do with the cold.

"Anna?" she tried again, louder this time. The mansion answered with a low, protracted creak, like the sound of ancient timbers shifting under their own weight, or perhaps something else entirely. It came from everywhere and nowhere, as if Hallowspire itself were stretching awake around her.

Mercy wrapped Anna's coat tighter around her shoulders and swung her feet to the floor. The marble was so cold it burned, stealing her breath in a sharp gasp that clouded visibly in the frigid air. She'd never known cold like this, not even during the harshest winters in Sévérité, when ice formed inside the windows and her mother had wrapped her in every scrap of fabric they owned. This cold was different. Unnatural. Almost alive.

A new sound emerged from the silence as she stood, one so faint at first that Mercy thought she might have imagined it.

A singing voice.

It was distant but drawing nearer, floating through Hallowspire's corridors like mist over water. The melody was simple, repetitive, but wrong somehow. The notes didn't progress as they should, didn't resolve where the ear expected. Instead, they circled back on themselves in spirals of sound that made Mercy's skin prickle with gooseflesh.

"Hush now, little flame, don't you cry. Sleep beneath a silent sky. Stars are holes in Heaven's floor. Watch them blink and close the door..."

Mercy found herself moving toward the sound, drawn by a curiosity she couldn't name and couldn't resist. Three steps brought her to the center of the Great Hall, beneath the iron chandelier with its hundred unlit candles.

The singing grew louder, more distinct. It came from the corridor that led toward the chapel wing.

"Mother's gone and won't be back. Follow her down spiral black..."

"Anna?" she called a third time, but even as the name left her lips, she knew Anna wasn't the source of that singing. The voice was higher, younger, and layered with harmonics that no human throat could produce.

"Hands will hold you, soft and tight. Sleep inside the endless night."

The temperature plummeted further. Mercy's breath plumed white and substantial before her face. The dying embers in the hearth sputtered, then flared briefly blue before subsiding into darkness, plunging the Great Hall into near-total blackness. Only the occasional burst of lightning from the windows remained—enough to see shapes and movement, but little else.

The singing stopped.

The silence that followed was absolute, pressing against Mercy's ears like cotton wool. She stood frozen in the center of the hall, heart hammering against her ribs, eyes straining to penetrate the darkness that surrounded her. When she could bear it no longer, she opened her mouth to call out again.

A soft, rhythmic pattering interrupted her. The sound of bare feet on marble, moving with deliberate slowness. It came from the chapel corridor, growing steadily louder—a child's gait, but measured and even, lacking the natural variation of human movement.

Mercy's throat closed around whatever words she'd meant to speak. She retreated a step, then another, until the backs of her thighs pressed against the velvet couch where she'd been sleeping. Her hands clutched Anna's coat with white-knuckled intensity, as if it might somehow shield her from whatever approached.

A small figure emerged from the corridor's mouth, silhouetted against the deeper darkness beyond. It stood motionless for a long moment, a child-sized shadow poised at the threshold between the passage and the hall. Then it moved forward, each step precise and identical to the last, crossing the marble floor with mechanical grace.

As it drew closer, details emerged from the gloom. A girl in a simple dress, its hem ragged and damp. Dark skin that seemed to be one with the shadows. Hair in wild disarray, standing out from her head as if suspended in water. And eyes—eyes that caught the faint gray light from the windows and reflected it back tenfold, luminous as a cat's but fixed and unblinking.

Effie.

But not Effie as Mercy had glimpsed her before. This was Effie transformed, Effie reshaped. Her movements were wrong—too fluid in some places, too rigid in others, as if her joints operated according to different principles than those of normal anatomy. Her head remained perfectly level as she walked, never bobbing with her steps. Her arms hung at her sides, fingers splayed at unnatural angles.

She stopped ten paces from Mercy, close enough that her features became visible in the gloom. Her face was expressionless, a mask of flesh pulled tight over her bone. Her lips were slightly parted, revealing teeth that gleamed too white in the darkness. But it was her eyes that fixed Mercy in place. They were no longer the eyes of a child but ancient things, wells that reflected centuries of patient hunger.

Mercy found her voice, though it emerged as little more than a whisper: "Effie?"

The girl's head tilted sharply to one side, a movement too quick and too far to be natural. The tendons in her neck stood out like cords. When she straightened, her head completed the motion with the same unsettling abruptness.

"They're waiting," Effie said, but the voice that emerged from her throat was not entirely her own. It contained fragments of her natural speech—the high, clear tones of a young girl—but beneath it ran something deeper and older, a bass note that resonated in the floor beneath Mercy's feet. "They've always been waiting."

Mercy pressed herself harder against the couch, as if she could somehow push through it and escape. "Who's waiting, Effie? Where have you been?"

Effie's expression didn't change, but something shifted behind her eyes—a flicker of awareness or recognition quickly submerged beneath the alien presence that controlled her. Her arm rose with the same mechanical precision as her walking, extending toward Mercy with fingers that moved independently of each other, curling and uncurling in sequence.

"Below," she said, and this time her voice was tripled—a child's voice layered over a woman's layered over something that wasn't human at all. "I walked the spiral."

Then she turned with that same unnatural fluidity and began walking back toward the chapel corridor, her bare feet making that same measured pattern on the marble. At the threshold, she paused and looked back, her luminous eyes fixed on Mercy with an expectation that bordered on command.

"Come," she said, and the word echoed through the Great Hall as if spoken by a multitude rather than a single child. "It's time."

Mercy hesitated at the edge of the Great Hall, watching Effie's small form recede into the darkness of the corridor. Every instinct screamed at her to run, to flee in the opposite direction, to find a way out of Hallowspire, to escape the unnatural child and whatever waited in the depths below.

But where would she go? Anna was missing. Micah and Juba were gone. Outside, the island was a maze of cliffs and caves with a storm approaching and the tide risen to claim the shores. And something in Effie's tripled voice tugged at her, a compulsion that wrapped invisible fingers around her will and pulled gently but insistently forward.

"Wait," Mercy called, her own voice thin and frightened. She clutched Anna's coat tighter around her shoulders and stepped into the corridor. The marble was ice beneath her feet, sending shivers up her legs with each step.

Effie didn't slow or acknowledge her call. She moved with that same mechanical precision, each footfall identical to the last, her head perfectly level, never turning to see if Mercy followed. The darkness swallowed her, leaving only a faint outline of her slim silhouette against the deeper shadows beyond.

Mercy hurried after her, heart hammering in her chest. The corridor stretched before her, longer than she remembered from their earlier exploration. The walls seemed farther apart, the ceiling higher, the distance to the first junction impossibly extended. She blinked, wondering if her eyes were playing tricks in the dim light, but the distortion remained. Hallowspire was reshaping itself around them.

"Effie," she tried again, her voice sounding strange in the stretched acoustics of the passage. "Effie, what happened to you?"

The child gave no sign of hearing. She glided forward, her movements fluid yet wrong, like a marionette controlled by an unpracticed hand. Where the corridor branched, she turned left without hesitation, though Mercy was certain that passage had led to the dining hall when they'd explored earlier. Now it sloped downward at a gentle angle, the wood-paneled walls giving way to dressed stone that glistened with moisture.

Mercy's breath clouded before her face in thick white plumes. The coat that had seemed so substantial in the Great Hall now felt thin as paper, offering little protection against the preternatural chill. Her fingers and toes had begun to ache, the cold seeping into her bones like poison.

They passed a door Mercy didn't recognize. It was narrow and arched, its wood black with age. A keyhole shaped like a spiral was located where the knob should have been. The door hadn't been there before; she was certain of it. As they passed, she thought she heard something behind it—a soft scratching, like fingernails on wood, and beneath that, a whisper so faint she couldn't make out the words.

Effie maintained her pace, her bare feet making no sound on the stone floor. The distance between them grew as Mercy slowed, disoriented by the architectural impossibilities surrounding her. She found herself counting her steps, trying to maintain some sense of distance and direction, but the numbers slipped away as soon as she thought them, replaced by the sensation of moving through thick syrup, each step requiring more effort than the last.

"Wait," she called again. "Effie, please, I can't—"

Effie paused, her head swiveling dreadfully slow until she faced Mercy. Her luminous eyes fixed on the older girl's face, unblinking.

"This way," she said, her tripled voice bouncing from the vaulted ceiling and returning as a choir of whispers. "We're almost there."

She turned and walked toward an archway on the far side of the chamber. Beyond lay darkness so complete it seemed solid, a wall of black that swallowed what little moonlight struggled through the windows.

Effie stepped through and disappeared.

Mercy followed, her legs moving against her will, drawn by the same invisible compulsion that had pulled her from the Great Hall. The darkness closed around her like cold water, pressing against her skin, filling her lungs with each panicked breath. For a terrible moment, she was blind and lost, surrounded by nothing but void.

Then light returned—sickly, greenish light that cast more shadows than it dispelled. Mercy found herself in a familiar corridor, its walls lined with niches holding relics too terrible to examine closely. The air smelled of cindered incense and burned bone. The Chapel of the Crucible lay ahead, its entrance marked by that bent-iron arch coiled with carvings of tongueless figures.

Effie stood in the chapel's doorway, waiting.

This, at least, was real; a place they had actually visited before. Mercy recognized the downward-sloping vault of the ceiling, the colored panes of the windows, the midnight floor veined with crimson marble. But changes had occurred since their last visit. The candles in the twisted iron sconces now burned with black flames that cast no light, yet somehow deepened the shadows. Fresh blood, steaming in the cold air, filled the basin atop the altar, not congealed wax. The empty alcove in the rear wall, where the chained mirror hung, was no longer empty. Or rather, the emptiness within it had taken form, a darkness denser than the surrounding gloom, shaped vaguely like a robed figure with no face.

Effie moved to the altar, her small hand trailing along its edge, leaving no mark in the dust that should have accumulated there. She circled it once, twice, a third time, each circuit tighter than the last, spiraling inward until the secret door groaned open, revealing the spiral staircase that wound downward into the blue-lit darkness of the vault beneath the chapel where they had found the iron door that refused to open.

Effie descended, her feet finding the steps with perfect precision despite the near-darkness. She glanced back once, her luminous eyes fixing Mercy in place.

"He said I'm the quietest one of all," she said, that tripled voice reverberating in the chapel's perfect acoustics. "That I'll sing the door open so he can come home."

"Effie, no—listen to me, you don't understand—"

"They said if I bring you back and stand in the middle, I'll get a new name. One that echoes forever."

Mercy's feet moved forward as if pulled by strings. She found herself at the top of the spiral stairs in the chapel, looking down into the blue gloom, where shadows were already engulfing Effie's small form. The cold intensified with each step downward, the air growing thick with dust and the lingering scent of old death.

They reached the vault floor, its polished surface reflecting the blue light from above. Ahead lay the iron door, its surface etched with those interlocked spirals, the silvery alloy in the grooves catching the light with an oily sheen.

The door that had resisted all their attempts to open it now stood wide open.

A sickly blue light spilled from beyond, casting Effie's shadow in elongated, distorted shapes across the floor. Not one shadow but three, each moving slightly out of sync with her actual movements.

Mercy halted at the threshold, her body instinctively recoiling from what lay beyond. Something waited there, something vast and hungry and patient. She could feel its attention turning toward her, a weight pressing against her skin from the inside out, as if her very soul were being crushed in a giant's fist.

Effie turned at the doorway, her small hand rising in

beckoning. For a moment—just a moment—her expression changed, the alien presence behind her eyes retreating to reveal the frightened child beneath. Her lips moved, forming words that might have been "help me" or "run away."

Then the moment passed, and the mask descended once more. Her face smoothed into that same expressionless stare, her eyes regaining their unnatural luminescence. When she spoke again, the tripled voice had returned, deeper and more commanding than before.

"They're waiting," she said, the words echoing from the iron door and returning distorted, as if spoken through water. "All of them. Waiting for so long."

Chapter 27

The door opened without sound, swinging inward on hinges that should have shrieked with rust but moved as if freshly oiled. Cold air rushed past Anna, carrying the unmistakable scent of seawater and something older—the reek of centuries-old bones washed by endless tides. She stepped through the doorway, the soul-stripped spirits flowing around her like water around a stone, their translucent forms illuminating the vast circular chamber beyond.

An ancient cistern unfolded before her. A perfect circle carved directly into the island's bedrock, its ceiling was a vaulted dome supported by pillars shaped like inverted ribs. The walls curved upward in smooth arcs, glistening with salt deposits that had formed their own organic patterns over decades of exposure to sea-mist. A wide basin filled with dark water lay in the center of the chamber, reflecting the ghostly light of the Quiet Ones in rippling patterns.

Anna crept forward, her boots making no sound on the stone floor. The chamber breathed around her, air currents swirling in subtle spirals that stirred her hair and cooled the sweat on her brow. The architecture felt ancient, older perhaps than Hallowspire itself. Thorne hadn't built this place; he had discovered it, recognized its power, and bent it to his purpose.

As the soul-stripped spirits entered the chamber, something extraordinary happened. The water in the central basin began to recede—not draining away through some hidden outlet, but pulling back as if drawn by an invisible tide, defying gravity and natural law. The liquid contracted toward the center, then continued to withdraw, revealing the basin's contents inch by inch with the deliberate slowness of a ritual unveiling.

Bones emerged from the retreating water. Hundreds of them arranged in precise geometric patterns across the basin floor. Not scattered or piled as in a common ossuary, but placed with mathematical precision to form interlocking spirals radiating from the basin's center. Femurs and tibias formed the spiral's primary arms, while smaller bones— fingers, toes, vertebrae—filled the spaces between with secondary patterns.

The bones were not the yellowed ivory of normal remains. As the last of the water pulled away, leaving them dry in the cold air, they started to emit a faint bioluminescent glow—a blue-green phosphorescence that pulsed in a slow, steady rhythm, as if the collective remains shared a single phantom heartbeat. The light grew stronger as Anna watched, casting eerie shadows that climbed the chamber walls and danced across the vaulted ceiling.

Along the basin's circumference, the rib-shaped pillars bore the now-familiar spiral sigils, etched deep into the stone and inlaid with some metallic substance that caught and amplified the bones' ghostly light. These markings flickered with residual power, as if responding to the presence of the soul-stripped spirits who had once been flesh connected to these very bones.

The Quiet Ones moved with sudden unified purpose, taking positions around the basin's edge. They kneeled in perfect synchronicity, translucent hands pressed flat against the stone floor, heads bowed as if in prayer or submission. The woman with the sewn mouth remained standing longest, her hollow eyes fixed on Anna with expectation before she too sank to her knees, completing the circle.

A Tide Ossuary, Rebecca's voice whispered. *This is where he disposed of their remains.*

Anna approached slowly, drawn by a compulsion beyond curiosity or Rebecca's urging. The bones seemed to grow more substantial as she neared them and lowered herself down into the empty cistern. Her hand reached out of its own accord, fingers extending toward the nearest configuration of bones.

"What happened here?" she whispered, though she wasn't sure if she spoke to Rebecca, the spirits, or the chamber itself.

Her fingertips made contact with the cold bone.

The world fractured.

Anna's consciousness split like light through a prism. The chamber around her remained visible but transparent, overlaid with another reality—memories pressed into the stone by extreme suffering, preserved by whatever power filled this place. Through this double-vision, she saw the ossuary as it had been decades earlier, the basin full not with water but with corpses arranged in the same pattern their bones would later form.

At the center of it all stood Thorne, tall and severe in a high-collared coat, his eyes reflecting the lantern light like polished onyx. In his right hand he held a curved blade of unusual design, its edge catching the light with an oily sheen. His left hand gripped the arm of a young girl. She was no more than twelve, with dark skin and eyes wide with terror.

The vision focused on this girl, as if the memory had originated with her. Anna felt herself drawn into a closer connection with this spectral remembrance, experiencing flashes of sensation and emotion that belonged to the child. Cold stone against bare feet. The bite of Thorne's fingers on thin arms. The smell of chalk and blood and the sea.

The girl's voice spoke directly into Anna's mind, not as words but as pure compressed meaning: *"He chose me to anchor the Gate. Said I was perfect—born during an eclipse, with the right measurements between heart and spine. Said I would be remembered as the keystone that opened the way through the Red Silence to the Inmost Dark. There were things waiting for him on the other side, he said. Things he wanted to welcome. But I think they were monsters."*

The vision shifted, showing Thorne placing the girl on the spiral altar in the chapel, binding her wrists and ankles with silver wire. The other twelve victims watched in silent horror, unable to move or speak, their souls already partially stripped through earlier rituals.

"But I failed," the girl's voice continued, her sorrow still raw across the decades. *"My soul wouldn't separate cleanly. The Gate opened, but not enough. He was so angry."*

The memory blurred with the girl's terror, fragments of what followed coming in disjointed flashes: Thorne's face contorted with rage. The knife descending. Blood flowing along the spiral groove. The girl's body convulsing as something was torn from it—not her life, but something deeper.

"He kept trying," the voice whispered. *"So many children after me. Always looking for the perfect vessel. The one who could hold the door open without breaking."*

The vision clarified again, showing Thorne at the altar once more, this time alone, carving names into the stone with methodical precision. Anna's perspective shifted, allowing her to see the names as if standing over Thorne's shoulder. Most had been scratched out, a line drawn through each failed attempt. But at the bottom, carved more recently and left intact, was a name that stopped Anna's breath in her throat:

Euphemia.

The girl's voice returned, fainter now, as if speaking from an increasing distance: *"He knew the bloodlines that could serve. Marked them through generations. The ones with the right kind of souls. Effie was chosen before she ever drew breath, the path laid out before her family ever fled their masters. The island has been calling to her since she was born. It was always meant to be Effie."*

The vision fractured, reality reasserting itself with jarring suddenness. Anna stumbled backward in the basin, her hand burning as if she'd pressed it against hot metal. Her lungs heaved, desperate for air that didn't taste of decades-old terror and despair.

The soul-stripped spirits remained in their circle, but their forms were fading, becoming more transparent with each passing second. The woman with the sewn mouth rose to her feet, her hollow eyes fixed on Anna with what might have been accusation or pleading. Her stitched lips worked against their bindings, forming words Anna couldn't hear but somehow understood:

"Save us. End this."

In the basin, the bones' glow dimmed as water began to flow back, seeping from invisible fissures in the rock and pooling around the careful arrangements. The liquid rose around Anna with unnatural speed, covering the femurs and skulls, climbing the spiral patterns until only the highest points remained visible beneath the dark surface.

Within seconds, the basin was full again, the water deceptively still and black as oil, concealing the osseous patterns beneath. The spirits had vanished completely, leaving Anna alone in the water with only the distant sound of droplets falling from the ceiling into the basin—a slow, measured rhythm like a heartbeat, or a countdown.

Rebecca's voice, silent during the vision, returned with renewed intensity: *Now you understand. If a soul can be stripped, it can also be restored. But it requires an open portal through which to pass—the Nocturne Gate. The girl is the key that will open the Gate fully... and through it, we can bring your mother back.*

Anna stared at the water's black surface, seeing in its reflection not her own face but Rebecca's—eyes gleaming with triumphant malice, lips curved in a smile that promised salvation at an unthinkable price.

Chapter 28

Mercy stepped through the iron doorway, passing beyond the threshold that had previously denied them entry. The air changed immediately—heavier, charged with something that tasted like metal and felt like static against her skin. Her ears popped as if she'd descended far beneath the earth, though the doorway had led straight ahead rather than down.

The Sanctum of Sundering unfolded before her, so vast that its dimensions seemed to defy the physical constraints of the island itself. This was no mere chamber carved from rock. This was a wound in reality, a space that existed partially outside the natural world.

The cavern was a perfect circle, its walls rising in smooth basalt curves to a vaulted dome of polished obsidian. That dome—black as the space between stars—was split by a clean fracture that ran from one side to the other, revealing not the expected stone or earth beyond, but an absolute void. The crack seemed to leak darkness rather than admit it, tendrils of pure black seeping downward like smoke underwater, dissolving before they reached the chamber floor.

Glyphs covered every surface: walls, floor, even the curved ceiling. Not carved, but pressed into the stone as if the basalt had once been soft as clay. They weren't the Latin or corrupted Enochian from Thorne's grimoire. These were older, their shapes suggesting meanings that human minds weren't meant to grasp. They pulsed with a sickly blue-green light that waxed and waned in a rhythm that matched nothing in nature—not heartbeat nor breath nor tide, but something more fundamental, as if reality itself were contracting around them.

The chamber floor spiraled downward like a giant limestone ammonite, each level a few inches lower than the last, creating a gradually descending path toward the center. And at that center...

Mercy's breath caught in her throat.

The Nocturne Gate was not what she had expected. There was no elaborate door or portal, no physical barrier to unlock or breach. Instead, there was simply nothingness—a perfectly circular pit, perhaps twenty feet across, that seemed to have no bottom. The darkness within wasn't merely the absence of light. It was something active and alive, a viscous pool of void that rippled and shifted like the surface of a black sea. As she watched, the darkness breathed, expanding slightly outward, then contracting inward, a slow, patient rhythm that had continued for centuries.

The edges of the pit were carved with the same spiral pattern they'd seen throughout Hallowspire, though here it was more precise, more perfect, as if this were the original from which all others had been copied. The spiral wasn't merely decorative; it formed a channel that wound from the outermost edge of the chamber floor all the way to the pit's rim, deepening as it approached the center. The channel glistened with residue. Not water, but something thicker that caught the pulsing light with an oily sheen.

Arranged in a perfect circle around the spiral's widest circumference were thirteen bodies—or what remained of them. They weren't skeletons, though they might have been more mercifully received if they were. Instead, they were desiccated corpses preserved in mounds of crystalline salt, each impaled through the center by an iron spike that emerged from their chests like malformed wings. Their skin was stretched tight over their bones, blackened and hardened like leather left too long in the sun. Their faces—God, their faces—were frozen in expressions of such perfect agony that Mercy felt her own muscles contort in sympathy.

Most horrifying was the evidence that these weren't ancient remains. The clothing still clung to their withered frames: simple cotton dresses, work-shirts with bone buttons, a child's knitted cap still pulled over a tiny, shrunken head. These were Thorne's victims, the thirteen souls he had stripped to anchor his gate, preserved not by accident but by design, their physical forms locked in the moment of their severance and denied even the mercy of decay.

Effie moved to the edge of the outermost spiral, her small form dwarfed by the chamber's immensity. She stood with her back to Mercy, facing the pit, her posture unnaturally straight. The blue-green light from the glyphs caught in her wild hair, transforming the dark curls into a halo of writhing shadows.

The air around Effie began to thicken, condensing into

shapes that at first seemed like mist or smoke. But as they solidified, horror bloomed anew in Mercy's chest. These were human figures, but wrong in every detail. They emerged from between the corpses, from cracks in the stone, from the very air itself.

The Thirteen. Quiet Ones no longer merely glimpsed from the corner of the eye but fully manifested.

They were translucent but grotesquely defined. Tattered remnants of clothing draped their emaciated frames, their skin ashen and stretched thin over their bones. Their faces were the worst: eyeless sockets weeping black, mouths gaping in permanent screams, though no sound emerged. They moved with jerky, uncoordinated motions, as if their limbs were being controlled by something that had never inhabited a human body.

One by one, they approached Effie. Their transparent hands reached for her, passing through her clothing, her flesh, to something deeper within. The girl didn't resist or cry out. Her body trembled but remained upright as the Thirteen surrounded her, their spectral figures forming a circle that mirrored the arrangement of their physical remains around the chamber.

"The Keystone returns," they intoned without tongues, their voices a chorus of wet, rotted music. *"The Final Anchor."*

Their hollow voices layered and multiplied, bouncing from the vaulted ceiling and returning as a hundred echoes, a thousand, until the chamber filled with their proclamation. The temperature plummeted further, frost forming along the spiral channel, creeping toward the pit at the center.

"The Wound will open," they continued, their synchronous

movement becoming more fluid, more purposeful. *"The Inmost Dark will dream through."*

They lifted Effie—not with physical strength, but with some force that made her small body rise several inches from the floor, her bare toes dangling just above the stone. Together, they carried her forward, floating her above the spiral path, moving inexorably toward the breathing darkness at the center.

Mercy wanted to scream, to run forward, to grab Effie and flee. But her body refused to obey. She could only watch, frozen in place, as the procession advanced toward the pit. The glyphs pulsed faster now, their light intensifying with each step the Thirteen took. The chamber itself seemed to contract around them, the vast space somehow focusing its attention on the small child floating toward the void.

When they reached the innermost spiral, mere feet from the pit's edge, they lowered Effie gently to the ground. Her feet touched the stone, and the moment they did, the entire chamber shuddered. A low, grinding sound rose from deep below—not mechanical but organic, like the groan of a leviathan stirring from ancient sleep.

Effie spoke, not in her own voice, not in the tripled voice from before, but in harmonics that no human throat should produce. The sounds created visible ripples in the air, concentric rings that expanded outward from her body and disappeared into the walls. Her hands rose, fingers tracing shapes in the air that left glowing trails behind them—sigils that matched those on the chamber walls but burned brighter.

The spiral beneath her feet began to turn—not the physical

stone, but something layered over it, a pattern of energy that rotated slowly counterclockwise. The pit at the center responded, the viscous darkness swirling in the opposite direction, creating a visual tension that made Mercy's eyes water and her head pound.

Effie's next words came clearer, though still layered with those impossible harmonics: "The thirteenth hour approaches. The Red Silence parts. That which waits beyond shall pass through me."

The air in the chamber grew thick and metallic, pressing against Mercy's skin with increasing weight. Each breath tasted of copper and ash, scorching her lungs and throat. Her stomach heaved, bile rising as her body rebelled against the wrongness permeating the sanctum. The pressure built behind her eyes until she thought they might burst from their sockets.

In the pit, something moved. A deeper darkness within the void shifted with deliberate purpose. The breathing rhythm accelerated, becoming shallow and eager. The blackness seemed to reach upward, stretching toward Effie's trembling form at the edge of the pit.

Mercy's paralysis broke. Terror propelled her backward, away from the scene unfolding before her. Her bare feet tangled beneath her, and she stumbled, nearly falling. The motion seemed to draw the attention of the Thirteen. Their eyeless faces turned toward her in perfect synchronicity, their sewn mouths working against their bindings.

She didn't wait to see more.

She turned and fled, her feet slapping against the stone floor of the vault, then the steps leading up to the chapel.

Behind her, Effie's voice rose in those terrible harmonics, the sounds chasing Mercy like physical things, clawing at her back as she ran.

The chapel blurred past—the black-flamed candles, the blood-filled basin, the faceless darkness in the alcove. Mercy didn't slow, didn't look back. Her mind had narrowed to a single thought, a single name: Anna.

Anna would know what to do, how to stop this, how to save Effie from whatever was rising from that bottomless pit.

Corridors stretched before her, twisting and turning in ways that defied her memory of Hallowspire's layout. Doors appeared and disappeared, passages branched where they should have continued straight, staircases led up when they should have led down. The mansion was shifting around her, trying to confuse her path, to lead her back toward the sanctum.

But Mercy had spent her life navigating the treacherous currents of fear and disorientation. She had fled through winter woods and hidden in root cellars while men with torches searched for the "witch-child."

She knew how to run, how to survive.

She fixed an image of Anna in her mind: tall and severe, dark hair falling around a face that promised both danger and protection—and she let that guide her. Not a direction, not a specific path, but a connection, a tether to the one person in Hallowspire who might stand a chance against what was awakening below.

"Anna!" she screamed as she ran, her voice bouncing off the shifting walls and returning distorted. "Anna, where are you? The Gate is opening! Anna!"

Chapter 29

Lightning crackled across the night sky, illuminating Hallowspire in stark relief against the churning darkness. Juba stood at the edge of the overgrown garden, rain plastering her clothes to her skin, her eyes fixed on the mansion's western wing where a strange blue light pulsed behind the leaded windows. Something was happening inside those walls, something that made the air taste like metal and fear. Beside her, Micah shivered from the cold. His face was a mask of determination and dread, the rain streaking down his cheeks like the tears he refused to shed.

"We shouldn't have left her," he whispered, his voice nearly lost beneath the storm's growl. "I shouldn't have—"

"Hush now," Juba cut him off. She reached into the folds of her shawl, fingers closing around the knife she kept hidden there. "What's done is done. We find Effie and we go—all three of us."

The servant's entrance lay half-hidden behind a tangle of briar roses, their thorns clawing at Juba's skirts as she forced her way through. The door itself was weathered oak banded with iron, swollen from decades of rain and salt. It should have been locked, perhaps even sealed by whatever force had claimed Hallowspire as its own. Instead, it swung inward at Juba's touch, hinges silent despite their apparent age and rust.

The mansion was expecting them.

They slipped inside, leaving the fury of the storm for a different kind of darkness. The narrow corridor stretched before them, its walls close enough that Juba could touch both sides with outstretched hands. The air hung thick and stale, carrying scents of mildew and something deeper—a pungent smell that reminded her of freshly turned earth or newly exposed bone.

Micah pressed close to his mother's side, his eyes darting to the shadows that pooled in corners and beneath the few pieces of abandoned furniture. These shadows moved wrong—not with the natural shifting of light and darkness, but with deliberate, sentient purpose. They stretched toward the intruders' feet like fingers, then retracted when met with Juba's unflinching gaze.

"They're watching," Micah whispered, his hand finding Juba's and squeezing tight.

"Let them watch," she replied, steel in her voice. "They took what's mine. I aim to take it back."

They moved deeper into Hallowspire's forgotten passages, following corridors that servants had once used to remain invisible to their master—and whatever he was doing.

From somewhere above came a sound. A high, sustained note that might have been singing or screaming. It lingered just at the edge of hearing, wavering between pitches that human vocal cords should not produce.

Juba's spine stiffened, recognition flashing across her features. "Effie," she breathed, her voice catching on the name.

"That's not Effie," Micah protested, though uncertainty threaded through his words. "That don't sound like her at all."

"It's her," Juba insisted, already moving toward a narrow staircase at the corridor's end. "I'd know my child's voice in heaven or hell."

The stairs led upward, each tread groaning beneath their weight despite their careful steps. As they climbed, the mansion's architecture shifted from the utilitarian plainness of the servant's quarters to the grand excess of its public spaces. They emerged into a high-ceilinged hallway lined with portraits in heavy gilt frames. The painted faces followed their progress, eyes swiveling in pigment that should have faded years ago.

The distant singing grew louder, drawing their attention upward. It echoed through Hallowspire's vaulted spaces, bouncing from walls and ceilings until it seemed to come from everywhere at once. The notes had shifted, organizing themselves into a pattern that made Juba's teeth ache and her vision blur. It was Effie's voice, but layered with others— older voices, hungrier ones.

They moved faster now, the air growing colder with each step, frost forming on the floor in delicate whorls that mimicked the spiral patterns carved throughout the mansion. Their breath clouded before their faces as they climbed the grand staircase, following the sound that called to them with maternal urgency.

The library doors stood open, an invitation or a trap. Beyond stretched the cavernous three-story chamber with its spiral staircases and constellation-painted dome. The air smelled of leather, dust, and something else—a subtle sweetness that Juba recognized from her mother's teachings. It was the scent of spirit-breach, of the Veil growing thin.

"The singing's coming from up there," Micah pointed to the library's upper gallery, where shadows seemed to concentrate despite the occasional lightning flash through the windows.

They climbed the wrought-iron spiral staircase to the upper gallery. It formed a complete circuit around the library's open center, with alcoves and reading nooks set at regular intervals. In one such alcove, partially hidden behind a hanging tapestry, something gleamed in the darkness. A small brass handle was set into what appeared to be solid paneling.

Juba approached cautiously, knife held ready in her right hand. The brass handle was shaped like a serpent devouring its own tail, the metal warm beneath her fingers despite the pervasive chill. When she turned it, a section of the wall swung inward with the soft sigh of well-oiled hinges, revealing a narrow spiral staircase that twisted upward into darkness.

The singing stopped abruptly, leaving a silence so complete it pressed against their eardrums like physical weight.

The stairwell breathed, a current of air flowing downward that carried the scents of burned herbs, dried blood, and older, stranger things.

With it came whispers. Dozens of them, layered over each other in a susurrus of pleading and warning.

"Don't go up," Micah begged, his fingers digging into Juba's arm. "Please, Mama. Whatever's up there... it's been waiting for us."

Juba hesitated, torn between maternal instinct and the crawling dread that worked its way up her spine. The knife in her hand suddenly seemed inadequate against what waited in the darkness above. But resolve quickly crystallized in her eyes. She gently removed Micah's hand from her arm and pressed a small stone into his palm. It was river-smooth and black as pitch, its surface etched with symbols older than the country they stood in.

"If I don't come back, you run," she instructed. "You get off this island however you can."

"I'm coming with you," Micah said, straightening his thin shoulders.

Juba nodded once, pride mingling with terror in her gaze. "Stay behind me. And if I tell you to run, you run. No arguing."

Together they began the ascent, the spiral staircase winding ever upward through stone that grew colder with each step. The air thickened, pressing against their skin like hands trying to hold them back. Whispers swirled around them, some in languages long dead, others in voices Juba recognized from the plantation—people she'd known, people who had died in chains.

At the top of the stairs, a door stood ajar, spilling sickly blue-green light onto the topmost steps. The reek of suffering hit them like a physical blow; the lingering residue of pain so intense it had seeped into the very stones. Micah gagged, pressing his sleeve against his mouth and nose. Juba's face hardened, the knife in her hand steady despite the fear that clawed at her chest.

"Effie?" she called, her voice stronger than she felt.

Silence answered.

The door swung wider, revealing the chamber beyond in all its terrible splendor. The Mourning Tower was where Thorne had conducted his darkest experiments, where he'd learned to strip souls from flesh and bind them to his terrible purpose.

Micah froze at the threshold, his body rigid with instinctive terror. "Don't," he whispered, the word barely audible. "Mama, don't go in there."

But Juba had already stepped across.

Thorne's laboratory sprawled before them in grotesque magnificence, a cathedral to pain disguised as scientific inquiry. Tall windows of leaded glass lined the eastern wall, their panes blackened with years of smoke from unspeakable burnings. The blue-green light that had beckoned them upward emanated not from candles or lamps, but from sigils etched into the stone floor. The same spiral pattern that appeared throughout Hallowspire was rendered here with a precision that made the eye ache to follow its curves.

"Effie?" Juba called again. Her voice fell dead against the stone walls, absorbed by the heavy tapestries that hung between the bookshelves. The knife in her hand felt too small to ward off the horror that permeated every inch of this place.

The air tasted of copper and ash, layered with the cloying sweetness of rot that no amount of incense or saltwater cleansing had managed to purge. Suspended from the ceiling on three copper chains hung the evidence of Thorne's methodical madness: aprons of thick leather, once white, perhaps, now stained the rusty brown of old blood. They hung at precise intervals, turning slowly in air currents that didn't exist. Below them, a drain sat in the center of the stone floor, its grate clogged with dark sediment that even decades of abandonment hadn't fully dried. The metal of the grate had been worked into yet another spiral, this one so tight it appeared almost as a solid circle until examined closely.

Juba approached it cautiously, her boots silent on the stone. She kneeled, bringing her face closer to the drain, and inhaled sharply through her nose—a practice her mother had taught her for identifying spirits and traces of the dead. What rose from that drain made her recoil instantly. Not just the expected scents of old blood and human remains, but something deeper and more wrong—the smell of souls rendered down like tallow, of essence extracted by force.

"They died screaming," she whispered, her voice tight with horror and rage. "Not just their bodies. Their spirits. He unmade them." Her fingers traced a protective sign in the air above the drain, a gesture so automatic she might not have realized she was doing it.

Micah remained at the threshold, one hand braced against the doorframe, his body leaning forward as if caught between the pull of his mother and the equally powerful urge to flee. His eyes darted from corner to corner, taking in the tools of Thorne's trade with the rapid assessment of a child who had learned early to identify threats.

The laboratory was divided into clear work areas, each dedicated to a different aspect of Thorne's research. To the left stood tables of alchemical apparatus: glass retorts with curved necks, crucibles blackened from intense heat, cracked beakers containing residue that still glistened wetly despite the years. Labels in precise handwriting identified mixtures with names like "Essence of Separation" and "Limbic Solvent #7." A cabinet nearby held rows of bell jars, each containing preserved organs suspended in a fluid that had long since turned cloudy. The organs themselves had shifted over time, growing strange protrusions or extra chambers that matched no known anatomy.

A massive oak writing desk dominated the center of the room, covered with scrolls and leather-bound journals. A quill sat in an inkpot that appeared to contain not ink but something thicker, darker—a fluid that refused to dry despite the decades. Scattered across the desk were diagrams of human figures with the skin peeled away to reveal not just muscles and organs, but glowing networks of lines that corresponded to no known system in the body. Not veins or nerves, but something else, something Thorne had seen that others could not.

Juba moved to the desk, her fingers hovering above but not touching the diagrams. "Soul maps," she murmured. "My grandmother spoke of such things. The pathways spirit takes through flesh." Her face hardened. "But these are wrong. Corrupted."

The eastern alcove contained what must have been Thorne's personal ritual space. A circle inscribed the floor, its edge inlaid with silver wire that still gleamed despite the dust. Inside the circle stood a pedestal of polished obsidian, and atop it sat an urn of the same material, its surface etched with minute spirals that seemed to shift position when viewed from different angles. A small brass plaque on its base read:

C. THORNE, 1761–1773.

"His sister," Micah said, finally stepping fully into the tower room. The door swung shut behind him with a soft click that made him flinch. "The reason he started all of this."

Juba's head snapped toward her son, eyes widening. "You understand what he did here?"

Micah nodded, his boyish face solemn. "The soul-stripping. Taking people apart until they weren't people anymore." He moved closer to his mother, carefully avoiding the drain in the floor. "The Quiet Ones showed me everything. Said it was so I'd understand what would happen if I didn't help them."

A soft humming emanated from the urn, a single note sustained just at the edge of hearing. The temperature in the tower dropped several degrees, frost forming along the edges of the windows. The urn's vibration intensified, rattling slightly against the pedestal's surface.

Across the room, something drew Micah to another object: a tall, oval mirror, currently veiled with a yellowed muslin cloth. The cloth rippled slightly, though no window was open, and no draft disturbed the tower's stale air. It moved as if something behind it was breathing, pressing gently against the fabric in a rhythm that matched the expansion and contraction of the tower walls.

"Don't touch that," Juba warned, but Micah was already reaching for the cloth's edge, his fingers grasping the yellowed fabric.

"I can see through it," he whispered, his voice oddly distant. "Without moving it. I can see... rooms. So many rooms. Not just in the house. Rooms that can't exist. Rooms that—" He broke off, his hand dropping away from the cloth as if burned. "Rooms where people are kept. Where they're still alive, even though they should be dead. Where they're still screaming."

The muslin continued to ripple, more forcefully now, as if whatever lay behind it had been roused by Micah's attention. Frost formed in delicate fractal patterns along the edges of the mirror, each crystalline branch another iteration of the spiral that dominated Hallowspire's design.

Juba moved swiftly to her son's side, pulling him away from the mirror. "Don't look at it!" she commanded, though her own eyes were drawn to the veiled glass. "That's how they trap you. Get you looking at what ain't meant to be seen."

The humming from the urn intensified, joined now by a similar tone from the mirror. The sounds intertwined, forming harmonies that set their teeth on edge. The frost spread from the mirror's edges, crawling across the floor toward them like living fingers reaching for their ankles.

Throughout the tower, candles that had been unlit suddenly blazed into life, their flames unnaturally tall and blue-white. They burned in perfect synchronicity, flaring higher, then dimming in a pattern that matched the humming from the urn and mirror. The laboratory apparatus began to vibrate, glass tinkling against glass, metal rattling against wood. The bloodstained aprons hanging from the ceiling started to sway, though no breeze stirred the air.

"We need to go," Juba said, backing toward the door with Micah's hand clutched tightly in hers. "Now."

But the door that had clicked shut behind them was no longer there—only smooth stone wall where an exit had been moments before. The tower had sealed them in, trapping them amid the instruments of Thorne's terrible science.

Their breath clouded before their faces in thick white plumes as the temperature plummeted further. The candles flared one final time, then extinguished simultaneously, plunging the tower into darkness, broken only by the faint glow of the sigils etched into the floor and the orange light that pulsed within the urn.

In that near-darkness, the muslin veil finally fell from the mirror, drifting to the floor with unnatural slowness. The polished surface beneath didn't reflect the room or its occupants. Instead, it showed a corridor stretching into infinite darkness, lined with doors behind which shapes moved with jerky, marionette precision. At the corridor's distant end, a figure approached—tall and thin, its movements too fluid to be entirely human.

"He's coming," Micah whispered, pressing against his mother's side. "He's been waiting for us all along."

Chapter 30

Anna's fingers clutched the edge of the stone basin, her body emerging from the submerged ossuary like a woman clawing her way from a grave. Saltwater dripped from her clothing, her hair hung in heavy ropes against her pale face, and her eyes—her eyes had seen things no living person was meant to witness. The cold certainty of what waited beneath Hallowspire had settled in her bones, a knowledge as terrible as it was unavoidable. She hauled herself up, boots scraping against ancient stone, just as the door to the chamber burst open with a sound like splintering bone.

Mercy stood framed in the doorway, her white hair wild around her face, her mismatched eyes wide with terror. She wore Anna's coat wrapped tight around her thin frame. The sleeves dangled past her fingertips, and the hem dragged on the floor. Her feet were filthy, leaving smeared prints on the stone. For a heartbeat, the two young women stared at each other across the chamber, mutual shock freezing them in place.

"Anna!" Mercy's voice broke the stillness, a sound so raw

with relief it bordered on pain. She lurched forward, her movements unsteady with exhaustion. "I thought… I couldn't find—" Words failed her as she stumbled toward Anna, her pale face contorted with fresh panic overlaying the momentary relief.

Anna stepped away from the basin, closing the distance between them. Her boots left wet impressions on the stone, the salt water seeping from her clothing marking her path like a sea creature emerging onto land. Something flashed behind her eyes as her awareness returned to the present, pushing back whatever cold calculation had settled there during her time in the ossuary.

"Effie," Mercy gasped as she reached her, doubling over to catch her breath. Her thin shoulders heaved beneath the coat, her entire body trembling. "They have Effie!"

Anna's hands clamped onto Mercy's shoulders, steadying the girl with a grip that betrayed her own tension. "Slow down," she commanded, though there was nothing slow in the sharp intensity of her gaze. "What about Effie? Where?"

"The iron door," Mercy managed between ragged breaths. Her fingers clutched at Anna's sodden sleeve, nails digging into the damp fabric. "It was open. They were waiting. The Quiet Ones… so many of them…"

"The Nocturne Gate," Anna's voice sharpened, focusing Mercy's scattered thoughts. "You found it."

Mercy nodded frantically, her white hair falling across her face. "A pit at the center of a spiral chamber. So dark—not just dark but—but wrong." She swallowed, struggling to find words for what she'd witnessed. "The floor spirals down toward it. And there were bodies—thirteen of them—

preserved in salt, arranged in a circle."

Anna's face hardened as Mercy's description confirmed the vision she'd seen in the ossuary. Her fingers tightened on the girl's shoulders, not to comfort her but to extract information with desperate efficiency. "And Effie? What were they doing with Effie?"

"They lifted her." Mercy's words tumbled out faster, propelled by the memory's fresh horror. "Not with hands. With something else. She floated. They called her the *Keystone* and the *Final Anchor*. They were moving her toward the center, toward the pit." Her voice cracked. "They're using her, Anna. Using her to open the Gate completely."

Anna's expression shifted as understanding dawned, confusion giving way to recognition, then blooming into full horror. The color drained from her face, leaving her lips bloodless, her eyes stark against her pallor. She had seen the ritual diagrams in the *Tenebric Sequence*, had felt the memories of the first child sacrificed at the spiral's center. Now Mercy's account completed the terrible puzzle, slotting the final piece into place with sickening clarity.

"Did you see anything else?" Anna's questions came rapid-fire now, her mind racing ahead to possibilities too terrible to fully contemplate. "Was there anyone else in the chamber? A man—tall, thin, with eyes like mirrors?"

"No one living." Mercy shook her head. "Just the spirits and Effie. But something was moving in the pit, Anna. Something reaching up toward her. And the whole chamber was changing—contracting, focusing on her."

Anna released Mercy's shoulders and stepped back, her mind calculating distances, timing, options. The ossuary had shown her Thorne's original ritual, the failed attempt to open a permanent breach in the Veil. But it had also revealed his contingency—the patient waiting game that had stretched across decades, the careful manipulation of bloodlines and circumstances to produce the perfect vessel.

"How much time do we have?" Anna asked, already moving toward the chamber door. "How far had the ritual progressed when you left?"

"They had just positioned her at the innermost spiral," Mercy said, falling into step beside Anna. "The floor was beginning to turn. Not the stone itself, but something on it, like a pattern of light. And Effie was speaking, but not in her voice. It was… wrong. Impossible."

Anna nodded grimly. "The Harmonic Invocation. Thorne described it in his grimoire. It's the final stage of the opening ritual." She glanced at Mercy, her eyes measuring the girl's exhaustion against the urgency driving them both. "We need to hurry. Once the harmonics align with the spiral's rotation, the barrier between worlds will thin enough for crossing."

"Crossing?" Mercy's voice rose in pitch. "Crossing what?"

"Whatever waits in the Inmost Dark beyond the Veil," Anna replied as she reached the chamber door. "Whatever has been wearing Thorne's face since he disappeared through the Gate."

The corridor outside stretched before them, its dimensions warping subtly as Hallowspire continued its unnatural reshaping. Anna paused, orienting herself in the shifting architecture.

"Show me the way," she said to Mercy. "And quickly. We're running out of time."

The mansion was changing around them, preparing itself for what was to come. Anna could feel it in the wood beneath her fingers, in the stone beneath her feet.

"The bones in the ossuary told a story," Anna said as they hurried through Hallowspire's shifting corridors. Her wet boots left ghostly prints on the wood, each step marking their desperate path through the mansion's labyrinth. "Thorne was building a circuit, a complete loop between different points on the island where the ley lines converge." She glanced at Mercy, who struggled to keep pace. "Whatever's happening with Effie now is the final piece of something Thorne started decades ago."

The corridors stretched and contracted around them, doorways appearing where none had been before, familiar passages suddenly ending in blank walls. Hallowspire was shifting, its architecture responding to the ritual unfolding beneath its foundations. The mansion itself seemed alive with anticipation, the wood creaking not with age but with a terrible awakening.

"I saw ritual marks in the chamber," Mercy added, her breath coming in quick gasps as she hurried alongside Anna. "The same spirals that are carved throughout the mansion, but older—like they were the originals. And they glowed, Anna. Not reflected light, but their own light, pulsing like a heartbeat." Her mismatched eyes darted toward Anna's face, seeking confirmation. "The Quiet Ones moved as if they were part of the pattern, positioning Effie where the spirals converged."

Anna nodded grimly. "The spirals aren't just symbols; they're conduits. I touched one of the bones in the ossuary, and I saw—" She hesitated, the memory still raw in her mind. "I saw Thorne performing the ritual with the first Thirteen. I felt what they felt." Her voice dropped to a whisper. "He was trying to create a permanent breach in the Veil, a gate that would stay open."

They turned a corner, entering a corridor Anna recognized despite the mansion's shifting. This passage led toward the chapel wing. The air grew colder with each step, frost forming on the walls, their breath clouding before their faces. The temperature drop was unnatural, a physical manifestation of the Veil thinning as the ritual progressed.

"The Tenebric Sequence isn't just about stripping souls," Anna explained, her voice tight with urgency. "The soul-stripping was preparation, rendering the Thirteen empty enough to serve as anchors for the Gate. Thorne positioned each victim at a specific point in the spiral, holding open a section of the breach like pins stretching fabric."

Mercy's pace faltered for a moment, her face paling further as understanding dawned. "But the fabric tore back," she said. "That's why they need Effie, why they called her the keystone."

"Yes," Anna said. "The original thirteen weren't enough to hold the Gate open permanently. Thorne disappeared through it, but the breach began to heal itself. What's left of him—or what's wearing his face—has been waiting for the right vessel to complete the circuit."

They reached the narrow staircase that would lead them to the chapel level. Anna took the steps two at a time, her body moving with focused precision despite her exhaustion. Behind her, Mercy struggled to keep up, her feet slapping against the cold stone, Anna's coat hampering her movements with its too-long sleeves.

"The Quiet Ones are positioning Effie at the center of the spiral," Mercy said between labored breaths as they climbed. "If she completes the ritual—"

"The Gate will fully open," Anna finished grimly. "And whatever's been waiting on the other side will have a permanent passage into our world."

They reached the chapel-level landing and paused for a moment while Mercy caught her breath. The corridor stretched before them, ending at the twisted iron arch that marked the Chapel of the Crucible's entrance. Beyond that lay the hidden door to the vault, and beyond that, the iron door to the sanctum—now open, waiting to receive them.

Use the girl instead...

Rebecca's voice slithered into Anna's mind with the intimate familiarity of a parasite that had made itself at home. Her presence expanded, a cold pressure behind Anna's eyes that made the edges of her vision blur with amber.

The albino child is a perfect vessel. If the slave girl is the key, then this child could be the lock. Her soul already walks the border between worlds. Her blood would seal the Gate forever. That is why the Quiet Ones wanted her dead.

Anna physically flinched from the suggestion, her hand rising to her temple as if she could physically push Rebecca's influence away.

One life for many, child. One strange girl who was never meant to survive anyway. A small price for your mother's soul.

Anna's hand dropped to her knife, fingers curling around the hilt with white-knuckled intensity. For one terrible moment, the possibility unfolded before her—so simple, so efficient. The girl was right here, trusting and vulnerable. It would be quick. It would be merciful. It would be—

"No!" The word tore from Anna's throat, startling Mercy, who stood watching her with concern. Anna's hand jerked away from her knife as if burned, her body shuddering as she fought Rebecca's influence. "Get out of my head," she hissed through clenched teeth.

"Anna?" Mercy stepped closer, her pale face tight with worry. "What is it? What's happening?"

Anna drew a shaky breath, forcing Rebecca's presence back into the corners of her consciousness. "Nothing."

Understanding dawned in Mercy's mismatched eyes—one blue, one red, both unnervingly perceptive. "You're thinking about why the Quiet Ones wanted me dead," she said, the words not a question but a statement of fact. "Because of what I am. What I've always been."

Anna didn't deny it. "You might have the qualities to stop the ritual," she admitted. "But that doesn't matter. We're going to save Effie and stop this, not find a different sacrifice."

They stared at each other, a silent understanding passing between them—two young women shaped by darkness but choosing, in this moment, to stand against it. Mercy nodded once, acceptance and determination hardening her delicate features into something stronger.

"We need to hurry," Anna said, turning back toward the chapel corridor. "If that thing inside Thorne leads what's waiting through the Veil..." She didn't finish the thought, the consequences too vast to articulate.

They moved forward again, their pace quickening as they approached the chapel entrance. The twisted iron arch loomed before them, its design suddenly clearer to Mercy's eyes. They weren't random coils of metal, but a precise representation of the spiral path that led to the Nocturne Gate. Thorne designed every part of Hallowspire as preparation, as an invitation.

"How do we stop it?" Mercy asked, her voice steadier now despite the terror that still widened her eyes. "How do we save Effie?"

"I don't know yet," Anna admitted, her mind racing through everything she'd learned from the ossuary and Thorne's writings. "But the ritual requires specific conditions. If we disrupt the spiral pattern, or remove Effie from the center before the breach fully opens…"

"They won't let her go easily," Mercy warned as they passed beneath the iron arch into the chapel proper. The black candles still burned with their lightless flames, the air thick with the scent of burned bone and something older, something that didn't belong in the human world at all.

"No," Anna agreed, her hand returning to her knife with renewed purpose. "But neither will I."

Ahead, the hidden door in the chapel wall stood open, revealing the spiral staircase that led down to the vault, and beyond that, to the Sanctum of Sundering where Effie waited at the center of Thorne's terrible design. Anna and Mercy paused at the threshold, gathering their strength for what lay ahead.

"Ready?" Anna asked, though there was no question of turning back.

Mercy nodded, fear and determination warring on her face. "Ready."

Together, they descended into darkness, toward the thing that breathed and waited below.

Chapter 31

The sigils on the floor of the Mourning Tower pulsed brighter, their blue-green light rising in tendrils that twisted and pulled at the eye and mind alike. The temperature dropped so low that the moisture in the air crystallized, falling as tiny ice shards that shattered against the stone floor.

Behind Juba and Micah, the mirror's surface rippled like disturbed water, the corridor within stretching and contracting as the figure drew ever closer. The tower itself seemed to hold its breath, waiting for what was about to emerge from the spaces between realities, conjured by the unholy ritual unfolding hundreds of feet beneath their feet.

Alistair Gilead Thorne manifested not in the gossamer translucence of the Quiet Ones, but as a wound in reality, a black silhouette framed by curling smoke that flickered like a half-remembered nightmare. He stepped through the mirror as if it were a doorway, the glass parting around his form like viscous liquid before solidifying again. His presence brought a pressure to the air, a weight that pressed against Juba and Micah's lungs, making each breath shallow and painful. The temperature dropped further still, cold enough that the moisture in their eyes threatened to freeze, forcing them to blink rapidly against the pain.

The specter bore only a passing resemblance to the man Thorne had been. His form was tall and thin, his silhouette draped in the tattered remnants of a black frock coat that moved according to currents no living person could perceive. Where his face should have been was a pale oval of translucent flesh stretched too tight across his skull. His eyes were mercury pools that reflected Juba and Micah's terror back at them with subtle distortions, showing not what was, but what could be, if fear claimed them completely.

"The boy who sees clearly," Thorne said, his voice strangely familiar yet otherworldly, each syllable echoing with harmonics that originated from somewhere beyond the room, beyond the house, beyond the world itself. "Micah. The one who knew enough to betray the witch."

Micah stiffened beside his mother, his thin shoulders straightening as if pulled by invisible strings. The name—*his* name—in Thorne's mouth was a violation, a hook that caught in his mind and pulled him half a step forward before Juba's hand on his arm arrested the movement.

"Don't listen," she hissed, her fingers digging into his flesh hard enough to bruise. "Don't look at his eyes."

But Micah was already caught. His gaze locked with the mercurial pools that had fixed upon him with predatory interest. Thorne's form rippled like heat distortion, the edges of his silhouette bleeding into the surrounding darkness and reforming with subtle alterations. One moment he appeared as the gentleman scholar he had been in life, the next as something older and more terrible—a shape with too many angles, limbs that bent in ways flesh should not permit.

"You were right to send them to the tide cave," Thorne continued, his voice intimate now, as if he spoke directly into Micah's mind rather than across the physical space that separated them. "You've seen their lies. The witch and her pale companion. They would take your sister from you. Use her for their own purposes."

Micah trembled, caught between Juba's restraining grip and Thorne's inexorable pull. "I didn't want to hurt them," he whispered, the words scraping his throat like ground glass. "I just wanted Effie back."

"Of course," Thorne's voice softened to velvet, his form solidifying further as he drew on Micah's attention like a lamp drawing sustenance from oil. "Family above all. I understand that necessity better than most." His gaze flicked to the urn containing his sister's remains, then back to Micah. "Let me show you how to protect your family—*truly* protect them. The witch cannot help you. But I can give you what you need."

Thorne extended one hand, the fingers elongated and needle-sharp, tapering to points that could pierce flesh. The air around his hand shimmered with possibility. Visions flickered too fast to fully comprehend but left impressions— Effie safe and whole; escape from the island; a future where Juba and her children never looked over their shoulders again.

Micah's free hand rose, trembling, inches from his body, drawn toward Thorne's impossible offer. His eyes had gone distant, unfocused, his pupils dilated so wide that almost no iris remained. His lips parted, forming words he hadn't yet spoken—acceptance, capitulation, surrender.

"No!" Juba's voice cracked through the tower like a whip, breaking the trance that had claimed her son. She stepped between Micah and Thorne, her back to the specter, forcing her child to look at her instead. From a pouch at her waist, she drew a handful of salt, casting it in a circle around them both with practiced precision. "You don't speak to my boy," she told Thorne without turning to face him. "You don't look at him. You don't breathe his name with that dead mouth of yours."

The temperature plunged again. Frost crept across the floor and walls in jagged patterns that mimicked the spiral sigils etched into the stone. The hanging aprons snapped taut, as if suddenly occupied by invisible bodies. The glass apparatus on the tables began to tremble, producing a high, thin tone that vibrated through bone and tooth.

"You have no power here, woman," Thorne's voice had changed, the scholarly cadence replaced by something ancient and cold, a voice that had never known human kindness or warmth. "This house is mine. This island is mine. And your children—" his gaze flicked to the urn again, a gesture full of terrible significance, "—will be mine. One way or another."

Juba pressed the small stone she'd given Micah earlier against her son's forehead, her lips moving in a whispered Gullah chant. The words were passed down from her grandmother, who had learned them from her grandmother before her, all the way back to ancestors who had been priestesses in a land across the sea.

"The dead don't own nothing," she said, her voice steady

despite the fear clawing at her chest. "Not land, not stone, not flesh." She turned slowly to face Thorne, keeping Micah behind her, the protective circle of salt their only barrier against what stood before them. "And you're not even properly dead, are you? Just stretched thin between here and somewhere worse."

Thorne's form distorted with rage, the edges of his silhouette blurring into smoke that lashed the air like whips. The mercury pools of his eyes expanded, threatening to swallow his entire face in reflective nothingness. When he spoke again, his voice was legion—not one entity but many, layered in a chorus that hurt the ear and mind alike.

"YOU KNOW NOTHING OF WHAT I AM."

The laboratory erupted with poltergeist force. Books flew from shelves, glass shattered against walls, and the chains holding the bloodstained aprons whipped through the air like metal snakes. The stone walls cracked with sounds like gunshots, fissures racing along their surface and converging into spiral patterns. The urn containing Thorne's sister toppled from its pedestal, striking the floor with a sound like a church bell tolling underwater, but didn't break. Instead, it rolled in a perfect spiral pattern toward the center of the room, leaving a trail of orange light in its wake.

Juba's salt circle held against the initial assault, the grains glowing with a pale blue light wherever Thorne's influence tried to cross the boundary. But the physical objects—the flying glass, the whipping chains—were another matter. A shard of a broken jar struck Juba's cheek, opening a thin line that welled with blood. A heavier piece of equipment crashed against the floor just outside their circle, shattering a bottle of amber liquid that spread across the stone in an expanding pool.

The stone in Juba's hand grew warmer, pulsing in time with her heartbeat. She pressed it harder against Micah's forehead, her chanting increasing in volume and urgency. The Gullah words weren't a prayer but a command—a binding, a banishing, a sealing of breaches. With each repetition, Thorne's form grew less substantial, the edges of his silhouette fraying like cloth subjected to too much strain.

"Mother to son, blood to blood," Juba's voice rose above the chaos, steady and implacable. "What's mine stays mine. What's yours stays yours. The line is drawn. The boundary set."

Thorne's rage found a new focus, concentrated now on the woman who dared to challenge him in his own domain. The mercury pools of his eyes fixed on Juba with such hatred that frost formed on her skin where his gaze touched. The air around him darkened further, cold smoke coalescing into tendrils that reached toward the salt circle with predatory intent.

"YOUR CHILDREN WERE MARKED BEFORE BIRTH," the chorus of voices thundered, the sound physically painful to human ears. "THE GATE MUST OPEN. THE RED SILENCE PARTS."

One of the whipping chains struck a candelabra, knocking it into the spreading pool of amber liquid. The substance ignited with a whoosh of blue-white flame, racing across the floor in a blazing spiral that followed the path of the sigils etched into the stone. Fire climbed the walls with unnatural speed, consuming the tapestries and bookshelves, turning ancient texts to ash in seconds. The heat was intense enough to blister paint and crack glass, yet the flames moved with purpose rather than the random hunger of natural fire.

The tower's sealed door reappeared in the wall behind them, blasted open by the force of Thorne's rage, or perhaps by the protective magic Juba had invoked. Beyond lay the spiral staircase, their only route of escape from the inferno that had engulfed the laboratory.

"Run!" Juba shouted, shoving Micah toward the open door. She scooped up a handful of salt, casting it directly at Thorne's form as she backed toward the exit. The crystals passed through his silhouette, but where they touched, his substance hissed and steamed like water on hot iron.

Thorne's scream of fury filled the tower, a sound so fundamentally wrong it seemed to tear at the fabric of reality itself. The mirror cracked from edge to edge, the fracture forming yet another spiral pattern within the glass. Through the crack poured more darkness—not smoke or shadow, but something deeper and more primordial, a substance that had never known light or form.

Juba grabbed Micah's arm and pulled him through the doorway just as a section of the ceiling collapsed, bringing down wooden beams wreathed in blue flame. They stumbled onto the spiral staircase, the heat of the fire at their backs pushing them forward as much as their own desperation to escape.

"The tower's burning," Micah gasped as they descended, the smoke already filling the stairwell despite the fire's unnatural properties. "The whole house will go up."

"Good." Juba's face was a mask of determination, blood

from the cut on her cheek trailing down to her jaw. "Let it burn. Let him burn with it."

They spiraled downward, the steps beneath their feet hot enough to feel through the soles of their shoes. Above them, the tower roared with flame, the fire spreading through walls and floors, following paths of energy laid decades ago when Thorne had designed Hallowspire according to the ritual geometry that would thin the barrier between worlds.

As they reached the library level, they saw that the fire had spread faster than physically possible, consuming the upper gallery and racing along the shelves where chained books screamed as they burned, releasing sounds no paper and ink should produce. Flames already wreathed the spiral staircases to the lower levels, cutting off their escape route.

"This way," Micah pulled his mother toward a narrow service door half-hidden behind a burning tapestry. Beyond lay another set of stairs, steep and cramped, designed for servants to move invisibly through the house. They plunged into this new passage, the air slightly clearer but still thick with smoke that stung their eyes and burned their lungs.

Behind them, the Mourning Tower's destruction continued, the sound of collapsing masonry punctuated by the higher, more terrible keen of whatever Thorne had become as his physical domain burned around him. The fire spread throughout the west wing with deliberate malice, following the spiral patterns built into Hallowspire's very bones, turning decades of occult architecture into a pyre visible for miles across the storm-tossed sea.

And somewhere beneath its burning, shifting form, Effie waited—no longer just a lost child but a key to something terrible, something that had been waiting in patient darkness since before Thorne had laid the first stone of his unholy design.

Chapter 32

The spiral staircase wound ever downward. Anna led the way, her wet boots sliding on the stone as she and Mercy descended deeper beneath Hallowspire's foundations. Above them, fire was consuming the mansion's west wing, but down here, in the lightless depths where the island's bedrock met the sea, a different kind of destruction was unfolding—one that would tear not just at wood and stone, but at the fabric of the mortal world itself.

"Hurry," Anna urged, her voice tight with desperation. The temperature dropped with each turn of the stairs, cold enough now that their breath hung in clouds before their faces, crystallizing on the damp walls like delicate funeral lace.

Mercy followed, Anna's coat still wrapped around her thin shoulders, bare feet numb against stone so cold it burned.

The mansion's architecture had shifted, distances warping as the ritual below progressed. What had been a journey of minutes during their earlier exploration now stretched and contracted like a living thing, the stairs sometimes doubling back on themselves in ways that defied natural geometry.

The walls around them changed as they descended, transitioning from Hallowspire's dressed stone to something older. These ancient surfaces were slick with condensation that moved wrong, droplets crawling upward rather than down, forming patterns that matched the spiral sigils carved into the rock at regular intervals. A low vibration thrummed through the stone, making their teeth ache and their vision blur at the edges. It wasn't a sound, precisely, but something deeper—a resonance that bypassed the ears and spoke directly to the bones.

They reached the landing where the spiral stairs ended and opened onto a short corridor. From beyond came a sound that made Anna stumble to a halt. A harmonized chanting in no human language, voices layered atop one another in impossible registers that scraped at the mind like knives across bone. The sound rose and fell in patterns that matched neither breath nor heartbeat, but some other, more fundamental rhythm—the pulse of something vast and ancient stirring from endless sleep.

Anna's hand flew to the knife at her belt. "Remember," she said, her voice barely audible beneath the chanting, "whatever happens, don't step onto the spiral. Once you're on it, the pattern claims you." Her eyes held a desperate intensity when they met Mercy's. "Stay behind me. If I tell you to run, you run—back up those stairs, out of the house, off this cursed island any way you can."

Mercy nodded, though fear had stolen her voice. Anna took a deep breath, steadied herself, and crossed the threshold.

The Sanctum of Sundering erupted before them in all its

terrible splendor—a perfect circular cavern carved directly into the island's living rock by the power of the three converging key lines. Its walls rose in smooth basalt curves to the vaulted ceiling and that cracked dome with its tendrils of void seeping downward like ink in water.

And down at the bottom of the spiral was the circular pit —the Nocturne Gate itself—not merely a hole in the floor but an absence, a perfect void that breathed and pulsed with terrible life. The darkness within it wasn't empty but glutted, swollen with forms that shifted and writhed just beyond perception.

The Thirteen stood arranged at perfect equidistance around the outer edge of the spiral. Their translucent forms had solidified into grotesque parodies of human shape, their emaciated frames draped in the tattered remnants of what they had worn in life. Their skin was ashen and pulled tight over their bones, pulsing with a sickly inner light that ebbed and flowed in time with their soundless chanting. Eyeless sockets wept black tears that never reached the floor, dissolving into smoke halfway down their gaunt cheeks. Their mouths gaped in eternal screams, lips pulled back from yellowed teeth, tongues missing from cavernous throats. They moved in perfect synchrony, hands raised toward the chamber's center, fingers contorted into tortured shapes.

Suspended above the innermost ring of the spiral at the edge of the black womb, floated Effie.

The child's small body hung three feet above the stone, arms outstretched as if crucified on invisible beams. Her wild hair stood out from her head, moving in currents that had nothing to do with air or gravity. Her skin had taken on a translucent quality, the blue-green light from the spiral showing through her like paper held before a flame, illuminating the delicate tracery of veins beneath. Most terrible were her eyes—rolled back in her head until only the whites showed, yet those whites now glowed with the same sickly luminescence that filled the chamber.

From her open mouth emerged not a child's voice but a chorus of layered harmonics that no human throat could produce, sounds that existed before language, before thought, before the division of light from darkness. The words, if they were words at all, seemed like physical things in the air, visible as ripples that expanded outward and disappeared into the chamber walls.

Anna froze at the edge of the spiral, her face contorting with horror. This was Thorne's ultimate design—not just to open a temporary breach, but to create a living gateway, a vessel through which the entities of the Inmost Dark could flow freely into the world. Effie wasn't just being sacrificed; she was being transformed into something that was neither dead nor alive, neither here nor there, but eternally between —a keystone in an arch that would never close.

"Dear God," Anna whispered, the words falling dead against the chamber's perfect acoustics. Her hand tightened on her knife, though she knew the blade would be useless against what she faced. This was no simple haunting to dispel, no ghost to banish with iron and graveyard dirt. This was the culmination of a design a lifetime in the making, a ritual that had claimed countless souls already and now reached hungrily for another.

The Thirteen turned as one, their eyeless faces fixing on the intruders with terrible awareness. Their chanting never faltered, but their bodies swayed toward Anna and Mercy like seaweed pulled by an invisible tide. The light pulsing through their translucent forms intensified, throwing their elongated shadows across the chamber floor, shadows that moved independently of their bodies.

"Anna," Mercy's voice cracked with terror, her small hand clutching at Anna's sleeve. "What do we do?"

The spiral beneath their feet glowed with increased intensity, the light spreading from the outer edges inward like a fuse burning toward powder. Effie's suspended body convulsed once, her back arching at an impossible angle, her mouth stretching wider to emit a higher harmonic that made the obsidian dome above them shudder and crack further.

The chamber's chill pierced Anna's bones, but another, more intimate and familiar cold spread through her mind like frost across a windowpane. Rebecca's presence, which had been a distant murmur since they'd entered the sanctum, now surged forward with renewed purpose. Her voice no longer whispered but spoke with clear, cutting precision inside Anna's skull, each word etched in ice.

One child's sacrifice opens, the other's closes, Rebecca intoned, her spectral voice carrying an authority that vibrated through Anna's very marrow. *Only blood taken in sorrow can generate enough power to seal the Gate.* The witch's consciousness expanded within Anna's mind, crowding out her own thoughts, forcing her attention toward Mercy, who stood transfixed by the horror before them.

"No," Anna whispered, the denial barely audible beneath the Thirteen's discordant chanting. She pressed her palm against her temple, as if the physical pressure might push Rebecca back into the recesses of her mind where she belonged.

The spiral path glowed brighter, its luminescence spreading from the outer edge inward. Effie's suspended body continued its unnatural movements, limbs twisting at angles that would break human bone, mouth stretched wide to emit those impossible harmonics. The Thirteen responded in kind, their eyeless faces turned toward the center, their own tongueless chanting rising in volume and complexity.

Look at the slave child, Rebecca pressed. *She is already half-gone. But the Gate—it can still be sealed if you hasten.* Her voice softened, taking on the reasonable tone of a mentor explaining a difficult but necessary truth. *If the slave girl is the key that opens it, then your pale companion's sacrifice is the lock that closes it. One life against countless. One strange, marked child against the world.*

The air in the sanctum grew heavy and electric, pressing against their skin and lungs with increasing weight. Breathing required conscious effort now, each inhalation drawing in something thicker than air, something that tasted of metal and ash. The obsidian dome above fractured further, darkness seeping through in viscous tendrils that writhed with half-glimpsed awareness.

"I won't," Anna hissed, her nails digging into her palms hard enough to draw blood. But even as she resisted, images flooded her mind—not her own thoughts, but visions planted by Rebecca: Mercy at the center of the spiral, her mismatched eyes wide with betrayal as Anna forced her into position; the Gate closing with Mercy's sacrifice, the ritual reversing; Effie falling safely to the stone as the breach in the Veil sealed itself. And beyond that, a glimpse of what she truly wanted—Abigail returning through the narrowing breach before it closed forever, mother and daughter reunited at last.

You're a hunter, child, Rebecca continued, her tone hardening. *You've spilled blood before. You've ended lives to save others. How is this different? The albino girl is already touched by darkness. Her red eye, her unnatural pallor; she was marked from birth for such a purpose. Would you trade one cursed child for another?*

Anna's gaze fixed on Mercy, seeing her anew through Rebecca's cold calculation. The girl stood transfixed by the ritual, her white hair glowing blue-green in the spiral's light, her thin body trembling with fear and cold beneath Anna's borrowed coat. So small, so vulnerable. And yet, as Rebecca suggested, perhaps already touched by something beyond the natural world. Her mismatched eyes had always seen more than they should, had recognized the darkness in Anna from their first meeting.

The chamber shuddered, stone groaning as the spiral's innermost rings continued to rotate physically, grinding against each other with the sound of millstones. The pit at the center—the Nocturne Gate itself—widened by inches, the darkness within churning with increased agitation. The Thirteen's bodies pulsed brighter, their forms growing more solid as they drew energy from the thinning Veil.

Think of your mother, Rebecca urged, striking at Anna's deepest vulnerability. *Abigail's soul hangs in the balance. Even now she waits beyond the Veil, counting on you to bring her back before the Devil claims what is his.* The witch's voice grew honeyed, persuasive. *This is why I drew you here to this island, to this moment. Everything has led to this choice. One sacrifice to save what you love most.*

Memories rose unbidden in Anna's mind. She saw Abigail teaching her to read by candlelight; Abigail bandaging her scraped knees; Abigail standing fierce and protective between her daughter and the monsters that haunted their lives. Then later memories: Abigail crumpled and bleeding on a granite ledge by the side of a waterfall, her body torn by werewolf's claws, her final spell casting her soul safely beyond the Veil rather than letting it be claimed by darkness.

The knife on Anna's belt seemed suddenly heavier, pulling at her awareness like an anchor. Her fingers twitched toward it, the movement not entirely her own. Rebecca's influence spread through her limbs like tendrils of ice, guiding her hand to the weapon's hilt.

Think how simple it would be, Rebecca whispered, her voice now intimate as a lover's. *One quick thrust. She would hardly feel it. And in that moment—that perfect moment when her life hangs between this world and the next—you place her at the center. Her blood completes the spiral. The Gate closes forever.*

Anna's hand closed around the knife, the familiar grip both comforting and terrible. She had killed countless times— monsters, mostly, but sometimes men who were monstrous enough to deserve death. Never an innocent. Never a child. Never someone who trusted her.

But Mercy wasn't just anyone. She was strange, marked, different—her albinism setting her apart even before the horror she'd endured at the hands of Cotton Barlow. Perhaps

Rebecca was right. Perhaps this was why their paths had crossed, why Anna had felt compelled to protect her. Not to save her, but to preserve her for this moment, for this purpose.

The blue-green light from the spiral crept up Mercy's bare legs as she stood at the edge of the pattern, unaware of the conflict raging in Anna's mind. The girl's attention remained fixed on Effie, her thin shoulders hunched with helpless concern beneath the too-large coat.

She won't suffer, Rebecca promised. *And when it is done, your mother will return. The debt will be paid. The Gate will close. No more children need be taken. Think of it as mercy, Anna. Is that not her name? Is that not what you will give her?*

The knife came free of its sheath with a soft hiss of steel against leather. The blade caught the spiral's light, reflecting it in fractured patterns across Anna's face. Her expression hardened, jaw set with terrible purpose, eyes growing distant as Rebecca's influence crowded out her own will.

At the center of the spiral, the Nocturne Gate pulsed wider, the darkness within parting like a mouth to reveal glimpses of what waited beyond the Veil. Not the peaceful afterlife of Christian teaching, not the restful shades of pagan belief, but something far older and more terrible—the Inmost Dark, where entities that predated human thought waited with patient, ancient hunger. Legions of the undead awaited their return, and behind them, things infinitely more terrifying. Tentacles of pure shadow lashed upward, testing the thinning barrier. Forms that defied description pressed against the membrane of reality, their geometries wrong in ways that hurt the mind to perceive.

Effie's suspended body convulsed again, her spine arching backward at an impossible angle, her mouth stretched in a silent scream as the harmonics poured from her throat with increased urgency. The Thirteen responded, their chanting accelerating, the words tumbling over each other in a cascade of impossible sounds. The ritual approached its culmination, the moment when the Veil would tear completely, allowing what waited beyond to pour through into the world.

"There's no other way," Anna whispered, her voice strange and distant to her own ears. The knife felt alive in her hand, eager for what came next. Behind her eyes, Rebecca's influence spread like black ink through water, drowning her conscience, her hesitation, her humanity.

She took a step toward Mercy's unprotected back, knife raised, Rebecca's cold triumph flooding her veins like poison.

Chapter 33

Mercy sensed the change, felt it in the air between them like the charge before lightning strikes. She turned, her white hair swinging in a pale arc, to find Anna three paces behind her, knife drawn, eyes strange and distant. For a heartbeat, neither moved—Mercy frozen in disbelief, Anna suspended between action and hesitation, the knife gleaming in her hand like a sliver of cruel moon.

"Anna?" Mercy's voice emerged small and confused, a child's voice in a chamber built for older, darker sounds. Her mismatched eyes widened, the blue one filling with tears, the red one seeming to glow in the spiral's uncanny light. "What are you doing?"

The knife in Anna's hand trembled slightly, catching the blue-green luminescence that pulsed through the chamber. Her face was a battlefield, features contorting as two wills fought for control—her own buried compassion against Rebecca's cold calculation.

"I have to," she said, the words scraping her throat like broken glass. "To close the Gate. To save my mother."

Beneath them, the Nocturne Gate pulsed wider, the darkness within it churning with increased agitation. The obsidian edges of the chasm cracked and splintered, widening the opening by inches. From those widening cracks rose tendrils of absolute darkness—not the absence of light but something deeper, more fundamental—the stuff of which nightmares were made before humans existed to dream them. They curled upward like smoke from a smothered fire, testing the air of the chamber, seeming to taste it with senses that had never known sight or smell or touch.

Mercy backed away, bare feet finding the edge of the spiral's outermost ring. One step back would take her into the pattern's embrace. One step forward would bring her within reach of Anna's blade. Her thin shoulders pressed against her ears, her body hunching inward as if trying to make herself a smaller target.

"Please," she whispered, palms raised in supplication. "You don't have to do this. There's another way."

Anna advanced a step, her movements sluggish, as if her limbs obeyed commands not entirely her own. Rebecca's presence surged behind her eyes, amber flecks appearing in her blue irises, her pupils contracting to pinpoints despite the chamber's dimness. The knife rose higher, its edge catching the light from the spiral in wicked gleams.

"What other way?" Anna's voice cracked, something of her true self breaking through Rebecca's control. "The Gate is opening. Effie is nearly gone. If I don't stop this—"

"The Quiet Ones told me," Mercy interrupted, her voice growing stronger despite her fear. Her gaze flicked to the translucent figures arranged around the spiral, their eyeless faces turned toward her with expectant hunger. "Not all of them are evil. Some are trapped here, like Effie. They want to be free."

The spiral's glow intensified, spreading inward at an accelerating pace. The stone floor beneath their feet vibrated with increasing intensity, dust and small fragments falling from the cracked obsidian dome above. Effie's suspended body convulsed again, her spine arching at an impossible angle, her mouth stretched wide in a scream that filled the chamber with cascading harmonics.

Kill her now, Rebecca's voice commanded inside Anna's mind, fury making the words burn like acid. *She lies. The Quiet Ones serve only their master. There is no other way.*

Mercy took a half-step forward, her courage outweighing her terror. "The woman with the sewn mouth—she found a way to speak to me in the tide cave. She said there's always been another sacrifice possible." Her mismatched eyes held Anna's with desperate intensity.

The knife wavered in Anna's hand, uncertainty battling against Rebecca's iron control. Memories flashed through her mind—not planted by Rebecca this time, but her own. Mercy trembling in her thin shift after the horror at Sévérité. Mercy's small hand in hers as they fled down moonlit paths. Mercy's rare smile, tentative and fragile as new ice, when Anna had shown her a kindness. The truth of their connection burned through Rebecca's manipulations like sunlight through fog.

She is using you, Rebecca hissed, her fury building like a storm. *The albino child knows nothing. Her empty promises will doom your mother's soul to Hell. Kill her now, while there is still time!*

The Gate yawned wider beneath Effie, the darkness within no longer static but churning like a whirlpool, drawing the chamber's light into its maw. The air grew thicker, harder to breathe, weighted with possibilities too terrible to name. The Thirteen's chanting reached a frenzied pace, their translucent bodies pulsing brighter with each syllable, their eyeless sockets fixed on the confrontation at the spiral's edge.

Something fragile and precious unfurled in Anna's chest—not hope, precisely, but its shadow; the possibility that there might be a path through this horror that didn't require Mercy's blood on her hands. The knife trembled violently now, her arm shaking with the effort of resisting Rebecca's control.

"Tell me," Anna managed, fighting for each word against Rebecca's tightening grip on her mind. "Tell me this other way."

LIES! Rebecca's voice thundered through Anna's consciousness, the force of her rage nearly driving Anna to her knees. *You weak, sentimental fool! The albino dies, or everything dies with her!*

The chasm widened further, cracks spreading across the chamber floor like lightning through dark water. Through the expanded opening, shapes became visible. Not just glimpses now, but clear visions of what waited in the Inmost Dark. Vast, ancient intelligences that had never known human morality or mercy, pressed against the thinning Veil with terrible patience.

Mercy's eyes filled with tears, but she didn't look away from Anna's face, didn't flinch from the blade that trembled between them. "Trust me," she said simply, the words falling into the chamber's chaos like stones into still water. "I trust you. I always have."

Something broke in Anna then—not her will, but the spell that had bound it. With a cry that was part defiance, part relief, she flung the knife away from her. It clattered against the stone floor, spinning across the polished surface until it came to rest at the edge of the spiral's outermost ring.

Rebecca howled in fury inside her mind, a scream of such hatred and rage that Anna's vision blurred with pain. The witch's presence thrashed within her, clawing at her consciousness like a trapped animal. *You've doomed us all!* Rebecca shrieked. *The Gate will open fully now! There is no stopping what comes!*

The chamber responded to Anna's choice with immediate, terrible consequence. The spiral's glow accelerated its inward rush, blue-green light racing toward the center like floodwater finding the lowest point. The Thirteen's chanting peaked in a crescendo of impossible sounds, their translucent bodies now blazing with inner light so bright it cast harsh shadows across the walls.

The Nocturne Gate convulsed, the chasm widening with a sound like the earth itself tearing apart. The darkness within parted like curtains, revealing not emptiness but a teeming, writhing infinity of horrors. Tentacled abominations pressed against the thinning barrier, shadow-beings composed of teeth and claws, entities that had waited for patient millennia for this moment of weakness.

From the center of it all, something vast and ancient turned its attention toward the mortal world. Not a creature but a presence—a consciousness so alien that merely sensing its awareness felt like drowning in ice water. It reached toward the breach with appendages that weren't physical but conceptual, extensions of will rather than flesh, hungry for what lay beyond the Veil it could never fully cross.

"Anna," Mercy's voice cut through the chamber's chaos, steady despite her fear. "The woman with the sewn mouth said there's still time. But we have to act now."

The Gate's maw gaped wider, ready to disgorge what decades of ritual and sacrifice had prepared it to release. Above it, Effie's small body hung suspended, no longer a child but a conduit, her humanity nearly burned away by the power flowing through her.

Anna stood at the precipice of decision, Rebecca's rage still howling inside her mind, the knife abandoned at her feet, and the world hanging in the balance.

Chapter 34

Flames danced along the ceiling beams of Hallowspire's west wing like perverse acrobats, leaping impossible distances and moving against natural drafts. Juba pressed her back against a wall that shuddered with heat. Her eyes narrowed against the stinging smoke as she pulled Micah closer to her side. They were trapped, the corridors behind them collapsed in a roar of timber and stone, the way forward obscured by rolling clouds of thick, unnatural smoke that seemed to reach for them with spectral fingers. The mansion's ancient timbers groaned beneath the weight of their own destruction.

But beneath that chorus of fire and falling wood lurked another sound. A distant, impossible singing that pulled at Juba's blood like the tide.

"She's still in here," she whispered, her voice scraping against a throat raw from smoke. "I can feel her."

The smoke churned around them in patterns too deliberate to be natural. Coiling tendrils formed and reformed into spiral configurations before dispersing. It carried scents beyond the expected reek of burning wood and fabric.

Cindered herbs, scorched metal, and something fouler: the stench of burned bone and rendered flesh.

"Stay low," Juba commanded, her voice ragged from the acrid air. She pulled the edge of her shawl over her mouth and motioned for Micah to do the same with his shirt. "Breathe through the cloth."

Micah crouched beside his mother, his eyes constantly scanning the billowing clouds for threats. "The fire's not right," he whispered against her ear. "It's not burning like normal fire. It's... hunting."

He was right. The flames advanced along the corridor ahead of them in staggered pulses, as if testing the air, sensing their presence. It followed patterns embedded in the mansion's very architecture, racing along the invisible lines of power that Thorne had laid into the foundation decades earlier. Where it touched wood, the flames didn't simply consume but transformed, blackening the grain into shapes that resembled screaming faces or grasping hands. The smoke it produced hung unnaturally thick, refusing to rise, coiling instead in spirals that mirrored the sigils carved throughout Hallowspire.

Juba reached into the pouch at her waist, fingers closing around her grandmother's stone. Its warmth pulsed against her palm in time with her heartbeat, a reminder that some protections remained even in this nightmare. With her free hand, she scattered a pinch of salt across the threshold before them, whispering words passed down through generations.

"Blood to bone, bone to stone, stone to earth, earth to sea. What walks without eyes cannot follow me."

The salt crystals flared with a pale blue light as they settled on the charred floorboards. The smoke withdrew from the barrier momentarily, creating a small pocket of clearer air. Juba pulled Micah forward, stepping across the threshold while the protection held.

"We need to find the main staircase," she said, orienting herself despite the mansion's shifting architecture.

They turned left at a junction, only to find themselves facing a corridor that stretched before them like a nightmare. It was impossibly long, the far end receding as they watched, as if the house were exhaling, extending itself to prevent their escape. Doors lined the walls, their frames warping in the heat, the wood contracting and expanding with sounds like stifled moans. As Juba and Micah approached the nearest door, it slammed shut with such force that the panel cracked down its center.

"It knows we're here," Micah whispered, his fingers digging into his mother's arm. "The house. It's trying to keep us."

A gilt-framed mirror hung on the wall beside them, its glass blackened by smoke but still reflective enough to show distorted versions of the corridor behind them—passageways that hadn't been there moments before, routes that promised escape but led nowhere. As Juba glanced at it, a face that wasn't hers stared back. The woman's features twisted in silent agony, mouth sewn shut with black thread, empty eye sockets weeping viscous darkness.

The glass cracked with a sound like ice breaking on a frozen pond, and the apparition pushed through—not just a reflection, but one of the Quiet Ones, a woman whose translucent form floated three inches above the floor, her mouth sewn shut with what looked like black wire, her eye sockets empty yet somehow still conveying desperate hunger. She drifted toward them, hands outstretched, fingers elongated beyond human proportion.

Others followed the woman, stepping through walls and rising from the floorboards. A man whose spine curved at impossible angles, a child with drill holes visible in its spectral skull, an elderly figure whose neck bore the marks of ritual separation, their soul-stripped bodies glowing with the same sickly blue-green light that pulsed from the sigils throughout Hallowspire.

They were once people—men, women, even children— their forms now twisted parodies of humanity. Their eyeless faces turned toward Juba and Micah with hungry awareness, sewn mouths working against their bindings as if trying to speak warnings or threats.

"Don't look at their eyes," Juba warned, pulling Micah closer to her side. Her hand dipped into the pouch at her belt, fingers closing around the smooth black stone. With her other hand, she scattered salt in a wide arc before them, her lips moving in a prayer that predated the Christian God by centuries.

The salt ignited where it struck the floor, a cold blue light that pushed the apparitions back. They retreated like mist before the wind, their forms dissolving at the edges only to reform several feet away. The sewn-mouth woman's neck craned at an unnatural angle, her hollow gaze fixed on Juba with what might have been contempt.

"They're everywhere," Micah whispered, his body pressed against his mother's side. His eyes darted from corner to corner, tracking movements that existed at the edge of perception. "But they're not trying to hurt us. They're trying to show us something."

A child-sized figure with drill holes visible through its skull pointed down the corridor with a spectral finger. The others followed, arranging themselves in a line, their translucent bodies forming a corridor of their own within the burning hallway. They pointed with spectral fingers down a path that hadn't existed moments before—a narrow side passage that shimmered like heat distortion in desert air.

"They were like Effie once," Micah said softly, his voice barely audible above the distant roar of the fire. "Before he took their souls away. They don't want it to happen again."

Juba hesitated, the salt still clutched in her palm. The black stone pulsed with warmth against her skin, not in warning but in confirmation. She closed her eyes, reaching out with senses her mother had taught her to trust above sight or sound.

"Effie," she breathed, her eyes snapping open. "She's below us. Deep below."

The mansion groaned around them, a deep, resonant sound that seemed to come from everywhere at once. Overhead, timber beams shifted and cracked with sounds like breaking bones. The corridor before them, which had stretched impossibly moments before, now contracted, walls squeezing inward, ceiling dropping lower, as if Hallowspire were attempting to crush them within its dying body.

"We need to find stairs going down," Micah said, already moving toward the passage the soul-stripped had indicated. "The servant stairs maybe, or—"

The house anticipated them. An open door slammed shut as they approached, the wood splintering outward as if struck by an invisible fist. The corridor to their left elongated impossibly, its end receding like a horizon viewed through the wrong end of a spyglass. Behind them, flames surged forward in a wave, consuming the corridor they'd just left with unnatural hunger.

"This way!" Juba cried, pulling Micah toward what appeared to be a narrow servant's passage. The air here was marginally clearer, though thin streams of smoke filtered through cracks in the walls. The passage descended at a gentle slope, confirming Juba's sense that they needed to go downward.

The way forward narrowed further, forcing them to turn sideways to continue. The walls pressed close on either side, the rough stone scraping against their shoulders. Smoke curled around their ankles, rising from below rather than filtering down from above. The air grew hotter rather than cooler, suggesting that fire had found its way to the lower levels as well.

The house shuddered around them, wood and stone protesting as flames consumed its structure. From somewhere above came the sound of a major collapse—support beams giving way, entire rooms surrendering to the inferno's hunger. Dust and fragments rained down from the ceiling, coating their hair and shoulders in gray ash.

"There," Micah pointed to a narrow opening half-hidden behind a rotting tapestry. "Servant stairs. They'll take us deeper."

The stairwell beyond was steep and cramped, the wooden

treads worn smooth by decades of invisible passage. It descended in a tight spiral, each step taking them further from the fire consuming the upper levels but closer to whatever horror awaited below. The walls here were bare stone rather than wood or plaster. They had passed beyond Hallowspire's later construction into the original foundation —perhaps even into chambers carved directly from the island's living rock.

"I can hear her," Juba said, her voice tight with urgency. "She's singing, but it's not her voice anymore. We have to hurry."

The house continued to die above them, its death throes echoing down the narrow passage. A deafening crack echoed through the narrow stairwell, the sound of centuries-old wood giving way. The steps beneath their feet shuddered, then began to collapse inward like a house of cards. Juba grabbed Micah by the collar of his shirt, hauling him backward onto the landing they'd just descended from. They tumbled together onto solid stone as the lower portion of the staircase disintegrated, wooden treads tumbling into darkness. The way down—their path to Effie—had vanished.

"This way," Juba commanded, pulling Micah through a doorway that opened onto a smoke-filled corridor. "The house won't keep us from her. Not while I still draw breath."

They had progressed perhaps twenty paces when the mansion voiced its displeasure again. A tremendous crack split the air, the sound so physical it struck them like a blow. The ceiling above began to give way. Ancient timbers— mortise and tenon joints that had held for centuries—finally surrendered to the unnatural fire that consumed them.

Juba looked up just as a massive oak beam, wreathed in blue-white flame, detached from the ceiling directly above her. There was no time to move, no space to dodge. The burning timber plummeted toward her with the terrible inevitability of a guillotine's blade, trailing sparks and burning debris in its wake.

"Mama!" Micah cried, his body moving with instinctive speed. He threw himself forward, colliding with Juba's side and partially shielding her with his own thin frame. The beam struck his shoulder with brutal force, driving him to his knees. The wood pinned him momentarily against his mother, its weight crushing, its heat searing through the rough fabric of his shirt. The smell of burning cloth mingled with the more terrible scent of scorched flesh.

"Micah!" Juba's cry tore from her throat, raw with maternal terror. She fell beside him, hands finding purchase on the smoldering beam, heedless of the blisters forming on her palms as she heaved against its weight. The wood was blackened and still burning along one edge, amber embers pulsing like malevolent eyes within the charred grain. It shifted reluctantly, groaning as if alive and unwilling to release its prey.

With a final surge of desperate strength, she wrenched the timber away, rolling it clear of her son's crumpled form. Micah remained on his knees, swaying slightly, his right shoulder hunched at an unnatural angle. His shirt had burned away in a rough circle where the beam had struck, revealing skin mottled an angry red and black beneath. Blood seeped from a dozen places where jagged splinters had punctured his flesh like primitive arrows. His face had gone ashen, the brown of his skin faded to a sickly gray that alarmed Juba more than the visible wound.

Juba's hands fluttered over the wound, afraid to touch yet desperate to help. "My boy," she whispered, her voice thick with restrained tears.

Micah looked up at her, lips pressed into a thin line against the pain. His eyes, however, remained clear and focused, holding her gaze with a steadiness that belied his years. "I'm fine, Mama," he insisted through gritted teeth. "We need to keep moving."

It was a lie, and they both knew it. The burn was deep; the splinters driven far into his muscle. In another time, another place, such a wound would demand a doctor's immediate attention. Here, trapped in a burning mansion haunted by the victims of a madman's experiments, it was merely one more burden to bear.

As if summoned by the scent of blood and pain, the air around them thickened with an unnatural presence. The soul-stripped apparitions had returned, more numerous than before, their translucent forms pressing closer with each passing second. The Quiet Ones glided through walls and flames alike, untouched by the physical destruction that threatened the living. Their eyeless faces turned toward the wounded boy with particular interest, drawn perhaps by the fresh blood or the vulnerability his pain created. The woman with the sewn mouth drifted to the forefront of the grim procession, her hollow sockets fixed on Micah's injury.

Juba's hand went to her belt, fingers closing around the protective stone. The pocketful of salt at her hip had torn during their flight, white crystals spilling across the floor in an unintended circle around them. Where the salt touched wood, it ignited with that same cold blue light, creating a barrier between the living and the dead.

"Stay back," she commanded, though whether she spoke to the soul-stripped or to some deeper presence in the house itself wasn't clear. "Blood to bone, bone to stone," she chanted, the words coming fast and urgent. "What stands between worlds cannot cross mine. What hungers without mouth cannot taste mine."

The Quiet Ones formed a loose circle around Juba and Micah, their presence dropping the temperature despite the inferno raging around them. Frost formed briefly on the floor where they hovered, melting instantly in the heat, creating a hissing steam that curled around their spectral forms like living shrouds. One by one, they pointed with spectral fingers toward a section of wall that appeared no different from any other—paneled in dark wood, stained with age and smoke.

Micah struggled to his feet, his good arm braced against the wall for support. "There," he said, voice thin with pain but certain. "They're showing us the way to Effie."

"Stay close," Juba warned as they approached the hidden door in the wall, her hand gripping Micah's uninjured arm. "Whatever's happening down there, we face it together. No matter what we find."

Chapter 35

The Sanctum of Sundering pulsed with increasing urgency, its blue-green light throbbing through the chamber like the heartbeat of some vast, dying creature. The glyphs etched into the basalt walls brightened and dimmed in sequences that hurt the eye to follow, their patterns shifting subtly with each cycle as if rewriting themselves into new and terrible configurations. At the center of it all, the Nocturne Gate yawned wider, its absolute darkness no longer contained within the perfect circle of the pit but spilling outward in viscous tendrils that probed the chamber floor like blind fingers seeking purchase in the world of the living.

Anna stood at the spiral's edge, her abandoned knife gleaming on the stone floor between her and Mercy. Her fingers trembled at her sides, the lingering sensation of Rebecca's control still burning through her veins like winter frost. The witch's presence had receded but not vanished. A sullen, furious pressure lingered behind her eyes, waiting for another opportunity to seize control. Anna could feel Rebecca's rage beating against the inside of her skull, wordless but potent.

Effie hung suspended above the expanding Gate, her small body stretched at unnatural angles, mouth open in a silent scream as impossible harmonics poured from her throat. The Thirteen maintained their positions around the spiral, their eyeless faces turned toward the confrontation at the edge, their sewn mouths working against their bindings as if trying to communicate some desperate message. The temperature in the chamber continued to plummet, frost forming along the edges of the stone grooves that made up the spiral pattern.

"What other way?" Anna demanded again, her voice brittle with strain. The words echoed against the glyph-etched walls, returning distorted and layered with harmonics that weren't present when she spoke. "What did they show you, Mercy? What did the Quiet Ones tell you?"

Mercy stepped forward, her feet leaving no imprints on the thin layer of frost that coated the chamber floor. Her white hair caught the pulsing light from the spiral, transforming it into a halo of blue-green fire around her pale face. Without breaking eye contact with Anna, she bent down and picked up the discarded knife, her thin fingers curling white-knuckled around the hilt.

"They showed me things," she said, her voice soft yet somehow cutting through the chamber's discordant sounds. "While we were in that sea cave. While the tide was rising. No words—pictures. Memories." The blade caught the eerie glow as she turned it over in her hands, examining its edge with a detached curiosity. "I thought I was dying. Maybe I was. But in that space between life and death, they could reach me."

The knife's edge glinted as Mercy tilted it, reflecting a fractured image of Anna's face back at her—distorted, divided, like looking at herself through shattered glass. The girl's mismatched eyes held Anna's gaze with an intensity that felt physically painful, as if she were staring directly into the secret chambers of Anna's soul.

"I know about her," Mercy said quietly. Each word dropped into the chaos like a stone into still water, creating ripples of silence that momentarily dampened the chamber's terrible sounds. "About Rebecca. The witch inside your head."

Anna's face drained of color, the blood retreating from her cheeks as if fleeing the exposure of her most closely guarded secret. Her lips parted, but no sound emerged, the confession she had never made to anyone dying unspoken in her throat. Her eyes widened with a vulnerability that transformed her features from their usual guarded severity into something raw and exposed.

"They showed me everything," Mercy continued, her voice gaining strength. "How she's been with you since birth. How she whispers to you in the dark. How she offers you power in exchange for your humanity." The knife trembled slightly in her grip, the only indication of the effort it took to speak these truths aloud. "I saw her face inside yours, Anna. I felt her rage. Her hunger."

Rebecca's presence surged again within Anna's mind, no longer words but pure emotion—hatred and fear intertwined, the desperation of a creature exposed to light after centuries of comfortable darkness. Anna pressed her palm against her temple, a futile gesture to contain what couldn't be physically restrained.

"No one knows," she whispered, the admission scraping her throat like broken glass. "No one has ever..." She swallowed hard, forcing herself to meet Mercy's steady gaze. "How did they show you?"

The obsidian dome above cracked further, darkness seeping through in greater quantities, pooling in the air like inverted puddles before drifting downward to join the churning void at the center. The Thirteen swayed more urgently now, their translucent forms pulsing brighter with each cycle of the chamber's unnatural light.

"You're like me," Mercy continued, her voice taking on an almost dreamlike quality. "Haunted. Marked since before you were born." Her mismatched eyes softened with something close to compassion. "They showed me how you fight her every day. How you've never surrendered, even when it would have been easier."

Anna's chest tightened, a pressure building behind her ribs that had nothing to do with the thinning air in the chamber. To be seen—truly seen, not just the mask she presented to the world but the war she fought silently within herself—was a vulnerability she had never allowed, never even imagined possible.

Mercy gripped the knife with trembling fingers, her knuckles white against the worn leather of the hilt. Her thin shoulders straightened beneath Anna's oversized coat, a strange dignity settling over her childish frame. The blue-green light from the spiral cast her face in sharp relief, transforming her pallor into something almost spectral—a living ghost making its final choice. When she spoke, her voice carried the weight of someone far older than her years, someone who had walked with death as a companion rather than an enemy.

"I understand now," she said, her mismatched eyes never leaving Anna's face. "I've seen what she does to you. How she twists your thoughts, how she uses your love for your mother to break your will. They showed me what happens if you let her finish what she started." Her fingers tightened around the knife, steadying its slight tremble.

The Nocturne Gate pulsed wider, its expansion accelerating as if responding to Mercy's words. The tendrils of darkness grew more substantial, coiling along the spiral's innermost ring like serpents preparing to strike. From within the void came shapes that defied description—entities composed of hunger and patience in equal measure. The ground beneath them trembled, stone grinding against stone as the Gate expanded further, darkness spilling across the innermost rings of the spiral like oil across water.

"But Rebecca was right about one thing," Mercy continued, her voice steady despite the horror unfolding before them. She took a half-step back, the knife in her hand catching the light from the spiral, its edge gleaming with terrible purpose. "Only a sacrifice will seal the Gate." Her pale lips curved in a small, sad smile. "But I can't let you lose yourself to her. Not for me. Not for anyone. The only way to keep your hands clean is if I do it myself."

Anna lunged forward as her voice tore from her throat, a desperate cry that shattered against the chamber's vaulted ceiling. "Mercy, don't—!"

But it was already too late.

With a swift, decisive movement, Mercy reversed the knife and plunged it deep into her own chest. The blade slid between her ribs with a sickening sound—steel parting flesh, scraping bone. For a fraction of a second, her face registered surprise rather than pain, as if she hadn't expected it to be so easy, so final.

Then the blood came.

It bloomed across her simple dress in a rapidly expanding stain, darker than darkness in the chamber's uncanny light. It soaked through the fabric in seconds, dripping onto the stone floor with a sound like rainfall against parched earth. Each droplet struck the spiral's grooves and ignited with sudden, crimson fire—not the blue-green phosphorescence that had filled the chamber before, but a deep, vital red that pulsed with the weakening rhythm of Mercy's heart.

Her legs buckled. The knife remained embedded in her chest, its hilt protruding obscenely from her slight frame, rising and falling with each labored breath. Her hands released from their grip on the weapon and hung limp at her sides, fingers already bluish at the tips as her life drained away. Yet her eyes—those mismatched windows—remained clear and focused, fixed on Anna with an expression that might have been triumph or regret or something too complex for any single word to capture.

"*No!*" Anna's scream split the air with such force it felt like something physical had been ripped from her body. She lunged forward, boots sliding on the frost-slick stone, arms outstretched to catch Mercy before she fell completely.

But as her foot crossed the outermost ring of the spiral, an invisible barrier repelled her with such force that she was thrown backward, landing hard on the chamber floor several feet away. The air between her and Mercy shimmered like heat rising from summer stone, though the temperature in the Sanctum continued to plummet. It was not heat but energy—raw, concentrated power generated by Mercy's freely given blood, creating a boundary that no living thing could cross.

Mercy staggered backward, leaving smeared, crimson footprints on the stone. Each step took her deeper into the spiral, her blood dripping onto the carved grooves, igniting them with that strange, red fire that raced along the pattern with unnatural speed. Where the crimson flame touched the blue-green light that had filled the chamber before, the colors fought and merged, creating a violet radiance that hurt the eye to look upon directly.

"I'm sorry," Mercy whispered, though whether to Anna or to herself wasn't clear. Her voice was thin now, weakening with each word, each breath. "It was always supposed to be me."

The Thirteen responded to the spreading crimson fire with increasing agitation, their translucent forms flickering like candles in a draft. The blue-green light that had sustained them began to fade, overwhelmed by the vital energy of Mercy's freely given blood. Their eyeless sockets turned toward her with what might have been recognition or gratitude or fear—emotions that transcended the boundaries of life and death, connecting them in this moment of terrible transformation.

Anna scrambled to her feet, throwing herself against the invisible barrier again and again, each impact sending lances of pain through her shoulders and palms. "Mercy!" she screamed, her voice breaking on the name. "Stop! Please!"

But Mercy continued her slow, faltering progress into the spiral, each step leaving a bloody print that ignited with crimson fire. The knife in her chest shuddered with each movement, the wound around it widening, spilling more of her life onto the ancient stone. Her white hair hung in lank strands around her face, blood from her mouth staining a few errant locks crimson. Despite the devastation of her body, her eyes remained clear and focused, carrying a purpose that transcended pain.

The chamber itself began to transform as Mercy's blood spread through the spiral. The glyphs etched into the walls brightened, then darkened, then flared with that same violet light produced by the merger of blood and ritual. The obsidian dome above fractured further, but now light poured through the cracks rather than darkness—a pure, blinding white that cut through the void like lightning through storm clouds. Conflicting energies thickened the air, making each breath a struggle, as if the very atmosphere were being rewritten by Mercy's sacrifice.

"I saw this," Mercy called, her voice surprisingly strong despite the blood that trickled from the corner of her mouth. "In the sea cave. I saw what would happen if you tried to save me." Her gaze locked with Anna's across the barrier, across the expanding rings of crimson fire. "Some of us aren't meant to be saved, Anna. Some of us are meant to save others."

Above the Nocturne Gate, Effie's suspended body convulsed violently, the harmonics pouring from her throat shifting in pitch and intensity. The darkness spilling from the pit seemed to hesitate, to pull back as if encountering an unexpected resistance. The tendrils of void that had probed the chamber floor began to retreat, coiling back toward their source like snakes returning to their nest.

Anna collapsed to her knees at the edge of the barrier, her palms pressed against the invisible wall that separated her from Mercy. Through the shimmering energy, she watched as the girl she had failed to protect took another staggering step toward the center of the spiral, toward the yawning darkness of the Gate, leaving another blazing footprint in her wake. The crimson fire had spread to cover nearly half the spiral now, working its way inexorably inward, transforming the ritual with each passing second.

"Please," Anna whispered, though she knew it was too late. The choice had been made. The blood had been spilled. The sacrifice had been offered—not taken, but given. Freely, fully, finally.

With each faltering step, Mercy moved deeper into the spiral, her blood tracing fiery paths through the ancient grooves carved into the stone. The knife lodged in her chest rose and fell with her increasingly shallow breaths, blood seeping in steady pulses that matched the slowing rhythm of her heart. Her crimson footprints flared with supernatural light, spreading outward like ripples in a pond, countering the flow of energy that had been building toward the Gate's opening. Where her blood touched the glyphs, their luminescence transformed—first to violent violet, then to pure, blinding white that scoured the shadows from the chamber's darkest corners.

The Thirteen began to disintegrate as the ritual reversed

itself. Their translucent forms, which had seemed so substantial moments before, now unraveled at the edges like cloth coming undone at the seams. The blue-green light that had animated them flickered and dimmed, overtaken by the spreading white fire of Mercy's sacrifice. One by one, they raised their spectral hands toward her in a gesture that might have been benediction or farewell. Their sewn mouths worked against their bindings one last time, not in pain but in what looked almost like relief. Then they dissolved—not into darkness but into motes of light that drifted upward toward the fractured dome, like embers rising from a dying fire.

The woman with the sewn mouth was the last to remain. Her eyeless face turned toward Anna, who still kneeled at the spiral's edge, hands pressed against the invisible barrier. For a moment, something passed between them. Not words, but understanding; a recognition of shared suffering and the terrible price of freedom. Then she dissolved as well, her form breaking apart into fragments of light that scattered throughout the chamber.

Above the constricting maw of the Nocturne Gate, Effie's small body convulsed violently. The impossible harmonics that had poured from her throat faltered, fractured, then ceased altogether. The tether that had bound her to the ritual snapped with an audible crack, like ice breaking on a frozen river. She dropped from her suspended position, limbs loose, head lolling, and collapsed onto the stone floor near the innermost ring of the spiral. She lay motionless except for the shallow rise and fall of her chest—alive but unconscious, her soul returned to her body but her mind still lost in whatever nightmare realm she had been forced to witness.

The Gate continued to close, its yawning darkness shrinking as Mercy approached the center of the spiral. The tendrils of void that had probed the chamber floor retreated, slithering back toward their source like creatures sensing approaching fire. The overwhelming presence that had reached through the breach—that vast, ancient intelligence from the Inmost Dark—withdrew, not in defeat but in rage, its attention focusing with terrible intensity on the small figure whose blood was unmaking decades of patient design.

"Almost there," Mercy whispered, her voice barely audible over the grinding of stone against stone as the spiral's innermost rings rotated in response to her presence. Her skin had grown translucent, the white fire spreading through her veins visible beneath the surface, tracing patterns that mirrored the glyphs etched into the chamber walls. "Almost done."

The air above the constricting Gate shimmered and twisted, reality bending as something forced its way partially through the narrowing breach. A figure materialized—not flesh but shadow given form, a silhouette cut from the fabric of darkness itself. Tall and thin, with limbs too long for human proportion, it wore the tattered remnants of what might have been a gentleman's frock coat. Where its face should have been was a blank oval, featureless except for two mirrored pools that reflected not the chamber but scenes of impossible horror—glimpses of the Inmost Dark, of realms no living eye was meant to witness.

Thorne. Or what had once been Thorne.

"YOU CANNOT!" The voice that emanated from the apparition wasn't a single voice but many, layered atop one another in a discordant chorus that made the air vibrate with its fury. "WE WILL BE REBORN!"

The wraith-like silhouette reached toward Anna with elongated fingers that tapered to points sharp enough to pierce flesh, to pierce soul. Its form flickered and distorted, unable to fully manifest in the physical world as the Gate continued to close, but its rage was palpable, a pressure that made blood vessels burst in Anna's nose and ears, that cracked the stone beneath her knees.

"YOU ARE NOTHING! INSECTS! VESSELS!" Each word tore at the air, leaving visible wounds in reality that bled darkness into the chamber. "WE HAVE WAITED EONS! WE WILL NOT BE DENIED!"

Mercy staggered forward, reaching the innermost ring of the spiral. She was only feet from the center now, from the edge of the constricting void. Her legs threatened to give way with each step, blood pooling beneath her feet, her skin growing more translucent by the second. The white fire had spread throughout her body, consuming her from within, transforming her flesh into something that was neither solid nor insubstantial but somewhere in between—a bridge between worlds, between states of being.

The barrier that had prevented Anna from entering the spiral shattered with a sound like breaking glass, fragments of energy dispersing throughout the chamber in a shower of sparks. She lurched forward, intent on reaching Mercy before the end, but found herself rooted in place by a new force—not a barrier this time, but the ritual's own power, holding her at the threshold of transformation.

"Let me go to her!" Anna screamed, her voice breaking

against the chamber's perfect acoustics. "Please!"

But the ritual had its own logic, its own requirements. And Anna's intervention was not part of the design.

Thorne's apparition lunged toward the center of the spiral, toward Mercy, its shadowy form elongating into a spear of absolute darkness. It moved with the desperate speed of a creature facing extinction, knowing that once the Gate closed, it would be forever banished to the Inmost Dark, trapped with the horrors it had sought to unleash upon the world. Its clawed hands reached for Mercy's throat, for the knife still embedded in her chest, for anything that might halt the ritual's reversal.

In that moment, the Sanctum's entrance burst open with a sound like splintering bone. Juba staggered through, supporting Micah, whose arm hung limp and burned at his side. Their faces, illuminated by the white fire that now filled the chamber, registered shock and horror and desperate hope in equal measure. Juba's eyes fixed on Effie's crumpled form near the inner spiral, a cry of anguish tearing from her throat. Micah's gaze, however, found Mercy at the center, understanding dawning in his young face with terrible clarity.

"No!" he shouted, his voice carrying across the chamber with surprising strength despite his injury

But his cry came too late. Mercy had reached the center of the spiral, the exact point where the Gate's maw had been widest. She stood at the edge of the constricting void, her white hair streaming upward as if caught in an invisible current, her mismatched eyes—one blue, one red—wide with wonder rather than fear. The knife in her chest pulsed with its own light now, the metal glowing white-hot, merging with her flesh, becoming part of the transformation that consumed her.

Thorne's apparition reached her just as the white fire bloomed outward from her chest, from the wound that had been a choice rather than a violation. The shadowy claws passed through her form like smoke trying to grasp water. His rage crystallized into a scream that transcended sound, that existed as pure vibration in the bones of those who heard it.

"I'm sorry," Mercy whispered, though whether to Anna or to Thorne or to herself wasn't clear. Her eyes met Anna's across the spiral, across the gulf of what could have been and what must be. "Tell William I wasn't afraid… At last."

Her body dissolved into radiance—not destroyed but transformed, converted into pure energy that expanded outward in a blinding surge. The white fire consumed Thorne's form, banishing him back through the narrowing Gate. His silhouette twisted and contorted as it was pulled inexorably into the void. The spiral blazed with light too intense to look upon directly, each glyph and sigil burning with the purest white fire, scouring away decades of corruption and dark purpose.

The Gate sealed with a thunderous boom that shook the foundations of Hallowspire and sent tremors through the island itself. The obsidian dome above shattered completely, raining fragments that dissolved into motes of light before they could strike the chamber floor. White fire surged upward through the opening, a pillar of radiance that pierced the night sky above the burning mansion, visible for miles across the storm-tossed sea.

And then, silence.

The chamber grew still, the white fire fading to a soft, ambient glow that emanated from the scorched spiral pattern etched into the stone. Where Mercy had stood, nothing remained—not blood, not bone, not even the knife that had pierced her heart. Only a perfect circle of white light at the center of the spiral, pulsing once, twice, like a final heartbeat, before fading to reveal nothing but blackened stone.

Anna kneeled at the spiral's edge, her face wet with tears she hadn't realized she was shedding. Across the chamber, Juba cradled Effie's unconscious form in her arms, rocking her gently, whispering prayers or promises or both. Micah stood at the threshold, his burned arm hanging limp at his side, his youthful face aged by what he had witnessed.

The Sanctum of Sundering was silent at last, the Nocturne Gate sealed by a sacrifice freely given, the Red Silence restored between worlds. Above them, Hallowspire continued to burn, consuming decades of dark purpose in cleansing flame. But here, in this chamber carved from the island's living rock, a different kind of fire had burned—brighter, purer, and infinitely more terrible in its beauty and its cost.

Chapter 36

The Womb Below, emptied of its terrible purpose, shuddered beneath them. The floor buckled, hairline fractures racing outward from the center where Mercy had stood moments before. Above them, the obsidian dome crumbled further, its structural integrity failing as its occult purpose died. The perfect geometry that had channeled and contained Thorne's rituals was unraveling, each fracture releasing decades of trapped energy. Spiderwebs of firelight raced across the black surface, connecting, branching, deepening until entire sections began to pull away from their ancient moorings.

"Move!" Anna shouted as the first chunk of obsidian, large as a man's torso, plummeted toward them. It struck the floor mere feet from where Juba kneeled, Effie's limp form cradled in her arms. The impact sent jagged shards skittering across the stone like black hail.

Through the widening holes in the dome, they could see Hallowspire burning above them. The unnatural fire had spread throughout the mansion, consuming decades of dark purpose with insatiable hunger. Flaming timbers crashed

358

downward, igniting the tapestries that had decorated the vault outside the sanctum. The air filled with choking smoke that poured into the chamber through the fractured dome, carrying the acrid stench of burning occult relics.

A fallen beam wreathed in flame now blocked their path back to the chapel and the upper levels. Anna's eyes scanned the chamber, searching desperately for another way out. The walls were seamless basalt, carved with glyphs but offering no obvious passages. But as another section of the dome crashed down, spilling more burning debris into the chamber, her gaze caught on something: a narrow archway, partially concealed behind a fallen column. Its edges were so perfectly matched to the surrounding stone that it was visible only from this precise angle, in this precise light.

"This way!" she shouted, pointing toward the hidden exit. Her voice cut through the rumble of collapsing stone and the hungry roar of the fire.

Juba struggled to her feet, Effie's small body a dead weight in her arms. The child remained unconscious, her face ashen, dark lashes stark against her cheeks. Whatever had used her as a conduit for the Gate's power had left her hollow, drained of something essential. She breathed, but barely, each inhalation shallow and labored.

Micah moved to help his mother, but his injured arm hung useless at his side, the burn angry and raw where the beam had struck him. Pain etched deep lines around his young mouth, but determination hardened his eyes as he placed his good hand against Juba's back, steadying her as she shifted Effie to a more secure position.

"I can carry her," Anna offered, stepping toward them.

Juba shook her head, her fierce maternal protectiveness flashing across her features. "She stays with me," she said, the words coming through clenched teeth. "Just show us the way out."

Anna nodded once, accepting both the refusal and the implied trust. She turned toward the hidden archway, but as she took her first step, a familiar cold spread through her mind—Rebecca's presence, diminished but not vanquished, slithering through her thoughts like frost across a windowpane.

Foolish girl, the witch whispered, her voice fainter than Anna had ever heard it, distant as a forgotten memory. The witch's consciousness felt fractured, weakened by whatever power had been unleashed when Mercy closed the Gate. *You think there's safety in that passage? It leads deeper, to older things than Thorne ever knew. There are worse fates than what awaits in the fire above.*

Anna pressed her palm against her temple, a futile gesture to silence the whispers that lived inside her own mind. Her fingers came away wet with blood. Her nose had begun to bleed, crimson droplets spattering the stone at her feet. The physical toll of Rebecca's influence, combined with the chamber's collapsing energies, was extracting a price from her flesh.

"Are you alright?" Micah asked, his expression tightened with concern.

Anna wiped the blood from her upper lip with the back of her hand, leaving a smeared crimson streak across her pale skin. "I'm fine. We need to move. Now."

Another section of the dome crashed down behind them,

sending a shower of burning debris across the chamber. The air grew thicker with smoke, each breath scraping their lungs like inhaled glass. Heat pressed against their skin, driving them toward the archway with more urgency than words ever could.

Anna led the way, stepping over fallen chunks of obsidian, skirting patches of blue-white flame that reached for her ankles with hungry persistence. She felt the absence of her knife like a phantom limb, her hand instinctively reaching for a weapon that wasn't there as she approached the unknown passage.

Behind her, Juba followed with Effie. The woman's face was set in a mask of maternal determination, her steps never faltering despite the burden in her arms. Micah brought up the rear, his good hand sometimes braced against the wall for support, his injured arm held tight against his chest. His eyes constantly scanned behind them, watching the chamber's accelerating collapse with the wary vigilance of a child who had learned early that safety was always temporary.

Anna paused as they reached the archway, studying the stone frame. It was older than the rest of the chamber, its surface worn smooth by the passage of something that wasn't time. The lintel bore carved symbols—not Thorne's glyphs or corrupted Enochian, but something more primal, shapes that suggested meaning without committing to it. The passage beyond was a throat of absolute darkness, swallowing the light from the burning chamber rather than reflecting it.

Rebecca's warning echoed in Anna's mind, but beneath it lay another thought, one entirely her own: Mercy hadn't died so they could perish here, trapped between fire and darkness.

The pale girl's sacrifice deserved more than that. It deserved survival. It deserved a witness.

"Stay close," Anna commanded, stepping through the archway into the darkness beyond. "And whatever you do, don't touch the walls."

Behind them, the Sanctum of Sundering gave one final, shuddering breath as its purpose died completely. The remaining sections of the obsidian dome collapsed inward, burying the spiral and the sealed Gate beneath tons of burning debris. A thunderous crash pursued them into the darkness of the hidden passage, the sound of one age ending and another, uncertain one beginning.

The passageway swallowed them whole, darkness pressing against their skin like a living thing. The air grew colder with each step away from the burning sanctum, heavy with the dank musk of places that had never known sunlight. Anna led the way, one hand trailing the stone wall despite her own warning, fingers reading the texture of the ancient carvings that covered every surface. These were of no human design. The patterns flowed like frozen waves, spiraling in configurations that suggested the movement of something vast and patient beneath the island's surface.

"These tunnels were carved by the Void Spiral ley line," Anna realized, her voice tight with controlled fear. "They're older than Hallowspire. Older than anything human on this island." The darkness forced them to move slowly, navigating by touch more than sight. The glow from the burning chamber behind them quickly faded, leaving only the faintest shimmer from the wall carvings themselves—a subtle, bluish phosphorescence that seemed to respond to their presence, brightening slightly when they passed, then dimming again in their wake.

Juba followed close behind, Effie's limp form slung across her back. The child's arms dangled over Juba's shoulders, her face pressed against the woman's neck, dark curls mingling with her mother's braids. Juba's breathing was labored but steady, each exhale carrying whispered fragments of protection spells her grandmother had taught her; phrases in a language older than the plantation, older than the ships that had brought her ancestors in chains across the sea.

"Blood to bone, bone to stone," she murmured, the words a rhythm that matched her footsteps. "What walks without eyes cannot follow we. What hungers without mouth cannot taste we." Her free hand traced small patterns in the air before them, invisible sigils that seemed to part the darkness for a few precious steps before it closed in again.

Micah brought up the rear, his injured arm cradled against his chest, his breath coming in pained gasps he tried to muffle. The burn on his shoulder throbbed in time with his heartbeat, each pulse sending fresh waves of agony through his thin frame. But he made no complaint, his eyes constantly scanning behind them, alert for signs of pursuit, whether from the collapsing structure or something less tangible that might have escaped the sealed Gate.

The catacombs narrowed as they progressed, forcing them to walk single file through passages barely wide enough for Juba's shoulders. The walls wept with condensation, slick moisture that collected in the carved grooves and ran down in rivulets that felt unnaturally warm against their fingers. The liquid carried the metallic tang of salt and a mineral bitterness that spoke of the earth's blood rather than anything human.

Smoke from the burning mansion above filtered down through cracks in the ceiling, filling the passageway with a gray haze that stung their eyes and scorched their lungs. It grew thicker as they moved deeper. The fire above had spread beyond the west wing to consume Hallowspire in its entirety.

"This way," Anna said, gesturing toward where the passage seemed to slope gently upward. "The carvings point to the surface."

But uncertainty flickered across her face, visible even in the dim phosphorescence of the tunnel walls. She had learned to read such patterns from books, from theoretical knowledge passed down through generations of occultists—never from direct experience navigating the bowels of an island built atop a convergence of dark energies. Each choice carried the weight of all their lives, and the burden settled in the tight line of her jaw, the tension between her shoulder blades.

They had progressed perhaps fifty yards along the path when a low rumble shook the tunnel, dislodging ancient dust from the ceiling and walls. The sound came not from behind them but from above—the death throes of Hallowspire as its foundations gave way. Cracks raced along the ceiling, splinters of stone raining down on their heads and shoulders.

"Move!" Anna shouted, pushing forward with renewed urgency. "The whole place is coming down!"

A larger tremor followed, violent enough to throw them against the walls. Juba stumbled, nearly dropping Effie as she fought to keep her balance on the uneven floor. Micah reached out instinctively to steady his mother, crying out as the movement sent fresh pain lancing through his burned shoulder.

The ceiling directly above him split with a sound like tearing fabric. Chunks of stone larger than his head began to fall, gathering momentum in the narrow space. One jagged piece, its edge sharp enough to cleave flesh from bone, plummeted toward his unprotected skull.

Juba moved with the speed of maternal terror, her free arm shooting out to grab her son by his good shoulder, yanking him forward with such force that his feet left the ground. He landed hard against her side as the stone crashed down exactly where he had stood, shattering on impact and sending razor-sharp fragments skittering along the passage floor.

"I got you," Juba whispered, her voice steady despite the fear that widened her eyes. "I always got you."

More debris fell, forcing them to hunch lower, pressing themselves against the walls as they moved forward at an awkward half-run. The air grew thicker, harder to breathe, heavy with dust and smoke and the acrid tang of fear.

"We're almost there," Anna called back to them, though the set of her shoulders betrayed her uncertainty. The passageway had widened slightly, allowing them to move two abreast, but the ceiling had lowered, forcing them to stoop as they hurried forward. "I can feel fresher air ahead."

Whether true or merely hopeful, the words gave them the strength to push on through the suffocating darkness. Each step was an act of faith now—faith in Anna's guidance, faith in the structural integrity of tunnels that had stood for millennia but might not survive the death of the mansion above, faith that there was indeed an exit waiting rather than a dead end that would become their tomb.

Effie stirred against Juba's back, her small body shifting for the first time since they'd fled the sanctum. Her eyes fluttered open, revealing irises that seemed to glow faintly in the darkness—not with the sickly blue-green light of the ritual, but with something cleaner, something that spoke of a mind returning to itself after a long absence.

"Mama?" she whispered, the word barely audible over their labored breathing and hurried footsteps.

Juba's stride faltered for half a step, her breath catching in her throat. "I'm here, baby," she said, her voice thick with emotion. "Mama's got you. You're safe now."

Effie's gaze drifted past her mother, focusing on something in the middle distance that none of them could see. Her lips curved in a small, puzzled smile.

"The Quiet Ones," she murmured, her voice dreamy and distant. "They're going home now. All of them. They're free."

Her eyes slid closed again, her body going limp against Juba's back. But her breathing seemed stronger now, more purposeful, as if whatever power had used her as a conduit had released its grip, allowing her true self to return.

Anna glanced back at the child's words, her face a complex mask of emotions—hope warring with suspicion, relief with wariness. She had seen too many apparent victories turn hollow, too many endings reveal themselves as mere preludes to greater horrors.

Mercy was the proof of that.

"Keep moving," she urged, turning back to the path ahead. "We're not safe yet."

The passage curved sharply to the right, then angled upward at a steeper incline. The walls here were different—

less finished, more natural, as if they'd moved beyond the carved sections into a tunnel formed by water or some natural process. The air carried a hint of salt and seaweed, the unmistakable breath of the Atlantic that surrounded Brimwatch Isle.

Behind them, deeper in the island's bones, something vast shifted with a sound like mountains sighing. The floor beneath their feet trembled, and a cold wind rushed past them, carrying whispers that might have been voices or merely the sound of stone grinding against stone as Hallowspire's foundations gave way completely.

They ran now, scrambling up the incline, the promise of escape driving them forward despite their exhaustion and injuries. Ahead, barely visible in the gloom, a faint gray light beckoned. Not sunlight, but something less artificial than the phosphorescence of the tunnel walls. The exit, or perhaps merely another false hope in a night that had offered little else.

They burst from the mouth of the sea cave into pearl-gray predawn light, salt spray stinging their faces as waves crashed against the rocky outcropping below. The hidden exit, concealed for centuries beneath Hallowspire's foundations, opened onto a narrow ledge twenty feet above the churning Atlantic. Behind them, the tunnel mouth exhaled a plume of dark smoke that dissipated quickly in the wind sweeping off the water. The air tasted clean after the choking confines of the catacombs. It was cold and sharp with salt, filling their lungs like the first breath after near-drowning.

"Keep moving," Anna commanded, her voice raw from smoke and exhaustion. "The cliff isn't stable."

They scrambled across the wet rocks, feet slipping on surfaces slick with sea spray and predawn dew. Juba still carried Effie, though the strain showed in the trembling of her legs, the tight lines around her mouth. The child remained unconscious but breathed steadily, her small face pressed against her mother's shoulder, dark lashes stark against her ashen cheeks. Micah followed, his injured arm held tight against his chest, his good hand reaching out to steady his mother when the rocks shifted beneath her feet.

Anna led them upward, following a natural formation in the cliff face that served as a crude stairway. Her movements were mechanical, driven by necessity rather than strength. She had pushed beyond exhaustion into that liminal space where the body continues only because stopping means death. Blood had dried in a rusty smear across her upper lip and chin, and her hands were raw, palms scraped bloody from their journey through the rough-hewn tunnel.

They reached a wider outcropping thirty feet above the water, a natural platform jutting from the cliff face with a clear view of Hallowspire—or what remained of it. The mansion burned against the lightening sky, silhouetted in terrible grandeur against the fading stars. Flames painted the predawn with lurid orange and that unnatural blue-white that had characterized the fire from its beginning in the Mourning Tower. But now the blaze was consuming not just the structure but its very foundations, eating downward into the island's flesh, following the paths of power that Thorne had tapped for his unholy purposes.

The ground beneath their feet trembled, a vibration that traveled up through stone and bone alike. It wasn't the movement of earth but the death throes of something that had never been merely a building—something that had lived and breathed and hungered in its own terrible way. Cracks raced along the cliff face, widening with each successive tremor, sending small cascades of stone tumbling into the churning sea below.

"It's going to collapse," Micah said, his voice steady despite the pain that tightened his features. "All of it."

As if summoned by his words, a terrible grinding emanated from Hallowspire's west wing. The Mourning Tower—where they had confronted Thorne's specter, where he had stripped so many souls from living flesh—began to tilt like a felled tree. Its stone walls, weakened by fire and the disruption of the ley lines that had sustained them, gave way first at the base, then in progressive failure upward. Windows shattered as the structure torqued, raining glass onto the burning ground below. The tower's uppermost level, where Thorne had conducted his darkest experiments, separated entirely, tumbling end over end before striking the cliff edge and breaking apart in a shower of stone and splintered wood.

"Get back!" Anna shouted, pulling Juba and Micah away from the cliff's edge as debris rained down around them. A chunk of masonry the size of a man's head struck their outcropping and bounded over the edge, narrowly missing Micah's feet.

The Mourning Tower's collapse triggered a chain reaction throughout Hallowspire's western wing. Walls buckled, roofs caved inward, centuries-old timbers snapped like kindling beneath the weight of falling stone. Fire pursued the destruction, racing along exposed beams and furnishings, consuming everything in its path with unnatural hunger.

Next came the Astral Spire—that perfect circle of stone and glass from which Thorne had mapped the convergence of the Trivium Tenebris. He had designed its elegant structure according to cosmic proportions, each angle and curve calculated to channel energy from the stars themselves. Now those same proportions worked against it, creating structural weaknesses that catastrophically failed as the supporting walls beneath gave way. The spire's glass dome imploded first, the enchanted panes—once capable of showing stars that no longer existed—shattering inward in a cascade of razor-sharp fragments. The skeletal ribs of the dome followed, collapsing like the fingers of a closing hand, drawing the entire tower downward into the burning heart of the mansion.

Throughout the destruction, the ground continued to tremble beneath their feet, the vibrations intensifying with each structural failure. Larger cracks appeared in the cliff face, some wide enough to swallow a child whole. Others vented plumes of steam or smoke from the island's wounded depths. The ledge they stood on remained stable, but its edge had begun to crumble, forcing them to retreat further with each successive tremor.

Then came the final catastrophe. The foundations—built upon the geometric center of the ley line convergence and designed to channel and contain the power of the Nocturne Gate—gave way completely. It happened not with violence but with a terrible grace, as if some invisible hand had simply withdrawn its support from beneath. The remaining walls and towers sank first by inches, then by feet, the entire structure sliding toward the sea like a ship being launched—a vessel bound for depths where light had never reached.

The cliff edge before Hallowspire crumbled, tons of earth and stone breaking free and plunging into the Atlantic. The mansion followed, its burning remnants striking the water with a hiss that became a roar as the fire met the sea in a violent confrontation of elements. Steam erupted in massive clouds, momentarily obscuring the destruction, but when the wind cleared the view, nothing remained of Hallowspire but scattered debris floating on the churning surface and the scars its passing had left on the island's face.

Massive waves radiated outward from the impact site, striking the cliffs with such force that spray rose higher than their vantage point. The outcropping they stood on shuddered with each impact, small fragments breaking free from its edge and tumbling into the abyss below. They retreated further, pressing their backs against the solid cliff face, seeking whatever stability remained in a world that seemed determined to shake itself apart beneath them.

For several minutes, no one spoke. The only sounds were the crash of waves, the distant hiss of fire meeting water, and their own ragged breathing as their bodies processed the narrow escape from death. The eastern sky had lightened further, the first tentative rays of dawn painting the horizon in pale gold and rose, throwing the destruction into stark relief against the new day.

"It's over," Micah said at last, his voice barely audible above the crashing waves. The words carried a weight beyond their simplicity—exhaustion and relief and disbelief that they had survived what should have been unsurvivable.

Juba made a soft sound that might have been agreement or

merely exhaustion, her arms tightening around Effie's delicate form. Her eyes remained fixed on the space where Hallowspire had stood, as if expecting it to reappear through some final malevolent trick. The morning light revealed the true extent of her ordeal—clothes torn and scorched, skin marked with cuts and burns, hair singed at the edges. Yet she stood straight, unbowed, a woman who had faced hell and emerged carrying what mattered most.

But Anna's expression remained guarded as she watched the churning waters where Hallowspire had disappeared. Her eyes narrowed against the rising light, searching the debris-strewn surface for something the others couldn't see. The tension never left her shoulders, her hand still half-raised as if reaching for the knife that was no longer at her belt—lost, like so much else, in the chamber where Mercy had made her sacrifice.

She had witnessed too many false endings, too many evils that merely slumbered rather than died. The Gate was closed and sealed by Mercy's freely given blood. The mansion was destroyed, its occult architecture erased from the physical world. But some things never truly died. They only waited, patient as the tide, for the right moment to return.

The sun crested the horizon, spilling true daylight across the wounded island. Brimwatch Isle would bear the scars of this night for generations—the collapsed cliff face, the blackened earth where Hallowspire had stood, the invisible fractures in the ley lines that had once converged beneath its foundations. But the island would heal in time. The question that lingered, unspoken but present in Anna's wary gaze, was whether those who had survived would heal as well—or whether they, like the island, would forever carry wounds too deep for the eye to see.

Epilogue

The Arcanium lay beneath Anna's Beacon Hill row house like a secret heart, its stone walls older than the city itself. Black candles burned in iron sconces in the Conjuring Chamber, their flames unnaturally still in the airless vault, casting long shadows across the pentagram carved into the stone floor. At its center lay Abigail, her body preserved by arts that defied natural decay, hands crossed over her chest in an inanimate repose. Anna stood at the edge of the sacred circle, the knife-edge certainty of her purpose the only thing keeping her upright after days of sleepless preparation.

She moved with deliberate precision, arranging the final components on the ebony altar: an athame with a bone handle worn smooth by generations of hands; a silver bowl of salt harvested from the shores of Brimwatch Isle; seven vials of blood, each taken under different phases of the moon. Beside them, Anna's Book of Shadows lay open. Inherited from Abigail and the long chain of witches who came before her, its yellowed pages were now covered with a new entry in Anna's own hand: her recollection of Thorne's Spiral of

Unbinding—the ritual that had stripped the souls from Thorne's victims, leaving them as the hollow Quiet Ones.

If Anna was correct, she could invert it, transform it, and use it to call her mother home.

But if she was wrong…

Weeks had passed since Brimwatch Isle. Weeks since Anna had watched Hallowspire collapse into the sea in a fury of unnatural fire and ancient stone. The memory of their rescue still felt dreamlike. Fishermen drawn by the flames visible for miles across the Sound found them huddled on the shore as dawn broke. The men's weathered faces had registered shock at the state of the island's survivors, at the story they pieced together of being trapped when the mansion caught fire. Simple men with simple explanations for the inexplicable.

Those same fishermen had later helped Juba secure passage to Canada with her children, no questions asked beyond the weight of coin in their palms. Anna had pressed extra funds into Juba's hands at their parting, watching as the woman's dark, knowing eyes measured her one last time.

"You sure about what you're fixing to do?" Juba had asked, Effie's sleeping form cradled against her chest.

Anna hadn't answered. Some truths were better left unspoken.

Now she stood alone in the chamber her mother had built for rituals far darker than Boston society could ever imagine.

The time approaches. Rebecca's voice curled through Anna's mind like frost spreading across a windowpane, familiar and alien at once. The witch's presence had grown stronger since their return. Anna's desperation had cracked open doors inside her mind that had previously remained sealed.

Her fingers traced the edge of her grimoire, lingering on the diagram that would guide her work. "You knew, didn't you? You knew she wouldn't come back through the Gate when Mercy closed it."

Rebecca's laughter rippled cold and clear inside her skull. *I told you what you needed to hear. Had you sacrificed the albino child as I instructed, Abigail would have returned. But that moment passed. Now we require... different methods.*

"You lied to me." Anna's voice echoed against the stone walls, brittle with exhaustion and fury. Her reflection scattered across the silver instruments on the altar. It was a woman she barely recognized, hollowed by grief and purpose, dark circles beneath eyes too bright with dangerous knowledge.

I offered you a chance to save your mother through simpler means, Rebecca countered, her tone sharpening. *You chose mercy over blood. Compassion over power.* The witch's disappointment cut through Anna's thoughts like a blade. *That is why we stand here now, preparing a ritual that will cost you far more than the quick death of one strange child.*

The candle flames stretched taller for a moment, as if pulled by an invisible current. Shadows deepened in the corners of the chamber, gathering like spectators to the work that would soon begin. Anna felt the weight of unseen eyes upon her—not just Rebecca's consciousness inside her own, but other presences drawn by the power gathering in the sacred space.

"We sealed the Gate," Anna said, her voice barely above a whisper. "Mercy gave herself to close it. To stop what was coming through."

Yes, Rebecca agreed with an odd pride coloring her spectral voice. *The child understood sacrifice better than you. She recognized necessity when it stared her in the face. But in closing the Nocturne Gate, she closed the path your mother might have walked to return to you.*

Anna's hand clenched around the athame, its blade catching the candlelight in a gleaming arc. "Then what makes you think this will work? If the Gate is sealed—"

The Nocturne Gate was but one doorway between worlds, Rebecca interrupted. *Others may be opened. Smaller. More… personal.* Her presence shifted within Anna's mind, pressing closer to the surface of consciousness. *The Spiral of Unbinding stripped souls from flesh. Reversed, it can call a soul home… but it requires a vessel prepared to receive it.*

Anna looked at her mother's body, preserved these long months in a state between death and decay. Abigail looked peaceful, almost as if she were merely sleeping—an illusion crafted by the spell that had kept her body intact while her soul wandered lost beyond the Veil.

"And a power source," Anna added, knowing where this led. She had studied Thorne's grimoire enough to understand the terrible symmetry of Thorne's work, how it might be inverted but never truly changed in nature. "Something to fuel the crossing."

Rebecca's approval flowed cold through her veins. *Yes. Thorne stripped the Quiet Ones of their humanity, piece by piece, until only hollow vessels remained. To restore a soul requires… the opposite. Not emptiness, but fullness. Not taking, but giving.*

The candles flickered as a change in air pressure signaled the approach of midnight. Anna felt it in her bones: the turning of the hour, the thinning of the Veil, the moment when such work became possible. Her hands trembled slightly as she reached for the chalk mixed with her own blood, prepared to draw the first lines of the spiral on the stone floor around her mother's body.

There can be no light left in you if we are to finish this work, Rebecca said, her voice cold and certain within Anna's thoughts. *No hesitation. No mercy. The vessel must be worthy of the soul it calls—and the price must be paid in full.*

Anna stared down at the chalk in her hand, at the grimoire open to the ritual that would call her mother back from beyond the Veil. The same ritual that would require the ultimate surrender of whatever humanity she had managed to preserve, despite Rebecca's constant presence in her mind. The choice had always been inevitable—from the moment of her birth, when Rebecca's darkness had bound itself to her in the womb.

"Some of us aren't meant to be saved," Anna murmured to herself.

Some of us are meant to save others, came Rebecca's mocking reply.

"I'm ready," Anna whispered, and kneeled to begin the work.

Her chalk-stained fingers hovered over the smooth stone floor. The mixture—powdered limestone infused with her own blood—felt warm against her skin, almost alive. She placed the first mark deliberately, not at the center as Thorne had done, but at the outermost edge of the circle. Where he had drawn inward to bind, she would draw outward to release. Where his spiral had pulled souls from flesh, hers would call one home from the spaces between worlds.

Her hand moved in a steady arc, the chalk leaving a rusty trail across the dark stone. The line curved away from her mother's body rather than toward it, beginning the intricate pattern that would unravel what death had done. The air in the Arcanium seemed to thicken with each stroke, pressing against her skin like something half-substantial.

Wider at the turning, Rebecca instructed, her voice no longer confined to Anna's thoughts but seeming to emanate from the shadows themselves. "The outward force must be gradual, then sudden. Like birth in reverse."

Anna's hand faltered at a critical juncture, the line wavering where it should flow smooth. Rebecca's displeasure manifested as a sharp pain behind her eyes.

Precision, the witch hissed. *Thorne understood the geometry of the soul. Each curve, each angle, must be perfect.*

Anna steadied her breathing, focusing on the pattern unfolding beneath her hands. The chalk felt heavier now, as if the mixture were drawing something from her with each mark she made. Sweat beaded on her forehead despite the chamber's chill, her body experiencing the toll that her mind had not yet registered.

Around them, the candle flames stretched unnaturally tall, reaching toward the vaulted ceiling like spectral fingers grasping at something just beyond reach. They no longer flickered but burned with a steady, impossible stillness, their light taking on a bluish tint that cast the chamber in the pallor of drowning. Shadows deepened in the corners, congealing into shapes that seemed to observe the proceedings with patient, ancient interest.

Anna reached for the Book of Shadows, confirming the next sequence of marks. What had been instructions for stripping away a soul now revealed their inverse: a pathway for restoration, for calling rather than banishing. She began to chant from the *Tenebric Sequence*, but backward, her voice falling into rhythms that her conscious mind could not have devised.

"Let the hollow refill. Let the gate rehook. Let the soul rise as embers rise—from shadow, from coil, from the hollow below."

The words tasted strange on her tongue; syllables that human mouths were not designed to form, sounds that existed in the spaces between language. Unlike Thorne's original ritual, this version required no circle of thirteen soul-stripped victims. Abigail's soul was already lost beyond the Veil, her body an empty vessel waiting to be filled. The ritual needed only a beacon strong enough to guide her home—and a sacrifice sufficient to power her return.

As Anna completed the first circuit of the spiral, the chalk lines began to glow with a pale blue light, pulsing in perfect rhythm with her heartbeat. Each beat sent a wave of luminescence flowing outward from her mother's body, as if the pattern were a visual manifestation of Abigail's absent pulse. The light seeped into the cracks between the bedrock, spreading beneath the floor like roots searching for water.

Continue, Rebecca urged, her presence now so close to the surface that Anna could almost see her—a shadow within her own shadow, moving just slightly out of sync. *The vessel is prepared. The path is forming. Now comes the final song.*

Anna reached for the athame, its blade gleaming with an

inner light that matched the glowing chalk lines. With a swift, practiced motion, she drew the edge across her left palm, opening a wound parallel to her lifeline. Blood welled immediately, dark and viscous in the strange light. She let it pool in her cupped hand before moving to the spiral's critical points; those junctures where Thorne's original design had bound souls most tightly.

At each point, she let exactly three drops fall onto the glowing chalk. The blood didn't spatter or run but sank directly into the stone as if it had struck parched earth, the floor drinking her offering with eager thirst. With each placement, the temperature in the chamber plummeted further, dropping well below freezing in the space of seconds. Frost crystallized on the stone walls, forming intricate patterns that mimicked the spiral on the floor. Anna's breath clouded before her face, her lips taking on a bluish tinge as the cold penetrated to her bones.

Yet she felt no discomfort, only a strange, floating detachment, as if she were observing the ritual from somewhere outside her own body. Rebecca's presence had spread through her limbs like ice through water, guiding her movements with increasing control. The boundary between them had grown thin, transparency replacing the wall that had separated their consciousnesses since Anna's birth.

The final arc, Rebecca whispered, the words forming on Anna's lips without her volition. *Complete the song. Sing your mother through.*

Anna's bloodied hand traced the last curve of the spiral, connecting it to the innermost circle that surrounded Abigail's body. The moment the line closed, the entire pattern surged with blinding white light that shot upward from the floor in a pillar that encompassed Abigail completely. The light was so intense that Anna was forced to shield her eyes, though she could still see the silhouette of her mother's body within the radiance—a dark shape that suddenly convulsed with violent force.

Abigail's back arched off the floor, her spine bending at an angle that would have broken a living woman's bones. Her arms flew outward, breaking the crossed position they had held in death. Her head snapped back, mouth opening in a silent scream as the light poured into her through every exit —eyes, mouth, nostrils, ears—filling her with radiance from within.

Then, as suddenly as it had appeared, the light receded, pulling back into the chalk lines, then into the stone itself, leaving the chamber in near-darkness. The candles had been extinguished by the surge of power. Only a single flame still guttered in the farthest sconce. In its weak light, Anna could see her mother's form, no longer rigid in death but softened, the chest now rising and falling with shallow breaths.

Silence fell, heavy and expectant. Anna crawled forward on hands and knees, ignoring the blood that still flowed from her palm, leaving smeared prints across the blackened stone. She reached the inner circle where her mother lay, her heart hammering against her ribs with hope so fierce it bordered on agony.

Abigail's eyes fluttered open.

They moved slowly, disoriented, before fixing on Anna's face hovering above her. Confusion gave way to recognition, and her lips parted.

"Anna?" Her voice was raspy from months of disuse, barely more than a whisper, but unmistakably hers. She lifted a trembling hand toward her daughter's face. "What have you done?"

The smile that spread across Anna's face wasn't her own—too wide, too knowing, too full of ancient triumph.

And when she spoke, the voice that emerged from her lips wasn't her own.

"Welcome back, granddaughter," said Rebecca, using Anna's mouth to form the words. "Your daughter has missed you terribly. Enough to give everything for your return." An icy laugh escaped from Anna's throat, familiar yet utterly foreign. "Absolutely everything."

Author's Note

Thank you, dear reader, for the generous gift of your time and attention. If you enjoyed this book and would like to see more, please consider taking a moment to leave a quick review on Amazon and/or Goodreads. A kind word from a reader like you is one of the best ways you can support independent authors and is very much appreciated.

Until next time, look under the bed, close the closet door, and whatever you do, don't turn around…

**She was innocent of witchcraft when they arrested her.
She was guilty when they hanged her.**

Step into a world of dark magic, fierce women, and terrifying evil with *A Firebrand of Hell*, a short story prequel to the best-selling *Book of Shadows* series, now available absolutely free!

Visit www.michaelpenning.com to download your copy!

BOOKS BY MICHAEL PENNING

Book of Shadows Series

All Hallows Eve
The Suicide Lake
The Wolf Society
The Damnation Chronicles
The Black Testament
The Hellfire House

Other Novels
Solitude
Devil Music

Michael Penning is a best-selling author and award-winning screenwriter of horror and dark fiction, crafting stories so chilling they could make a ghost shiver. As the macabre mind behind the *Book of Shadows* series, he has been weaving nightmares since before he could finish his own sack of trick-or-treat candy. When he's not conjuring new ways to make readers sleep with one eye open, he enjoys traveling, photography, and brewing beer. He lives in Montreal with his wife and daughter, who have yet to flee in terror. For updates and free giveaways, visit www.michaelpenning.com and follow Michael on social media @michaelpenningauthor.